If We Were Villains

If We Were
Villains

M. L. Rio

FLATIRON
BOOKS
NEW YORK

IF WE WERE VILLAINS. Copyright © 2017 by M. L. Rio. All rights reserved. Printed in the United States of America. For information, address Flatiron Books, 175 Fifth Avenue, New York, N.Y. 10010.

www.flatironbooks.com

Names: Rio, M. L., author.
Title: If we were villains / M. L. Rio.
Description: First edition. | New York : Flatiron Books, 2017.
  Identifiers: LCCN 2017288580 | ISBN 9781250095282 (hardcover) | ISBN 9781250154958 (international) | 9781250095305 (ebook)
Subjects: College students—fiction. | Actors—fiction.
  BISAC: FICTION / Coming of Age. | FICTION / Literary. | FICTION / Thrillers / Suspense.
Classification: PS3618.I564 I35 2017 | DCC 813/.6—dc23
LC record available at https://lccn.loc.gov/2017288580

ISBN 978-1-250-09529-9 (trade paperback)

Our books may be purchased in bulk for promotional, educational, or business use. Please contact your local bookseller or the Macmillan Corporate and Premium Sales Department at 1-800-221-7945, extension 5442, or by e-mail at MacmillanSpecialMarkets@macmillan.com.

First Flatiron Books Paperback Edition: April 2018

20 19

For the many weird and wonderful thespians whom I have had the good fortune to call my friends. (I promise this is not about you.)

ACT I

PROLOGUE

I sit with my wrists cuffed to the table and I think, *But that I am forbid / To tell the secrets of my prison-house, / I could a tale unfold whose lightest word / Would harrow up thy soul.* The guard stands by the door, watching me, like he's waiting for something to happen.

Enter Joseph Colborne. He is a graying man now, almost fifty. It's a surprise, every few weeks, to see how much he's aged—and he's aged a little more, every few weeks, for ten years. He sits across from me, folds his hands, and says, "Oliver."

"Joe."

"Heard the parole hearing went your way. Congratulations."

"I'd thank you if I thought you meant it."

"You know I don't think you belong in here."

"That doesn't mean you think I'm innocent."

"No." He sighs, checks his watch—the same one he's worn since we met—as if I'm boring him.

"So why are you here?" I ask. "Same fortnightly reason?"

His eyebrows make a flat black line. "You would say fucking 'fortnight.'"

"You can take the boy out of the theatre, or something like that."

He shakes his head, simultaneously amused and annoyed.

"Well?" I say.

"Well what?"

"*The gallows does well. But how does it well? It does well to those that do ill,*" I reply, determined to deserve his annoyance. "Why are you here? You should know by now I'm not going to tell you anything."

"Actually," he says, "this time I think I might be able to change your mind."

I sit up straighter in my chair. "How?"

"I'm leaving the force. Sold out, took a job in private security. Got my kids' education to think about."

For a moment I simply stare at him. Colborne, I always imagined, would have to be put down like a savage old dog before he'd leave the chief's office.

"How's that supposed to persuade me?" I ask.

"Anything you say will be strictly off the record."

"Then why bother?"

He sighs again and all the lines on his face deepen. "Oliver, I don't care about doling out punishment, not anymore. Someone served the time, and we rarely get that much satisfaction in our line of work. But I don't want to hang up my hat and waste the next ten years wondering what really happened ten years ago."

I say nothing at first. I like the idea but don't trust it. I glance around at the grim cinder blocks, the tiny black video cameras that peer down from every corner, the guard with his jutting underbite. I close my eyes, inhale deeply, and imagine the freshness of Illinois springtime, what it will be like to step outside after gasping on stale prison air for a third of my life.

When I exhale I open my eyes and Colborne is watching me closely.

"I don't know," I say. "I'm getting out of here, one way or the other. I don't want to risk coming back. Seems safer to let sleeping dogs lie."

His fingers drum restlessly on the table. "Tell me something," he says. "Do you ever lie in your cell, staring up at the ceiling, wondering how you wound up in here, and you can't sleep because you can't stop thinking about that day?"

"Every night," I say, without sarcasm. "But here's the difference, Joe. For you it was just one day, then business as usual. For us it was one day, and every single day that came after." I lean forward on my elbows, so my face is only a few inches from his, so he hears every word when I lower my voice. "It must eat you alive, not knowing. Not knowing who, not knowing how, not knowing why. But you didn't know *him*."

He wears a strange, queasy expression now, as if I've become unspeakably ugly and awful to look at. "You've kept your secrets all this time," he says. "It would drive anyone else crazy. Why do it?"

"I wanted to."

"Do you still?"

My heart feels heavy in my chest. Secrets carry weight, like lead.

I lean back. The guard watches impassively, as if we're two strangers talking in another language, our conversation distant and insignificant. I think of the others. Once upon a time, *us*. We did wicked things, but they were necessary, too—or so it seemed. Looking back, years later, I'm not so sure they were, and now I wonder: Could I explain it all to Colborne, the little twists and turns and final *exodos*? I study his blank open face, the gray eyes winged now by crow's-feet, but clear and bright as they have always been.

"All right," I say. "I'll tell you a story. But you have to understand a few things."

Colborne is motionless. "I'm listening."

"First, I'll start talking after I get out of here, not before. Second, this can't come back to me or anyone else—no double jeopardy. And last, it's not an apology."

I wait for some response from him, a nod or a word, but he only blinks at me, silent and stoic as a sphinx.

"Well, Joe?" I say. "Can you live with that?"

He gives me a cold sliver of a smile. "Yes, I think I can."

SCENE 1

The time: September 1997, my fourth and final year at Dellecher Classical Conservatory. The place: Broadwater, Illinois, a small town of almost no consequence. It had been a warm autumn so far.

Enter the players. There were seven of us then, seven bright young things with wide precious futures ahead of us, though we saw no farther than the books in front of our faces. We were always surrounded by books and words and poetry, all the fierce passions of the world bound in leather and vellum. (I blame this in part for what happened.) The Castle library was an airy octagonal room, walled with bookshelves, crowded with sumptuous old furniture, and kept drowsily warm by a monumental fireplace that burned almost constantly, regardless of the temperature outside. The clock on the mantel struck twelve, and we stirred, one by one, like seven statues coming to life.

"*'Tis now dead midnight*," Richard said. He sat in the largest armchair like it was a throne, long legs outstretched, feet propped up on the grate. Three years of playing kings and conquerors had taught him to sit that way in every chair, onstage or off. "And by eight o'clock tomorrow we must be made immortal." He closed his book with a snap.

Meredith, curled like a cat on one end of the sofa (while I sprawled like a dog on the other), toyed with one strand of her long auburn hair as she asked, "Where are you going?"

Richard: "*Weary with toil, I haste me to my bed—*"

Filippa: "Spare us."

Richard: "Early morning and all that."

Alexander: "He says, as if he's concerned."

Wren, sitting cross-legged on a cushion by the hearth and

oblivious to the others' bickering, said, "Have you all picked your pieces? I can't decide."

Me: "What about Isabella? Your Isabella's excellent."

Meredith: "*Measure*'s a comedy, you fool. We're auditioning for *Caesar*."

"I don't know why we bother auditioning at all." Alexander—slumped over the table, wallowing in the darkness at the back of the room—reached for the bottle of Scotch at his elbow. He refilled his glass, took one huge gulp, and grimaced at the rest of us. "I could cast the whole bastarding thing right now."

"How?" I asked. "I never know where I'll end up."

"That's because they always cast you last," Richard said, "as whatever happens to be left over."

"Tsk-tsk," Meredith said. "Are we Richard tonight or are we Dick?"

"Ignore him, Oliver," James said. He sat by himself in the farthest corner, loath to look up from his notebook. He had always been the most serious student in our year, which (probably) explained why he was also the best actor and (certainly) why no one resented him for it.

"There." Alexander had unfolded a wad of ten-dollar bills from his pocket and was counting them out on the table. "That's fifty dollars."

"For what?" Meredith said. "You want a lap dance?"

"Why, are you practicing for after graduation?"

"Bite me."

"Ask nicely."

"Fifty dollars for what?" I said, keen to interrupt. Meredith and Alexander had by far the foulest mouths among the seven of us, and took a perverse kind of pride in out-cussing each other. If we let them, they'd go at it all night.

Alexander tapped the stack of tens with one long finger. "I bet fifty dollars I can call the cast list right now and not be wrong."

Five of us exchanged curious glances; Wren was still frowning into the fireplace.

"All right, let's hear it," Filippa said, with a wan little sigh, as though her curiosity had gotten the better of her.

Alexander pushed his unruly black curls back from his face and said, "Well, obviously Richard will be Caesar."

"Because we all secretly want to kill him?" James asked.

Richard arched one dark eyebrow. "*Et tu, Bruté?*"

"*Sic semper tyrannis*," James said, and drew the tip of his pen across his throat like a dagger. *Thus always to tyrants.*

Alexander gestured from one of them to the other. "Exactly," he said. "James will be Brutus because he's always the good guy, and I'll be Cassius because I'm always the bad guy. Richard and Wren can't be married because that would be gross, so she'll be Portia, Meredith will be Calpurnia, and Pip, you'll end up in drag again."

Filippa, more difficult to cast than Meredith (the femme fatale) or Wren (the ingénue), was obliged to cross-dress whenever we ran out of good female parts—a common occurrence in the Shakespearean theatre. "Kill me," she said.

"Wait," I said, effectively proving Richard's hypothesis that I was a permanent leftover in the casting process, "where does that leave me?"

Alexander studied me with narrowed eyes, running his tongue across his teeth. "Probably as Octavius," he decided. "They won't make you Antony—no offense, but you're just not *conspicuous* enough. It'll be that insufferable third-year, what's his name?"

Filippa: "Richard the Second?"

Richard: "Hilarious. No, Colin Hyland."

"Spectacular." I looked down at the text of *Pericles* I was scanning, for what felt like the hundredth time. Only half as talented as any of the rest of them, I seemed doomed to always play supporting roles in someone else's story. Far too many times I had asked myself whether art was imitating life or if it was the other way around.

Alexander: "Fifty bucks, on that exact casting. Any takers?"

Meredith: "No."

Alexander: "Why not?"

Filippa: "Because that's precisely what'll happen."

Richard chuckled and climbed out of his chair. "One can only hope." He started toward the door and leaned over to pinch James's cheek on his way out. "*Goodnight, sweet prince—*"

James smacked Richard's hand away with his notebook, then made a show of disappearing behind it again. Meredith echoed Richard's laugh and said, "*Thou art as hot a Jack in thy mood as any in Italy!*"

"*A plague o' both your houses,*" James muttered.

Meredith stretched—with a small, suggestive groan—and pushed herself off the couch.

"Coming to bed?" Richard asked.

"Yes. Alexander's made all this work seem rather pointless." She left her books scattered on the low table in front of the fire, her empty wineglass with them, a crescent of lipstick clinging to the rim. "Goodnight," she said, to the room at large. "Godspeed." They disappeared down the hall together.

I rubbed my eyes, which were beginning to burn from the effort of reading for hours on end. Wren tossed her book backward over her head, and I started as it landed beside me on the couch.

Wren: "To hell with it."

Alexander: "That's the spirit."

Wren: "I'll just do Isabella."

Filippa: "Just go to bed."

Wren stood slowly, blinking the vestigial light of the fire out of her eyes. "I'll probably lie awake all night reciting lines," she said.

"Want to come out for a smoke?" Alexander had finished his

whiskey (again) and was rolling a spliff on the table. "Might help you relax."

"No, thank you," she said, drifting out into the hall. "Good-night."

"Suit yourself." Alexander pushed his chair back, spliff poking out of one corner of his mouth. "Oliver?"

"If I help you smoke that I'll wake up with no voice tomorrow."

"Pip?"

She nudged her glasses up into her hair and coughed softly, testing her throat. "God, you're a terrible influence," she said. "Fine."

He nodded, already halfway out of the room, hands buried deep in his pockets. I watched them go, a little jealously, then slumped down against the arm of the couch. I struggled to focus on my text, which was so aggressively annotated that it was barely legible anymore.

PERICLES: *Antioch, farewell! for wisdom sees those men*
Blush not in actions blacker than the night
Will 'schew no course to keep them from the light.
One sin, I know, another doth provoke;
Murder's as near to lust as flame to smoke.

I murmured the last two lines under my breath. I knew them by heart, had known them for months, but the fear that I would forget a word or phrase halfway through my audition gnawed at me anyway. I glanced across the room at James and said, "Do you ever wonder if Shakespeare knew these speeches half as well as we do?"

He withdrew from whatever verse he was reading, looked up, and said, "Constantly."

I cracked a smile, vindicated just enough. "Well, I give up. I'm not actually getting anything done."

He checked his watch. "No, I don't think I am either."

I heaved myself off the sofa and followed James up the spiral stairs to the bedroom we shared—which was directly over the library, the highest of three rooms in a little stone column commonly referred to as the Tower. It had once been used only as an attic, but the cobwebs and clutter had been cleared away to make room for more students in the late seventies. Twenty years later it housed James and me, two beds with blue Dellecher bedspreads, two monstrous old wardrobes, and a pair of mismatched bookshelves too ugly for the library.

"Do you think it'll fall out how Alexander says?" I asked.

James pulled his shirt off, mussing his hair in the process. "If you ask me, it's too predictable."

"When have they ever surprised us?"

"Frederick surprises me all the time," he said. "But Gwendolyn will have the final say, she always does."

"If it were up to her, Richard would play all of the men and half the women."

"Which would leave Meredith playing the other half." He pressed the heels of his palms against his eyes. "When do you read tomorrow?"

"Right after Richard. Filippa's after me."

"And I'm after her. God, I feel bad for her."

"Yeah," I said. "It's a wonder she hasn't dropped out."

James frowned thoughtfully as he wriggled out of his jeans. "Well, she's a bit more resilient than the rest of us. Maybe that's why Gwendolyn torments her."

"Just because she can take it?" I said, discarding my own clothes in a pile on the floor. "That's cruel."

He shrugged. "That's Gwendolyn."

"If I had my way, I'd turn it all upside down," I said. "Make Alexander Caesar and have Richard play Cassius instead."

He folded his comforter back and asked, "Am I still Brutus?"

"No." I tossed a sock at him. "You're Antony. For once I get to be the lead."

"Your time will come to be the tragic hero. Just wait for spring."

I glanced up from the drawer I was pawing through. "Has Frederick been telling you secrets again?"

He lay down and folded his hands behind his head. "He may have mentioned *Troilus and Cressida*. He has this fantastic idea to do it as a battle of the sexes. All the Trojans men, all the Greeks women."

"That's insane."

"Why? That play is as much about sex as it is about war," he said. "Gwendolyn will want Richard to be Hector, of course, but that makes you Troilus."

"Why on earth wouldn't *you* be Troilus?"

He shifted, arched his back. "I may have mentioned that I'd like to have a little more variety on my résumé."

I stared at him, unsure if I should be insulted.

"Don't look at me like that," he said, a low note of reproach in his voice. "He agreed we all need to break out of our boxes. I'm tired of playing fools in love like Troilus, and I'm sure you're tired of always playing the sidekick."

I flopped on my bed on my back. "Yeah, you're probably right." For a moment I let my thoughts wander, and then I breathed out a laugh.

"Something funny?" James asked, as he reached over to turn out the light.

"You'll have to be Cressida," I told him. "You're the only one of us pretty enough."

We lay there laughing in the dark until we dropped off to sleep, and slept deeply, with no way of knowing that the curtain was about to rise on a drama of our own invention.

SCENE 2

Dellecher Classical Conservatory occupied twenty or so acres of land on the eastern edge of Broadwater, and the borders of the two so often overlapped that it was difficult to tell where campus ended and town began. The first-years were housed in a cluster of brick buildings in town, while the second- and third-years were crowded together at the Hall, and the handful of fourth-years were tucked away in odd isolated corners of campus or left to fend for themselves. We, the fourth-year theatre students, lived on the far side of the lake in what was whimsically called the Castle (not really a castle, but a small stone building that happened to have one turret, originally the groundskeepers' quarters).

Dellecher Hall, a sprawling red brick mansion, looked down a steep hill to the dark flat water of the lake. Dormitories and the ballroom were on the fourth and fifth floors, classrooms and offices on the second and third, while the ground floor was divided into refectory, music hall, library, and conservatory. A chapel jutted off the west end of the building, and sometime in the 1960s, the Archibald Dellecher Fine Arts Building (generally referred to as the FAB, for more than one reason) was erected on the east side of the Hall, a small courtyard and honeycomb of corbeled walkways wedged between them. The FAB was home to the Archibald Dellecher Theatre and the rehearsal hall and, ergo, was where we spent most of our time. At eight in the morning on the first day of classes, it was exceptionally quiet.

Richard and I walked from the Castle together, though I wasn't due to audition for another half hour.

"How do you feel?" he asked, as we climbed the steep hill to the lawn.

"Nervous, like I always am." The number of auditions under my belt didn't matter; the anxiety never really left me.

"No need to be," he said. "You're never as dreadful as you think you are. Just don't shift your weight too much. You're most interesting when you stand still."

I frowned at him. "How do you mean?"

"I mean when you forget you're onstage and forget to be nervous. You really listen to other actors, really hear the words like it's the first time you've heard them. It's wonderful to work with and marvelous to watch." He shook his head at the look of consternation on my face. "I shouldn't have told you. Don't get self-conscious." He clapped one huge hand on my shoulder, and I was so distracted I pitched forward, my fingertips brushing the dewy grass. Richard's booming laugh echoed in the morning air, and he grabbed my arm to help me find my balance. "See?" he said. "Keep your feet planted and you'll be fine."

"You suck," I said, but with a grudging smirk. (Richard had that effect on people.)

As soon as we reached the FAB, he gave me another cheery smack on the back and disappeared into the rehearsal hall. I paced back and forth along the crossover, puzzling over what he had said and repeating *Pericles* to myself like I was saying a string of Hail Marys.

Our first semester auditions determined which parts we would play in our fall production. That year, *Julius Caesar*. Tragedies and histories were reserved for the fourth-years, while the third-years were relegated to romance and comedy and all the bit parts were played by the second-years. First-years were left to work backstage, slog through general education, and wonder what the hell they'd gotten themselves into. (Each year, students whose performance was deemed unsatisfactory were cut from the program—often as many as half. To survive until fourth year was proof of either talent or dumb luck. In my case, the latter.) Class photos from the past fifty years hung in two neat rows along the wall in the crossover. Ours was the last and certainly the sexiest, a publicity photo from the previous year's production of *A Midsummer Night's Dream*. We looked younger.

It was Frederick's idea to do *Midsummer* as a pajama party. James and I (Lysander and Demetrius, respectively) wore striped boxers and white undershirts and stood glaring at each other, with Wren (Hermia, in a short pink nightgown) trapped between us. Filippa stood on my left in Helena's longer blue nightdress, clutching the pillow she and Wren had walloped each other with in Act III. In the middle of the photo, Alexander and Meredith were wrapped around each other like a pair of snakes—he a sinister and seductive Oberon in slinky silk bathrobe, she a voluptuous Titania in revealing black lace. But Richard was the most arresting, standing among the other rude mechanicals in clownish flannel pajamas, enormous donkey ears protruding from his thick black hair. His Nick Bottom was aggressive, unpredictable, and totally deranged. He terrorized the fairies, tormented the other players, scared the hell out of the audience, and—as always—stole the show.

The seven of us had survived three yearly "purges" because we were each somehow indispensable to the playing company. In the course of four years we were transformed from a rabble of bit players to a small, meticulously trained dramatic troupe. Some of our theatrical assets were obvious: Richard was pure power, six foot three and carved from concrete, with sharp black eyes and a thrilling bass voice that flattened every other sound in a room. He played warlords and despots and anyone else the audience needed to be impressed by or afraid of. Meredith was uniquely designed for seduction, a walking daydream of supple curves and skin like satin. But there was something merciless about her sex appeal—you watched her when she moved, whatever else was happening, and whether you wanted to or not. (She and Richard had been "together" in every typical sense of the word since the spring semester of our second year.)

Wren—Richard's cousin, though you never would have guessed it by looking at them—was the ingénue, the girl next door, a waifish thing with corn silk hair and round china doll eyes. Alexander was our resident villain, thin and wiry, with long dark curls and sharp canine teeth that made him look like a vampire when he smiled.

Filippa and I were more difficult to categorize. She was tall, olive-skinned, vaguely boyish. There was something cool and chameleonic about her that made her equally convincing as Horatio or Emilia. I, on the other hand, was average in every imaginable way: not especially handsome, not especially talented, not especially good at anything but just good enough at everything that I could pick up whatever slack the others left. I was convinced I had survived the third-year purge because James would have been moody and sullen without me.

Fate had dealt us a good hand in our first year, when he and I found ourselves squashed together in a tiny room on the top floor of the dormitories. When I'd first opened our door, he looked up from the bag he was unpacking, held out his hand, and said, *"Here comes Sir Oliver! You are well met,* I hope." He was the sort of actor everyone fell in love with as soon as he stepped onstage, and I was no exception. Even in our early days at Dellecher, I was protective and even possessive of him when other friends came too close and threatened to usurp my place as "best"—an event as rare as a meteor shower. Some people saw me as Gwendolyn always cast me: simply the loyal sidekick. James was so quintessentially a hero that this didn't bother me. He was the handsomest of us (Meredith once compared him to a Disney prince), but more charming than that was his childlike depth of feeling, onstage and off. For three years I enjoyed the overflow of his popularity and admired him intensely, without jealousy, even though he was Frederick's obvious favorite in much the same way that Richard was Gwendolyn's. Of course, James did not have Richard's ego or temper and was liked by everyone, while Richard was hated and loved with equal ferocity.

It was customary for us to watch whichever audition followed our own (performing unobserved was compensation for performing first), and I paced restlessly along the crossover, wishing that James could have been my audience. Even when he didn't mean to be, Richard was an intimidating onlooker. I could hear his voice from the rehearsal hall, ringing off the walls.

Richard: *"Therefore take heed how you impawn our person,*
   How you awake our sleeping sword of war:
   We charge you, in the name of God, take heed.
   For never two such kingdoms did contend
   Without much fall of blood; whose guiltless drops
   Are every one a woe, a sore complaint,
   'Gainst him whose wrongs give edge unto the swords
   That make such waste in brief mortality."

I'd seen him do the same speech twice before, but that made it no less impressive.

At precisely half past eight, the door to the rehearsal hall creaked open. Frederick's familiar face, wizened and droll, appeared in the gap. "Oliver? We're ready for you now."

"Great." My pulse quickened—a flutter, like little bird wings trapped between my lungs.

I felt small walking into the rehearsal hall, as I always did. It was a cavernous room, with a high vaulted ceiling and long windows that gazed out on the grounds. Blue velvet curtains hung on either side of them, hems gathered in dusty piles on the hardwood floor. My voice echoed as I said, "Good morning, Gwendolyn."

The redheaded, stick figure woman behind the casting table glanced up at me, her presence in the room disproportionately enormous. Bold pink lipstick and a paisley head scarf made her look like some sort of gypsy. She wiggled her fingers in greeting, and the bangles on her wrist rattled. Richard sat in the chair to the left of the table, arms folded, watching me with a comfortable smile. I was not Leading Man material and therefore didn't qualify as competition. I flashed him a grin and then tried to ignore him.

"Oliver," Gwendolyn said. "Lovely to see you. Have you lost weight?"

"Gained it, actually," I said, my face going warm. When I left for summer break she had advised me to "bulk up." I spent hours at the gym every day of June, July, and August, hoping to impress her.

"Hm," she said, gaze descending slowly from the top of my head to my feet with the cold scrutiny of a slave trader at auction. "Well. Shall we get started?"

"Sure." Remembering Richard's advice, I straightened my feet on the floor and resolved not to move without reason.

Frederick eased back into his seat beside Gwendolyn, removed his glasses, and wiped the lenses on the hem of his shirt. "What do you have for us today?" he asked.

"Pericles," I said. He had suggested it, the previous term.

He gave me a small, conspiratorial nod. "Perfect. Whenever you're ready."

SCENE 3

We spent the rest of the day at the bar—a dimly lit, wood-paneled hole-in-the-wall where the staff knew most Dellecher students by name, accepted as many fake IDs as real ones, and didn't seem to find it odd that some of us had been twenty-one for three years. The fourth-years had finished auditioning by noon, but Frederick and Gwendolyn had forty-two other students to see, and—allowing for lunch and dinner breaks and deliberation—the cast lists probably wouldn't be posted until midnight. Six of us sat in our usual booth at the Bore's Head (as clever a joke as Broadwater was capable of), collecting empty glasses on the table. We all drank beer except Meredith, who was mainlining vodka sodas, and Alexander, who drank Scotch and drank it neat.

It was Wren's turn to wait at the FAB for the cast list to go up. The rest of us had taken ours already, and if she reappeared empty-handed it would be back to the beginning of the rotation. The sun had set hours before, but we weren't finished dissecting our auditions.

"I fucked it up completely," Meredith said, for what might have been the tenth time. "I said 'dismember' instead of 'dissemble,' like an absolute idiot."

"In the context of that speech it hardly matters," Alexander said, wearily. "Gwendolyn probably didn't notice and Frederick probably didn't care."

Before Meredith could reply, Wren burst in from outside, a single sheet of paper clutched in her hand. "It's up!" she said, and we all leapt to our feet. Richard guided her to the table, sat her down, and snatched the list. She had already seen it and suffered herself to be shunted into a corner while the rest of us bent over the table. After a few moments' silent, furious reading, Alexander sprang up again.

"What did I tell you?" He slapped the list, pointed at Wren, and shouted, "Barkeep, let me buy this lady a drink!"

"Sit down, Alexander, you preposterous ass," Filippa said, grabbing his elbow to pull him back into the booth. "You weren't all right!"

"I was so."

"No, Oliver's playing Octavius, but he's also playing Casca."

"Am I?" I had stopped reading once I saw the line drawn between my name and Octavius's and leaned in for a second look.

"Yeah, and I've got three—Decius Brutus, Lucilius, and Titinius." She offered a stoic smile to me, her fellow persona non grata.

"Why would they do that?" Meredith asked, stirring what remained of her vodka and sucking the last drops off her little red straw. "They've got plenty of second-years to use."

"But the third-years are doing *Shrew*," Wren said. "They'll need all the bodies they can get."

"Colin's going to be a busy boy," James remarked. "Look, they've got him playing Antony *and* Tranio."

"They did the same thing to me last year," Richard said, as if we didn't all already know. "Nick Bottom with you all and the Player King with the fourth-years. I was in rehearsal eight hours a day."

Sometimes third-years were chosen to take a role in a fourth-year cast that couldn't be trusted to a second-year. It meant classes from eight until three, then rehearsal with one cast until six thirty and rehearsal with another cast until eleven. Secretly, I didn't envy Richard or Colin.

"Not this time," Alexander said, with a wicked little smirk. "You'll only have rehearsal half the week—you die in Act III."

"I'll drink to that," Filippa said.

"*How many fond fools serve mad jealousy!*" Richard declared.

"Oh, shut up," Wren said. "Get us another round and perhaps we'll put up with you a little while longer."

He rose from his seat and said, "*I would give all my fame for a pot of ale!*" as he made his way to the bar.

Filippa shook her head and said, "If only."

SCENE 4

We left our things in the Castle and ran wildly through the trees, down the hillside stairs to the edge of the lake. We laughed and shouted at one another, sure we wouldn't be heard and too tipsy to care if we were. The dock stretched out into the water from the boathouse, where a collection of useless old tools crumbled and rusted. (There hadn't been a boat kept on the south side of the lake since they turned the Castle into student housing.) We spent many warm nights and some of the cold ones smoking and drinking on the dock, dangling our feet over the water.

Meredith, who was in by far the best shape and much faster than the rest of us, ran with her hair snapping like a flag behind her and got there first. She stopped and draped her arms over her head, a pale stripe of her back visible above her waistband. *"How sweet the moonlight sleeps upon this bank!"* She turned and grabbed both my hands, because I was closest. *"Here will we sit and let the sounds of music / Creep in our ears: soft stillness and the night / Become the touches of sweet harmony."* I pretended to protest as she dragged me to the end of the dock and the others tumbled down the stairs to join us, one by one. Alexander brought up the rear, wheezing.

"Let's go skinny-dipping!" Meredith said, already kicking her shoes off. "I haven't been swimming all summer."

"The chariest maid is prodigal enough," James warned, *"if she unmask her beauty to the moon."*

"For God's sake, James, you're no fun." She swatted the backs of my thighs with one of her shoes. "Oliver, won't you come in the water with me?"

I didn't trust that mischievous smile of hers at all, so I said, "Last time we went skinny-dipping I fell on the dock buck naked and spent the rest of the night facedown on the couch with Alexander pulling splinters out of my ass."

The others laughed exhaustively at my expense, and Richard let out a long wolf whistle.

Meredith: "Come on, somebody swim with me!"

Alexander: "You can't keep your clothes on for twenty-four hours, can you?"

Filippa: "Maybe if Rick could keep her happy she wouldn't be such a slut around the rest of us."

More laughter, more whistling. Richard gave Filippa a lofty sort of look and said, "*The lady doth protest too much, methinks.*"

She rolled her eyes and sat beside Alexander, who was busy crumbling weed into a cigarette paper.

I breathed in and held the sweet woody air in my lungs for as long as I could. A sweltering summer in suburban Ohio had made me impatient to return to Dellecher and the lake. The water was black by night, deep blue-green like jade by day. Dense forest surrounded it on all sides except one, the north shore, where the trees were thinner and a strip of sandy white beach shimmered like diamond dust in the moonlight. On the south bank we were just far enough away from the firefly lights of the Hall that there was little danger of our being seen and even less of being overheard. At the time, we liked our isolation.

Meredith lay back, eyes closed, humming peacefully. James and Wren sat on the opposite edge of the dock, looking toward the beach. Alexander finished rolling his joint, lit it, and handed it to Filippa. "Have a hit. We've got nothing to do tomorrow," he said, which wasn't entirely true. We had our first real day of classes and convocation later in the evening. Nevertheless, she accepted the joint and took a long drag before passing it to me. (We all indulged on special occasions, except Alexander, who was at least a little bit stoned all the time.)

Richard sighed, a sound of profound satisfaction that rumbled in his chest like a big cat's purr. "This is going to be a good year," he said. "I can feel it."

Wren: "Could that be because you've got the part you wanted?"

James: "And half as many lines to learn as the rest of us?"

Richard: "Seems fair, after last year."

Me: "I hate you."

Richard: "Hatred is the sincerest form of flattery."

Alexander: "That's imitation, dickhead."

A few of us snickered, still pleasantly buzzed. Our squabbling

was good-natured and usually harmless. We had, like seven siblings, spent so much time together that we had seen the best and
worst of one another and were unimpressed by either.

"Can you believe it's our last year?" Wren said, when the lull
after our laughter had lingered long enough.

"No," I said. "Seems like just yesterday my dad was shouting
at me for throwing my life away."

Alexander snorted. "What was it he said to you?"

" 'You're going to turn down a scholarship at Case Western
and spend the next four years in makeup and panty hose, making love to some girl through a window?' "

"Art school" alone was enough to provoke my rigidly prac-
tical father, but more often than not Dellecher's dangerous
exclusivity was the cause of raised eyebrows. Why should intelligent, talented students risk forcible ejection from their school
at the end of each year and graduate without even a traditional
degree to show for their survival? What most people who lived
outside the strange sphere of conservatory education didn't realize was that a Dellecher certificate was like one of Willy Won-
ka's golden tickets—guaranteed to grant the bearer admission to
the elite artistic and philological sodalities that survived outside
of academia.

My father, even more staunchly opposed than most, refused
to accept my decision to waste my university years. Acting was
bad, but something so niche and old-fashioned as Shakespeare
(at Dellecher, we didn't do anything else) was exponentially
worse. Eighteen and vulnerable, I'd felt for the first time the ex-
traordinary dread of wanting something desperately and watching it slip through my fingers, so I took the risk of telling him
I would go to Dellecher or nowhere. My mother persuaded
him to pay my tuition—after weeks of ultimatums and circular
arguments—on the grounds that my elder sister was on her way
to failing out of Ohio State and they were relying on me to be
the one they bragged about at dinner parties. (Why they didn't

have higher hopes for Leah, the youngest and most promising of us, was a mystery.)

"I wish my mother had been so furious," Alexander said. "She still thinks I'm at school in Indiana." Alexander's mother had given him up for foster care at an early age and made only the barest efforts to stay in touch. (All she'd deigned to tell him about his father was that the man was either from Puerto Rico or Costa Rica—she couldn't remember which—and had no idea Alexander existed.) His tuition was paid by an extravagant scholarship and a small heap of money left to him by a dead grandfather, who had only done it to spite his own profligate offspring.

"My dad's just disappointed I wasn't a poet," James added. Professor Farrow taught the Romantic poets at Berkeley, and his much younger wife (scandalously, a former student) was a poet herself until she suffered a Plath-like breakdown when James was in grade school. I'd met them two summers before when I visited him in California and had my suspicions that they were interesting people but disinterested parents unequivocally confirmed.

"My parents don't give a damn," Meredith said. "They're busy with Botox and tax evasion and my brothers are taking good care of the family fortune." The Dardennes split their time between Montreal and Manhattan, sold fantastically expensive wristwatches to politicians and celebrities, and treated their only daughter more like a novelty pet than a member of the family.

Filippa, who never spoke about her parents, said nothing.

"*A little more than kin, and less than kind,*" Alexander said. "My God, our families are miserable."

"Well, not all of them," Richard said. His and Wren's parents were three seasoned actors and a director living in London, making frequent appearances in the West End theatres. He shrugged. "Our parents are thrilled."

Alexander exhaled a stream of smoke and flicked his spliff away. "Lucky you," he said, and shoved Richard off the dock.

He hit the water with a monstrous splash, which sent water

crashing over all of us. The girls squealed and threw their arms over their heads, while James and I yelped in surprise. A moment later we were all sopping wet, laughing and applauding Alexander, too loud to hear Richard swearing when his head burst through the surface again.

We lingered by the water for another hour before, one by one, we began the slow climb back to the Castle. I was the last man standing on the dock. I didn't believe in God, but I asked whoever was listening not to let Richard's prediction jinx us. A good year was all I wanted.

SCENE 5

Eight in the morning was far too early for Gwendolyn.

We sat in a ragged circle, legs folded like storybook Indians, yawning and clutching mugs of coffee from the refectory. Studio Five—Gwendolyn's lair, festooned with colorful tapestries and cluttered with scented candles—was on the second floor of the Hall. There was no furniture to speak of, but instead a generous collection of floor pillows, which only increased the temptation to stretch out and sleep.

Gwendolyn arrived her usual quarter after the hour ("fashionably late," she always told us), swathed in a spangled shawl, gold rings thick as knuckle dusters gleaming on her fingers. She was brighter than the pale morning sun outside and almost painful to look at.

"Good morning, darlings," she trilled. Alexander grunted half a greeting, but nobody else replied. She stopped, standing over us, hands on her bony hips. "Well, this is just shameful. It's your first day of class—you ought to be bright-eyed and bushy-tailed." We stared at her until she flung her hands up and said, "On your feet! Let's go!"

The next half hour was devoted to a series of painful yoga

positions. Gwendolyn, for a woman in her sixties, was disturbingly limber. As the minute hand inched toward the nine, she straightened up from her King Pigeon Pose with an ecstatic sigh that must have made someone besides me uncomfortable.

"Isn't that better?" she said. Alexander grunted at her again. "I'm sure you've all missed me over the summer," she continued, "but we'll have plenty of time to catch up after convocation, so I'd like to dive right in and let you know that things are going to work a little differently this year."

For the first time, the class (besides Alexander) showed signs of life. We shifted, sat up straighter, and began to really listen.

"So far, you've been in the safe zone," Gwendolyn said. "And I feel it's only fair to warn you that those days are no more."

I looked sideways at James, who frowned. I couldn't tell if she was being her usual dramatic self or if she really meant to make a change.

"You know me by now," she said. "You know how I work. Frederick will coax and cajole you all day long, but I'm a pusher. I've pushed you and pushed you, but"—she held up one finger— "never too far." I didn't entirely agree. Gwendolyn's teaching methods were merciless, and it wasn't unusual for students to leave her class in tears. (Actors were like oysters, she explained when anyone wanted justification for this emotional brutality. You had to crack their shells and break them open to find the precious pearls inside.) She plowed ahead. "This is your last year and I'm going to push you as far as I have to. I know what you're capable of, and I'll be damned if I don't drag it out of you by the time you leave this place."

I shared another nervous look, this time with Filippa.

Gwendolyn adjusted her shawl, smoothed her hair, and said, "Now, who can tell me—what is our biggest impediment to good performance?"

"Fear," Wren said. It was one of Gwendolyn's many mantras: On the stage, you must be fearless.

"Yes. Fear of what?"

"Vulnerability," Richard said.

"Precisely," Gwendolyn said. "We're only ever playing fifty percent of a character. The rest is *us*, and we're afraid to show people who we really are. We're afraid of looking foolish if we reveal the full force of our emotions. But in Shakespeare's world, passion is irresistible, not embarrassing. So!" She clapped her hands and the sound made half of us jump. "We banish the fear, beginning today. You can't do good work if you're hiding, so we're going to get all of the ugliness out in the open. Who's first?"

We sat in surprised silence for a few seconds before Meredith said, "I'll go."

"Perfect," Gwendolyn said. "Stand up."

I eyed Meredith uneasily as she climbed to her feet. She stood in the middle of our little circle, shifting her weight from foot to foot until she found her balance, tucking her hair out of the way behind her ears—her usual method of centering herself. We all had one, but few of us could make it look so effortless.

"Meredith," Gwendolyn said, smiling up at her. "Our guinea pig. Breathe."

Meredith swayed on the spot, as if at the push and pull of a breeze, eyes closed, lips slightly parted. It was strangely relaxing to watch (and, at the same time, strangely sensual).

"There," Gwendolyn said. "Are you ready?"

Meredith nodded and opened her eyes.

"Lovely. Let's start with something easy. What is your greatest strength as a performer?"

Meredith, normally so confident, hesitated.

Gwendolyn: "Your greatest strength."

Meredith: "I guess—"

Gwendolyn: "No guessing. What is your greatest strength?"

Meredith: "I think—"

Gwendolyn: "I don't want to hear what you think, I want to

hear what you *know*. I don't care if you sound stuck up, I care what you're good at, and as a performer you need to be able to tell me. *What is your greatest strength?*"

"I'm physical!" Meredith said. "I feel everything with my whole body and I'm not afraid to use it."

"You're not afraid to use it, but you're afraid to say what you really mean!" Gwendolyn was nearly shouting. I glanced back and forth between them, alarmed at how quickly things had escalated. "You're tiptoeing around it because we're all sitting here staring at you," Gwendolyn said. "Now, out with it. *Out*."

Meredith's easy elegance was gone, and instead she stood with her legs locked, arms held rigidly at her sides. "I have a great body," she said. "Because I work fucking hard at it. I love looking this way and I love people looking at me. And that makes me magnetic."

"You're damn right, it does." Gwendolyn leered at her like the Cheshire Cat. "You're a beautiful girl. It sounds bitchy, but you know what? It's true. More important than that, it's *honest*." She jabbed one finger at her. "*That* was honest. Good."

Filippa and Alexander both fidgeted, avoiding Meredith's eyes. Richard was looking at her like he wanted to rip her clothes off on the spot, and I had no idea where to look. She nodded and made to sit back down, but Gwendolyn said, "You're not done." Meredith froze. "We've established your strengths. Now I want to hear about your weaknesses. What are you most afraid of?"

Meredith stood glowering at Gwendolyn, who, to my surprise, didn't interrupt the silence. The rest of us squirmed on the floor, eyes flicking up at Meredith with a mixture of sympathy, admiration, and embarrassment.

"Everyone has a weakness, Meredith," Gwendolyn said. "Even you. The strongest thing you can do is admit it. We're waiting."

In the excruciating pause that followed, Meredith stood impossibly still, eyes burning acid green. She was so exposed that

staring at her seemed invasive, voyeuristic, and I grappled with
the impulse to yell at her to just fucking say something.

"I'm afraid," she said, after what felt like a year, speaking very
slowly, "that I'm prettier than I am talented or intelligent, and
that because of that no one will ever take me seriously. As a performer or a person."

Dead silence again. I forced my eyes down, glanced around at
the others. Wren sat with one hand over her mouth. Richard's
expression was softer than I had ever seen it. Filippa looked slightly
nauseous; Alexander was fighting back a nervous grin. On my
right, James peered up at Meredith with keen, evaluative interest,
as if she were a statue, a sculpture, something shaped a thousand
years ago in the likeness of a pagan deity. Her unmasking was
harsh, mesmeric, somehow dignified.

In a weird, bewildered way, I understood that this was exactly what Gwendolyn wanted.

She held Meredith's gaze so long it seemed like time had
stopped. Then she exhaled enormously and said, "Good. Sit.
There."

Meredith's knees bent mechanically, and she sat in the center
of the circle, spine straight and stiff as a fence post.

"All right," Gwendolyn said. "Let's talk."

SCENE 6

After an hour of interrogating Meredith about her insecurities
(of which there were more than I ever would have guessed),
Gwendolyn dismissed us, with the promise that everyone else
would be subjected to the same rigorous questioning over the
next two weeks.

On our way up the stairs to the third floor, second-year art
students bustling around us on their way down to the conservatory, James fell in step beside me.

"That was ruthless," I said, sotto voce. Meredith walked a few steps ahead of us, Richard's arm around her shoulders, though she didn't seem to have noticed it. She moved determinedly forward, avoiding direct eye contact with anyone.

"Again," James whispered, "that's Gwendolyn."

"I never thought I'd say this, but I'm looking forward to being shut in the gallery for two hours straight."

While Gwendolyn taught the more visceral elements of acting—voice and body, heart over head—Frederick taught the intimate particulars of Shakespeare's text, everything from meter to early modern history. Bookish and diffident as I was, I much preferred Frederick's classes to Gwendolyn's, but I was allergic to the chalk he used on his blackboard and spent most of my time in the gallery sneezing.

"Let's go," James said, quietly, "before Meredick steals our table." (Filippa had coined that particular term at the end of our second year, when the two of them were newly in love and at their most obnoxious.) Meredith's expression was still distracted as we edged past them on the stairs. Whatever Richard had said to soothe her, it wasn't working.

Frederick preferred to conduct fourth-year classes in the gallery, rather than the classroom he was forced to use for the more numerous second- and third-years. It was a narrow, high-ceilinged room that had once stretched the entire length of the third floor but was unceremoniously divided into smaller rooms and studios when the school opened. The Long Gallery became the Short Gallery, barely twenty feet from end to end, walled on two sides with bookshelves and dotted with portraits of long-dead Dellecher cousins and offspring. A love seat and a low-slung sofa faced each other under the elaborate plasterwork ceiling, while a small round table and two chairs basked in the light of the diamond-paned window on the south side of the room. Whenever we had tea with Frederick (which we did twice a month as third-years and daily during class as fourth-years), James and I made a beeline for the table. It was farthest from the nefarious chalk dust and offered a sparkling view of the lake and surrounding woods, the conical Tower roof perched on top of the trees like a black party hat.

Frederick was already there when we arrived, wheeling the chalkboard out from an odd little spear closet wedged between a bookshelf and the noseless bust of Homer at the end of the room. I sneezed as James said, "Good morning, Frederick."

He looked up from the blackboard. "James," he said. "Oliver. Lovely to have you both back. Pleased with casting?"

"Absolutely," James said, but there was a note of wistfulness in his voice that puzzled me. Who would be disappointed to be playing Brutus? Then I remembered his remark from two nights previous, about wanting a little more variety on his résumé.

"When's our first rehearsal?" he asked.

"Sunday." Frederick winked. "We thought we'd give you a week to settle back in."

Because of their unsupervised residence in the Castle and their infamous penchant for overindulgence, the fourth-year theatre students were generally expected to throw some kind of kickoff party at the beginning of the year. We had planned it for Friday. Frederick and Gwendolyn and probably even Dean Holinshed knew about it but gamely pretended not to.

Richard and Meredith finally came in from the hall, and James and I hurried to dump our things on the table. I sneezed again, wiped my nose on a tea napkin, and peered out the window. The grounds were soaked in sunlight, the lake rippling gently at the touch of a breeze. Richard and Meredith sat on the smaller sofa, leaving the other for Alexander and Filippa to share. They no longer bothered to leave room for Wren, who (endearingly, like a child excited for story time) preferred to sit on the floor.

Frederick poured tea at the sideboard, so the room smelled, as it always did, of chalk and lemon and Ceylon. When he had

filled eight cups—tea drinking in Frederick's class was mandatory; honey was encouraged, but milk and sugar were contra-
band—he turned around and said, "Welcome back." He twinkled
down at us like a bookish little Santa Claus. "I enjoyed your auditions yesterday, and I am eager to work with you again this semester." He passed the first teacup to Meredith, who passed it to
Richard, who passed it to James, and so on until it ended up in
Wren's hands.

"Fourth year. The year of the tragedy," Frederick said, grandly,
when the tea tray was empty and everyone had a cup and saucer.
(Drinking tea from mugs, we were often reminded, was like
drinking fine wine from a Solo cup.) "I will refrain from telling
you to take the tragedies any more seriously than the comedies. In
fact, one might argue that comedy must be deadly serious to the
characters, or it is not funny for the audience. But that is a conversation for another time." He took his own teacup off the tray,
sipped delicately, and set it down again. Frederick had never had a
desk or lectern, and instead paced slowly back and forth in front of
the blackboard as he taught. "This year, we will devote our attention to Shakespeare's tragic plays. What might that course of study
encompass, do you think?"

I sneezed as if in response to his question, and there was a
brief pause before we began suggesting topics.

Alexander: "Source material."

Filippa: "Structure."

Wren: "Imagery."

Meredith: "Conflict, internal and external."

Me: "Fate versus agency."

James: "The tragic hero."

Richard: "The tragic villain."

Frederick held up a hand to stop us. "Good. Yes," he said.
"All of those things. We will, of course, touch on each of these
plays—*Troilus and Cressida* and other problem plays included—

but naturally we will begin with *Julius Caesar*. A question: Why is *Caesar* not a history play?"

James was first to answer, with characteristic academic eagerness. "The history plays are confined to English history."

"Indeed," Frederick said, and resumed his pacing. I sniffed, stirred my tea, and sat back in my chair to listen. "Most of the tragedies include some element of history, but what we choose to call 'history' plays, as James has said, are truly *English* history plays and are all named after English monarchs. Why else? What makes *Caesar* first and foremost a tragedy?"

My classmates exchanged curious glances, unwilling to offer the first hypothesis and risk being wrong.

"Well," I ventured, when nobody else spoke, my voice thick with congestion, "by the end of the play most of the major characters are dead, but Rome is still standing." I stopped, struggling to articulate the idea. "I think it's more about the people and less about the politics. It's definitely political but if you look at it next to, I don't know, the *Henry VI* cycle, where everybody's just fighting over the throne, *Caesar*'s more personal. It's about the characters and who they are, not just who's in power." I shrugged, unsure whether I'd managed to make any part of my point.

"Yes, I think Oliver is onto something," Frederick said. "Permit me to pose another question: What is more important, that Caesar is assassinated or that he is assassinated by his intimate friends?"

It wasn't the sort of question that needed an answer, so no one replied. Frederick was watching me, I realized, with the proud, fatherly affection he usually reserved for James—who gave me a faint but encouraging smile when I glanced across the table.

"That," Frederick said, "is where the tragedy is." He looked around at all of us, hands folded behind his back, the midday sunlight glinting on his glasses. "So. Shall we begin?" He turned to the blackboard, took a piece of chalk from the tray, and began to write. "Act I, Scene 1. A street. We open with the tribunes and the commoners. What do you suppose is significant about that? The cobbler has a battle of wits with Flavius and Murellus, and upon further questioning introduces our eponymous hero-tyrant . . ."

We rummaged around in our bags to find notebooks and pens, and as Frederick carried on, we scribbled down almost his every word. The sun warmed my back and the bittersweet scent of black tea drifted up into my face. I stole furtive glances at my classmates as they wrote and listened and occasionally posed questions, struck by how lucky I was to be among them.

SCENE 7

Convocation was traditionally held in the gold-spangled music hall on the ninth of September, Leopold Dellecher's birthday. (He'd moved north from Chicago and had the house built sometime in the 1850s. It wasn't turned into a school until a half century later, when the upkeep proved to be too much for the rapidly shrinking Dellecher family.) Had old Leopold somehow evaded death, he would have been turning one hundred and eighty-seven. An enormous cake with exactly that many candles was waiting upstairs in the ballroom to be cut and distributed to students and staff following Dean Holinshed's welcome speech.

We sat on the left side of the aisle, in the middle of a long row filled in by second- and third-years. The theatre students, always the loudest and most likely to laugh, sat behind the instrumental and choral music students (who kept mostly to themselves, apparently determined to perpetuate the stereotype that they were the most complacent and least approachable of the seven Dellecher disciplines). The dancers (a collection of underfed, swan-like creatures) sat behind us. On the opposite side of the aisle sat the studio art students (easily identified by their unorthodox hair-styles and clothing perpetually spattered with paint and plaster), the language students (who spoke almost exclusively in Greek and Latin to one another and sometimes to other people), and the philosophy students (who were by far the weirdest but also the most amusing, prone to treating every conversation as a social experiment and tossing off words like "hylozoism" and "compossibility" as if they were as easily comprehensible as "good morning"). The staff sat in a long line of chairs on the stage. Frederick and Gwendolyn perched side by side like an old married couple, conversing quietly with their neighbors. Convocation was one of the rare times that we all melted together, a sea of people in what we all knew as "Dellecher blue," because nobody wanted to call it "peacock." School colors were not, of course, mandatory, but nearly everyone was wearing the same blue sweater, with the coat of arms stitched above the left breast. A larger version of the family crest hung on a banner behind the podium—a white saltire on a blue field, a long gold key and a sharp black quill crossed like swords in the foreground. Below was the motto: *Per aspera ad astra*. I'd heard a variety of translations, but the one I liked best was *Through the thorns, to the stars.*

As always, it was one of the first things Holinshed said at convocation.

"Good evening, everyone. *Per aspera ad astra.*" He had appeared onstage from the shadows of the wings, a spotlight on his face striking the rest of us into silence. "Another new year. To the first-years among you I must simply say welcome, and that we are delighted to have you. To the second-, third-, and fourth-years, welcome back, and congratulations." Holinshed was a strange man—tall but stooped, quiet but forceful. He had a large hooked nose, wispy copper hair, and little square glasses so thick that they magnified his eyes to three times their natural size. "If you are sitting in this room tonight," he said, "it means you have been accepted into the esteemed Dellecher family. Here you will make many friends, and perhaps a few enemies. Do not let the latter prospect frighten you—if you haven't made any enemies in life, you've been living too safely. And that is what I wish to discourage." He paused, chewed on his words for a moment.

"He's gone a bit off the wall," Alexander muttered.

"Well, he has to recycle his speeches at least every four years," I whispered. "Can you blame him?"

"At Dellecher, I encourage you to live boldly," Holinshed continued. "Make art, make mistakes, and have no regrets. You have come to Dellecher because you prized something above money, above convention, above the kind of education that can be evaluated on a numeric scale. I do not hesitate to tell you that you are remarkable. However"—his expression darkened—"our expectations are adjusted to match your enormous potential. We expect you to be dedicated. We expect you to be determined. We expect you to dazzle us. And we *do not like* to be disappointed." His words boomed through the hall and hung in the air like an odorous vapor, invisible but impossible to ignore. He let the unnatural quiet linger far too long, then abruptly leaned back from the podium and said, "Some of you have joined us at the end of an era, and when you leave you will be emerging into not only a new decade and a new century, but a new millennium. We plan to prepare you for it as best we can. The future is wide and wild and full of promise, but it is precarious, too. Seize on every opportunity that comes your way and cling to it, lest it be washed back out to sea."

His gaze settled unmistakably on us, the seven fourth-year thespians.

"*There is a tide in the affairs of men / Which, taken at the flood, leads on to fortune,*" he said. "*On such a full sea are we now afloat, / And we must take the current when it serves / Or lose our ventures.* Ladies and gentlemen, never waste a moment." Holinshed smiled dreamily, then checked his watch. "And on the subject of waste, there is an enormous cake upstairs that needs devouring. Goodnight."

And he was gone from the stage before the audience could even begin to clap.

SCENE 8

It was a week before anything else interesting happened. After Frederick's class (where a discussion of the fine line between homosocial and homoerotic in the infamous "tent scene" had us all teetering between amusement and embarrassment), we descended the stairs together, complaining of our hunger. The refectory—once the Dellecher family's grand dining room—was crowded at noon, but our usual table was empty and waiting.

"I'm fucking starving," Alexander declared, attacking his plate before the rest of us had even sat down. "Drinking all that damn tea makes me feel ill."

"Maybe if you ate breakfast that wouldn't happen," Filippa said, watching with disgust as he shoveled mashed potatoes into his mouth.

Richard arrived late, with an envelope in his hand, which he'd already opened. "There's mail," he said, and sat down at the end of the table between Meredith and Wren.

"For all of us?" I asked.

"I'd expect so," he said, without looking up.

"I'll go," I said, and a few of them muttered their thanks at me as I stood. Our mailboxes were at the end of the refectory, and I found my name first on the wall of little wooden cubbies. Filippa's was closest to mine, then James, and the rest were increasingly spread out at the far ends of the alphabet. The same square envelope waited in each of our mailboxes, our names written on the front in Frederick's small, elegant script. I took them back to the table and passed them around.

"What are they?" Wren asked.

"Dunno," I said. "We can't be getting midterm speech assignments yet, can we?"

"No," Meredith said, already tearing into hers. "It's *Macbeth*."

The rest of us immediately stopped talking and ripped our
own envelopes open.

A few traditional performances took place every year at Dellecher. While the weather was warm, the art students re-created
van Gogh's *Starry Night* with sidewalk chalk. In December the
language students did a reading of " 'Twas the Night Before
Christmas" in Latin. The philosophy students rebuilt their Ship
of Theseus every January and held a symposium in March, while
the choral and instrumental students did *Don Giovanni* on Valen-
tine's Day and the dancers performed Stravinsky's *Rite of Spring* in
April. The theatre students did scenes from *Macbeth* on Halloween and scenes from *Romeo and Juliet* at the Christmas masque.
Because the first-, second-, and third-years were barely involved, I
had no idea how they were cast.

I broke the seal on my envelope and pulled out a card that
bore five more lines of Frederick's tiny writing:

> *Please be at the trailhead at a*
> *quarter to midnight on Halloween.*
> *Come prepared for Act I, Scene 3, and Act IV, Scene 1.*
>
> *You will be playing* BANQUO.
>
> *Report to the costume shop at 12:30 p.m.*
> *on October 18th for a costume fitting.*
> *Do not discuss this with your peers.*

I stared at it, wondering if there had been some clerical error.
I checked the envelope again, but it said, unmistakably, *Oliver*. I
glanced up at James to see if he had noticed anything unusual,

but his face was blank. I would have expected him to be playing
Banquo to Richard's Macbeth.

"Well," Alexander said, looking faintly bemused, "I take it
we're not supposed to talk about this."

"No," Richard said. "It's tradition. The Christmas masque is
the same, we're not meant to know who's playing whom before
the performance." I had momentarily forgotten that he'd played
Tybalt the previous year.

I struggled to read the girls' faces. Filippa seemed unsurprised.
Wren looked excited. Meredith, slightly suspicious.

"Do we get to rehearse at all?" Alexander asked.

"No," Richard said again. "You'll get a cue script in your
mailbox tomorrow. Then you just learn your lines and show up.
Excuse me." He pushed his chair back and left the table without
another word. Wren and Meredith exchanged a quizzical look.

MEREDITH: "What's wrong with him?"

WREN: "He was fine half an hour ago."

MEREDITH: "Do you want to go or should I?"

WREN: "Be my guest."

Meredith left the table with a sigh, her shepherd's pie only half
eaten. Alexander, who had finished his own, had the good grace
to wait a full three seconds before he said, "You think she's coming back for that?"

James pushed the plate at him. "Eat it, you savage."

I glanced over my shoulder. In the corner by the coffee urns,
Meredith had caught Richard and was listening to him talk with
a hard frown. She touched his arm, said something, but he
shrugged away and left the refectory, confusion hanging like a
shadow over his eyes. She watched him go, then returned to the
table to tell us he had a migraine and was going back to the Castle.
Apparently oblivious to the fact that her plate had gone missing,
she sat down again.

As lunch dragged on, I ate and listened to the others talk,
lamenting the volume of lines they had to learn for *Caesar* before

off-book day, which was another week away. The envelope felt heavy in my lap. I watched James across the table. He was quiet, too, not really listening to the conversation. I looked from him to Meredith to Richard's empty chair, and couldn't help feeling that the balance of power had somehow shifted.

SCENE 9

Combat class was held after lunch in the rehearsal hall. We dragged battered blue mats out of the storage closet, spread them on the floor, and began to stretch halfheartedly, waiting for Camilo. Camilo—a young Chilean guy whose dark beard and gold earring made him look a bit like a pirate—was our fight choreographer, personal trainer, and movement coach. Second- and third-year movement classes were devoted to dance, clowning, animal work, and all the basic gymnastics an actor might need. First semester of fourth year was devoted to hand-to-hand combat, second semester to swordplay.

Camilo arrived at exactly one o'clock and, because it was a Monday, lined us all up to be weighed.

"You've put on five pounds since start of term," he said, when I stepped on the scale. He'd been pleased with my progress over the summer, even if Gwendolyn hadn't. "Are you sticking to the program I gave you?"

"Yes," I said, which was mostly true. I was supposed to be running, lifting, eating well, and not drinking much. We unanimously ignored Camilo's responsible drinking policy.

"Good. Keep at the weights, but don't kill yourself." He leaned closer, as if to share a secret. "It's fine for Richard to look like the Hulk, but frankly you don't have the metabolism for it. Keep your protein intake up and you'll be lean and mean."

"Great." I stepped off the scale and let Alexander—who was taller than I was but always too skinny because he couldn't stop smoking or wake up in time for breakfast—take my place. I eyed my reflection in the long mirrors on the wall opposite the windows. I was fit enough, but I wanted a little more weight, a little more muscle. I stretched and glanced at James, who was the smallest of us boys—barely five ten, slim but not skinny. There was something almost catlike about him, a kind of primal agility. (For animal work, Camilo had assigned him the leopard. He spent a month prowling around our room in the dark before he was sufficiently absorbed in the role to pounce on me in my sleep. I spent the next half hour waiting for my heart to stop hammering while I assured him that, yes, my cry of terror had been entirely genuine.)

"No Richard today?" Camilo asked, when Alexander stepped off the scale.

"He's not feeling well," Meredith said. "Migraine."

"Pity," Camilo said. "Well, we must carry on without him." He stood looking down at the six of us, sitting like ducklings in a neat little row on the edge of the mat. "What did we finish with last week?"

Filippa: "Slaps."

Camilo: "Yes. Remind me of the rules."

Wren: "Make sure you're not too close. Make eye contact with your partner. Turn your body to hide the nap."

Camilo: "And?"

James: "Always use a flat, open hand."

Camilo: "And?"

Meredith: "You have to sell it."

Camilo: "How?"

Me: "Sound effects are most convincing."

"Perfect," Camilo said. "I think we're ready to try something with a little more force. Why don't we learn the backhand?" He cleared his throat, cracked his knuckles. "The backhand—you can do this with your fist or a flat hand, depends what you're going for—is different from a straight slap because you should never cross the body."

"How do you mean?" Meredith asked.

"James, may I borrow you?" Camilo said.

"Certainly." James climbed to his feet and let Camilo position him so they were standing face-to-face. Camilo extended his arm so the tip of his middle finger was a hairsbreadth from the end of James's nose.

"When you slap someone, you have to move your hand across the middle of their body." He moved his hand across James's face in slow motion, without touching him. James turned his head in the same direction. "But with a backhand, you don't want to do that. Instead, my hand is going to go straight up along his side." Camilo's right fist moved vertically from his left hip up past the crown of James's head. "See? One long straight line. You don't ever want to cross the face doing this because you could just about take somebody's face off. But that's all there is to it. Shall we try it full speed? James, I'll have you do the nap."

"All right."

They locked eyes, and James gave Camilo a little nod. Camilo's arm flashed across the space between them, and there was a solid crack as James smacked his own thigh and lurched away. It happened so fast it was impossible to tell they'd never made contact.

"Excellent," Camilo said. "Let's talk about when or why you might want to use this move. Anyone?"

Filippa was the first to answer. (In Camilo's class, she often was.) "Since you're not crossing the body, you can stand closer together." She tilted her head, looking from Camilo to James as if she were rewinding and replaying the blow in her mind. "Which makes it almost intimate, and especially jarring precisely *because* it's so intimate."

Camilo nodded. "It's remarkable how the theatre—and Shakespeare in particular—can numb us to the spectacle of violence. But it's not just a stage trick. When Macbeth has his head chopped off, or Lavinia has her tongue cut out, or the conspirators bathe their hands in Caesar's blood, it should affect you, whether you're the victim, the aggressor, or only a bystander. Have you ever seen a real fight? It's ugly. It's visceral. Most importantly, it's emotional. Onstage we have to be in control so we don't hurt other actors, but violence has to come from a place of violent feeling, or the audience won't believe it." He glanced from one of us to the next until his eyes landed on me. A grin flickered under his moustache. "Oliver, would you join us?"

"Sure." I pushed myself to my feet and took Camilo's place across from James.

"Now," Camilo said, putting one hand on each of our shoulders, "you two are famously good friends, aren't you?"

We smirked at each other.

"James, you're going to try the backhand on Oliver. Don't say it out loud, but I want you to think of what he would have to do to make you hit him. And don't move a muscle until you feel that impulse."

James's smile faded, and he watched me with a close, confused sort of look, eyebrows pinched tightly over the bridge of his nose.

"Oliver, I want you to do the opposite," Camilo said. "Imagine you've provoked this attack, and when it happens, let the feeling hit you even though the fist doesn't."

I blinked, already at a loss.

"Whenever you're ready," he said, and stepped back. "Take your time."

We stood there, motionless, staring at each other. James's eyes were keen bright gray, but standing so close I could see a little ring of gold around each pupil. Something was moving, working, in his mind—accompanied by a tightening at the corners of his jaw, a nervous twitch of his lower lip. James had never really been angry with me, to my knowledge. Transfixed by the strangeness of it, I completely forgot my own part of the exercise and simply watched the pressure build, his shoulders rising, fists clenched tight at his sides. He gave me a small, curt nod. I knew what was coming, but some incongruous reflex made me lean forward, tilt toward him. His hand slashed up toward my head, but I didn't react, didn't do the nap or the turn, just flinched as something sharp flicked across my cheek.

It was weirdly still and quiet in the room. James frowned at me, the spell of animosity broken. "Oliver? You didn't— Oh!" He took my chin in one hand and turned my head, brushed the side of my face. Blood. "God, I'm sorry."

I grabbed his elbow to steady myself. "No, it's all right. Is it bad?"

Camilo edged James out of the way. "Let's see," he said. "No, just a scratch, caught the corner of his watch. You okay?"

"Yeah," I said. "I don't know what happened, I just spaced out and leaned into it." I gave him an awkward shrug, suddenly aware that he and the four classmates I'd forgotten about were all staring at me. "It's my fault. I wasn't ready." James, not forgotten—how could he be?—stood watching me with such profound concern that I almost laughed. "Really," I said. "I'm fine."

But when I went back to my seat I nearly staggered, as dizzy as if he really had hit me.

SCENE 10

Our first off-book rehearsal did not go well.

It was also our first rehearsal in the space. The Archibald Dellecher Theatre sat five hundred people and was decorated with all the modesty of a baroque opera house. The seats were upholstered in the same blue velvet as the grand drape, and the chandelier was so impressive that some people seated in the balcony spent more time staring at it than watching whatever play they'd come to see. With six weeks of rehearsal left, none of the actual platforms or set pieces had been built, but they were all taped out on the stage. It felt like standing on a giant jigsaw puzzle.

I knew my Casca lines, but I hadn't spent as much time on Octavius, since he didn't enter until Act IV. I crouched in a third-row seat, furiously rereading my upcoming speeches as Alexander and James faltered through what we had started calling The Tent Scene, which by that point was one part martial strategy dispute, one part lovers' tiff.

James: *"Should I have answered Caius Cassius so?*
　　When Marcus Brutus grows so covetous
　　To lock such rascal counters from his friends,
　　Be ready, gods, with all your thunderbolts;
　　Dash him to pieces!"

Alexander:　　　　*"I denied you not!"*

James: *"You did!"*

Alexander: *"I did not: he was but a fool that brought*
　　My answer back. Brutus hath rived my heart.
　　A friend should bear his friend's infirmities,
　　But Brutus makes mine greater than they are."

They glared at each other for so long that I glanced toward the prompt table before James blinked and said, "Line."

I felt a sympathetic twinge of embarrassment. Richard, waiting in the wings to enter as Caesar's ghost, shifted his weight, arms folded tightly.

"I do not, 'til you practice them on me," Gwendolyn called from the back of the house. I could tell from her exaggerated emphasis on the meter that she was getting tired of delays.

James: *"I do not, 'til you practice them on me."*

Alexander: *"You love me not."*

James:　　　　　　*"I do not like your faults."*

Alexander: *"A friendly eye could never see such faults."*

James: *"A flatterer's would not, though they do appear*
　　As huge as high Olympus!"

Alexander: *"Come, Antony, and young Octavius, come,*
　　Revenge yourselves alone on Cassius,
　　For Cassius is aweary of the world . . . Line?"

Gwendolyn: *"Hated by one he loves—"*
Alexander: *"Hated by one he loves; braved by his brother;*
    Cheque'd like a bondman; all his faults observed,
    Set in a note-book . . . Damn. Line?"
Gwendolyn: *"—learn'd and conn'd by rote—"*
Alexander: "Right, sorry, *learn'd and conn'd by rote,*
    To cast into my teeth. O, I could weep
    My spirit from mine eyes!"

Alexander proffered an imaginary blade (we didn't have props yet) and tore the neck of his shirt open. "*There is my dagger,*" he exclaimed, "*And here my naked breast; within, a heart / Dearer than Pluto's*—No, sorry—*Plutus' mine.* Is that right? Fuck me. Line?" He looked toward the prompt table, but before Gwendolyn could feed him the text, Richard emerged into the work lights from the stage left wing.

"I'm sorry," he said, deep voice ringing in the mostly empty auditorium. "Are we going to spend the whole night on this scene? Clearly they don't know the lines."

In the answering silence I stared at James, openmouthed, afraid to turn around. He and Alexander both glowered at Richard like he'd said something obscene, while Meredith had frozen where she sat on the floor in the aisle, one leg extended to stretch out a kink in her hamstring. Wren and Filippa craned their necks to peer into the darkness over my shoulder. I risked glancing behind me. Gwendolyn was on her feet; Frederick sat beside her with his hands folded, frowning down at the floor.

"Richard, that's enough," Gwendolyn said, sharply. "Take five and don't come back until you've cooled off."

Richard didn't react at first, as if he hadn't understood, then abruptly turned on his heel and left through the wings without a word.

Gwendolyn looked down on James and Alexander. "You two take five as well, look over your lines, and come back ready to work. In fact, everyone take five. Go." When nobody moved, she flapped her hands to shoo us out of the auditorium, like we were so many unwelcome chickens. I loitered until James brushed past me, then followed him out to the loading dock. Alexander was already there, already lighting a spliff.

"That son of a bitch," he said. "He's got half as many lines as we do and he's got the nerve to interrupt our first off-book run? *Fuck* him." He sat down, sucked hard on the spliff, then passed it up to James, who took one short drag and handed it back.

"You're not wrong," he said as he exhaled, a cloud of white smoke issuing from his lips. "But neither is he."

Alexander looked mutinous. "Well, fuck you, too."

"Don't pout. We *should* know our lines better. Richard's called us out on it, is all."

"Yeah," I said, "but he was a major dick about it."

One corner of James's mouth twitched toward a smile. "True."

The door opened and Filippa appeared, arms folded against the nighttime chill. "Hey. You guys okay?"

Alexander took another long pull and let his mouth hang open, the smoke pouring out in a long, lazy stream.

"It's been a long night," James said, flatly.

"If it makes you feel any better, Meredith's just bitten Richard's head off."

"What for?" I asked.

"For being a jackass," she said, as if it should have been obvious. "Just because she's sleeping with him doesn't mean she can't see when he's being a shithead."

James: "I'm confused. Is he a jackass or is he a shithead?"

Filippa: "Honestly, I think Richard could be both."

Me: "At least he won't be getting laid for a while."

Alexander: "Yeah. Great. That'll make him much more cooperative."

"Actually, he apologized," Filippa said. "To Meredith, anyway. Said it was childish and he regretted it already."

"Really?" Alexander said, smoke curling around his head like he was about to combust. "So not only is he a jackass shithead major dick son of a bitch, but he's already apologized?" He threw his spliff on the concrete and ground it out with his heel. "That's just perfect, now we can't even stay mad. Seriously, fuck him." He finished pulverizing the spliff and looked up at the rest of us. We stood in a loose ring around him, lips pressed tight together, struggling to keep straight faces. "What?"

Filippa caught my eye and we both burst out laughing.

SCENE 11

Time travels in divers paces with divers persons. With us it ambled, trotted, and galloped all through October. (It never stood still until the morning of November the twenty-second, and it seems, to me at least, that it hasn't really moved since then.)

We had long ago finished cataloging our strengths and weaknesses. Alexander followed Meredith and declared his ability to frighten people rather proudly, but confessed the concern that he was the villain in his own life's story. Wren presented a double-edged sword: she was intimately in touch with her emotions but, as a result, too sensitive for such a competitive artistic environment. Richard told us what we all knew already—that he was unfailingly confident, but his ego made him difficult to work with. Filippa made her statement without any trace of embarrassment. She was versatile, but because she didn't have a "type," she would be stuck playing secondary characters forever. James—speaking slowly, deep in thought, seeming not to even see the rest of us— explained that he immersed himself completely in every character he played, but sometimes he couldn't quite leave them behind and learn to be himself again. By the time my turn came we had grown so numb to one another's insecurities that my saying I was the least talented person in our year didn't seem to surprise anyone. I couldn't think of any great strength I had and admitted as much, but James interrupted me to say, "Oliver, you make every scene you're in about the other people in it. You're the nicest person and the most generous actor here, which is probably more important than talent anyway." I immediately shut my mouth, certain he was the only one who thought so. Oddly, nobody else argued.

On October 16, we took our usual places in the gallery. Outside, a perfect autumn day had lit the trees around the lake aflame. The blaze of color—tawny orange, sulfurous yellow, arterial red—shimmered upside down on the surface of the water. James peered out the window over my shoulder and said, "Apparently Gwendolyn has the art classes stewing up stage blood to splatter all over the beach."

"Won't that be fun."

He shook his head, mouth quirked up at one corner, and slid into the chair opposite mine. I pushed a cup and saucer toward him and watched as he lifted the cup to his lips, still smiling. The others rattled in from the hall, and the spell of lazy tranquility faded into the air like steam.

Officially, we had left off our lessons on *Caesar* and moved on to *Macbeth*, but *Caesar*'s familiar words leapt readily to our lips, and with them came a kind of bristling tension. Weeks of difficult rehearsals and Gwendolyn's psychological puppeteering had made neutrality impossible. That day, what began as a simple discussion of tragic structure quickly devolved into an argument.

"No, that's not what I'm saying," Alexander said, halfway through our lesson, impatiently pushing his hair out of his face. "What I'm saying is that the tragic structure is staring you in the face in *Macbeth*; it makes *Caesar* look like a telenovela."

Meredith: "What the hell does that mean?"

Frederick: "Language, please, Meredith."

Wren sat up straighter on the floor, returning her teacup to the saucer between her knees. "No," she said, "I understand."

Richard: "Then explain it to the rest of us, won't you?"

Wren: "Macbeth's a textbook tragic hero."

Filippa: "Tragic flaw: ambition."

Me: [sneeze]

"And Lady M is a textbook tragic villain," James added, glancing from Wren to Filippa, soliciting their agreement. "Unlike Macbeth, she doesn't have a single moral qualm about murdering Duncan, which paves the way for every other murderous thing they do."

"So what's the difference?" Meredith said. "It's the same in *Caesar*. Brutus and Cassius assassinate Caesar and set themselves up for disaster."

"But they're not villains, are they?" Wren asked. "Cassius maybe, but Brutus does what he does for the greater good of Rome."

"*Not that I loved Caesar less, but that I loved Rome more*," James recited.

Richard made an impatient sort of noise and said, "What's your point, Wren?"

"Her point is my point," Alexander said, shifting forward to perch on the very edge of the couch, long legs bent so his knees were almost as high as his chest. "*Caesar*'s not in the same category of tragedy as *Macbeth*."

Meredith: "So, what category is it in?"

Alexander: "Fuck if I know."

Frederick: "Alexander!"

Alexander: "Sorry."

"I think you're making it too complicated," Richard said. "*Caesar* and *Macbeth* have the same setup. Tragic hero: Caesar. Tragic villain: Cassius. Wishy-washy middleman: Brutus. I guess you could equate him with Banquo."

"Wait," I said. "What makes Banquo—"

But James interrupted: "You think *Caesar* is the tragic hero?"

Richard shrugged. "Who else?"

Filippa pointed at James. "Um, duh."

"It has to be Brutus," Alexander said. "Antony makes it plain as day in Five-Five. It's your cue, Oliver, what does he say?"

Me: *"This was the noblest Roman of them all:*
    All the conspirators, [sneeze] *save only he,*
    Did that they did in envy of great Caesar;
    He only, in a general honest thought
    And common good to all, made one of them."

"No," Richard insisted. "Brutus can't be the tragic hero."

James was affronted. "Why on earth not?"

Richard almost laughed at the look on his face. "Because he's got like fourteen tragic flaws!" he said. "A hero's only supposed to have *one*."

"Caesar's is ambition, just like Macbeth," Meredith said. "Simple. Brutus's only tragic flaw is that he's dumb enough to listen to Cassius."

"How can Caesar be the hero?" Wren asked, glancing from one of them to the other. "He dies in Act III."

"Yes, but the play's named after him, isn't it?" Richard said, the words and his breath coming out together in a rush of exasperation. "That's how it goes in all the other tragedies."

"Really," Filippa said, voice flat. "You're going to base your argument on the *title* of the play?"

"I'm still waiting to hear what these fourteen flaws are," Alexander said.

"I didn't mean there are *exactly fourteen*," Richard said, thinly. "I meant it would be impossible to isolate *one* that leads to him skewering himself."

"Couldn't you argue that Brutus's tragic flaw is his insurmountable love of Rome?" I asked, looking across the table at

James, who was watching Richard with narrowed eyes. Frederick stood in front of the blackboard, lips pursed, listening.

"No," Richard said, "because besides that you've got his pride, his self-righteousness, his vanity—"

"Those are all essentially the same, as you of all people ought to know." James's voice cut across Richard's and the rest of us were startled into silence.

"What was that?" Richard asked. James clenched his jaw and I knew he hadn't meant to say so much out loud.

"You heard me."

"Yes, I fucking did," Richard said, and the cold snap of his voice made every hair on the back of my neck stand up. "I'm giving you a chance to change what you said."

"*Gentlemen.*" I'd nearly forgotten Frederick was there. He spoke softly, faintly, and for a moment I wondered if the shock of it might knock him out. "*Enough.*"

Richard, who had been leaning forward like he might leap off the couch and throw himself at James, eased back against the cushions again. One of Meredith's hands alighted on his knee.

James averted his eyes. "Richard, I'm sorry. I shouldn't have said that."

Richard's face was blank at first, but then the anger vanished and left him looking dejected. "I suppose I deserve it," he said. "Never properly apologized for my little outburst on off-book day. Truce, James?"

"Yes, of course." James looked up again, shoulders sinking an inch in relief. "Truce."

After a slightly awkward pause in which I exchanged quick baffled glances with Filippa and Alexander, Meredith said, "Did that just happen? For God's sake, it's just a *play*."

"Well." Frederick sighed, removed his glasses, and began to polish them on the hem of his shirt. "Duels have been fought over less."

Richard raised an eyebrow at James. "Swords behind the refectory at dawn?"

James: "Only if Oliver will be my second."

Me: *"I've hope to live, and am prepared to die."*

Richard: "Very well, Meredith can be mine."

Alexander: "Thanks for the vote of confidence, Rick."

Richard laughed, all apparently forgiven. We returned to our
debate and proceeded civilly, but I watched James out of the corner of my eye. There had always been small rivalries between us,
but never before such an open display of hostility. With a sip of
tea I persuaded myself that we were all simply overreacting. Actors are by nature volatile—alchemic creatures composed of incendiary elements, emotion and ego and envy. Heat them up, stir
them together, and sometimes you get gold. Sometimes disaster.

SCENE 12

Halloween approached like a tiger in the night, with a soft rumble of warning. All through the second half of October, the skies
were bruised and stormy, and Gwendolyn greeted us every
morning by saying, "What dreadfully *Scottish* weather we're having!"

As the ill-omened day crept closer, it was impossible to suppress a buzz of mounting excitement among the students. The
morning of the thirty-first, whispers chased us around the refectory as we poured our coffee. What, everyone wanted to know,
would happen on the windswept beach that evening? We were too
restless to focus on our lessons, and Camilo dismissed us early, with
the instruction that we "go and prepare our enchantments." Back
in the Castle, we avoided one another, slunk into corners, and
muttered our lines to ourselves, like the inmates of a lunatic asy-
lum. When witching hour arrived, we set off through the woods,
one by one.

The night was eerily warm, and I struggled to follow the crooked forest path in darkness plush as velvet. Unseen roots reached up to snatch at my ankles, and once I lost my footing and fell to the ground, the damp smell of the coming storm swelling in my nose. I brushed myself off and proceeded more carefully, my heartbeat quick and shallow, like the pulse of a nervous rabbit.

When I reached the trailhead, I was afraid for a moment that I was late. My costume (pants, boots, shirt, and coat in culturally ambiguous military style) did not include a watch. I hovered at the edge of the trees, looking back up the hill toward the Hall. Dim lights burned in three or four windows, and I imagined the few students too cautious to brave the beach peeping timidly out. A twig snapped in the shadows and I turned.

"Someone there?"

"Oliver?" James's voice.

"Yeah, it's me," I said. "Where are you?"

He emerged from between two black pines, his face a pale oval in the gloom. He was dressed much the same as I was, but silver epaulettes glinted on his shoulders. "I had hoped you might be my Banquo," he said.

"I suppose congratulations are in order, Thane of Everything."

With my suspicions confirmed, I felt a little pinch of pride. But at the same time something prescient stirred, an indistinct disquiet. No wonder Richard wasn't happy on the day of scene assignments.

Midnight: the low boom of the chapel clock rippled through the still night air and James gripped my arm hard. "*The bell invites me*," he said, words light and breathless with excitement. "*Hear it not, Duncan, for it is a knell / That summons thee to heaven, or to hell!*" He let go and vanished into the shadows of the underbrush. I followed, but not too close, afraid of tripping again and dragging both of us to the ground.

The belt of trees between the Hall and the north shore was dense but narrow, and soon a dusky orange light began to filter between the branches. James—I could see him clearly by then, or the outline of him at least—stopped, and I tiptoed up behind him. Hundreds of people were crowded on the beach, some sitting in long cramped rows on the benches, others in tight little clumps on the ground, their silhouettes black against the fulgent glow of the bonfire. A murmur of thunder smothered the lap of the waves against the shore and the crackling flames. Excited whispers rose from the spectators as the sky overhead, oil-painted in furled fore-boding violet, flushed white with lightning. Then the beach was quiet again, until a high, shrill voice said, "*Look!*"

A solid black shape was approaching on the water, a long rounded dome, like a hump of the Loch Ness Monster.

"What is that?" I breathed.

"It's the witches," James said slowly, the firelight reflected like red sparks in both his eyes.

As the bestial shape crept closer, it came slowly into focus, enough that I could tell it was an overturned canoe. Judging by the height of the hull on the water, there would be just enough room for a pocket of air underneath. The boat drifted into the shallows, and for a moment the surface of the lake was smooth as glass. Then there was a ripple, a shudder, and three figures emerged. A collective gasp rushed out from the audience. The girls looked less like witches at first than phantoms, their hair hanging sleek and wet over their faces, filmy white dresses melt-ing from their limbs, swirling in spirals behind them. As they rose from the water their fingertips dripped and the fabric clung so closely to their bodies that I could tell who was who, though their faces remained downcast. On the left, Filippa, her long legs and slim hips unmistakable. On the right, Wren, smaller and slighter than the other two. In the middle, Meredith, her curves bold and dangerous under the thin white shift. Blood pounded in my ears. James and I, for the time being, forgot each other.

Meredith lifted her chin just high enough that her hair slid back from her face. "*When shall we three meet again?*" she asked, her voice low and lush in the balmy air. "*In thunder, lightning, or in rain?*"

"*When the hurlyburly's done,*" Wren answered, slyly. "*When the battle's lost and won.*"

Filippa's voice, throaty and bold: "*That will be ere the set of sun.*"

A drum echoed from somewhere deep in the trees and the audience shivered with delight. Filippa looked toward the sound, straight up the path to where James and I stood hidden in the shadows. "*A drum, a drum! Macbeth doth come.*"

Meredith raised her hands from her sides and the other two came forward to grasp them.

ALL: "*The weird sisters, hand in hand,*
    Posters of the sea and land,
    Thus do go, about, about,
    Thrice to thine, and thrice to mine,
    And thrice again to make up nine."

They came together in a triangle and pushed their open palms up toward the sky.

"*Peace!*" Meredith said. "*The charm's wound up.*"

James inhaled suddenly, like he'd forgotten to breathe before, and stepped out into the light. "*So foul and fair a day I have not seen,*" he said, and every head turned toward us. I walked close behind him, not afraid of stumbling now.

"*How far is't call'd to Forres?*" I said, and then stopped dead. The three girls stood side by side, staring up at us. "*What are these / So wither'd and so wild in their attire, / That look not like the inhabitants o' the earth, / And yet are on't?*" We descended more slowly. A thousand eyes followed us, five hundred pairs of lungs holding their breath.

Me: "*Live you? or are you aught*
    That man may question? You seem to understand me—"
James: "*Speak if you can.*"

Meredith sank down in a crouch in front of us. *"All hail Macbeth, hail to thee, Thane of Glamis!"*

Wren came to kneel beside her. *"All hail Macbeth, hail to thee, Thane of Cawdor!"*

Filippa didn't move, but said, in a clear ringing voice, *"All hail Macbeth, that shalt be King hereafter!"*

James twitched backward. I caught his shoulders and said, *"Good sir, why do you start, and seem to fear / Things that do sound so fair?"*

He looked sideways at me and I let him go, reluctantly. After a moment's hesitation I slid past him, stepped down from the last sandy stair to stand among the witches.

Me: *"I' the name of truth,*
  Are ye fantastical or that indeed
  Which outwardly ye show? My noble partner
  You greet with present grace and great prediction
  Of noble having and of royal hope,
  That he seems rapt withal. To me you speak not.
  If you can look into the seeds of time,
  And say which grain will grow and which will not,
  Speak then to me, who neither beg nor fear
  Your favors nor your hate."

Meredith was on her feet in an instant. *"Hail!"* she said, and the other girls echoed her. She darted forward, came too close, her face only an inch from mine. *"Lesser than Macbeth and greater."*

Wren appeared behind me, fingers drumming on my waist, peeking up at me with an impish smile. *"Not so happy, yet much happier."*

Still, Filippa stood off. *"Thou shalt get kings, though thou be none,"* she said—indifferent, almost bored. *"So all hail, Macbeth and Banquo."*

Wren and Meredith continued to pet and paw me, plucking at my clothes, exploring the lines of my neck and shoulders, pushing back my hair. Meredith's hand wandered all the way up to my mouth, fingertips tracing my lower lip, before James—who had indeed been looking on with a kind of rapt revulsion—started and spoke. The girls' heads snapped toward him and I swayed on the spot, weak-kneed at the loss of their attention.

James: *"Stay, you imperfect speakers! Tell me more.*

By Sinel's death I know I am Thane of Glamis;
But how of Cawdor? The Thane of Cawdor lives,
A prosperous gentleman; and to be King
Stands not within the prospect of belief."

They only shook their heads, put their fingers to their lips, and slunk back into the water. When they had completely disappeared beneath the surface and we had recovered most of our wits, I turned to James, eyebrows raised expectantly.

"Your children shall be kings," he said.

"You shall be king."

"And Thane of Cawdor too. Went it not so?"

"To the selfsame tune and words." Footsteps approached from the trees and I looked toward them. *"Who's here?"*

The rest of the scene was short, and when I wasn't speaking, I kept a watchful eye on the water. It was still again, reflecting the tempestuous purple sky. When the time came, I and the two lucky third-years playing Ross and Angus exited right, out of the firelight.

"We're done," one of them whispered. "Break legs."

"Thanks." I ducked behind the shed on the edge of the beach. It was no bigger than an outhouse, and if I glanced around one corner I could see the fire, the canoe resting on the water, the stretch of sand where James now stood alone.

"Is this a dagger which I see before me, / The handle toward my hand?" He groped into the empty air before him. *"Come, let me clutch thee."*

It was a speech I had never expected to hear him give. He was too spotless to talk of blood and murder like Macbeth, but in the red glare of the fire he no longer looked so angelic. Instead he was handsome the way you think of the devil as handsome—forbiddingly so.

James: *"Thou sure and firm-set earth,*
   Hear not my steps, which way they walk, for fear
   The very stones prate of my whereabout,
   And take the present horror from the time,
   Which now suits with it. Whiles I threat, he lives:
   Words to the heat of deeds too cold breath gives.
   I go, and it is done."

He condemned Duncan once more, then stole away to meet me on the edge of the firelight as the audience waited, whispering to one another, for the next scene to begin.

"What now?" I said when he was close enough to hear.

"I think—wait." He shrank back, bumped against me.

"What?"

"*Hecate*," he hissed.

Before I could even catch the substance of the word, Alexander exploded out of the water. Little shrieks of surprise went up from the audience as waves crashed back down around him. He was soaking wet, naked to the waist, his curls loose and wild around his face. He threw his head back and howled up at the sky like a wolf.

"Literally wicked," I said.

The girls emerged from the water again, and no sooner had Meredith said, "*Why how now, Hecate, you look angerly!*" than Alexander grabbed her by the back of the neck, flinging water everywhere.

"*Have I not reason, beldams as you are,*" he snarled, "*Saucy and over-bold? How did you dare / To trade and traffic with Macbeth / In riddles and affairs of death?*"

James seized my arm. "Oliver," he said. "*Blood-bolter'd Banquo smiles upon me.*"

"Oh. Oh, *shit.*"

He bullied me into the shed, the door squealing treacherously behind us. Inside, the floor was cluttered with oars and lifejackets, leaving barely enough space for the two of us to stand face-to-face. A gallon bucket waited on one low shelf.

"Jesus," I said, hastily unbuttoning my jacket. "How much blood did they think we needed?"

"Loads, apparently," James told me, bending down to wedge the lid off. "And it *reeks*." A sweet, rotten odor filled the room as I wriggled out of my boots. "I suppose we have to give them points for authenticity."

My arm was tangled in a shirtsleeve. "*Shit* shit shit, I'm stuck, ouch, fuck—James, help—!"

"Hush! Here." He stood, took my shirt by the hem, and yanked it up over my head. My head got caught in the collar and I crashed against him. "Can you get blood on those pants?" he asked, catching at my waistband to steady me.

"Well, I'm not going naked."

He reached for the bucket. "Fair enough. Close your mouth."

I clamped my mouth and eyes shut and he poured the blood over my head, like some kind of perverse pagan baptism. I spluttered and coughed as it ran down my face. "What *is* this shit?"

"I don't know. And I don't know how much time you have." He grabbed my head. "Hold still." He smeared the blood around my face and chest and shoulders, raked his fingers through my hair to make it stand on end. "There." For a split second he just stared at me, somehow looking impressed and completely revolted at the very same time.

"How do I look?"

"Fucking incredible," he said, then nudged me toward the door. "Now go."

I stumbled out of the shed and sprinted into the trees, swearing as sharp stones and pine needles jabbed at my bare feet. It was certainly spooky, showing up at midnight with no idea who we'd meet in the dark, but it was troublesome, too. I only knew

my scenes, so I could hardly guess how much time I had before
I was due to enter as Banquo's ghost. A branch whipped across my
face but I ignored it and clambered up the hill, over roots and
rocks and creeping vines. Another scratch on my cheek wouldn't
matter; I was already covered in blood. My skin felt sticky as it
cooled in the raw night air, and my heart was pounding again—
half from the effort of climbing to the trailhead, half from petty
fear that I would miss my second entrance.

As it turned out, I made it back to the tree line in plenty of
time. I arrived slowly and clumsily, twigs cracking under my feet,
but the audience was watching James's second conference with the
witches with anxious attention and paid me no mind. I lurked
under a low-hanging branch, the keen scent of pine cutting
through the ripe stench of stage blood on my skin.

Wren: *"By the pricking of my thumbs,*
   Something wicked this way comes!"
James: *"How now, you secret, black, and midnight hags!*
   What is't you do?"

The girls danced in a ring around the fire, hair loose and
tangled, green lakeweed clinging to their skirts. Every now
and then one of them tossed a handful of sparkling dust in the
fire and a cloud of colored smoke burst above the flames. I shifted
in my hiding place, waiting. I was the last in a series of visions,
but how would they appear? I searched the crowd of spectators
for familiar faces, but it was too dark to make out many distin-
guishing features. I spotted Colin's blond head on the house left
side, and the firelight glinted on a coppery curl that I thought
might belong to Gwendolyn. I couldn't help but wonder—where
in the world was Richard?

An unearthly shriek of laughter from Wren pulled my attention back down to the beach.

Meredith: *"Speak!"*
Wren: *"Demand!"*
Filippa: *"We'll answer."*

Meredith: *"Say, if thou'dst rather hear it from our mouths,*
   Or from our masters?"
James: *"Call 'em; let me see 'em."*
The girls' voices rose in a high, discordant chant. James stood
looking on, brooding and uncertain.

Meredith: *"Pour in sow's blood, that hath eaten*
   Her nine farrow; grease that's sweaten
   From the murderer's gibbet throw
   Into the flame—"
ALL: *"Come, high or low;*
   Thyself and office deftly show!" .

Filippa threw something on the fire and the flames roared
up above their heads. A voice bellowed across the beach, tremendous and terrifying as some primordial god. Unmistakably,
Richard.

"MACBETH. MACBETH. MACBETH. BEWARE MACDUFF."

He was nowhere to be seen, but his voice pressed in on us
from all sides, so loud it rattled in my bones. James was no less
alarmed than I or anyone else and stumbled over his words when
he spoke. *"What'er thou art, for thy good caution, thanks; / Thou hast
harp'd my fear aright: but one word more—"*
Richard interrupted, deafeningly.

Richard: *"BE BLOODY, BOLD, AND RESOLUTE; LAUGH TO*
   SCORN
   THE POWER OF MAN, FOR NONE OF WOMAN BORN
   SHALL HARM MACBETH."
James: *"Then live, Macduff: what need I fear of thee?"*
Richard: *"BE LION-METTLED, PROUD; AND TAKE NO*
   CARE
   WHO CHAFES, WHO FRETS, OR WHERE CONSPIRERS
   ARE:
   MACBETH SHALL NEVER VANQUISH'D BE UNTIL
   GREAT BIRNAM WOOD TO HIGH DUNSINANE HILL
   SHALL COME AGAINST HIM."

James: *"That will never be—*
Who can impress the forest, bid the tree
Unfix his earth-bound root? Sweet bodements! good!
Rebellion's head, rise never till the wood
Of Birnam rise, and our high-placed Macbeth
Shall live the lease of nature, pay his breath
To time and mortal custom. Yet my heart
Throbs to know one thing: tell me, if your art
Can tell so much: shall Banquo's issue ever
Reign in this kingdom?"

The witches all cried out at once, *"Seek to know no more!"*

James: *"I will be satisfied: deny me this,*
And an eternal curse fall on you! Let me know."

ALL: *"Show his eyes, and grieve his heart;*
Come like shadows, so depart!"

Eight cloaked figures rose in the back row of the audience. A girl sitting beside them squealed in surprise. They glided toward the center aisle and began to descend (more third-years? I wondered) while James watched in wide-eyed horror. *"What,"* he said, *"will the line stretch out to the crack of doom?"*

My heart leapt up into my throat. I stepped into the light for the second time, blood slick and gleaming on my skin. James gaped up at me, and the audience all turned together. Stifled screams fluttered on the surface of the silence.

"Horrible sight," James said, weakly. I started down the stairs again, raising my arm to point and claim the eight cloaked figures as my own. *"Now, I see, 'tis true; / For the blood-bolter'd Banquo smiles upon me, / And points at them for his."*

I lowered my hand again and they disappeared, melted into the surrounding shadows as if they had never existed. James and I stood ten feet apart before the fire. I gleamed crimson, grim and bloody as a newborn baby, while James's face was ghostly white.

"*What, is this so?*" he said—it seemed—to me. A strange, swelling silence followed. We both leaned forward without moving our feet, waiting for something to happen. Then Meredith came between us.

"*Ay, sir,*" she said, and dragged James's gaze away from me. "*All this is so: but why / Stands Macbeth thus amazedly?*"

He allowed himself to be led away, back to the fire and the tempting attentions of the witches. I climbed to the top of the steps, stopped there and lingered, to haunt him. Twice his eyes wandered my way, but the audience was watching the girls again. They reeled around the fire, cackling up at the stormy sky, and began to sing once more. James looked on for a moment, aghast, then turned and fled the firelight.

ALL: "*Double double, toil and trouble;*
 Fire burn and cauldron bubble—
 Scale of dragon, tooth of wolf,
 Witches' mummy, maw and gulf . . ."

While Meredith and Wren carried on the dance, their movement wild and violent, Filippa lifted up a bowl that had been hidden deep in the sand. A red and viscous liquid sloshed against the sides, the same false blood that prickled on my skin.

ALL: "*Double double, toil and trouble,*
 Fire burn and cauldron bubble.
 Cool it with a baboon's blood,
 Then the charm is firm and good."

Filippa upended the bowl. There was a sickening splash, and everything went black. The audience surged to its feet in a roar of glee and confusion. I sprinted back into the cover of the trees.

When the lakeside lights came on—weak orange bulbs flickering weirdly at the edges of the beach—the shore was alive with shouts and laughter and applause. I doubled over in the cool forest darkness, hands on my knees, breathing heavily. I felt like I'd just outrun a landslide. All I wanted was to find the other fourth-years and share a sigh of relief.

But quiet celebration was not to be had. Halloween demanded a party of bacchanalian proportions, and it didn't take long to begin. As soon as the faculty and the more timorous first- and second-years had gone, kegs appeared as if conjured by some lingering magic, and music came thudding through the speakers that had so eerily magnified Richard's voice. Alexander was the first of us to emerge, staggering out of the water like a drowned man reanimated. Admirers and friends from other disciplines (there were many of the former, few of the latter) surrounded him, and he regaled them with a thrilling tale of treading water for over an hour. I waited in the safety of the trees a little longer, well aware that I was covered in blood and it would be impossible not to draw attention to myself. Only when I spotted Filippa did I venture back out onto the beach.

As soon as the light hit me, people shouted congratulations, reached out to slap my back and tousle my hair before they realized how sticky I was. By the time I made my way to Filippa, two plastic cups foaming over with beer had been forced into my hands.

"Here," I said, and passed one to her. "Happy Halloween."

Her eyes flicked from my bloody face to my dirty bare feet and back again. "Nice costume."

I plucked at the sleeve of her dress, which was still damp and mostly transparent. "I like yours better."

She rolled her eyes. "Think they'll try to get all of us completely naked this year?"

"There's always the Christmas masque."

"Oh God, bite your tongue."

"Seen the others?"

"Meredith's off looking for The Voice. No clue about James and Wren."

Alexander excused himself from his audience and barged between us, hooking an arm around each of our necks. "That went about as well as could be expected," he said. Then, "What the fuck? Oliver, you're *filthy*."

"No, I'm Banquo." (He had been back under the boat for both of my scenes.)

"You smell like raw meat."

"You smell like pond water."

"Touché." He grinned and rubbed his palms together. "Shall we get this party properly started?"

"How do you propose we do that?" Filippa asked.

"Get drunk, get loud, get lucky." He pointed a finger pistol at her. "Unless you have a better idea."

She put both hands up in surrender and said, "Lead on."

Halloween seemed to bring out a sort of sybaritic hysteria in the Dellecher students. What I remembered of it from my first three years was quickly forgotten, as being a fourth-year was a little like being a celebrity. People I didn't know, barely knew, barely recognized, heaped compliments on me and all the others, asked how long we'd been rehearsing, and expressed appropriate amazement when they learned that we hadn't, at all. For an hour or so I accepted proffered drinks and drags on spliffs and cigarettes, but the close press of people soon began to suffocate me. I scanned the crowd with some urgency, in search of one of my fellow fourth-year thespians. (I'd been separated from Alexander and Filippa, though at that point I didn't recall when or how.) I shook off a desperately flirtatious second-year girl by saying I needed another drink, found one, and wandered toward the edge of the light. I breathed a little more freely, content to watch the debauchery for a while without participating. I sipped slowly at my beer until I felt a hand on my arm.

"Hello there."

"Meredith." She had detached herself from a group of studio art boys (probably begging her to pose for a drawing class) and followed me to the periphery of the party. She was still in her witch dress, and in my foggy state it was impossible not to stare at her through the fabric.

"Tired of hearing how fabulous you are?" she asked.

"Mostly they just want to touch the blood."

She smiled and walked her fingers from my elbow up to my shoulder. "Sick little freaks." She'd definitely been drinking, but she held her liquor better than the rest of us. "Then again, maybe they just want an excuse to touch *you*." She licked a spot of stage blood off the tip of one finger and winked, thick black eyelashes like ostrich-feather fans. It was unbearably sexy, which irritated me for some reason. "You know," she said, "the bare-chested, covered-in-blood look, it's working for you."

"The braless, wearing-a-bedsheet look, it's working for you," I said, without thinking, and only half sarcastic. A slow-motion movie of Richard kicking my teeth in reeled through my head and I added, loudly, "Where's your boyfriend? I don't think I've seen him."

"He's sulking, trying to keep me and everyone else from having fun." I followed her gaze back to the beach, where Richard was sitting on a bench by himself, nursing a drink and watching the revelers as if he found their partying profoundly offensive.

"What's wrong with him now?"

"Who cares? It's always something." She tugged my fingers and said, "Come on, James is looking for you."

I pulled my hand away but followed obediently, downing most of my drink in one gulp. I could feel Richard glaring at me.

Someone had built the fire up to blazing again, and James and Wren stood beside it, talking to each other and ignoring everyone else. As we approached he offered her his coat; she pulled it close around her shoulders, then looked down and laughed. The hem hung halfway to her knees.

"How on earth did all four of you fit under that canoe?" James asked, when I was near enough to hear.

"Well, it was very cozy," she said. "I must've accidentally almost kissed Alexander five times."

"Lovely. Give him a few more drinks and he'll be telling everyone how badly you want him."

Wren turned toward us and gave a little gasp, clutching the collar of James's coat with both hands. "Oliver, you startled me! You still look frightful."

Me: "I'd love to wash off, but that water looks very cold."

Wren: "It's not terrible once you're in it up to your waist."

Me: "Says the girl standing by the fire, wearing someone else's coat."

"Wren," Meredith said, glancing over her shoulder toward the benches, "will you please talk to Richard? I've had enough of him."

Wren offered the rest of us a wan smile and said, "*My gentle cousin.*"

James watched her pick her way through the crowd. Meredith peered into his half-empty cup, took it from him, and reached for mine. "You two stay here," she said. "I'll be back with more drinks."

"Oh good," I said. "I can't wait."

When she was gone, James turned to me and asked, "All right?"

"Yes," I said. "Fine."

I could tell from his skeptical smile that he didn't believe me, but mercifully he chose to change the subject. "You know, you *do* look frightful. Scared me half to death coming out of the trees like that."

"James, you did this to me."

"Yes, but in the dark in that tiny little shed, it wasn't the same. With all the light on you and that look on your face . . ."

"Well," I said, "*blood will have blood.*"

"Well, I plan never to get on your bad side."

"Likewise," I said. "You make a surprisingly convincing villain."

He shrugged. "Better me than Richard. He looks really murderous."

I glanced toward the benches again. Richard and Wren sat side by side, heads bent together. An ominous frown darkened his face as he spoke, looking down at his hands. That half-buried unease pushed up toward the surface again. I told myself it was just a stomachache, too much booze drunk too quickly. "*Sound and fury*," I said, "*signifying nothing*. Don't mind him."

Another hour went by, or maybe two or three. The sky was so dark that it was impossible to tell how time was passing, unless you measured the minutes by the number of drinks you had. I lost count after seven, but my hand was never empty. The younger students retreated to the Hall, weaving through the trees, laughing and swearing as they tripped over protuberant roots and spilled what was left of their beer on themselves. Fourth-years of every discipline and a few precocious third-years lingered. Someone decided that the night couldn't end without everyone soaking wet, and slippery, wobbling chicken fights had begun.

After a dozen rounds, Alexander and Filippa were the reigning champions. They looked more like one creature than two, Filippa's long legs wound so tightly around Alexander's shoulders that they could have been a terrifying set of Siamese twins. He stood waist-deep in the water, barely swaying, gripping her knees. Unlike Meredith, his drunkenness was obvious, but it only seemed to make him invincible.

"Whozenext?" he yelled. "*Undefeated*, that's what we are."

"If someone defeats you, will you call it a night?" James asked. The rest of us sat in the sand, our bare feet at the edge of the water, forgotten drinks hanging heavily from our fingertips. The air was unseasonably temperate for October, but cold waves nipped at our toes, a forewarning of approaching winter.

Alexander listed to the left and let go of Filippa's leg to point at us; she grabbed for his other hand to keep from falling off. "'Sgotta be you guys," he said.

I shook my head at James. We had been happy to heckle and cheer them on as they thrashed the remaining third-years.

Meredith: "Well, I'm not getting back in the water."

Filippa: "What's the matter, Mer? Afraid of a little rough play?"

The thirty or so onlookers hooted and whistled.

Meredith: "I know what you're doing. You're baiting me."

Filippa: "Duh. Is it working?"

Meredith: "You bet, bitch. Bring it on."

People whooped and Filippa grinned. Meredith stood, brushed the sand from her backside and called over her shoulder, "Rick! Let's teach these morons a lesson."

Richard, who had deigned to come down to the beach but was sitting a yard or so behind the rest of us, said, "No. Make a spectacle of yourself if you want. I'm staying dry."

Another round of laughter, meaner this time. (Meredith was much admired but also much envied, and any misstep of hers was jealously savored by at least a few.)

"Fine," she said, coolly. "I will." She grabbed her skirt and tied it up in a knot high on her hip. She waded into the water, turned, and said, "Coming, Oliver?"

"What, me?"

"Yeah, you. Someone has to help me sink these idiots, and James sure as fuck isn't going to do it."

"She's right," James said, blithely. "I'm sure-as-fuck not." (Unlike the rest of us, who were all attracted to Meredith in some biological, unavoidable way, James seemed to find her overt sex appeal somehow repulsive.) He smirked at me. "Have fun."

Meredith and I stared at each other for a moment, but the fierceness of her expression didn't make refusal feel like an option. People I didn't even know shouted encouragement at me until I climbed, a little sloppily, to my feet. "This is a bad idea," I said, mostly to myself.

"Don't worry." Wren nudged James with her elbow. "I'll make him fight the winners with me."

He protested, but I didn't hear what he said because Meredith had grabbed my arm and was dragging me into the water. "Get on your knees," she ordered.

"I bet she says that to all the boys," Alexander said. *"Have you no modesty, no maiden shame, / No touch of bashfulness?"*

I glared at him as I crouched down in the water. The cold nearly knocked the wind out of me, seizing onto my stomach and chest like a sheet of ice. "Jesus," I said. "Hurry up and get on!"

"I bet he says that to all the girls," Filippa said, with a wink. *"Perforce I must confess, / I thought you lord of more true gentleness!"*

"Okay," I said to Meredith, as more lewd laughter bubbled in my ears. "Let's kill them."

"That's the spirit." She swung one leg over my shoulder, then the other, and I nearly toppled her right off. She wasn't heavy, but I was drunk, and I hadn't realized quite how drunk until just then. She hooked her feet under my armpits and I straightened up slowly. There was a smattering of applause as I tried to find my balance, wishing the water would stop pushing and pulling at me. Some of the stage blood loosened from my skin and snaked down my abdomen to my waistband.

Colin, our cocky young Antony, seemed to be the acting referee. He sat straddling the overturned canoe, double-fisting Solo cups. "Ladies, keep your claws to yourselves," he said. "No plucking out of eyeballs, please. First to knock a girl in the water wins."

I struggled to focus on Alexander, wondering how to upend him. With Meredith's thighs wet and glistening on either side of my face it was difficult to concentrate.

"Fie, fie!" Filippa said, delightedly. *"You counterfeit, you puppet you!"*

"*Ay, that way goes the game,*" Meredith said. "*How low am I, thou painted maypole? Speak!*"

"*Oh, when she's angry she is keen and shrewd!*" Filippa replied. "*She was a vixen when she went to school!*" More scandalized laughter.

"*Will you suffer her to flout me thus?*" Meredith said. "*Let me come to her!*"

And we lurched forward. I wove underneath Meredith, fighting to stay upright. The girls grappled violently, the churning water and Alexander's manic laughter loud and disorienting. Meredith lost her balance, and the shift of her weight pulled me sharply backward.

I threw my body in the opposite direction and slammed against Alexander. Filippa nearly kicked me in the face and the whole world reeled, but an idea sparked at the very same time. I lunged headfirst at Alexander again, and when I saw the white flash of Filippa's foot, I risked letting go of Meredith's leg to grab it. We leaned hard to the side but I shouted, "Meredith, *now!*"

I flung Filippa's foot upward and Meredith shoved her hard. She tilted immediately backward, pulling Alexander with her, and after one brief suspended moment, arms windmilling at their sides, they both crashed down in the water. Meredith and I careened to the right and I clamped my free hand on her thigh again. The spectators clapped and hollered, but I could barely hear them because Meredith was hugging my head with her legs, one hand clutched in my hair. I turned dizzily on the spot and tried to smile.

Filippa and Alexander came up from under the water, choking and sputtering.

"Right," Alexander said. "Some'n gimme a drink, I'm done."

"I think we're all done," Filippa said.

"Oh no," Meredith said, to my dismay. "Wren said she'd play winner."

Colin smacked the side of the canoe. "Hear hear!"

"I'm up for it if James is," Wren said.

I wiped the water from my eyes and looked at him. He sat fidgeting in the sand with a sheepish half smile. Suddenly I wanted him to play. "C'mon, James," I said. "Let us make a fool of you and we can all go home."

"Go on, get some revenge for us," Filippa said, standing on the beach, wringing the water out of her skirt.

"Well," he said, "if I must."

Wren climbed to her feet and offered James her hands to help him up. She tied her skirt in a more modest knot than Meredith's and started into the water. Some of the spectators had wandered off, but there were about ten of them left and they called out reassurances. Meredith had begun to feel heavy on my shoulders, so I jostled her a little farther forward. She combed my hair back out of my eyes with her fingertips and said, "You okay down there?"

"I'm too drunk for this."

"You're my hero."

"Just what I've always wanted."

Wren waded out to where we were and said, "God, it's cold!"

"*'Tis a naughty night to swim in.*" James winced as he trudged in after her. "Let me help you up." He crouched down as I had done, taking one of her hands as she put her leg over his shoulder.

But before she could finish climbing on, a voice we'd barely heard all night said, "Actually, I think there's been enough of this."

I turned, slowly and carefully. Richard stood on the beach, scowling.

"You didn't want to play," Meredith said. "Why do you get an opinion?"

"It's just a bit of fun," Wren said. She had only made it half-way up and was perched, parrot-like, on James's shoulder. His eyes were fixed on Richard.

"It's fucking stupid and somebody's going to get hurt. Get down."

"Come on, Rick," Alexander said from where he was sprawled in the sand with another drink. "She'll be fine."

"Shut up," he said. "You're drunk."

"And you're not?" Filippa said. "Mellow out, it's just a game."

"Fuck off, Filippa, this has nothing to do with you."

"Richard!" Wren said. Filippa glared up at him, mouth slightly open in surprise.

"Okay, I think the show's over," Colin said, sliding off the canoe. "C'mon guys, clear out." The few onlookers left grumbled their disappointment and began to trickle away. Colin hesitated, looking from Richard to the rest of us like he wasn't sure whether we still needed a referee.

"Would you both stop screwing around?" Richard said, his voice carrying across the water as if it had once again been magically magnified.

"Oh, I see," Meredith said. "You can't stand us having a good time because you're busy pouting? Because you didn't get the last bow for once?" His face went white—livid—and I squeezed her knees hard, trying to warn her not to say too much. She didn't feel it, didn't understand, or didn't care. "Fuck that," she said. "It's not always about you."

"That's rich coming from a world-class attention whore."

"Richard, what the hell?" A flash of anger made my head feel suddenly hot. My grip on Meredith's legs tightened reflexively. The instinct to defend her was unexpected, unwarranted, but I didn't have time to be confused about it. She was dangerously quiet.

Richard started to say something else, but James interrupted. "That's enough," he said, and there was a bite in his voice I had never heard before. "Why don't you take five, and come back when you've cooled off?"

Richard's eyes burned black. "Take your hands off my cousin and I'll—"

"And you'll *what?*" Wren splashed down but stayed close to James. "What is the matter with you? It's just a game."

"Yeah, okay," Richard said, striding into the water. "Let's play a game. Wren, move, it's my turn."

"Richard, don't be an idiot." Meredith swung one leg off my shoulder and I grabbed her around the waist to help her down. Without her extra weight I felt like I was filled with helium. I blinked hard, trying to clear my head.

"No, I want to play," Richard said again. How much had he drunk? He was speaking clearly, but his movement was loose and reckless. "Wren, get out of the way."

"Come on, Richard, he hasn't done anything," I said.

He rounded on me. "Oh, don't worry—I'll be with you in a minute."

I leaned back. I didn't like my odds if he was determined to start a fight with someone.

"Leave him alone," James said, sharply. "He only played because you didn't want to and he was trying to be nice."

"Yes, we all know how *nice* Oliver is."

"Richard," Meredith said. "Don't be an asshole."

"I'm not, I want to play now. Come on, I thought you wanted one last game." He reached around Wren and shoved James backward. There was a soft splash as the water caught him.

"Richard, stop!" Wren said.

"What's the matter?" he asked. "One more game!" He pushed James again and James knocked his arm away.

"Richard, I'm warning you—"

"What? I want to play."

"I'm not playing," James told him, every muscle in his body taut and rigid. "Don't fucking do that again."

"So you'll play with the girls and Alexander and Oliver but not with me?" Richard demanded. "COME ON!"

"Richard, stop!" We yelled it all together, but we'd waited

too long. He shoved James again, and there was nothing playful about it. James hit the water hard, arms smacking the surface as he tried to catch himself. As soon he was back on his feet, he lunged at Richard, hit him with all his weight, plowed him backward. But Richard was laughing as the water seethed around them—he was so much bigger, it was impossible for the fight to be fair. I was moving toward them, my legs dragging, when Richard's laugh turned into a snarl and he plunged James face-first into the water.

"RICHARD!" I shouted.

Maybe he didn't hear me over James's thrashing, or maybe he just pretended not to. He kept him under, one arm locked around his neck. James beat one fist on his side, but I couldn't tell if he was fighting back or just fighting to get loose. The girls and Colin and Alexander crashed toward them, but I got there first. Richard shook me off and the cold water slapped me across the face, jumped into my mouth and nose. I threw myself at him again, latched on like a parasite.

"STOP! YOU'RE CHOKING HIM—" His shoulder hit my chin and I bit my tongue hard. Colin appeared out of nowhere, hauled on the arm keeping James under as I yelled, "YOU'RE GOING TO FUCKING DROWN HIM, *STOP!*"

Meredith grabbed Richard around the neck, then Filippa seized his elbow, and by the time he finally let go of James we were all tangled together, the water surging around us, icy and vicious.

James burst through the surface with a gasp, and I caught him before he could sink again. "James," I said. "James, are you okay?" He hung on my neck with one arm, choking, water and bile coming up together and splashing down his front.

Meredith was pounding on Richard's chest with her fists, screaming at him, forcing him out of the water and onto the beach. "*Are you out of your mind? You could have killed him!*"

"What is *wrong* with you?" Wren yelled, her voice cracking, tears spilling down her cheeks.

"James?" I propped him up as best I could, my arms in an awkward loop around his ribs. "Can you breathe?"

He nodded feebly and coughed again, eyes squeezed shut. The back of my throat felt tight, stretched like a bowstring.

"Jesus H. Christ," Colin said, quietly. "What the hell was that?"

"I don't know," Filippa said, from where she stood between us, gaunt and shivering. "Let's get him out of the water."

Colin and I helped James to the beach, where he collapsed in the sand on his side. His hair hung limp and wet in his eyes, his whole body trembling as he breathed. I crouched beside him and Filippa hovered over us. Alexander looked dumbstruck. Colin, absolutely terrified. Wren cried silently, little hiccups making her shoulders jerk and twitch. I'd never seen Meredith so angry, cheeks burning crimson even in the weak moonlight. And Richard just stood there, bemused.

"Richard," Alexander said, carefully. "That was fucked up."

"He's all right, isn't he? James?"

James stared up at him from the ground, eyes bright and hard like steel. Silence settled, and I was struck by the senseless idea that we and everything around us were made of glass. I was afraid to breathe, afraid to move, afraid something might break.

"We were just playing," Richard said, with a thin smile. "Just a game."

Meredith took one step to put herself between Richard and the rest of us. "Walk away," she said. He opened his mouth to reply, but she cut him off. "Go back to the Castle and go to bed before you do something dumb enough to get yourself expelled." She looked like a fury, eyes blazing, hair hanging in wet tangled ropes around her shoulders. "Go. *Now.*"

Richard glared at her, looked around at the rest of us, then turned and trudged back up the beach. Relief rushed through

me and made me light-headed, like blood flooding back to an
unfeeling limb.

As soon as he was out of sight, fading into the shadows of the
trees, Meredith deflated. "Jesus." She bent halfway over,
pressed the heels of her palms against her eyes, mouth twisted up
like she was trying not to cry. "James. I'm so sorry."

He pushed himself up so he was sitting cross-legged in the
sand. "It's okay," he said.

"It's *not* okay." She still had her hands over her face.

"It's not your fault, Mer," I said. The idea of Meredith crying
was so bizarre, so unsettling, I didn't think I could watch it.

"You're not responsible for him," Filippa said. She glanced at
Wren, whose eyes were fixed on the ground, tears running down
her face, clinging to her chin before they dripped down into the
sand. "None of us are."

"*The night has been unruly,*" Alexander said, significantly more
sober than he'd been half an hour before. "God, what a shit-
show."

Meredith finally lowered her hands. Her eyes were dry, but
her lips were cracked and colorless, like she was about to throw
up. "I don't know about the rest of you, but I want to get cleaned
up and go to bed and pretend this didn't happen for like at least
eight hours."

"I think some sleep would be good for everyone," Filippa
said, and there was a murmur of agreement.

"You guys go," James said. "I just—I'll be there in a minute."

"You sure?" Colin asked.

"Yeah. I'm fine, I just want a minute."

"All right."

Slowly, we straggled up the beach. Meredith went first, after
one last apologetic look at James—and one, for some reason, at
me. Filippa followed, one arm around Wren's shoulders. Colin
and Alexander wandered up the trail together. I lingered, under
the pretense of getting the rest of my costume out of the shed.

When I came out, James was sitting right where we'd left him, looking out at the lake.

"You want me to stay?" I asked. I didn't want to leave him.

"Please," he said, in a small voice. "I just couldn't deal with the rest of them, for a while."

I dropped my stuff in the sand and sat beside him. Sometime during the party, the storm had passed over. The sky was clear and quiet, stars peering curiously down at us from a wide dome of indigo. The water, too, was still, and I thought, what liars they are, the sky and the water. Still and calm and clear, like everything was fine. It wasn't fine, and really, it never would be again.

A few stubborn drops of water clung to James's cheeks. He didn't quite look like himself, somehow. He seemed so fragile I was afraid to touch him. He started to say something—maybe my name—but only the ghost of a sound slipped out before he stopped, pressed the back of his hand against his mouth. My chest ached, but the ache went deeper than muscle and bone, like some sharp thing had ripped a little hole right through me. I risked reaching toward him. He let out a small shuddering sigh, then breathed more easily. For a long time we sat side by side without speaking, my hand on his shoulder.

The lake, the broad black water, lurked in the background of every scene we played after that—like a set from a play we did once, shuffled to the back of the scene shop where it would have been quickly forgotten if we didn't have to walk past it every day. Something changed irrevocably, in those few dark minutes James was submerged, as if the lack of oxygen had caused all our molecules to rearrange.

ACT II

PROLOGUE

The first time I leave the facility in ten years, the sun is a blinding white orb in a gray dishwater sky. I have forgotten how enormous the outside world is. At first I'm paralyzed by the vastness of it, like someone's pet goldfish dropped unexpectedly into the ocean. Then I see Filippa, leaning on the side of her car, the light glinting off her aviators. I barely resist the urge to run at her.

We embrace roughly, like brothers, but I hold her longer than that. She's solid and familiar and it's the first affectionate human contact I've had in far too long. I bury my face in her hair. It smells like almonds, and I inhale as deeply as I can, press my hands flat against her back so I can feel her heartbeat.

"Oliver." She sighs and squeezes the back of my neck. For one wild moment I think I'm going to burst into tears, but when I let go of her she's smiling. She doesn't look any different. Of course, she's been back to see me every two weeks since they put me away. Besides Colborne, she's the only one who has.

"Thank you," I say.

"For what?"

"For being here. Today."

"*My poor prisoner,*" she says, laying one hand on my cheek, "*I am as innocent as you.*" Her smile fades and she withdraws her hand. "Are you sure you want to do this?"

For a second or two, I really do think about it. But that's all I've done since Colborne's last visit, and I've made up my mind. "Yeah. I'm sure."

"All right." She pulls the driver's door open. "Get in."

I climb into the passenger seat, where a pair of men's jeans and a T-shirt are neatly folded. I move them into my lap as she starts the car. "These Milo's?"

"He won't mind. I didn't think you'd want to show up wearing the same clothes you left in."

"These aren't the same clothes."

"You know what I mean," she says. "They don't fit. You look like you've gained about twenty pounds. Don't most people lose weight in prison?"

"Not if they want to get out in one piece," I tell her. "Besides, there's not much to do."

"So you exercise incessantly? You sound like Meredith."

Afraid I'm going red, I pull my shirt off, hoping she won't notice. Her eyes seem to be on the road, but her glasses are mirrored, so I can't really tell. "How is she?" I ask, as I look for the tag in the other shirt.

"Certainly not struggling. We don't talk much. None of us do anymore."

"What about Alexander?"

"Still in New York," she says, which isn't the answer to the question I'm asking. "Took up with some company that does really intense immersive stuff. Right now he's playing Cleopatra in a warehouse filled with sand and live snakes. Very Artaud. They're doing *The Tempest* next, but it might be his last show."

"Why?"

"Well, they want to do *Caesar* and he refuses to be in that ever again. He thinks that's the play that fucked us all up. I keep telling him he's wrong."

"You think it was *Macbeth* that fucked us up?"

"No." She stops at a red light and glances at me. "I think we were all fucked up from the start." The car rumbles to life again, slides into first gear, then second.

"I don't know if that's true," I say, but neither of us pursues the subject.

We drive in silence for a while, and then Filippa turns the stereo on. She's listening to an audiobook—Iris Murdoch, *The Sea, the Sea*. I read it in my cell a few years ago. Apart from exercising and hoping to go unnoticed, that's what a fledgling Shakespeare scholar does in prison. By the midpoint of my ten-year tenure I'd been rewarded for my good (i.e., unobtrusive) behavior with a job shelving books instead of peeling potatoes.

Because I know the story, I barely listen to the words. I ask Filippa if I can roll the window down, and I hang my head out like a dog. She laughs at me, but says nothing. The fresh Illinois air skips across my face, weightless and flighty. I look out at the world through my eyelashes, alarmed by how bright it is even on this overcast day.

My mind wanders down the road to Dellecher, and I wonder, will I recognize it? Maybe they've torn the Castle down, razed the trees to make room for real dormitories, and put up a fence to keep kids out of the lake. Maybe now it looks like a children's summer camp, sterile and safe. Or maybe it, like Filippa, has hardly changed at all. I can still see it, lush and green and wild, in some tiny way enchanted, like Oberon's wood, or Prospero's island. There are things they don't tell you about such magical places—that they're as dangerous as they are beautiful. Why should Dellecher be any different?

Two hours go by, and then the car is parked in the long empty drive at the Hall. Filippa gets out first and I follow slowly. The Hall itself is the same, but I look immediately beyond it to the lake, resplendent under the bloodless sun. The surrounding forest is as thick and savage as I remember, the trees stabbing fiercely up at the sky.

"You all right?" Filippa asks. I haven't moved from the side of the car.

"*This is as strange a maze as e'er men trod.*"

Panic flutters softly around my heart. For a moment I'm twenty-two again, watching my innocence slip through my fingers with equal parts eagerness and terror. Ten years of trying to explain Dellecher, in all its misguided magnificence, to men in beige jumpsuits who never went to college or never even finished high school has made me realize what I as a student was willfully blind to: that Dellecher was less an academic institution than a cult. When we first walked through those doors, we did so without knowing that we were now part of some strange fanatic religion where anything could be excused so long as it was offered at the altar of the Muses. Ritual madness, ecstasy, human sacrifice. Were we bewitched? brainwashed? Perhaps.

"Oliver?" Filippa says, more gently. "Are you ready?"

I don't answer. I never was.

"C'mon."

I trail behind her as she walks. I've braced myself for the shock of seeing Dellecher again—unchanged or otherwise—but what I'm not expecting is the sudden ache in my chest, like longing for an old lover. I've missed it, desperately.

"Where is he?" I ask, when I catch up with Filippa.

"He wanted to wait at the Bore's Head, but I wasn't sure you should go back yet."

"Why not?"

"Half the same people still work there." She shrugs. "I didn't know if you'd be ready to see them."

"I'd be more concerned that they're not ready to see me," I say, because I know that's what she's really thinking.

"Yeah," she says. "That, too."

She leads me through the front doors—the Dellecher coat of arms, Key and Quill, staring disapprovingly down at me as if to say, *You are no longer welcome here.* I haven't asked Filippa who else knows I'm coming back. It's summer and the students are gone, but the staff often linger. Will I turn a corner and find myself face-to-face with Frederick? Gwendolyn? God forbid, Dean Holinshed.

The Hall is eerily empty. Our footsteps echo in the wide corridors, usually so tightly packed with people that any small sound is trampled underfoot. I peer curiously into the music hall. Long white sheets hang over the windows, and the light falls in wide pale stripes across the vacant seats. It has the haunted feeling of an abandoned cathedral.

The refectory, too, is empty, almost. Sitting alone at one of the student tables, nursing a cup of coffee and looking distinctly out of place, is Colborne. He stands hastily and offers one hand. I grasp it without hesitation, strangely glad to see him.

Me: "Chief."

Colborne: "Not anymore. Turned in my badge last week."

Filippa: "Why the change of heart?"

Colborne: "Mostly my wife's idea. She says if I'm going to risk getting shot on a regular basis, I ought to at least be paid well for it."

Filippa: "How touching."

Colborne: "You'd like her."

Filippa laughs and says, "Probably."

"And how are you?" he asks. "Still hanging around this place?" He glances down at the empty tables, up at the corniced ceiling, as though he's not quite sure where he is.

"Well, we live in Broadwater," she says. "We," I assume, refers to her and Milo. I didn't know they'd moved in together. She is almost as much a mystery to me now as she was ten years ago, but I don't love her any less for it. I know more than most about desperately kept secrets. "We don't come out here much during the summer."

Colborne nods. I wonder if he feels at all awkward around her. He knows me—he knew all of us once—but now? Does he look at her and see a suspect? I watch him closely and hope I won't have to remind him of our bargain.

"Can't be much reason to," he says, amiably enough.

"We've got to decide on a season for next year, but we can do that in town."

"Any ideas yet?"

"We're thinking about *Twelfth Night* for the third-years. We have two that actually share some DNA for the first time since—

well, since Wren and Richard." There's a brief, uncomfortable pause before she continues. "And we really have no idea what to do with the fourth-years. Frederick wants to branch out and try *Winter's Tale*, but Gwendolyn's insisting on *Othello*."

"Good group this year?"

"Good as ever. We picked more girls than boys for once."

"Well, that can't be a bad thing."

They share a fast grin, and then Filippa looks pointedly at me. She raises her eyebrows, just barely. *Now or never.*

I turn to Colborne, mimic her expression. He checks his watch. "Shall we take a walk?"

"Whatever you want," I tell him.

"All right," he says to me. And then, to Filippa: "Coming?"

She shakes her head, somehow frowning and smiling at the same time. "I don't need to," she says. "I was there."

Colborne's eyes narrow. Unperturbed, she touches my arm, says, "I'll see you tonight," and walks out of the refectory, Colborne's unasked questions hanging in the air behind her.

He watches her leave, then asks, "How much does she know?"

"She knows everything." He frowns, eyes nearly disappearing beneath his thick brows. "People always forget about Filippa," I add. "And later they always wish they hadn't."

He sighs, like he doesn't have the energy to be really disgruntled. He contemplates his coffee for a moment, then abandons it on the table. "Well," he says. "Lead the way."

"Where?"

"You'd know better than I would."

I'm silent, thinking. Then I sit. It's as good a place as any.

Colborne chuckles reluctantly. "You want some coffee?"

"I wouldn't say no."

He disappears into the kitchen, where two coffee urns stand in the corner. (They've been there at least fourteen years. They're always full, though I never—even as a student—saw who filled them.) He comes back with a full mug, sets it in front of me. I watch the milk swirl as he sits down in the same chair he just got up from.

"Where do you want me to start?" I ask.

He shrugs. "Wherever you think is best. See, Oliver, I don't just want to know what happened. I want to know the how and the why and the when. I want to make sense of it."

For the first time in a long time, that little rip in the middle of me, the black bruise on my soul that's been struggling to heal for nearly a decade, throbs. Old feelings come softly thronging back. Bittersweetness, discord, and confusion.

"I wouldn't count on that," I tell Colborne. "It's been ten years and I still can't make sense of it."

"Then maybe this will be good for both of us."

"Maybe."

I sip my coffee pensively. It's good—it has flavor, unlike the brownish slime we drank in prison, which only vaguely reminded me of coffee, even on good days. The heat soothes the swelling pain in my chest, for a moment.

"So," I say, when I'm ready. The mug warms my palms, and the memories flood through me like a drug, razor sharp, crystal clear, kaleidoscopic. "Fall semester, 1997. I don't know if you remember, but it was a warm autumn that year."

SCENE 1

Two weeks before opening night we had our photos taken for publicity, and the FAB was an absolute madhouse. In order to take photos we needed costumes, and everyone was running back and forth from the dressing rooms to the rehearsal hall, changing ties and shirts and shoes until Gwendolyn was satisfied. The previous year's election had inspired Frederick to do *Caesar* as a presidential race, so we were all dressed as White House hopefuls. I had never worn a suit that really fit me in my

life, and my own reflection surprised me more than once. For
the first time, I entertained the idea that I could be handsome,
with enough effort. (Previously, I'd thought of myself as attrac-
tive only in a forgettable, inoffensive way—an idea reinforced by
the fact that the few girls I'd been mixed up with inevitably
seemed to realize that they liked me better onstage as Antonio
or Demetrius than offstage as my mild-mannered self.) Of course,
among my classmates I might as well have been invisible. Alexander looked like a mafioso in shimmering charcoal gray, an
onyx tiepin glinting on his chest. James, immaculate in deep ink
blue, could have been the heir apparent of some small European
monarchy. But Richard, in pale pearl gray and a blood-red tie,
cut the most impressive figure of us all.

"Is it just me or does that suit actually make him taller?" I
asked, looking through the door of the rehearsal hall, where
they'd set up a black screen to be our backdrop. They wanted
Richard first, for the "campaign poster shot," as Gwendolyn kept
calling it.

"I think his ego just makes him look bigger," James said.

Alexander craned his neck to see between us. "Maybe so. But
you can't deny, the guy looks *good*." He glanced at me and added,
"So would you, if you could learn to tie a Windsor knot properly."

Me: "Is it *still* crooked?"

Alexander: "Have you seen yourself?"

Me: "Just fix it, will you?"

Alexander tipped my chin up to adjust my tie and carried on
whispering to James. "Honestly, I'm glad we've got a night off
from rehearsal for this. Every time we do The Fucking Tent
Scene with Gwendolyn's commentary, I just want to lie down
and die."

"Arguably, that's sort of how you should feel."

"Look, I expect to be emotionally exhausted after a show,
but she makes that scene so real that I look at you *off*stage and I
can't decide if I want to kiss you or kill you."

I snorted out a laugh and Alexander jerked on my tie. "Stop squirming."

"Sorry."

Filippa appeared behind us from the girls' dressing room. (She had at least three costumes; at that particular moment it was a pin-striped pantsuit, not flattering.) "What are we talking about?" she whispered.

Alexander: "I might make out with James tomorrow."

James: "Lucky me."

Filippa: "Could be worse. Remember *Midsummer*, when Oliver head-butted me in the face?"

Me: "In my defense, I tried to kiss you nicely, but I couldn't see because Puck squirted his love juice right in my eye."

Alexander: "There was so much innuendo in that sentence I don't even know where to start."

Across the room, Gwendolyn clapped her hands and said, "Well, I don't think we're going to get anything better than that. What's next? The couples? Fine." She turned toward us and called, "Filippa, go and find the other girls, won't you?"

"Because they couldn't *possibly* want me here for any other reason," Filippa muttered, and disappeared into the dressing room again.

"Honestly," James said, shaking his head, "if they don't give her a decent role in the spring, I'm boycotting the show."

When the other girls appeared it was immediately clear that wardrobe had spent more time on them. Wren was in a tasteful navy dress, while Meredith wore something red that hugged her curves like a coat of paint, her hair blown out to its full volume like a lion's mane.

"Where do they want us?" Meredith asked.

"In the centerfold, I'd imagine," Alexander said, looking her up and down. "Did they have to pour you into that?"

"Yeah," she said. "And I'll need five people to pry me out of it." She seemed annoyed about it more than smug.

"Well," James said, "I'm sure there will be no shortage of volunteers." He didn't make it sound like something to be smug about.

"James!" Gwendolyn barked. "I need you and the girls over here, yesterday."

They made their way across the room, Meredith carefully tiptoeing between the tangled extension cords in gleaming patent pumps.

"So," Filippa said, "I don't even count as a girl now."

"No offense," Alexander said, "but not in that outfit you don't."

"Quiet in the hall, please!" Gwendolyn called, without even turning around.

Filippa made a face like she'd just bitten into a rotten apple. "God, spare me," she said. "I'm going for a smoke."

She didn't elaborate, but she didn't need to. As Gwendolyn and the photographer arranged Richard, Meredith, James, and Wren under the lights, it was impossible to ignore the blatant display of favoritism. I sighed, barely bothered, and watched James— hardly aware of the camera, unintentionally charming—as Gwendolyn jostled him and Wren together. I was only half listening when Alexander leaned close to my ear and said, "Are you seeing what I'm seeing?"

"Huh?"

"Okay, actually pay attention for a minute and *then* tell me if you see it."

At first I had no idea what he was talking about. But then I did see something—just a twitch at the corner of Meredith's mouth as Richard's hand brushed her back. They stood side by side, turned slightly toward each other, but Meredith didn't quite look like Calpurnia, the perfect politician's wife, adoring to the point of distraction. Her hand lay flat on Richard's lapel, but it looked stiff and unnatural there. At the photographer's instruction, he put one arm around her waist. She lifted her own arm, just barely, so their elbows weren't touching.

"Trouble in paradise?" Alexander suggested.

After the Halloween "incident," as I kept thinking of it, we had all proceeded largely as though nothing out of the ordinary had happened, dismissing it as a bit of drunken horseplay gone too far. Richard offered James a perfunctory apology, which was accepted with proportionate insincerity, and from that point forward, they were rigidly cordial to each other. The rest of us were making a commendable (if doomed) effort to get back to normal. Meredith was the unexpected exception: for the first few days of November, she refused to speak to Richard at all.

"Aren't they sleeping in the same room again?" I asked.

"Not as of last night."

"How do you know?"

He shrugged. "The girls tell me things."

I looked sideways at him. "Anything interesting?"

He gave me a quick once-over and said, "Oh, you have *no* idea."

I could tell he wanted me to ask what, so I didn't. I peeked back through the door, hoping to reach a conclusion on the state of affairs with Meredick, but another small movement distracted me. At Gwendolyn's instruction, Wren tilted her head to rest on James's shoulder.

"Don't they look the perfect American couple," Alexander remarked.

"Yeah." The camera flashed. James played idly with a strand of Wren's hair, but at the nape of her neck, where I was fairly sure the photographer wouldn't catch it. I frowned, squinted across the room. "Alexander, are you seeing what I'm seeing?"

He followed my gaze with only a vague show of curiosity. James continued winding one lock of Wren's hair around his finger.

I couldn't tell if either of them even realized he was doing it. Wren smiled—maybe for the camera—as if she had a secret.

Alexander gave me a queer, sad sort of look. "Are you just seeing this now?" he said. "Oh, Oliver. You're as oblivious as they are."

SCENE 2

The following night's dress rehearsal was our first on a finished set. Twelve grand Tuscan columns made a half circle on the top platform, and a flight of shallow white steps led down into what we called the Bowl: a flat faux-marble disc on the floor, eight feet in diameter, where the infamous assassination took place. Behind the columns the scrim glowed softly, cycling through a full spectrum of celestial colors, from dusky twilight purple to the orange blush of sunrise.

A new set always presented challenges we hadn't anticipated during early rehearsals, and we all returned to the Castle short-tempered and sore. James and I went immediately up to the Tower.

"Is it just me, or did that run somehow take about ten hours?" I asked, falling backward onto my bed. The mattress caught me and I groaned. It was after midnight and we'd been on our feet since five.

"Feels like it." James sat on the edge of his bed and ran his hands through his hair. When he lifted his head again he looked tousled and tired, even a little bit ill. There wasn't enough color in his face.

I propped myself up on my elbows. "You okay?"
"Why?"
"You seem really, I don't know, worn out."
"I haven't been sleeping well."
"Something bothering you?"

He blinked at me, as if he hadn't understood the question, then said, "No. It's nothing." He stood and pulled his shoes off.

"Are you sure?"

He turned his back to me as he unbuttoned his jeans and let them slide to the floor. "I'm fine." His voice sounded flat, wrong, as if someone had struck a false note on the piano. I pushed myself off the bed and crossed slowly to his side of the room.

"James," I said, "don't take this the wrong way, but I kind of don't believe you."

He glanced over his shoulder at me. "*I never in my life / Did hear a challenge urged more modestly.* You know me too well." He folded his jeans and dropped them on the foot of his bed.

"So tell me what's wrong."

He hesitated. "You have to promise me you're going to keep it to yourself."

"Yeah, of course."

"You won't want to," he warned.

"James," I said, more urgently, "what are you talking about?"

He didn't answer—he just pulled his shirt off and stood there in his underwear without speaking. I stared at him, bewildered and inexplicably anxious. A dozen different questions tangled together in my mouth before my own awkwardness made me glance down and I realized what he was trying to show me.

"Oh my God." I seized both his wrists and pulled him toward me, the abashment of the previous moment forgotten. Bruises in raw, vivid blue spotted the undersides of his arms, all the way to his elbows. "James, what *is* this?"

"Finger marks."

I let go of his left arm like I'd been electrocuted. "What?"

"The assassination scene," he said. "When I stab him the last time, he goes down on his knees and grabs my arms and . . . well."

"Has he seen this?"

"Of course not."

"You have to show him," I said. "He might not even know he's hurting you."

He looked up at me with a flash of annoyance. "When was the last time you left a mark like this on someone and didn't know you were doing it?"

"I've never left a mark like that on anyone, ever."

"Exactly. You'd know if you had."

I realized I was still holding his other wrist and abruptly let go. He rocked backward, unbalanced, as if I'd been pulling him forward before. He brushed his fingers along the inside of his arm, biting hard on his bottom lip like he was afraid to open his mouth, afraid of what might come out.

Suddenly I was furious, my pulse throbbing softly in my ears. I wanted to give Richard ten bruises for every one he'd put on James, but I could never hope to hurt him, not like that, and my own inefficacy made me angrier than anything else.

"You have to tell Frederick and Gwendolyn that he's doing this," I said, more loudly than I meant to.

"Like a snitch?" James said. "No, thank you."

"Just Frederick then."

"No."

"You have to say *something*!"

He pushed me back a step. "*No*, Oliver!" He glanced away, into some empty corner of the room. "You promised me you wouldn't say a word, so don't."

I felt a little prick of pain, as if something had stung me. "Tell me why."

"Because I don't want to give him the satisfaction," he said. "If he knows how easily he can hurt me, what's going to make him stop?" His eyes darted back to my face, a glint of gray. Imploring and apprehensive. "He'll give up if he doesn't think it's working. So promise me you're not going to say anything."

My guts clenched like someone had kicked me in the stomach. What I wanted to say was elusive, inapproachable, just out of reach. I grasped the nearest bedpost and leaned on it. My head was heavy with confusion, fury, and some other fierce thing I couldn't identify.

"James, this is so fucked up."

"I know."

"What are we going to do?"

"Nothing. Not yet."

SCENE 3

During dress rehearsal the following night I didn't take my eyes off Richard, but as it happened, when he went too far I wasn't the only one watching.

We had just finished Act II, Scene 1, which included Brutus's conference with the conspirators, his conference with Portia, and his conference with Ligarius. (How on earth James kept all of his lines straight, I had no idea.) Wren and Filippa had exited stage right and were peering curiously around the curtain. James and Alexander and I had exited stage left and waited restlessly in the dense darkness of the wings for our next entrance: Three-One, the assassination scene.

"How much time do you think I have?" Alexander asked, a hoarse whisper over his shoulder.

"For a smoke?" I said. "Enough, if you go now."

"If I'm late coming back, stall for me."

"How am I supposed to do that?"

"Pretend you've forgotten a line or something."

"And invoke the wrath of Gwendolyn? No."

Wren put her finger to her lips on the opposite side of the stage, and James nudged Alexander with one elbow. "Stop talking. They can hear you on the other side."

"What scene is this?" Alexander asked, in a lower voice.

Richard had already entered—tieless and coatless—and was

talking with a servant, played by one of our inexhaustible second-years.

"Calpurnia," I murmured.

As if I had somehow summoned her, Meredith appeared between the two center columns, barefoot and wearing a short silk bathrobe, arms tightly folded.

Alexander whistled under his breath. "Would you look at her legs? I guess that's one way to sell tickets."

"You know," James said, "for a boy who likes other boys, you provide a lot of heterosexual commentary."

Alexander: "I might make an exception for Meredith, but she'd have to be wearing that robe."

James: "You're disgusting."

Alexander: "I'm adaptable."

Me: "Shut up, I want to hear this."

James and Alexander exchanged a look, which I didn't understand and chose to ignore.

"*What mean you, Caesar? Think you to walk forth?*" Meredith asked, when the servant had exited. "*You shall not stir out of your house today.*" She stood with one hand on her hip, expression dark and judgmental. The scene had changed since last I saw it; Meredith descended into the Bowl, and as she described her dream it sounded more like a threat than a warning. Richard, judging by the look on his face, was having none of it.

"Well," Alexander said, "I wouldn't count on him remaining at home."

The servant entered again, clearly terrified to even be on the same stage with the two of them.

Richard: "*What say the augurers?*"

Servant: "*They would not have you stir forth today.*
     Plucking the entrails of an offering forth,
     They could not find a heart within the beast."

Richard rounded on Meredith.

Richard: *"The gods do this in shame of cowardice:*
 Caesar should be a beast without a heart,
 If he should stay at home today for fear!
 No, Caesar shall not."

He seized her shoulders and she twisted in his grip.

"Is that the blocking?" I asked. Neither James nor Alexander answered.

Richard: *"Danger knows full well*
 That Caesar is more dangerous than he:
 We are two lions litter'd in one day,
 And I the elder and more terrible—"

Meredith squirmed and let out a cry of pain. Filippa caught my eye from the opposite wing and shook her head, just barely.

"And Caesar," Richard bellowed, *"shall go forth!"* He thrust Meredith away from him so roughly that she lost her balance and fell backward onto the stairs. She threw her arms out to catch herself and there was a sharp crack as her elbow hit the wood. That same vindictive reflex I'd felt on Halloween made me lurch forward—to do what, I had no idea—but Alexander grabbed my shoulder and whispered, "Easy, tiger."

Meredith pushed her hair out of her face and looked up at Richard with wide, angry eyes. The auditorium was silent except for the soft buzz of the lights for a split second before she said, "I'm sorry, what the fuck just happened?"

"Hold!" Gwendolyn yelled, from the back of the house, her voice shrill and distant.

Meredith climbed to her feet and whacked Richard's chest with the back of her hand. "What was that?"

"What was *what?*" He, for some unfathomable reason, looked even angrier than she did.

"That wasn't the blocking!"

"Look, it's a big moment, I got caught up in it—"

"And you decided to *throw me on the fucking stairs?*"

Gwendolyn was running down the center aisle, shouting, "Stop! Stop this!"

Richard grabbed Meredith's arm and yanked her so close he could have kissed her. "Are you really going to make a scene right now?" he said. "I wouldn't."

I bit back a curse word, knocked Alexander's hand off my shoulder, and ran out onto the stage with James right behind me. But Camilo got there first, jumping up out of the front row. "Whoa," he said. "Break it up. C'mon, calm down." He wedged an arm between them and pried Meredith away from Richard.

"What's going on here?" Gwendolyn said, when she reached the edge of the stage.

"Well, *Dick* decided to improvise some blocking," Meredith said, pushing Camilo away. She winced when his hand brushed her arm and her eyes flicked down; a drop of blood snaked out of her sleeve. My own vicarious outrage—overlapping and confused, half for James, half for Meredith—roared up in my chest and I ground my teeth together, fighting a suicidal urge to tackle Richard into the orchestra pit.

"I'm bleeding," Meredith said, staring at the spots of red on her fingertips. "You son of a bitch." She turned and flung the tab curtains back, ignoring Gwendolyn as she called, "Meredith, wait!"

Richard's anger flickered off like a bad lightbulb and left him looking uneasy.

"Everyone take ten," Gwendolyn told the rest of us. "Hell, take fifteen. We're having intermission now. Go."

The second- and third-years were first to move, leaving the auditorium two by two, whispering to one another. I felt Alexander hovering behind me and took a bracing breath in.

"Camilo, would you make sure she's all right?" Gwendolyn asked. He nodded and exited upstage. She turned to Richard. "Go and apologize to that girl," she ordered, "and so help me God, don't pull anything else like that or I'll have Oliver learn your lines and you can watch from the front row on opening night."

"I'm sorry."

"Don't apologize to *me*," she said, but her ire was already fading to exasperation.

Richard nodded—almost humbly—and watched her make the slow walk back to the top of the house. Not until he turned around did he seem to realize that the other five of us were standing there, glaring at him. "Oh, relax," he said. "I didn't really hurt her. She's just angry."

Beside me, James had clenched his fists so hard his arms were quivering. I shifted my feet, too agitated to stand still. Alexander leaned forward, like he was ready to throw himself between the two of us and Richard if he had to.

"For God's sake," Richard said, when nobody replied. "You all know what a drama queen she is."

"Richard!" Wren said.

He looked guilty, but only for a moment. "Really," he said, "do I have to apologize to all of you, too?"

"No, of course not," Filippa said, in a calm, even voice that distracted me from the sound of my own pulse in my ears. "Why would you? You've only interrupted our run, fucked up Gwendolyn's blocking, forced Milo to break up a fight, possibly ruined a costume, maybe damaged the set, and injured one of our friends—not for the first time either. Now Oliver might have to learn all your lines and play your part and save the show when you inevitably fuck up again. And you have the balls to blame it on Meredith being a drama queen?" Her blue eyes were cold as frostbite. "You know, *Rick*, people aren't going to put up with your bullshit for much longer."

She turned her back on him before he had time to respond and disappeared between the tabs. She'd said what we all wanted to say, and, ever so slightly, the tension eased. I exhaled; James unclenched his fists.

"Just don't, Richard," Wren said, when he opened his mouth again. She shook her head, with a tight, pinched expression not unlike disgust. "Just don't." And she followed Filippa.

Richard sniffed, then said to me, James, and Alexander, "Anything else?"

"No," Alexander said, "I think she pretty much covered it." He gave one warning look to me and James before he exited through the wings, already fumbling in his pockets for rolling papers.

Only three of us left. James, Richard, me. Gunpowder, fire, fuse.

Richard and James stared at each other for a moment, as if I wasn't there, but neither spoke. The silence between them was unstable, precarious. I waited, wondering which way it would tilt, the apprehension making all my muscles tighten under my skin. At last, James gave Richard the tiniest smile—a glimmer of petty triumph—then turned and followed Alexander out.

Richard's eyes settled on me, and I thought they might burn right through me.

"Don't start learning my speeches yet," he said.

And he left me onstage alone. I was quiet. Motionless. In my own estimation, *pointless*. A fuse with no fire and nothing to ignite.

SCENE 4

When we finished our run (thankfully without further incident), I avoided the dressing rooms. I lurked in the lobby until I thought everyone else would have gone, then made my way back through the theatre. The house lights had all been turned off, and I fumbled between the seats with numb hands, grunting at the armrests that reached out to smack my kneecaps in the dark.

The crossover lights buzzed as I let myself into the men's

dressing room, and I was relieved to find it empty. Mirrors on one wall showed me my own reflection, and a costume rack was pushed against the other, tightly packed with two or three suits for each of a dozen actors. The refuse of the theatre was strewn on every surface—forgotten clothing, combs and hair gel, broken eyeliner pencils.

I began to peel my costume off, for once without bumping elbows with four other boys. Normally I would have enjoyed the luxury of *space*, but I hadn't fully recovered from the second-act disaster and I was only vaguely relieved not to have to share the room with Richard. I hung my shirt, jacket, and pants carefully on one hanger, then stowed my shoes underneath the rack. My own clothes had been scattered around the room, likely picked up and discarded during the frenzy following Act V when everyone scrambled to get dressed and go home. I found my jeans crumpled in a corner, my shirt hanging off the mirror. One of my socks was hiding under the counter, but the other never surfaced. I fell heavily into a chair and had just finished pulling my shoes on—damn the sock—when the door creaked open.

"There you are," Meredith said. "We didn't know where you went."

She was still wearing the robe. I risked one glance at her, then concentrated intensely on tying my shoes. "Just needed some room to breathe," I said. "I'm fine."

I stood and moved toward the door but she was in the way, leaning on the frame, one leg folded up like a flamingo, knee tucked perfectly in the curve of her instep. There was something introspective and uncertain in her expression, but her face was flushed, like the heat of anger hadn't quite left her.

"Meredith, do you need something?"

"A distraction, maybe." She offered half a smile, waiting for me to catch on.

Comprehension hit me with a little jolt like an electric shock, and I leaned back, eased away from her. "I don't think that's a good idea."

"Why not?" She seemed genuinely confused, almost impatient—I had to remind myself she was a natural actress.

"Because this is the sort of game where people get hurt," I said. "I don't particularly care about Richard just now, but I don't want to be one of them."

She blinked, and the impatience was gone, replaced by something softer, not so self-assured. "I won't hurt you," she said. She came cautiously closer, as if she were afraid of startling me. I was paralyzed, watching the silk move like water on her skin. A bruise was already swelling beneath her collarbone, and I couldn't help but think of Richard's hands and how much damage they could do.

"I can think of someone who might," I said.

"I don't want to think about him." Her voice had a raw, tender quality, which I didn't immediately recognize for what it was: shame.

"Right, you want to be distracted."

"Oliver, it's not like that."

"Really? Then what is it like?" It was a desperate question. I didn't know what it was meant to do—dissuade her or tempt her or challenge her; call her bluff, force her hand, make her show me. Perhaps all at once.

The only thing it didn't do was dissuade her. She was still looking up at me, but in a way she'd never looked at me before, something reckless gleaming in her sea-glass eyes. "It's like this."

I felt her hands on my chest, her palms warm through the thin fabric of my shirt. My heart stuttered at her touch, and I wondered suddenly if she was wearing anything under the robe. Part of me wanted to rip it off and find out, and another part wanted to crack her head against the wall and knock some sense into her. She leaned into me and the press of her body overthrew all my logical objections. My hands moved automatically, without my permission, rising to find the curve of her waist, smoothing the silk against her skin. I could smell her perfume, sweet and lush and tantalizing, the fragrance of some exotic flower. Her fingers, softly insistent on the back of my neck, pulled my face toward hers. My pulse crescendoed in my ears, my imagination rushing treacherously forward.

I turned my head abruptly and the tip of my nose brushed her cheek. If I kissed her, what would follow? I didn't trust myself to stop.

"Meredith, why are you doing this?" I couldn't look at her without staring at her mouth.

"I want to."

All my latent anger came bubbling up like acid.

"You want to," I said. "Why? Because James won't touch you, and Alexander doesn't like girls? Because you want to make Richard furious and I'm the easiest way to do it?" I pushed her back so we were no longer touching. "You know what he's like when he's furious. You're lovely, but you're not worth that."

The last words were out of my mouth before I could catch them, before I even realized how awful they were. She stared at me for a moment, motionless. Then she turned and wrenched the door open. "You know, I guess you're right," she said. "People do get hurt."

As the door swung shut behind her, I was transported back to our first day of Gwendolyn's class, two months before. It was maddening how beautiful she was—but did that make the rest of her any less real? I dragged one hand across my face, feeling sick. "Hell," I said, quietly. It was all I could manage.

I gathered my things, shouldered my bag, and left the building, furious by then at both of us. When I got back to the Castle, I paused outside her door on my way up to the Tower. One vagrant line of verse wandered through my head. *Courage, man; the hurt cannot be much.*

I knew better than to believe it.

SCENE 5

The following morning, James dragged me out of bed a little after seven to go for a run. The bruises on his arms had faded to a rotten green, but he wore a sweatshirt with the sleeves pulled down to his wrists. It was cold enough by then that it didn't look peculiar.

We often ran the narrow trails that wound through the woods on the south side of the lake. The air was cool and sharp, the morning overcast, our breath coming out in long plumes of white. We kept a good pace together for a two-mile loop, talking in short stilted bursts.

"Where'd you go last night?" he asked. "I couldn't find you after final curtain."

"Didn't want to deal with Richard in close quarters so I waited in the lobby."

"Did Meredith ambush you?"

I frowned at him. "How did you know?"

"I thought she might."

"Why?"

"Just the way she's been looking at you lately."

I stumbled over a root and fell a little bit behind him, then doubled my speed to catch up.

Me: "How has she been looking at me?"

James: "Like she's a shark and you're an oblivious fur seal."

Me: "Why is that the word everyone's using to describe me lately?"

James: "Who else called you a fur seal?"

Me: "Not that. Never mind."

I watched the ground for a moment, thinking. The dull ache

in my left side intensified whenever I inhaled. The air smelled of earth and evergreen and approaching winter.

"So, are you going to tell me what happened?" James asked.

"What?"

"With Meredith." He said it lightly, teasing, but there was apprehension there, too. Guilt made my face warmer than exertion already had.

"Nothing happened," I said.

"Nothing?"

"Not really. I told her I wasn't interested in becoming Richard's next punching bag and she left."

"Is that the only reason?" I could tell from his tone that he wasn't convinced.

"I mean, I don't know." I'd lain awake most of the night repeating the scene in my head, agonizing over those last few words, thinking up a thousand things I should have said instead, wishing it had gone a different way. I couldn't pretend I was immune to Meredith; I'd always admired her, but from what I thought was a safe distance. By coming closer she'd confused me. I didn't believe she really wanted me, just that I was the easiest mark. But I couldn't admit that to James— because I was embarrassed, and because I was afraid I was wrong.

He watched me, waiting for me to elaborate.

"It's like Alexander said the other day," I told him. "I couldn't decide if I wanted to kiss her or kill her." We jogged on in an awkward silence softened by the twittering of whatever dimwitted birds hadn't yet flown south for the winter. We passed the trail leading back to the Castle and started up the steep hill toward the Hall. When we were halfway up I asked, "What do you think?"

"About Meredith?"

"Yeah."

"You know how I feel about Meredith," he said, with a note of finality that discouraged further questions. But it wasn't really an answer—there was something unsaid, something trapped behind his teeth. I wanted to know what he was thinking but didn't know how to ask, so we climbed the rest of the way up the hill without speaking.

My calves were burning by the time we landed on the wide lawn behind the Hall, doubled over, breathing hard. As our bodies cooled, the November chill crept in. My shirt was stuck to my back, beads of sweat sliding out of my hair and down my temples. James's face and throat glistened feverish red, but the rest of his skin was pale from sleeplessness, and the contrast made him look distinctly unwell.

"Water?" I said. "You don't look good."

He nodded. "Yeah."

We trudged across the wet grass to the refectory. At eight a.m. on a Saturday, it was mostly empty. A few teachers and early risers sat reading quietly, mugs of coffee and breakfast plates in front of them. At one table, a cluster of dancers clad in black spandex stretched their long legs. At another, a choral music student sat inhaling steam from a cereal bowl filled with hot water, perhaps hoping to counteract the effects of what looked like a murderous hangover on her vocal chords. A small mixed group had accumulated at the far wall where the mailboxes were.

"What do you suppose that's about?" I asked.

James grimaced. "I have a fairly good idea."

I followed him over, and the little crowd parted easily to let us through—maybe because we were flushed and sweaty, but maybe not.

In the middle of the wall was a long corkboard reserved for general campus announcements. Usually it was thatched with club flyers and tutoring advertisements, but that day everything else was hidden behind an enormous campaign poster of Richard. He glared out at the viewer in monochrome red, his handsome features sharpened by deep black shadows. Below the immaculate knot of his tie but above the smaller text detailing the production information white block letters proclaimed,

ALWAYS I AM CAESAR

James and I stood staring at it for long enough that most of the other people who had come to investigate lost interest and wandered away.

"Well," he said, "that's bound to get people's attention."

I was still staring, annoyed that James wasn't more annoyed. "Fuck this," I said. "I don't want him watching me like Big Brother from every wall for the next two weeks."

"*He doth bestride the narrow world / Like a Colossus,*" James remarked, "*and we petty men / Walk under his huge legs and peep about / To find ourselves dishonorable graves.*"

"Fuck that also."

"You're starting to sound like Alexander."

"Sorry, but after last night I think the odds of Richard ripping my head off went up like a hundred percent."

"Keep that in mind next time Meredith throws herself at you."

"It wasn't quite like that," I said, and immediately wished I hadn't spoken.

"Be careful, Oliver," he said, knowingly, as if he could read my mind. "You're much too trusting. She did this to me, too, first year. We were partners for voice class—that weird humming thing. Remember?"

"Wait, she did what?"

"Decided she wanted me and assumed I wanted her, because doesn't everyone? When I told her no she changed her mind. Acted like it never happened and went after Richard instead."

"Are you serious?"

He gave me a wry sort of look in reply.

"Jesus." I glanced away, around the refectory, curious what sort of secrets everyone else was keeping. How little we wondered about the inner lives of other people. "Why didn't you tell me?"

"It didn't seem important."

I thought of him twirling a strand of Wren's hair around his finger and asked, "Anything else I should know, while we're on the subject?"

"No. Honestly." If he was hiding something, his expression— at ease, unaffected—didn't give it away. Maybe Alexander was right and James and I were equally oblivious.

I shifted my weight. I felt like Richard was watching me, the poster a garish red blotch in my peripheral vision. I turned, sighed at it, and said, "I guess the good news is that after yesterday's drama he'll have to stop trying to break your arms in Act III."—

"You think so?"

"You don't?"

He shook his head in a sad, distracted way. "He's too smart for that."

"So . . . what do you think he'll do?"

"He'll lay off, but just for the next few days. He'll wait for opening night. Gwendolyn's not going to run onstage and stop the show." His eyes flicked back and forth across the poster. For a moment he might have forgotten I was there.

James: *"Now, in the names of all the gods at once,*
Upon what meat does this our Caesar feed,
That he is grown so great?"

I was quiet for a while, then spoke one of my own lines in reply, unsure of where exactly it had come from.

Me: *"Hold, my hand:*
Be factious for redress of all these griefs,
And I will set this foot of mine as far
As who goes farthest."

James's gray eyes sparkled gold as he looked back at me and said, "*There's a bargain made.*" There was something unfamiliar in his smile, some fierce gladness that made me at once eager and uneasy. I grinned back as best I could, then followed him to the kitchen to get a glass of water. My mouth was unbearably dry.

SCENE 6

Richard's face haunted me for the rest of the week, but his wasn't the only one. Posters of James had also appeared—his done in royal blue, bearing the slogan *Soul of Rome.* Other publicity photos—featuring Alexander; Wren and Meredith; and then me, Colin, and our Lepidus together—appeared in the lobby of the FAB and the school newspaper. Campus began to hum again with anticipation for an upcoming production.

On opening night, there wasn't a single empty seat in the house. Dellecher's production quality was legendary, and the prospect of seeing the next big actor, artist, or virtuoso before fame snatched them away attracted more than the obvious collection of students and faculty. The house was packed with local Bardolators, students on field trips, and season ticket holders. (In the spring, the best seats would be reserved for a troop of agents invited from New York to watch us perform.) The lights came up on a group of excitable second-years, the common Romans, giddy at the idea of being onstage at Dellecher for the first time. The rest of us, more experienced and only half as agitated, waited in the wings.

The play climbed through the first two acts until the tension was so great that the whole auditorium seemed to be holding its breath. The assassination was swift and violent, and as soon as James directed the conspirators to disperse, I stumbled offstage, ears ringing.

"*Fuck!*" I blundered into the heavy black curtains on stage left. Someone caught me by the shoulders and guided me out of the tabs as the secondary conspirators shuffled past on their way back to the dressing rooms. The house rang with Antony's impassioned soliloquy over Caesar's body.

Colin: "*O, pardon me, thou bleeding piece of earth,*
   That I am meek and gentle with these butchers!
   Thou art the ruins of the noblest man
   That ever livèd in the tide of times.
   Woe to the hand that shed this costly blood!"

I groped toward the wall in the dark, one hand over my ear. The same someone turned me around so I didn't fall face-first into the fly lines.

"Are you all right?" Alexander whispered. "What happened?"

"He hit me right in the ear!"

"When?" James's voice.

"When I stabbed him, he turned around and smashed me with his elbow!" A bolt of pain so acute it felt solid had lodged in my skull like a railroad spike. I perched on the locking rail, leaning forward on my knees. A warm hand landed on the back of my neck; I didn't know whose.

"That's not the blocking," Alexander said.

"Of course it fucking isn't," James said. "Breathe, Oliver."

I unclenched my jaw and inhaled. James's hand slid to my shoulder. "Did he try to snap your wrists again?" I asked.

"Yeah." He glanced toward the light slanting in between the downstage legs. Colin had finished his speech and was conversing with a servant.

"Is he doing this shit on purpose?" Alexander said. "He about took my head off when I stabbed him but I thought he'd just gotten carried away again."

"Have you seen James's arms?"

James hushed me but unfastened his left cuff button and peeled his sleeve back. Even in the gloom of the wings we could see blotches of blue and purple on his skin. Alexander let out a string of obscenities all in one breath.

James shook his cuff back down. "Exactly."

"James," I said, "we have to do something."

He turned, the light from the stage turning his face a sickly malarial yellow. It was nearly time for intermission. "All right," he said. "But we leave Frederick and Gwendolyn out of it."

"How?"

There was a growl in Alexander's voice as he said, "If he wants a fight, let's give him a fight."

I tugged at my earlobe. A faint, shrill ringing pestered me like a fly. "Alexander," I said, "that's suicide."

"I don't see why."

"He's bigger than all of us."

"No, Oliver, idiot. He's bigger than *each* of us." He gave me a very pointed look.

The lights onstage were suddenly doused, and the audience erupted into applause. All at once people were rushing by. In the darkness it was impossible to tell who was who, but we knew one of them must be Richard. Alexander pushed me and James both back against the line sets, and the heavy ropes wobbled and groaned behind us like a ship's rigging. His hand was a vise on my shoulder, the audience thundering in my ears. "Listen," he said, "Richard can't fight off all three of us at once. Tomorrow, if he tries anything, instead of assassination we give him a righteous ass-kicking."

"*Here is my hand*," James said, after a split second's hesitation. "*The deed is worthy doing.*"

I hesitated also, a split second longer. "*And so say I.*"

Alexander squeezed my arm. "*And I and now we three have spoke it*, let the stupid bastard do his worst."

He let go of us abruptly as the house lights came up and the audience all rattled to their feet on the other side of the curtain. A few first-year technicians in black had already hurried onstage and were cleaning up the mess left after the assassination. The three of us shared a grim look, and said nothing else, but went single file to the dressing room. I trailed after James, limbs tingling with the same restless feeling from the week before, both eager and uneasy.

SCENE 7

Apart from Richard's unnecessary roughness, opening night had gone well, and the following morning praises were lavished on us in the hallways. The choral and orchestral students remained aloof—unimpressed by anyone who didn't have the discipline for something so refined as *music*—but the others regarded us with wide-eyed admiration. How could we explain that standing on a stage and speaking someone else's words as if they are your own is less an act of bravery than a desperate lunge at mutual understanding? An attempt to forge that tenuous link between speaker and listener and communicate something, anything, of substance. Unable to articulate it, we simply accepted their compliments and congratulations with the appropriate (and, in some cases, entirely contrived) humility.

In class, we were easily distracted. I barely listened to Frederick's lecture and my mind wandered so far during one of Camilo's balance exercises that I let Filippa knock me over backward. Alexander gave me an impatient sort of look that clearly meant, *Get your shit together.* As soon as we were dismissed, I retreated to the Tower with a mug of tea and René Girard's *Theatre of Envy*, hoping to distract myself from a dozen distressing premonitions of the night ahead. By then I felt no sympathy for Richard—the relentless, catchall antagonism he'd practiced over the last few weeks left a deeper impression than three years of placid friendship had—but I knew that no retaliation on our part would go unpunished. Any impartial observer would have dismissed it as a grandiloquent grudge match, but when I tried to persuade myself that that was all it was, Frederick's voice quietly reminded me that duels had been fought over less.

The prospective comeuppance of our feud with Richard, enormous as it loomed, was not the only thing weighing on my mind. Friday night was the night of the cast party; an hour after final curtain, most of Dellecher's theatre students and the bolder ones from other disciplines would invade the first floor of the Castle to celebrate a good opening and drink to the coming close. Meredith and Wren, neither of whom appeared onstage after Act II, had graciously agreed to sneak back between intermission and curtain call to get everything ready for a night of riotous revelry. When the rest of us arrived, we would have nothing to do but give our thanks to Dionysus and indulge.

At half past six I closed my book and took the stairs down to the dining room. The table and chairs had already been cleared away to make enough space for a dance floor. A set of speakers surreptitiously borrowed from the sound booth was stacked in one corner, cables trailing along the baseboards toward the nearest outlets. I left the Castle and began the long walk to the FAB with a fretful, anxious feeling that became more and more like dread with each passing minute.

It must have been showing on my face by the time I opened the door to the dressing room, because Alexander grabbed the front of my jacket, hauled me out to the loading dock, and stuck a lit spliff in my mouth.

"Don't get jittery," he said. "Everything's going to be fine."

(I'm not sure anyone has ever been so wrong.)

I puffed obediently on the spliff until there was only a half inch left. Alexander took it, sucked it down to his fingertips, threw it on the ground, and led me back inside. My misgivings faded to a vague paranoia at the back of my brain.

Time moved slowly as I put on makeup and costume pieces and went through the motions of a vocal warm-up. James,

Alexander, Wren, Filippa, and I leaned on the wall in the crossover, hands splayed on our diaphragms, chanting, *"Howl, howl, howl, howl—O, you are men of stones."* When a first-year with a headset appeared to tell us we had five minutes to places, my personal time lag collapsed and everything started to move as if on fast-forward.

The second-years vacated the dressing rooms and scrambled to find their places in the wings, hastily buttoning shirts and cuffs, or hopping down the hall as they tried to get their shoes tied. Filippa threw me in a chair in the girls' dressing room and attacked me with a comb and a tube of hair gel as the lights came up and the first lines of the play crackled through the backstage speakers.

Flavius: *"Hence! home, you idle creatures, get you home:*
    Is this a holiday?"

Filippa gave me a smart little slap to the forehead. "Oliver!"

"Fuck, what?"

"You're done, get out of here," she said, scowling down at me, one hand on her hip. "What is the matter with you?"

"Sorry," I said, as I climbed out of the chair. "Thanks, Pip."

"Are you high?"

"No."

"Are you full of crap?"

"Yes."

She pursed her lips and shook her head, but didn't reprimand me further. I wasn't entirely sober, but neither was I entirely stoned, and she probably knew that Alexander was mostly to blame. I left the girls' dressing room and loitered in the crossover until Richard brushed past, taking no more notice of me than he did of the paint on the walls. I followed a half step behind him, emerged into the glaring lights, and said, with as much sincerity as I could muster, *"Peace, ho! Caesar speaks."*

Acts I and II passed not unlike the first rainy front of a hurricane. There was rumble and bluster and a sense of impending peril, but we and the audience knew that the worst was yet to come. When Calpurnia entered, I watched from the edge of the wings. Richard and Meredith seemed to have overcome their difficulties, or had at least put them on hold for the duration of the run. He was rough with her but not violent; she was impatient with him but not provocative. Before I knew it, James was shaking me by the shoulder and whispering, "Let's go."

Act III opened with the silhouette of the colonnade against the scrim, which glowed scarlet—a raw, dangerous dawn. Richard stood between the two center columns, the rest of us arranged in a ring around him as Metellus Cimber knelt in the Bowl and pleaded for his brother. I was standing closest, so close that I could see the tiny tic of a nerve in Richard's jaw. Alexander, waiting with predatory, feline patience on the opposite side of the circle, caught my eye and flicked the front of his jacket open to reveal the paper knife tucked in his belt. (They were more in keeping with the theme than daggers would have been, but no less threatening.)

Richard: *"I could be well moved, if I were as you:*
 If I could pray to move, prayers would move me:
 But I am constant as the northern star,
 Of whose true-fix'd and resting quality
 There is no fellow in the firmament."

He looked around at the rest of us with bright gleaming eyes, daring us to contradict him. We shifted our feet and fingered our narrow blades, but kept our silence.

Richard: *"The skies are painted with unnumber'd sparks,*
 They are all fire and every one doth shine,
 But there's but one in all doth hold his place:
 So in the world; 'tis furnish'd well with men,
 And men are flesh and blood and apprehensive.
 Yet in the number I do know but one
 That unassailable holds on his rank,
 Unshaked of motion: and that I am he!"

His voice filled every corner of the auditorium, like a crack opening in the earth's crust, the boom and tremor of an earthquake. On my right, Filippa raised her chin, just barely.

Richard: *"Let me a little show it, even in this;*
   That I was constant Cimber should be banish'd,
   And constant do remain to keep him so."

Cinna began to object, but I had no ears for him. My eyes were fixed on James and Alexander. They mirrored each other's movements, turning slightly downstage so the audience could see the steel glinting on their belts. I licked my bottom lip. Everything felt too close, too real, like I was sitting in the front row of a movie theatre. I squeezed my eyes shut, fist clenched on the hilt of my knife, listening for the five fatal words that would spur me to action.

Richard: *"Doth not Brutus bootless kneel?"*

I opened my eyes, and all I saw was James, one knee bent in genuflection, staring up at Richard with bold contempt in his face.

"Speak hands, for me!" I shouted, and leapt at Richard, thrusting my blade under his upstage arm. The other conspirators came suddenly to life and swarmed on us like wasps. Richard glared at me, teeth bared and grinding hard together. I wrenched my knife away and made to move back, but he seized me by the collar, crushing the fabric so tightly around my throat that I couldn't breathe. I dropped the knife, groping at his wrist with both hands as his thumb jabbed into my carotid artery.

My vision was already swimming when Richard released me, with a roar of pain—Alexander had grabbed him by the hair and yanked him backward. I fell heavily on my tailbone, one hand flying to my neck. Someone had Richard's arm bent behind his back and the other half-dozen conspirators lunged to take their stabs at him, all blocking abandoned. In the confusion he lashed out wildly and hit Filippa right in the stomach, hard enough to knock her sprawling. She landed in a heap on the stairs—I'd made it to my feet just in time to watch her fall, and an inarticulate sound of outrage stuck in my throat. I shoved Cinna aside and dropped to my knees beside her. She lifted her head, clutching her stomach, gulping futilely, all the wind knocked out of her.

Suddenly the bedlam subsided, and I turned halfway around, kneeling over Filippa, who was quiet but gripping my leg hard. Richard stood surrounded by panting conspirators, arms pinned to his sides, Alexander's fist still clenched in his hair. James stood just out of his reach, suit disheveled, knife clutched tightly in his hand.

Richard's words were thick with hatred as he said, "*Et tu, Bruté?*"

James took one step forward and placed the blade against his neck.

Richard: "*Then fall, Caesar.*"

James's face was unnervingly blank. He slid the knife quickly forward—Richard made a short choking sound, then let his head loll against his chest. Alexander and the rest of the conspirators released him one by one, and he slumped to the floor. When they straightened up again, the second- and third-years looked from me to James to Alexander, wide-eyed, painfully aware of the audience and the fact that the scene had spiraled completely out of control. One of them had a line, but she must have forgotten, because nobody spoke. Alexander waited as long as he could, then spoke for her.

"*Liberty! Freedom! Tyranny is dead!*" He gave the nearest second-year a small shove. "*Run hence, proclaim, cry it about the streets.*" The rest shifted, exhaled, relieved. Filippa gasped as the air rushed into her lungs again. I helped her sit halfway up while Alexander continued barking orders. "*Some to the common pulpits, and cry out, / 'Liberty, freedom, and enfranchisement!'*"

"*People and senators, be not affrighted,*" James said to the conspirators, and his calmness seemed to reassure them. "*Fly not; stand still; ambition's debt is paid.*"

We relaxed into the text again, as if nothing at all unusual had happened. But as Filippa and I climbed to our feet, I couldn't help glancing down at Richard. He lay motionless except for the angry twitch of his eyelids, a vein bulging and throbbing in his throat.

SCENE 8

My head cleared as Brutus and Cassius's coup collapsed. Richard had disappeared out the door during intermission, and no one saw him again until Act IV when he returned as Caesar's ghost— an apparition doubly sinister for its stony solemnity. The final curtain fell at ten thirty, and my body ached with fatigue, but the layered drama of the assassination scene and anticipation for the party kept me awake and alert. By the time I'd washed my face, gotten my costume off, and dressed myself again, most of the second- and third-years had gone. James and Alexander were waiting in the crossover with four fat spliffs rolled already (one for each of us and one for Filippa, who had already gone back to the Castle to change). We left the FAB and strolled down the path through the woods with our hands in our pockets. We didn't mention the Three-One incident, except for Alexander saying simply, "I hope he's learned his lesson."

When we were only thirty feet from the Castle, the sultry party light began to soak through the thick shadows of the trees. We stopped to finish smoking and stamped the roaches down in the damp pine needles. Alexander turned to us and said, "We've had a long week. I plan to make a long night of it, and if you two aren't royally fucked by midnight I will take it upon myself to see that you *are* fucked, royally or otherwise, by morning. Understand?"

Me: "You make it sound a lot like date rape."

Alexander: "Do as I've said and it won't come to that."

James: "You're both of you going to hell."

Alexander: "Directly."

Me: "Posthaste."

Alexander: "*Every man put himself into triumph; some to dance, some to make bonfires, each man to what sport and revels his addiction leads him.* Go."

Obediently, we went.

The front door opened and a wave of noise crashed out to meet us. The Castle was crammed with people, some drinking, some dancing, sparkling in their party clothes. (The boys didn't look too terribly different from usual—only better dressed, better groomed—but the girls were hardly recognizable. Night had fallen, and with it came short slinky dresses and dark mascara and satin lipstick, transforming them from mere *girls* to a coven of bewitching nocturnal creatures.) The welcoming roar washed over us; hands reached out to snatch our clothes and drag us help-lessly inside.

Two kegs sweated in the downstairs bathtub, tightly packed in with ice and bottles of water. Stacks of Solo cups cluttered the kitchen counter, while handles of cheap rum, vodka, and whiskey were arranged in a bowling-pin pyramid on the stove (mostly paid for by Meredith's exorbitant monthly allowance, with more modest contributions from the rest of us). The good stuff was stashed in Alexander's bedroom. As soon as we arrived, Filippa nipped upstairs and returned with a Scotch and soda for each of us. Immediately thereafter, James and Alexander both disappeared, sucked away into the crowd. Most of the theatre students had assembled in the kitchen, where they talked and laughed twice as loudly as they needed to, still performing, ob-served by less obnoxious onlookers from the art, language, and philosophy departments. Choral and orchestral students eager to criticize the music selection and dancers eager to show off had filled the dining room, which was so poorly lit that they either had only a dim idea who they were dancing with or simply didn't

care. Music thundered through the floorboards, every bass note
a tiny earthquake, the footstep of a slow-approaching dinosaur.
The surface of my drink shivered and vibrated until Filippa
threw a handful of ice in it.

"Thanks," I said. Her expression was distant, distracted.
"You okay?"

"Fine," she said, with a pained sort of smile. "Got a wicked
bruise but not where anyone will see."

"You look good to me," I said, lamely. She wore a short blue
something that showed off her long legs. Mercifully, she wasn't
too made-up and still looked human.

"It happens every now and then," she said, exhaling, allowing herself to relax. "Where've you been?"

"Outside. Alexander rolled you a spliff if you want it."

"God bless the filthy hedonist. Where is he now?"

"On the dance floor," I said, "prowling for first-years who
don't know they're gay yet."

"Where else?" she said, and left the kitchen, deftly weaving
between the people at the counter fighting to get a hold of
the rapidly diminishing mixers. I took a long drink of Scotch
and soda, wondering how long the cross-fade would take. Colin
and several other third-years paused on their way out to the
driveway—where people would be smoking and chatting and
waiting for their eardrums to stop throbbing—to congratulate
me on a good show. I thanked them, and when they filed out,
Colin hovered on the threshold. I bent my head close to his to
hear him.

"Three-One went off the rails today," he said. "Everything
all right?"

"I think so," I said. "Pip got knocked around a bit, but she's
tough. Have you seen Richard?"

"He's upstairs, throwing back whiskey like it's keeping him
alive."

We shared a look that was one part disdain, one part concern.

We both remembered all too well what had happened the last time Richard drank too much.

"What about Meredith?" I asked, wondering if she might be a contributing factor to Richard's foul mood, or if James and Alexander and I were solely to blame.

"Holding court in the garden," Colin said. "She hung all the lights out there. I think she's watching to make sure no one tears them down."

"Sounds about right."

He grinned. (Though we had originally compared him to Richard, the comparison didn't stick. He played the same bombastic roles, but offstage his cockiness was endearing more than infuriating.) "Want to come out for a smoke?" he said.

"I've had one, but you should find Pip in the yard."

"Great," he said, and stepped out after his friends. I turned to scan the kitchen, wondering where James had gotten to.

For maybe an hour, maybe longer, I wandered from room to room, conversation to conversation, accepting drinks and congratulations with polite disinterest. The music in the dining room was so loud I could hardly hear what anyone said. The dull red light and constant surge and sway of bodies exacerbated my state of intoxication, and when I began to feel dizzy, I ventured out into the driveway. As soon as I set foot outside, the same flirtatious girl from Halloween spotted me. I did an abrupt 180 and escaped around the side of the building to the garden.

The garden—less an actual garden than a small plot of grass bordered on three sides by trees—wasn't as crowded. People stood in clumps of three or four, talking and laughing or gazing up at the string lights, which had been painstakingly stretched from tree to tree. The yard twinkled as though several hundred obliging fireflies had decided to attend the party. Meredith sat on the table in the middle with her legs crossed at the knee, a drink in one hand and a toothpick speared through two olives in the other. (She, apparently, was sipping martinis while everyone else made do with well liquor and Coke.) I hovered uncertainly at the edge of the yard. We hadn't said more than a few words to each other since the dressing room incident, and I wasn't sure where we stood. Before long I found myself staring at her legs. Her calves tapered perfectly to slender ankles and black pumps with five-inch heels. I considered the possibility that she was sitting on the table because she couldn't stand on the soft ground without sinking into it.

When she realized I was there she smiled—without resentment, it seemed. (The boy beside her—he played cello with the orchestral students, though I didn't know which year he was— carried on talking, unaware that her attention had shifted.) A little ripple of relief went through me. She turned toward the cellist again but looked down into her drink, stirring slowly with her olives.

I was about to go back inside when I felt an arm slide around my waist.

"Hello, you," Wren said, with the cuddly, kittenish affection she always displayed when she'd been drinking. She was wearing something pale green and floaty that made her look like Tinker Bell.

I ruffled her hair. "Hello. Having a good time?"

"Splendid, only Richard's being a snot."

"I'm shocked."

Her nose crinkled as she frowned. She was still hugging me around the waist and I wondered vaguely if she could stand up on her own. "I don't know what's gotten into him," she said, with an edge of bitterness in her voice I hadn't heard before. "He's always been a bit of a pig, but now he's . . . I don't know. Mean."

It was such an innocent word that I felt a twinge of something protective, big-brotherish. I squeezed her against my side and said, "I don't know if 'mean' does it justice."

"Why not?"

"I don't know, it's not just mean—it's sadistic. He's been battering us onstage. Opening night he about busted my eardrum, Filippa's got a bruise the size of Australia, and James—" I stopped, belatedly remembering my promise to keep it to myself. My verbal and visual filters weren't working properly.

"What's he done to James?" she demanded, with a kind of fearful uncertainty. She was trying to keep up, but the whiskey wouldn't let her.

"I said I wouldn't tell anyone. But he'll tell you, if you ask him." I thought of him twirling a strand of her hair, and it occurred to me that he'd do just about anything she asked him to. Something clenched uncomfortably in my chest.

She frowned again. Her arms had gone loose around me, as if she'd forgotten they were there. "You know, he scares me sometimes."

"James?" I asked, bewildered.

She shook her head. "Richard. I'm afraid he'll really hurt someone, or himself. He's just . . . reckless, you know?"

It wasn't the word I would have chosen, but I nodded anyway. "You should tell him that. You're probably the only person he'd listen to."

"Maybe. But it'll have to wait 'til morning. Right now he's completely plastered."

"Well," I said, "if he's too drunk to stand up this party might turn out okay."

I had a strange, sinking feeling just then. Richard, no matter how much he drank, had never been fully incapacitated by alcohol. It only made him more, if I used Wren's word, *reckless*.

Meredith slid off the table and excused herself from her admirers (of which there were four, by that time). She crossed the yard with surprising steadiness, cocked her head, and said, "Aren't you two precious." Up close and in my less than lucid state, I couldn't stop staring at her. She wore a snug black sheath, one shoulder bare, a strap of tiny jet beads glittering on the other. In those shoes, she was almost as tall as I was.

"The garden looks amazing, Mer," Wren said.

"Yes." She smiled up at the lights. "I hate to leave it. *And I must lose / Two of the sweet'st companions in the world.*" She winked. Her eye shadow—dark plum purple—somehow made her eyes even greener.

"Where are you going?" Wren asked.

"Inside for another drink." She raised her empty cup. "Refill?"

Wren hiccupped. "I think I'm done."

"I think you are, too," Meredith said, barely scolding, almost sisterly. She turned to me. "Olive, Oliver?" She raised her toothpick, one last olive speared on the end.

"You have it," I said, unable to suppress a smirk. "If I did it would be cannibalism."

She gave me such a piercing look that my temperature shot up about ten degrees, then bit the olive off the toothpick and disappeared inside. I watched her go and stared dumbly at the empty doorway until Wren spoke.

"She doesn't seem to be suffering much."

"What?"

"She and Rick are 'taking some time off,'" she said, making quotation marks in the air with only one hand. "I figured you knew."

"Uh, no. I didn't."

"Her idea. He's not exactly pleased about it but you know how he is, he won't apologize for anything." She made a face. "If he'd just swallowed his pride she might have changed her mind."

"Oh."

She yawned, pressed the back of her hand to her mouth. "What time is it?"

"Dunno," I said. "Late." My own eyelids felt a little heavy.

"I'll go find out."

"I don't want to know."

She let go of me, pushing herself off my side to stand up straight. "Okay, I won't tell you." She petted my arm, like I was a dog, then meandered up the steps, a bit of her skirt pinched between two fingers.

The yard had mostly emptied during our conversation. People were either heading back inside or (I hoped) going home. I ventured out into the middle of our little clearing and closed my eyes. The night air was chilly, but it didn't bother me. It soothed my warm skin like a salve, rinsed the smoke from my lungs, evicted Meredith's velvet shadow from my head. When I opened my eyes I was surprised to see a patch of blue between the dark treetops, a white sliver of moon grinning down at me. A sudden desire to see the whole sky urged me to take the trail down to the lake. But when I made to move, James's voice held me in place.

"*Well shone, Moon. Truly the moon shines with a good grace.*" I turned to find him standing behind me, hands in his pockets.

"Where've you been all night?"

"Honestly?"

"Yeah, honestly."

"I was making the rounds for a while, but I got overwhelmed and snuck upstairs to do some reading."

I laughed. "You utter dork. What brought you back down?"

"Well, it's after midnight, and I can't disappoint Alexander."

"By now I doubt he even remembers telling us that."

"Probably not." He tilted his head back to admire the sky. "It looks farther away when there's so little of it."

For a while we just stood there, faces upturned, not speaking. The noise from the Castle was a dull rumble in the background, like the clamor of car engines on a road in the distance. An owl hooted softly, somewhere. It occurred to me (for the first time, I think) how alone we were when the Castle was empty, when there wasn't a party, when the other students were all half a mile away at the Hall. It was just *us*—the seven of us and the trees and the sky and the lake and the moon and, of course, Shakespeare. He lived with us like an eighth housemate, an older, wiser friend, perpetually out of sight but never out of mind, as if he had just left the room. *Much is the force of heaven-bred poesy.*

There was a soft fizz of electricity; Meredith's lights flickered and went out. I looked back toward the Castle in the deep gloom. The kitchen lights were on and the music audible, so I assumed we hadn't blown a fuse.

"Wonder what happened."

James was not curious enough to tear his eyes away from the sky. "Look," he said.

With the lights out we could see stars, tiny pinpricks of white scattered around the moon and glinting like sequins. The world was perfectly still for one precious instant. Then there was a crash, a shout, and something inside shattered. At first, neither of us moved. We stood staring at each other, hoping—silently, desperately, pointlessly—that someone had simply knocked a bottle off the counter, or slipped on the stairs, or some other clumsy, innocent thing. But before either of us could speak again, voices inside started screaming.

"Richard," I said, my heart already in my throat. "I bet anything." We raced back toward the Castle, in as straight a line as we could manage.

The door was hanging open but people had blocked it completely, filled up the gap. James and I shoved them aside to get into the kitchen, where at least a dozen others had made a ring around the edge of the room. James broke through the circle first, knocking two second-year linguists out of his way. I wasn't sober enough to judge the distance and slammed into him when he stopped, but the close press of people kept both of us from falling over.

The cellist who'd been talking to Meredith outside sat crumpled on the floor with one hand over his face, blood dribbling out between his fingers. Filippa crouched beside him, perched on her toes in a glittering mess of broken glass. Meredith and Wren stood facing Richard, and all three of them were shouting at once, their words overlapping and indistinguishable as music and laughter churned in from the next room. Alexander hovered in the doorway behind Richard, but he was leaning on Colin and in no condition to intervene, so James and I pushed forward to arbitrate.

"What happened?" I asked, hollering to be heard over the racket.

"Richard," Filippa said, giving him a dirty look over her shoulder. "Came downstairs and sucker punched him."

"What the hell? *Why?*"

"He was watching the yard from the upstairs window."

"Everyone calm down!" James ordered. Wren fell silent, but Richard and Meredith ignored him.

"You're out of control!" she yelled. "You need to be in a straitjacket."

"Well, maybe we could share one."

"This is not a fucking joke! You could have knocked his teeth out!"

The boy on the floor groaned and leaned forward, a long thread of blood and saliva hanging from his bottom lip. Filippa stood up swiftly and said, "Yeah, I think he probably did. He needs to go to the infirmary."

"I'll take him," Colin said. He left Alexander leaning on the doorjamb and gave Richard a wide berth as he came across the kitchen. He and I and Filippa got the cellist to his feet and draped his arm around Colin's shoulders. They weren't even out of the room before Richard and Meredith resumed their shouting match.

Meredith: "Are you happy now?"

Richard: "Are you?"

"Both of you, *stop!*" Wren's voice had climbed to a danger-ously high pitch. "Just *stop*, can't you?"

Richard rounded on her and she took one wary step back. "This isn't your problem, Wren."

"No," Filippa said, sharply, "you've made it *everybody's* problem."

"Don't be a bitch, Filippa—"

James and I both moved forward, but Meredith spoke first and Richard froze, all the muscles between his shoulders bunched and bulging.

"Don't talk to her like that. Turn around and look at me," she said. "Stop bullying everyone else like a fucking schoolboy and *look* at me."

He turned and lurched toward her so suddenly that everyone jumped back, but Meredith didn't move an inch—she was either brave or crazy.

"Shut your mouth—" he started, but she didn't let him fin-ish.

"Or what? You'll knock my teeth out, too?" she asked. "Do it. I *dare* you."

I decided that perhaps "brave" and "crazy" were not mutu-ally exclusive. "Meredith," I said, carefully.

Richard swung toward me, and James and Filippa shifted closer, closing ranks. "Don't tempt me," he said. "You I'll send to the infirmary in *pieces*."

"Back off!" Meredith shoved him, both hands hitting his chest with a flat thump; before she could withdraw again he grabbed her by the wrist. "It's not about him. You're making it about him because you can't hit me and you're just desperate to hit someone!"

"You'd like that, wouldn't you?" Richard said, jerking her forward. She twisted her arm against his grip until her flesh went white. "If I knocked you around a bit, gave everyone something to stare at? We all know how you like everyone staring at you. You *slut*."

Between the six of us, we'd called Meredith some version of "slut" a thousand times, but this was horrifically different. Everything seemed to go silent, despite the music pounding in the next room.

Richard grabbed her chin, tilting her face up toward his. "Well. It was fun for a while."

My last thin thread of hesitation snapped. I lunged at him, but Meredith was closer. People screamed as she backhanded him across the face—it was nothing like Camilo's class, not precise or controlled, but a wild, savage blow meant to do as much damage as possible. Richard swore obscenely, but before he could get to her James and Alexander crashed into him like a pair of linebackers. Even their combined weight wasn't enough to knock him down, and he kept bellowing curses, snatching at every inch of Meredith he could reach. I grabbed her around the waist, but he already had a fistful of her hair and she cried out in pain as he yanked on it. I lifted her right off the ground and wrenched her away from him, crushing her against my chest as I lost my balance and stumbled into Filippa. Richard, James, and Alexander pitched backward and fell against the cabinets, half a dozen people rushing to catch them before they hit the floor.

I pawed Meredith's hair away from my face, one arm locked tight around her, unsure whether I was trying to protect her or control her or both. "Meredith—" I said, but she elbowed me in the stomach and shoved me off. Filippa seized my shirt when I staggered and held on, like she was afraid of what I might do if she let go. Meredith stared straight past us at Richard, arms rigid at her sides, chest heaving. Slowly, he pushed himself upright. James had already backed away, and the few people still holding on to Richard hastily removed their hands. Alexander cursed softly, touching his fingertips to a bloody lip. Everyone else's eyes were fixed on Meredith, but it wasn't the kind of staring she was used to. Everything she felt was written on her face—shame, fury, paralytic disbelief.

"You *bastard*," she said. She turned and shouldered past me and Filippa, scattering terrified first-years as she made her way to the stairs.

Richard and I stood facing each other, like unarmed fencers. Alexander flickered in my peripheral vision, reaching up for a napkin to wipe his mouth. I could hear Wren whimpering, but the sound was distant. James stood behind Richard like a shadow, watching me with a shell-shocked expression, one part dread, one part indignation. Anger bristled on my skin, trapped there by the fabric of my shirt pulled tight against my body. I wanted to hurt Richard like he'd hurt Meredith, like he'd hurt James, like he would hurt any one of us who gave him half a reason. I glanced at Filippa because I didn't trust myself not to attack him any more than she did.

"I'll go," I said, stiffly. She nodded and let go of my shirt, and I didn't wait. The crowd parted as easily for me as it had for Meredith. I turned into the hall between the kitchen and dining room and pressed my back flat against the wall, breathing slowly through my nose until my head stopped spinning. I didn't even know what I was drunk on anymore—whiskey and weed and howling rage. I took one last long breath, then ducked through the doorway to the stairwell.

"Meredith," I said, for the third time. She was the only one there, halfway up the stairs. Music droned in the walls, half muted. Warm pink light leaked in from the kitchen.

"Leave me alone."

"Hey." I climbed the first three steps behind her. "Wait."

She stopped, one hand trembling on the banister. "For what? I'm done with this fucking party, with all of them down there. What do you want?"

"I just want to help."

"Is that right?"

I stared up at her—dress disheveled, arms folded, face flushed—and felt a tiny, painful thud in the pit of my stomach. She was too stubborn. "Forget it," I said, and turned down the stairs again.

"Oliver!"

I gritted my teeth, turned back around. "Yes?"

She didn't say anything at first, just glared at me. Her hair was tangled and caught in her earring where Richard had grabbed it. That little rip in the middle of me opened wider and it burned— raw and tender, red and angry.

"You really want to help?" she asked. It was only half a question—tentative, suspicious of the answer.

"Yes," I said again, too fiercely, stung by her doubt.

That same brazen, fearless look she'd given me in the dressing room flashed across her face. In one impulsive motion, she came down the three steps between us and kissed me, caught me, both hands curled tight around the back of my neck. I was startled but still, oblivious to everything but the unexpected heat of her mouth on mine.

We separated an inch and looked at each other with wide, unguarded eyes. Nothing about her had ever seemed simple, but she was, then. Simple and close and beautiful. A little tousled, a little damaged.

We kissed again, more urgently. She forced my lips apart, stole my breath right out of my mouth, pushed me backward until I hit the banister. I grabbed her hips and pulled her against me, ready to feel every inch of her.

An unfamiliar voice interrupted the thick noise of music through the wall. "Oh, shit."

She disengaged, broke away, and I nearly lost my balance in the sudden absence of her body. Some nameless first-year was standing at the foot of the stairs, drink in hand. His eyes slid from me to Meredith with dull, unfocused surprise. "Oh, *shit*," he said again, and staggered out toward the kitchen.

Meredith reached for my hand. "My room," she said. I would have followed her anywhere, and I didn't care who knew— Richard (who deserved so much worse than such petty betrayal) or anyone else.

We climbed the stairs hastily, clumsily, impeded by her high heels, my drunkenness, and our foolish refusal to keep our hands off each other. We ran down the hall on the second floor, crashing against the wall and locking lips again before we stumbled into her bedroom. She threw the door shut and turned the bolt behind her. We collided more than embraced, the whole feverish scene shot through with flashes of pain—she clenched her fingers in my hair, caught my bottom lip between her teeth, shuddered when the rough stubble on my jaw scraped her throat. The bass from the dining room downstairs thudded under everything like some savage tribal drumbeat.

"You look fucking amazing," I said, in the split second I had to speak when she pulled my shirt up over my head.

She tossed it across the room. "Yeah, I know."

The fact that she knew was somehow sexier than pretending she didn't. I fumbled for the zipper on the side of her dress and said, "Great, just making sure."

The rest of our clothes came off and were carelessly discarded, everything but our underwear and Meredith's shoes. We kissed and gasped and grasped at each other like we were afraid to let go. My head swam, the floor shifting and tilting under me whenever I closed my eyes. I ran one hand from the nape of her neck to the small of her back, her skin electric under my fingertips. The warm silk touch of her lips against my ear made me groan and clutch her closer—delirious, addicted, furious that I'd ever pretended not to want her.

We were halfway to the bed when a fist boomed on the door, made it shake in its frame. Another fist followed, and another, pounding and pounding like a battering ram. "OPEN THE DOOR! OPEN THIS FUCKING DOOR!"

"Richard!" I reeled back, but Meredith grabbed me fast around the neck.

"He can bang on the door all night if he wants."

"He'll break it down," I said, and the words disappeared between her lips before they even left mine, the thought forgotten before I finished it. My pulse was wild.

"Let him try." She shoved me backward onto the bed, and I didn't argue.

Everything after that was disjointed and confused. Richard hammered on the door, bellowing curses and threats I could barely hear—his voice only part of a heavy rhythm, *"I'LL KILL YOU, I'LL KILL YOU, I SWEAR TO GOD I'LL KILL YOU BOTH."* It was impossible to listen with Meredith between me and him, tangible, intoxicating, the tiny intake of her breath enough to drown out his riot of noise. He faded out, like the end of a bad song, and I didn't know whether he'd left or I'd gone deaf to everything but Meredith. My head was so light that without her weight on top of me I might have floated away. Inch by inch, my brain and body reconnected. I let her have her way for a little longer, then rolled her over on her back and pinned her down, unwilling to be entirely submissive.

When I collapsed beside her on the mattress, my muscles were quivering under my skin. We were too hot to touch by then, and we lay with only our legs tangled together. Our shallow breaths lengthened, deepened, and sleep pulled me swiftly down like gravity.

I didn't sleep long, and I slept like a man on a raft, waves rolling underneath me—seasick more than drunk. My eyes opened before I even knew I was awake, and I stared up at the unfamiliar ceiling. Meredith lay beside me, one hand pressed under her cheek, the other arm tucked tight against her chest. A tiny line had appeared between her eyebrows, as though whatever she was dreaming troubled her.

The lamp on the nightstand leaked watery orange light across the bed. I reached carefully over her to turn it off but paused, my arm outstretched. Meredith's breath fluttered against the back of my hand. I couldn't help staring—not, for once, because she was beautiful, but because the small dark spots on her body I'd mistaken in my drunken fervor for shadows and tricks of the light hadn't faded. The delicate line of her wrist was marred by tiny blooms of purple, like budding violets on her skin. Older marks, weak as watercolors now, showed where a heavier hand than mine had touched her, where phantom fingers had squeezed too hard: the nape of her neck, the curve of her knee. She was every bit as bruised as James. I felt nauseous, but the sick feeling settled in my chest instead of my stomach.

I risked brushing a strand of hair off her cheek, then turned the light out. The room shrank in around me, the eager darkness encroaching at last. I lifted the sheet and put my feet on the floor. I wanted water, badly, to soothe my dry throat and clear my head. Halfway across the room I pulled my underwear on.

Before I opened the door, I pressed my ear against it. Was Richard crazy enough to wait outside all night for one of us to emerge? Hearing nothing, I opened it just a crack. The hall stretched empty and dark in both directions. The lights and music downstairs had been shut off and the whole building felt skeletal, like an empty shell where some soft spineless creature used to live. I crept toward the bathroom, wondering if I was the only person awake. Evidently not—Alexander's door was open, his bed empty. I moved quietly, hoping not to rouse anyone. I knew a confrontation of some kind was unavoidable, but I didn't want to face it any sooner than I had to. Not before I could convince myself that it had all actually happened—my memory of the party had the gauzy, chimerical quality of a dream. Part of me wanted to believe that was all it was.

Assuming an inebriated partygoer had left the light on, I opened the bathroom door without knocking. In the instant it took my eyes to adjust, a crouching figure sprang up from the floor.

"Jesus!"

"Hush, Oliver, it's me!" James reached around me to pull the door shut. His arm brushed across my bare stomach and I shivered at the dampness of his skin. He took one step back, naked and dripping wet. The shower drummed softly in the background.

"What are you doing?"

He pushed the toilet handle down and the water swirled away as he wiped his mouth. "Just been sick," he said.

"You okay?"

"Yeah. Drank too much is all. What are you doing up?"

"Needed some water," I said, averting my eyes. We'd shared a room for three years and James naked was nothing I hadn't seen before, but I'd surprised him and it felt somehow intrusive.

"Do you care if I get back in?" His hand rose briefly from his side, a loose abortive gesture toward the shower. "I feel disgusting, I hate vomiting."

"Go ahead." I slid past him to get to the sink and cupped cold water into my mouth as he stepped over the side of the tub. The spray hit his skin with a hiss, and he pulled the curtain halfway closed.

"So," he said, a little too casually. "Did you just come from Meredith's room?"

"Um. Yeah."

"You think that's a good idea?"

"Not especially."

My reflection was messy, disheveled. I surreptitiously wiped a smear of lipstick from the corner of my mouth. In the mirror I could see James leaning on the shower wall, water dripping from his nose and chin.

"I guess everyone knows," I said. I splashed my face, hoping my skin would cool.

"One of the first-years came in from the stairwell and basically announced it to the room."

"I really hate first-years." I shut the faucet off, then closed the toilet lid and sat on it.

"So. How was it?"

I glanced up at him, anxiety prickling sorely on my skin. "You do know Richard's going to kill me."

"That did seem to be his plan."

James turned his face into the water, eyes squeezed shut. My limbs felt heavy and useless, as if the muscles and bones had dissolved and been replaced with half-mixed concrete. I raked my wet fingers through my hair and asked, "Where is he, anyway?"

"Don't know. Disappeared into the woods with a bottle of Scotch after Pip and Alexander stopped him kicking Meredith's door down."

"Christ." I hung my head for a moment, then pushed myself to my feet before I felt too heavy to move.

"Are you going back to her room?" James asked. His back was to me, the water slithering down between his shoulder blades in two narrow streams (for a moment I indulged the idea that maybe it would wash his bruises off like paint).

"I don't want to just leave her in there, like a one-night stand."

"Is that not what this is?"

I couldn't remember ever being angry with James before. The feeling surged up unexpectedly—broad and vulnerable, raw as a burn. "No," I said, too loudly.

He glanced over his shoulder, brow furrowed in confusion. "Oh?"

"Look, I know she's not your favorite but she's not just some girl either."

He blinked. "I guess not," he said, and turned his back to me again.

"James," I said, with no idea what I meant to say after.

He turned the water off, one hand lingering on the handle. A few tiny drops clung to his eyelashes, rolled down his face like tears. "What?" he said, slightly delayed.

I struggled to form words—I felt the shape of them, but not the substance—until a smudge on his cheek distracted me.

"I— You've got puke on your face," I blurted.

His expression was blank as the odd sentence registered, and when it did he blushed to the roots of his hair. "Oh."

Suddenly we were both embarrassed (which seemed absurd, after the last five minutes of intimate conversation and casual nakedness).

"I'm sorry, that's vile," he said.

"It's fine." I stooped down to grab his towel from the floor. "Here." We'd both reached for it, and when I stood up again we nearly bumped heads. I eased back, enormously aware of my own body and how clumsy it was. He looked wide-awake, almost alarmed. I felt my own face going hot.

I garbled a goodnight, put the towel in his hand, and hastily left the room.

SCENE 10

An hour or so later I woke again, to the sound of someone banging on the door. There was a voice, too—female. Not Richard. I propped myself halfway up and Meredith stirred beside me. Whoever it was knocked again, more insistently.

"Oliver, I know you're in there," Filippa said. "Get up."

She sounded hollow, like a bad recording of herself. I didn't want her to wake Meredith, so I slid out of the bed and opened the door without bothering to find my jeans.

Filippa's face was drawn and pale. "Get dressed," she said. "Both of you. You need to come down to the dock. Now."

She left, walking quickly, head bent. I stood in the doorway for a moment, surprised by her failure to make some scathing remark. Something was wrong—wrong enough that my waking up *déshabillé* in Meredith's room didn't matter. I closed the door again and began grabbing my clothes off the floor. "Meredith," I said, urgently. "Wake up."

We went down to the dock together, bleary-eyed and puzzled.

"What the fuck is going on?" she asked. "It's not even light out."

"I don't know," I said. "Filippa seemed upset."

"About *what*?"

"She didn't say."

We stumbled down the rickety wooden stairs built into the side of the hill in partial darkness. A soft muffled cold, like a blanket of snow, pressed in around me and made me shiver, even though I'd pulled a coat and a sweatshirt on. The steps were littered with rocks and twigs, and the danger of stumbling was so great that I kept my eyes on my feet until the last step finally flattened out and I glanced up. A few stubborn stars still peered down from a sky barely lighter than the jagged black branches of the trees. I paused as my eyes adjusted to the sunless, twilit world. Shadow shapes solidified as James, Alexander, Wren, and Filippa—all standing there on the dock, staring out at the water. I couldn't see past them, see what it was they were looking at.

"What is it?" I said. "Guys?"

Alexander was the only one to turn my way, and he just shook his head—a tiny, labored motion.

"What's going on?" Meredith said. There was finally a note of worry in her voice.

I pushed between James and Wren, and the vast expanse of the lake opened up in front of me, mist blurring the lines of the banks. Tiny ripples murmured around a grotesque pale shape, partly submerged where the water should have been glassy and smooth. Richard floated on his back, neck twisted unnaturally, mouth gaping, face frozen in a Greek mask of agony. Blood crawled dark and sticky across his face from the crush of tissue and bone that used to be an eye socket, a cheekbone—now cracked and broken open like an eggshell.

We stood numb and silent on the dock as the earth ceased to turn. A terrible stillness held our six warm breathing bodies and Richard—unmoving, inanimate thing—in the same unbreakable thrall. Then there was a sound, a soft groan; Richard stretched one hand feebly toward us, and the whole world lurched. Wren stifled a scream and James grabbed my arm.

"Oh, *God*." He choked on the word. "He's still alive."

ACT III

PROLOGUE

Colborne and I emerge into the early afternoon together. The day feels primeval, prehistoric, the sun bright and blinding behind a thin layer of clouds. Neither of us has sunglasses, and we grimace against the light like reluctant, newborn babies.

"Where to now?" he says.

"I'd like to walk around the lake."

I start across the lawn and he walks close beside me. Mostly, he's been silent, just listening. Every now and then his face responds to something I've said—a subtle lift of the eyebrows, or a twitch at the corner of his mouth. He's asked a few questions, little things, like "This was when?" Though the timeline is clear in my head, explaining it to someone else is a curious task, simple in theory but painstaking in practice, like assembling a long line of dominoes. One event inevitably leads to the next.

We walk all the way down to the woods without speaking. The trees are taller than I remember—I don't have to duck under the branches anymore. I wonder how much a tree grows in ten years and reach out to brush the bark, as if each knotted trunk is the shoulder of an old friend I touch as I pass, without thinking. I reconsider: I don't have any old friends except Filippa. How do the others think of me now? I haven't seen them. I don't know.

We emerge from the copse onto the beach, which looks exactly the same. Coarse white sand like salt, rows and rows of weather-beaten benches. The little shed where James poured blood all over me on Halloween is listing slightly to the side—a diminutive Tower of Pisa.

Colborne's hands hide in his pockets as he looks out over the water. We can see the opposite shore, just barely, a hazy line drawn between the trees and their reflections. The Tower sticks up out of the forest like a fairy-tale turret. I count three across to find the window that was beside my bed, a narrow black slot in the gray stone wall.

"Was it cold that night?" Colborne says. "I don't remember."

"Cold enough." I wonder if there's still a clear patch of sky over the garden, or if the branches have all tangled together to block it out. "At least, I think it was. We'd all been drinking, and we always drank way too much, like it was something we were just supposed to do. The cult of excess: drink and drugs, sex and love, pride and envy and revenge. Nothing in moderation."

He shakes his head. "Every Friday night I lie awake wondering what dumb thing some drunk kid's going to do that I'll have to clean up in the morning."

"Not anymore."

"Yeah. Just got my own kids to worry about."

"How old are they now?"

"Fourteen," he says, like he can't quite believe it. "Starting high school this fall."

"They'll be all right," I tell him.

"How do you know?"

"They've got better parents than we did."

He smirks, not quite sure whether I might be mocking him. Then he nods toward the Castle. "You want to walk around to the south bank?"

"Not yet." I sit down in the sand and peer up at him. "This is a long story. There's a lot you don't know yet."

"I've got all day."

"You going to stand until nightfall?"

He makes a face but bends his knees to sit beside me as a breeze blows off the lake. "So," he says. "How much of what you told me about that night was true?"

"All of it," I say, "in one way or another."

A pause. "Are we going to play this game?"

"*Wherein I am false I am honest; not true, to be true*," I say.

"I thought they would have beaten that bullshit out of you in prison."

"That bullshit is all that kept me going." One thing I'm sure Colborne will never understand is that I need language to live, like food—lexemes and morphemes and morsels of meaning nourish me with the knowledge that, yes, there is a word for this. Someone else has felt it before.

"Why don't you just tell me what happened? No performance. No poetics."

"For us, everything was a performance." A small, private smile catches me off guard and I glance down, hoping he won't see it. "Everything poetic."

Colborne is quiet for a moment and then says, "You win. Tell it your way."

I gaze across the lake at the top of the Tower. A large bird—a hawk, maybe—soars in long lazy circles over the trees, an elegant black boomerang against the silvery sky.

"The party started around eleven. We were all wrecked by one o'clock, Richard worst of all. He broke a glass, punched a kid in the mouth. Things got ugly and confused and out of control, and by two I was upstairs in bed with Meredith."

I can feel his eyes on the side of my face, but I don't look up.

"That was the truth?" he asks, and I sigh, exasperated by the note of surprise in his voice.

"Weren't there enough witnesses?"

"Twenty shitfaced kids at a party, and only one of them actually saw anything."

"Well, he wasn't blind."

"So there was something between you two."

"Yes," I say. "There was something."

I don't know how to continue. Of course, I was at Meredith's mercy. Like Aphrodite, she demanded exaltation and idolatry. But what was her weakness for me, tame and inconsequential as I was? A thing of mystery.

As I tell the story to Colborne, guilt wriggles, wormlike, in the pit of my stomach. Our relationship was a point of significant interest, but Meredith refused to testify at my trial, stubbornly insisting that she didn't remember what everyone wanted to know. She spent a few weeks being hounded by press people, which proved to be too much attention even for her. After I was convicted she went back to the Manhattan apartment and, for a month or so, didn't come out. (Her brother Caleb made the news before she did, when he broke a paparazzo's jaw with his briefcase. After that, the vultures lost interest, and I thought of Caleb more fondly.)

Meredith did eventually make her way to TV—she stars now in some legal drama loosely based on the *Henry VI* cycle. It was popular in prison, not because of its Shakespearean source material, but because she spends a lot of time on the show lounging around in slinky nightgowns that show off her figure. She came to visit me—only once—and when the rumor that I'd had some sort of affair with her surfaced, it won me unprecedented respect among the other inmates. If pressed for details I told them only what could be found on the Internet or was obvious: that she was a natural redhead, had a small birthmark on her hip, wasn't shy about sex. The more intimate truths I kept to myself: that our lovemaking was as sweet as it was savage; that despite her normally foul mouth the only noise she ever made in bed was to murmur "Oh God, Oliver" in my ear; that we might have even loved each other, for a minute or two.

I give Colborne only the trivial details.

"You know, she came to see me one night," he says, digging his heels into the sand. "Rang the bell until it woke us up, and when I opened the door she was standing there on the porch in this ridiculous dress, glittering like a Christmas tree." He almost laughs. "I thought I was dreaming. She barged in and said she needed to talk to me, said it couldn't wait, that there was a party on and it was the only time you all wouldn't miss her."

"When was this?"

"The same week we arrested you. Friday, I think."

"So that's where she went." He glances at me and I shrug. "I did miss her."

We lapse into silence—or as close to silence as we can get with the distant cries of birds, the murmur of the wind between the pine needles, the tiny wash of waves licking at the shore. The story has changed; we both feel it. It happens just like it did ten years ago: we find Richard in the water and we know nothing will ever be the same.

SCENE 1

Richard had reached toward us and wrenched the world right out of orbit. Everything tilted, hurtled forward. As soon as those three words—*He's still alive*—were out of James's mouth, he was running headlong to the end of the dock.

"Richard!" Wren croaked, the sound involuntary and compulsive, like a cough. Her cousin lay convulsing in the water, blood bubbling vivid red on his lips as one hand groped toward us.

"*James!*" Alexander's voice, shrill and frantic, pierced through the gloom. "Oliver, grab him!"

I stumbled into a sprint, feet pounding on the wet planks, seized by the senseless fear that James would throw himself into the water and let Richard drag him under.

"James!" My fingers scraped off the back of his jacket, closed on nothing. "Stop!" I made one more reckless grab and caught him clumsily around the waist. He lost his balance and pitched forward with a cry of surprise. For one terrible moment the water rushed up to meet us, but just as I gasped to go under, James slammed into the dock chest-first and I crashed down on top of him. Pain went howling through my limbs but I didn't let go, hoping that my weight would be enough to hold him down.

Wren tried to call out again but gagged and swallowed her voice.

"Can he hear us?" Alexander said. "Jesus, can he even hear us?"

My head hung over the edge of the dock, pulse pounding between my temples, eyes open wide. Richard, just out of reach, gulped against the thick slime of blood in his mouth. His limbs were twisted and bent around him like the broken wings of a bird—pushed too soon from the nest, unready for flight. *Hamlet* stirred in my memory. *There's a special providence*, he says, *in the fall of a sparrow.*

"He's not dead!" James writhed underneath me. "*He's not dead, get off!*"

"No!" Alexander said, sharply. "Wait—"

Filippa's voice broke through, closer than Alexander's. "Oliver!" I felt her hands on my shoulders, dragging me away from the edge. "Get up," she said, "get him away from there—"

"James, come on!" I hauled him backward, pulled him to his feet. He strained feebly against my arms, and I worried for a moment that I might have broken his ribs. Behind us, Wren was on her knees, moaning, and Meredith crouched beside her, face livid—her expression less like terror than rage.

"Let go of me!" James said, half trying to push me off. "Let *go*—"

"Not if you're going to do something crazy," Alexander said. "Just wait a minute—"

"We can't wait, he's *dying*—"

"And we're going to what, leap in and save him? All the king's horses and all the king's men? Shut up and think, for one fucking minute!"

"Think about *what*?" I asked, still holding James but not sure why.

"I mean, how did this even happen?" Alexander asked, of nobody in particular.

"Well, he fell," Filippa said, immediately. "He must have—"

"He just *fell*?" I said. "Pip, look at his *face*—"

"So he smashed his head on something," Meredith said. "After how much he drank, are you really surprised?"

"God, Richard," Wren said again, but seething now, wiping angrily at her eyes. "Richard, you *idiot*—"

"Hey! Stop that." Alexander yanked her up off her knees. "Don't cry over him, it's his own fucking fault—"

"Are you all insane?" James demanded, looking wildly from one of them to each of the others. He'd stopped straining against my grip, as if he'd forgotten I was holding him. "We have to help him!"

"Do we?" Alexander asked, whirling around, taking one impulsive step toward him. "I mean, do we really?"

"Alexander, he's *still alive*—"

"Yeah, exactly."

"What?" I said, but neither of them seemed to hear me.

"We can't just stand around arguing about how it happened, we have to *do* something—" James started, but Alexander cut him off.

"Look, I know you have a pathological need to play the hero, but right now you need to stop and ask yourself if that's really what's best for everyone."

I stared at him, appalled.

"What are you saying?" James asked, faintly, as if he already knew the answer.

Alexander stood with his long arms braced at his sides, twitching with a kind of crazed potential energy. He glanced over his shoulder at the water. Richard's last convulsion had subsided and he lay unnervingly motionless, as if he were playing dead. The water was smooth and dark as velvet now except for the weak flutter of his exhalations that gave him away. *If it be now*, I thought, *'tis not to come.*

"All I'm saying is, let's not do anything before we've thought it through," Alexander said, sweat gleaming on his temples despite the raw November chill. "I mean, do you not remember what he's been like the last few weeks? Clobbering us onstage, we're covered in bruises, he nearly drowned you on Halloween, and last night?" He looked at me. "You and Meredith?" There was a sharp, stabbing pain in my chest. "Richard completely lost his mind. You didn't hear him ranting about what he'd do when he got his hands on you. If he wasn't in the water right now, you probably would be."

"We had to stop him breaking in," Filippa said. I'd forgotten how close she was standing beside me, one hand on my back, until she spoke and I felt the vibration of her voice. "He almost put Alexander through the wall."

"Never mind me, what about Wren?" Alexander said, but he was appealing to James, not her. "You were there, you *saw* it."

"What did he do?" Meredith said, when James didn't answer. Wren squeezed her eyes shut. "What did he do to her?"

"She tried to stop him storming off," Filippa said, talking quietly, whispering, like Richard might hear. Like she was afraid to wake him. "He threw her across the yard. He could have broken every bone in her body."

"You think all that's going to stop?" Alexander asked, with a throb of fear in his voice. "You think we'll pull him out of the water and he'll be fine and we'll all be friends again?"

A thin silence answered him. *If it be not to come, it will be now.*

Alexander forced one nervous hand into his pocket and found the stub end of a cigarette. His lighter flared and he cupped his fingers around the flame as if it were something unspeakably precious. At the first breath in he shivered, and when he exhaled again his voice was lower, if not quite steady. "Don't say it out loud if you don't want to. But five minutes ago when we thought he was dead, what did you feel?"

Filippa's face was ashen but unreadable. Silver tear tracks glistened on Wren's cheeks. Beside her, Meredith was upright and immovable as a statue. James stood suspended between her and me, mouth open in abject, childlike horror. Around us the trees' bristling black silhouettes stood eerily straight and motionless, and thin clouds strung across the milky sky like smoke. The world was no longer dark; a cold light had broken and crouched low on the horizon, prowling the no-man's-land between night and day. I forced myself to look down at Richard. If he was breathing I couldn't hear it, but even in that silence he was snarling, teeth bared and seamed with blood. I felt it on the tip of my tongue, the compulsion to confess that in that perilous instant when I thought he was dead, all I'd really felt was relief.

"So," Meredith said—and it seemed, somehow, that she was speaking for all of us. Her warm vivacity was gone, and there was something about how coldly sober and steady she looked that sent pins and needles prickling down my spine. "What do you suggest we do?"

Alexander shrugged, and there was something terribly momentous in that simple, meaningless gesture. "Nothing."

For a long time, nobody spoke. Nobody protested. I was stunned by their reticence until I realized—I hadn't spoken either.

James's voice finally stirred in the dead air. "We have to help him. We *have* to."

"Why, James?" Meredith said, quietly, reproachfully, as if he had somehow betrayed her. "You of all people should understand . . . We don't owe him anything."

James averted his eyes—perhaps in defiance, perhaps in shame—and Meredith turned her gorgon gaze on me. Every tiny intimacy of the previous night came creeping back to mind: her lips against my skin and Richard's ugly fingerprints on hers, neither more persuasive than the other. I swallowed a hard lump in my throat. *If it be not now, yet it will come.*

Alexander was fidgeting, on the verge of interrupting, but he shut his mouth when I moved, shifted, put myself between James and the rest of them. He twitched at the weight of my hands on his shoulders. *"Since no man knows aught of what he leaves, what is't to leave betimes?"* I said. He looked at me with unbearable mistrust, as if I were a stranger, someone he didn't recognize. I pulled him just an inch closer, trying to tell him in some impossible way that I wanted him and the others unhurt and unafraid more than I wanted Richard alive, and we couldn't have both anymore. "James, please. *Let be.*"

He stared at me a moment longer, then let his head droop again. "Wren?" he said, turning just enough that he could see her from the corner of his eye. She looked impossibly young, huddled between Meredith and Alexander, arms wrapped tight around her stomach, as if they wouldn't unwind. But she seemed to have wept all the softness out of her cool brown eyes. She didn't speak, didn't even open her mouth—just nodded, slowly. *Yes.*

Something wretchedly like a laugh slipped out between James's lips. "Do it, then," he said. "Let him die."

That loathsome opiate, relief, raced through my veins again— sharp and lucid at the initial prick, before everything went numb. I heard one of the others, maybe Filippa, exhale and I knew I wasn't the only one who felt it. The moral outrage we should have suffered was quietly put down, suppressed like an unpleasant rumor before it had a chance to be heard. Whatever we did—or, more crucially, did not do—it seemed that so long as we did it together, our individual sins might be abated. There is no comfort like complicity.

Alexander tried to say something, but a wet spluttering sound made us all look toward the lake. Richard's head had lolled to one side, low enough that the water lapped at his nose and mouth

and left a cloud of dark hematic red around his face. His whole
body stiffened, seized up, the muscles in his neck and arms bulging
like steel cables, though he didn't seem to be able to move his
limbs. The rest of us watched in a state of rigid paralysis. There
was a distant groan, the sound trapped somehow inside his body,
unable to find a way out. One last little spasm went through him,
the hand that had so futilely stretched toward the sound of our
voices opening up like a flower. The fingers flexed, closed again,
shrank back toward the palm. Then everything was still.

At long last Alexander rolled his shoulders forward, and all
the smoke he'd been holding in his lungs spilled out at once.
"Well," he said to the rest of us, suddenly calm and placid as the
lake that lay behind him. "What now?"

The question was so absurd and the way he said it so ludi-
crously casual that I had to clench my teeth against a psychotic
impulse to laugh. My classmates shifted around me, turning inward, toward one another, away from the water. Their faces were
smooth, impassive, the panic of a minute before forgotten. No
reason to fuss now. No rush. I couldn't help but wonder if my
own expression was so staid, if perhaps I was a better actor than
I'd always thought and none of them suspected that there was
some sick, silent laughter trapped in my throat.

Filippa: "We need to decide what to tell the police about what
happened."

Alexander: "To him? Who knows. I don't even know where
I was half the night."

Meredith: "You can't say that. Someone's dead and you *don't
know* where you were?"

Me: "Jesus, it's not like one of us did this."

Filippa: "No, of course not—"

Me: "He was drunk. He drank himself blind and went crashing into the woods."

Wren: "They're going to want to know why one of us didn't
go after him."

Alexander: "Because he's a violent fucking lunatic and he chucked you across the yard?"

Meredith: "She can't say that, you idiot—it sounds like a motive."

James: "Then you had better not say where you were either."

He spoke so softly I almost didn't hear him. He watched Meredith without embellishing, his face white and stiff as a plaster cast.

"Sorry," she said, "what motive do I have to kill my boyfriend?"

"Well, what I remember about last night is your *boyfriend* calling you a slut in front of everyone and you rushing upstairs to revenge-fuck Oliver. Or have I left something out?" He looked from her to me, and that pain in my chest was back, like he'd grasped an invisible dagger and twisted it between my ribs.

"Look, he's right," Filippa said, before Meredith could argue. "We don't know what happened to Richard, but there's no sense making this more difficult for ourselves. Least said, soonest mended."

"Okay, but we can't avoid the fight in the kitchen because half the school was there," Alexander said, then gestured from Meredith to me. "And someone saw these two morons making out in the stairwell."

"He was drunk," Meredith snapped. "Drunker than you, and you don't even know where you were."

Filippa talked over them. "We were all drinking, so any question you don't want to answer, just say you don't remember."

"And the rest?" James asked.

"What do you mean?" Wren said. " 'The rest.' "

"You know. Before."

Filippa, as always, was quickest to understand. "Not a word about Halloween," she said. "Or the assassination scene, or anything else."

"So, what," Alexander said, "before last night, everything was just fine?"

Filippa's face was perfectly blank, and I could already picture her sitting across from some rookie police officer, back straight, knees together, ready to answer whatever question he threw at her. "Yes, precisely," she said. "Before last night, everything was fine."

Wren scuffed her toes against the dock, glancing away, avoiding everyone's eyes. "And this morning?" she said, in a very small voice.

"Nobody ever comes out here besides the seven of us," Alexander said. "So we say we've just found him."

"And what are we supposed to have been doing up 'til now?" I asked.

"Sleeping," Meredith said. "The sun's not even up." But as she spoke, the shrill call of a bird echoed between the trees and we knew—it wouldn't be long. I glanced toward the end of the dock where Richard lay unmoving in the water, unable to push Hamlet's poor fallen sparrow out of my head. *The readiness is all.*

Alexander said as much, in humbler words: "What time is it? Are we sure he's . . . shuffled off?"

"No," Filippa said. "But before we call the police, we need to be."

Another silence, just long enough for the fear we'd briefly forgotten to come creeping back.

"I'll do it," Meredith said. She dragged her fingers through her hair, then let her arms fall to her sides again. I'd seen her do it a thousand times before: push her hair back from her face, steel herself, and step into the spotlight. But to watch her disappear into the freezing water was more than I could stomach.

"No," I said. "I'll go."

Everyone looked at me like I'd lost my mind except Meredith. A kind of desperate gratitude flitted across her face, so fast I almost didn't see it. "All right," she said. "Go."

I nodded, mostly to myself. When I'd spoken, I'd done it thinking only of her, not of what I would have to do in her place. The others drifted apart, leaving a narrow path for me to walk to the end of the dock. I stood numb and unmoving for a second or two, then put one foot forward. Three slow steps put them all behind me. I paused, reached down to pull my shoes off. Three more steps. I unzipped my jacket and dropped it on the dock, tugged my sweatshirt off over my head. The cold air stung my bare skin, and goose bumps crept from my scalp down my spine and my arms and legs until every hair on my body was standing on end. Three more steps.

The lake had never seemed so enormous, so dark or so deep. Richard had sunk almost beneath the surface, like a toppled statue, and only marmoreal fragments emerged—three fingers loosely curled, the slope of a collarbone, sensuous twist of the throat. Misery set in stone. A thin film of crimson clung to his skin, too bright, too lurid, for that place of misty grays and evergreen. Fear seized my heart in a pitiless grip and crushed it to a small, hard lump like a cherry stone.

I stared down at him until I thought my blood would freeze if I didn't move. I looked back to tell the others that I couldn't do it—couldn't go any closer, couldn't plunge into that black water, couldn't prod his crooked throat in search of a pulse. But the sight of them huddled together, like five children afraid of the dark, watching me and waiting for some kind of reassurance, made my own fear seem selfish.

I held my breath, closed my eyes, and stepped off the dock.

SCENE 2

Two hours later I hadn't stopped shivering. We sat in a line against the wall in a third-floor hallway, where it was more than warm enough. I'd been given a blanket and a dry pair of jeans but no time to shower. Worse than the lingering chill was the sensation of the lake water and Richard's blood seeping into my skin, burning and itching on every inch of my body. Filippa, sitting uncomfortably close on my left, lifted one hand without looking at me and placed it so lightly on the inside of my wrist that I barely felt it. She, James, Alexander, and Wren had already given their statements. Meredith was in the office giving hers, while I waited, in a state of catatonic anxiety, to give mine.

The door opened with a heavy scrape and Meredith reappeared. I tried unsuccessfully to catch her eye until I heard Holinshed say, "Mr. Marks."

Filippa's hand slid off my arm. I stood and moved toward the door with the brittle, mechanical motion of the Tin Man. Pausing on the threshold, I glanced at my classmates again. They sat with their faces all turned away, looking anywhere but at me or one another—except Alexander, who gave me the smallest secret nod. I bowed my head and ducked into the room.

It was bigger than I expected, like the gallery but lower-ceilinged, not as bright. The windows gazed out over the long sweeping drive at the front of the hall, the stately iron gate reduced to thorny black bars in the distance. I twitched as the door boomed shut behind me. There were four other people in the room—Frederick, standing in the corner by the window; Holinshed, leaning on the enormous claw-footed desk with his chin tucked against his chest; Gwendolyn, sitting behind the desk with her head in her hands; and a younger, broad-shouldered man with sandy hair, wearing a brown bomber jacket over a shirt and tie. I'd already caught a glimpse of him down at the Castle, before they herded us up to the Hall.

"Morning, Oliver." He extended a hand, which I shook with clammy fingers, realizing that I must look vaguely ridiculous, what with a moth-eaten blanket hanging from my shoulders like some derelict sovereign's cape.

"This is Detective Colborne," Holinshed said. He peered at me over the rims of his glasses, expression unforgiving and severe. "He's going to ask you some questions about Richard."

Gwendolyn gave a small whimper and covered her mouth.

"Okay," I said. My tongue felt like sandpaper.

"There's no need to be nervous," Colborne said, and that same hysterical laughter from two hours earlier echoed in my brain. "I just need you to tell me what happened, and if you don't remember, it's all right to tell me you don't remember. No information is better than wrong information."

"Okay."

"Why don't you sit? Might make things easier." He gestured to the chair waiting behind me. There was another one in front of Holinshed's desk, facing me, empty.

I lowered myself into the chair, wondering if it would vanish before I got there and let me fall to the floor. In that moment, nothing seemed certain or solid—not even the furniture. Colborne sat across from me in the other chair and reached into his pocket. His hand emerged again with a small black tape recorder, which he placed behind him on the edge of Holinshed's desk. It was already on, a little red light glaring at me.

"Do you mind if I record this?" Colborne asked, politely enough, but I knew I couldn't refuse. "If I don't have to write everything down I can pay closer attention to what you're saying."

I nodded and adjusted my blanket. Dignity was immaterial, and I didn't know what else to do with my hands.

Colborne leaned forward and said, "So, Oliver. All right if I call you Oliver?"

"Sure."

"And you're a fourth-year theatre student."

I didn't know if I was expected to answer, so I said, a half second too late, "Yes."

Colborne didn't seem to notice, only offered another non-question. "Dean Holinshed tells me you're from Ohio."

"Yes," I said again, again too late.

"You miss home at all?" he asked, and I was almost relieved.

"No." I could have told him that as far as I was concerned, Dellecher was home, but I didn't want to say any more than I had to.

Colborne: "How big is your hometown?"

Me: "Average, I guess. Bigger than Broadwater."

Colborne: "Did you do theatre in high school?"

Me: "Yes."

Colborne: "Did you like it? How was it?"

Me: "It was all right. Not like here."

Colborne: "Because here is . . . ?"

Me: "Better."

Colborne: "Are you close? The six of you."

It sounded alien. The six of us. We had always been seven.

"Like siblings," I said, and immediately regretted it, uncertain how quickly the word "rivalry" would come to mind.

"You share a room with James Farrow," Colborne said, more quietly. "Is that where you slept last night?"

I nodded, not quite trusting myself to speak. We'd decided that James would account for me. The fact that one drunk first-year saw me on the stairs with Meredith didn't mean we had to admit to what had happened after.

"And what time did you go to bed?" Colborne said.

"Two? Two thirty? Something like that."

"Okay. Talk me through what happened at the party, and be as specific as possible."

My eyes flicked from Colborne to Frederick to Holinshed. Gwendolyn sat staring down at the top of the desk, her hair limp and tired-looking.

"There aren't any wrong answers," Colborne added. His voice had a soft scratch to it that made him sound older than he was.

"Right, yeah. I'm sorry." I tightened my grip on the blanket, wishing my palms would stop sweating. "Well. James and Alexander and I walked down from the FAB a little after ten thirty, and we weren't in a rush so we probably got to the Castle about eleven. We got drinks, and then we all got separated. I just, I don't know, wandered around for a while. Someone told me Richard was upstairs, drinking by himself."

"Any idea why he wasn't socializing with everyone else?" Colborne asked.

"Not really," I said. "Figured he'd come down when he was ready."

He nodded. "Go on."

I looked toward the window, to the long winding road that led away from Dellecher, disappearing into the gray. "I went outside. Talked to Wren. Talked to James. Then there was a—a bunch of noise, I guess, from inside. So we went in to see what was happening. It was just me and James by then. I don't know where Wren went."

"And you were in the yard, is that right?"

"Yes."

"When you went inside, what happened?"

I shifted in my chair. Two different memories were fighting for dominance: the truth and the version of it we'd agreed to tell. "It was confusing," I said, feeling some fleeting comfort in the honesty of those three words. "The music was loud and everyone was talking at the same time, but Richard had hit somebody—I don't remember his name. Colin brought him up to the infirmary."

"Allan Boyd," Holinshed said. "We'll be discussing this with him, too."

Colborne didn't acknowledge the interjection, his attention fixed on me. "And what then?"

"Meredick—I mean, Richard and Meredith—were arguing. I don't know exactly what it was about." More accurately, I wasn't sure how much Meredith had told them.

"The others made it sound like Allan had been paying her a

little more attention than Richard was comfortable with," Colborne said.

"Maybe. I don't know. Richard was drunk—I mean, beyond drunk. Belligerent. He said some pretty nasty things. Meredith was upset and she went upstairs, to get away from everybody. I went after her, just to make sure she was all right. We were talking in her room—" A few vivid moments of Meredith flashed in my brain—strands of auburn hair caught in her lipstick, black silk lines at the edges of her eyelids, the strap of her dress sliding down off her shoulder. "We were talking in her room and Richard came up and started pounding on the door," I said, too quickly, hoping Colborne wouldn't notice how warm my face and throat had gotten. "She didn't want to talk to him and she told him as much—through the door, we were sort of afraid to open it—and eventually he went away."

"What time was this?"

"God, I don't remember. Late. One thirty, maybe?"

"When Richard left, do you know where he went?"

"No," I said, exhaling a little more easily. Another scrap of truth. "We didn't come out for a while."

"And when you did?"

"Everyone was gone, really. I went up to bed. James was already there, but not quite asleep." I tried to picture him rolling over on his side to whisper to me across the room. But all I could see was the dim yellow light of the bathroom, steam and hot water warping his features in the mirror. "He told me Richard had gone off into the woods with a bottle of Scotch."

"And that was the last you heard of him?"

"Until Alexander found him?" The prismatic memories of the previous night fell away, and the cold of the morning crept through me. I could feel the water on my skin, in my hair, under my fingernails. "Yes."

"All right," Colborne said. He spoke gently, the way you talk to spooked horses and crazy people. "Now, I'm sorry to ask this, but I need you to tell me what you saw this morning."

I could still see it. Richard suspended on the surface of life, bloodied, gasping—and the rest of us simply watching, waiting for the curtain to drop. *Revenge tragedy*, I wanted to say. Shakespeare himself couldn't have done it better.

"I saw Richard," I told him. Not a proper dead man, not really floating. "Just sort of *hanging* there. But broken and crushed, like everything was bent the wrong way."

"And you—" He cleared his throat. "You got in the water." It was the first time he hesitated.

"Yes." I pulled the blanket closer, as if it could somehow thaw me, shield me from the feeling of cold water closing in around me. I knew, sitting there in the dry warmth of Holinshed's office, that I'd never forget it—how my lungs shrank so suddenly I thought they would shatter, gasping more in shock than for oxygen. Richard's face, much too close, white as bone. The sour iron smell of blood. That insane urge to laugh was back, as strong as the urge to vomit, and for one harrowing moment I thought I would be sick all over the carpet at Colborne's feet. I swallowed again, choked everything down. He mistook my wave of nausea for emotion and respectfully waited for me to compose myself.

Eventually I managed to say, "Someone had to."

"And he was dead?"

I could have told him how it felt, to reach for Richard's throat and find the flesh cold, that vein that had once bulged and throbbed in anger flat and finally still. Instead all I said was "Yes."

He stared at me, with a brittle sort of look, deliberately blank, like a bad poker face. Before I could guess what he didn't want me to see he blinked, leaned back. "Well, that can't have been easy. I'm sorry."

I nodded, unsure of whether I was supposed to thank him or if condolences were in his job description.

"Just one more question, if you're up for it."

"Whatever you need."

"Tell me about the last few weeks," he said, loosely, as if it were only a matter of course. "You've all been under a lot of pressure, Richard maybe most of all. Was he behaving strangely?"

Another mosaic of memories took shape like a stained-glass window, shards of color and light. The white glow of the moon on the water at Halloween, the blue bruises on James's arms, the bright ripe red of blood creeping out of Meredith's silk sleeve. My stomach, knotted and clenched a moment before, unexpectedly unwound. My pulse slowed.

"No," I said. Filippa's words echoed softly in my head. "Before last night, everything was fine."

Colborne watched me with curious closeness. "I think that's all for now," he said, after what felt like too long a pause. "I'm going to give you my contact information. If you think of anything else, please don't hesitate to tell me."

"Of course," I said. "I will."

But, of course, I wouldn't. Not until ten years later.

SCENE 3

Up on the fifth floor of Dellecher Hall was a secret cache of rooms reserved for the school's more illustrious guests. This peculiar apartment had three bedrooms, one bathroom, and a large central drawing room that contained a fireplace, a collection of elegant Victorian furniture, and a baby grand piano. Hallsworth House (as it was called, after Leopold Dellecher's wealthy in-laws) was where the faculty decided to hide the six remaining fourth-years while the south shore of the lake was crawling with police.

Dean Holinshed had called an emergency assembly in the music hall that evening, but he decided that we should not be present. He didn't wish, he explained, to subject us or the other students to the temptation to gossip. So, as the rest of the school sat in dumbstruck silence four floors below, Wren, Filippa, James, Alexander, Meredith, and I were prisoners at the fireside in Hallsworth House. Frederick and Gwendolyn didn't like the idea of leaving us entirely alone, so one of the nurses from the infirmary had been placed as a sentinel outside the door to the rest of the fifth floor, where she sat sniffling into a tissue as she half-heartedly filled in a crossword puzzle.

I strained my ears against the suffocating quiet, acutely aware of our schoolmates, all gathered together without us. Exile was intolerable. It felt somehow Damoclean, a period of suspended judgment, dreading condemnation by a jury of our peers. (*O, my prophetic soul.*) Our mercenary relief at having Richard gone was quickly turning sour. Already I'd found a thousand things to be afraid of. What if one of us let something slip? Talked in our sleep? Forgot how the story was supposed to go? Or perhaps we'd walk on tiptoes the rest of our lives, waiting for the thread to snap, the axe to fall.

Alexander must have been infected by the same anxiety. "Do you think they're going to tell everyone we're up here?" he asked, staring hard at the carpet as though he might suddenly develop X-ray vision and be able to see what was going on downstairs.

"I doubt it," Filippa said. "They won't want anyone sneaking up." The lines on either side of her mouth were deep and dark, as if she had aged ten years in as many hours. The others were silent, listening uselessly for a sound from downstairs. James sat with his knees pinned tightly together, arms folded over his chest, like he was cold. Wren was listless, limp, her limbs bent into her chair at odd clumsy angles, like those of a dropped doll. Meredith sat on the couch beside her, cross-legged, fists clenched, tension making every elegant line of her body hard and angular.

"What do you think they'll do about *Caesar*?" Alexander said, when he couldn't stand the quiet anymore.

"They'll call it off," Filippa said. "It'd be tasteless to just replace him."

"So much for 'the show must go on.'"

I tried—for one abortive moment—to imagine someone, anyone, else assuming Richard's role. The threat Gwendolyn had made to have me learn his lines and take his place echoed from my memory and I balked, recoiled from the idea. "Honestly," I said, afraid I'd have to scream if I didn't do something else with my voice, "do you really want to get back onstage without him?"

A few heads shook; nobody spoke. Then—

"Is it just me," Alexander said, "or is this the longest day of everyone else's life?"

"Well," James said. "Certainly not Richard's."

Alexander gaped at him, eyes wide and glaring.

"James," Meredith said. "What the fuck."

Filippa breathed out in a hiss, rubbing her forehead. "We're not doing this," she said, then looked up, from one of them to each of the others. "We are not going to bicker and bitch at each other—not about this. *Things without all remedy / Should be without regard: What's done is done.*"

Alexander laughed a thin, humorless laugh I didn't like at all. "*To bed, to bed, to bed!*" he said. "God, I need a smoke. I wish they hadn't stuck the nurse outside." He clambered to his feet, turned on the spot, moving in the quick, restless way he did when he was upset. He wandered around the room in an aimless zigzag, struck a few random notes on the piano, then started opening cupboards and fumbling around on the bookshelves.

"What are you doing?" Meredith asked.

"Looking for booze," he said. "There must be something hidden in here. The last guest they had was the guy who wrote the Nietzsche book and I bet my ass he's an alcoholic."

"How can you possibly want to drink right now?" I said. "My insides still feel like liquid from last night."

"Hair of the dog. Aha." He emerged from a cabinet in the back of the room with a bottle of something amber in one hand. "Anyone for brandy?"

"Go on," Filippa said. "Maybe it'll take the edge off."

Glasses clinked together as he rummaged deeper in the cabinet. "Anyone else?"

Wren didn't speak, but to my surprise James and Meredith both said, "Yes, please," at precisely the same time.

Alexander returned with the bottle in one hand, four glasses stacked and tilting in the other. He poured himself enough brandy to burn the Hall down, then passed it to Filippa. "I don't know how much you want," he said. "Personally I plan to drink myself to sleep."

"I'm not sure I'll ever sleep again," I said. Richard's half-smashed face—garish as a carnival mask—leapt at me every time I closed my eyes.

James, staring into the fire, chewing a fingernail, said, *"Methought I heard a voice cry, 'Sleep no more!'"*

"Where are we sleeping?" Meredith asked, ignoring him. "There's only three rooms."

"Well, Wren and I can share," Filippa said, with a sidelong look at her. She didn't acknowledge that she'd heard.

"Who wants to share with me?" Alexander said. He waited for a reply but didn't get one. "Don't everyone jump up at once."

"I'll stay out here," I said. "I don't mind."

"What time is it?" Meredith said. She lifted her glass to her lips, with a pained expression, as if that simple motion were monumentally taxing.

Filippa squinted at the carriage clock on the table beside her. "Quarter after nine."

"Is that all?" I said. "It feels like midnight."

"It feels like Judgment Day." Alexander threw back an enormous gulp of brandy, gritted his teeth as he swallowed, and reached for the bottle again. He filled his glass almost to the brim and stood clutching it tightly. "I'm going to bed," he announced. "If someone decides they don't want to crash in the living room, well, we all know I'm not picky about who I sleep with. Goodnight."

He left the room, with a small stiff bow. I watched him go and propped my head on one hand, unsurprised by how heavy it felt. Exhaustion pumped sluggishly through my veins, dampening everything else. In the raw dark of the morning I'd felt relief rather than dismay at the spectacle of Richard's death, and now that it was dark again—after all we'd done and said during the long hypnotic hours in between—I was too tired for sadness or pity. Perhaps it was absent because I didn't quite believe it. I half expected Richard to burst through the door, wiping stage blood from his face, laughing cruelly at how he'd had us fooled.

Filippa finished her drink, and the sound of her glass touching down on the table made me look up. "I'm going to go to bed, too," she said, pushing herself to her feet. "I want to just lie down for a while, even if I don't sleep. Wren? Why don't you come to bed?"

Wren was still for a moment, then reanimated, unfolded herself from the chair, eyes bleary, out of focus. She accepted Filippa's proffered hand and followed her out, without protest.

"Are you sleeping here?" Meredith asked, when they'd gone. She spoke to me as if James wasn't there. He didn't react or respond, as if he hadn't heard her.

I nodded. "You take the other bedroom."

She straightened up—slowly, gingerly, like everything hurt.

"Going to sleep?" I asked.

"Yeah," she said. "I hope I never wake up."

The first real pang of sadness stuck me like a needle, but it had nothing to do with Richard, not really. I wanted to say something but couldn't find a single adequate word and so I sat silent and immobile on the couch as she, too, left the room, half her brandy undrunk. When the door closed behind her I deflated, slumped against the pillows behind me, dragged my hands across my face.

"She doesn't mean it," James said.

I frowned behind my fingers. "Is that meant to be comforting or critical?"

"It's not meant to be anything," he said. "Don't be angry with me, Oliver, I can't take it right now."

I exhaled and lifted my hands off my face. "I'm sorry. I'm not angry. I'm just . . . I don't know. Drained."

"We should sleep."

"Well. We can try."

We lay down—I on one couch, James on the other—but didn't bother trying to find sheets or proper pillows. I smashed a decorative bolster under my head and pulled a throw blanket down over my legs. On the other couch, James did the same, pausing to finish his brandy and what was left of Meredith's. When he was settled, I turned out the lamp on the table behind me, but the room was still saturated with firelight. The flames had shrunk to small buds of yellow, flickering between the logs.

As I watched the wood blacken and crumble and collapse, my lungs constricted, refused to take in sufficient air. How swiftly, how suddenly everything had gone wrong. Where did it even begin? Not with Meredith and me, I told myself, but months earlier—with *Caesar*? *Macbeth*? It was impossible to identify Point Zero. I squirmed, unable to dismiss the idea that some huge invisible weight was crushing down on me like a boulder. (It was that ponderous crouching demon Guilt. At the time I didn't know him, but in the months to come he would climb onto my chest every night and sit snarling there, an ugly Fuselian nightmare.) The fire burned down to embers and its light slowly left the room, leaking out through the cracks. Lacking oxygen, light-headed, I tilted back toward unconsciousness, and it was more like suffocating than falling asleep.

A whisper brought me back to life.

"Oliver."

I sat up and blinked against the gloom at James, but it wasn't he who had spoken.

"Oliver."

Meredith had appeared, a pale shape in the dark void of her bedroom door. Her head drooped against the doorframe like a flower bud swollen with rainwater, and for one odd moment I wondered what the weight of her hair was, if she felt it hanging down her back.

I pushed my blanket off and crept across the room with another furtive look at James. He lay on his back, head turned to the side, away from me. I couldn't tell if he was dead asleep or trying too hard to fake it.

"What is it?" I whispered, when I was close enough for her to hear me.

"I can't sleep."

My hand twitched toward her, but it didn't get far. "It's been a bad day," I said, lamely.

She exhaled, gave me a weak nod. "Will you come in?"

I leaned away from her, forcibly reminded of that night in the dressing room when I'd withdrawn in exactly the same way. She could tempt anyone, but Fate didn't seem like a good target. We had one casualty already. "Meredith," I said, "your boyfriend's dead. He *died* this morning."

"I know," she said. "It's not that." Her eyes were glassy, unapologetic. "I just don't want to sleep alone."

That little prick of sadness burrowed deeper, touched me at the quick. How well I'd been trained to mistrust her. And by whom? Richard? Gwendolyn? I glanced over my shoulder at James again. All I could see was a shock of his hair sticking up behind the arm of the couch.

It didn't really matter where I slept, I decided. Nothing mattered much after that morning. Our two souls—if not all six— were forfeit.

"All right," I said.

She nodded, only once, and went back into the room. I followed, closed the door behind me. The blankets on the bed were already disheveled, kicked around, messy. I slid between the sheets in my jeans. I'd sleep in my clothes. We'd sleep. That was all.

We didn't touch, didn't even speak. She climbed into the bed beside me and lay down on her side, one arm folded under her pillow. She watched me as I settled myself, propped my own pillow up a little higher. When I stopped moving, she closed her eyes—but not before a few tears leaked out, slipped between her eyelashes. I tried not to feel her trembling against the mattress, but it was like the tick of the mantel clock in the Castle: soft, persistent, impossible to ignore. After what might have been as long as an hour, I lifted my arm, without looking at her. She shifted closer, tucked her head against my chest. I curled my arm around her.

"*God*, Oliver," she said, her voice small and stifled, one hand pressed over her mouth to keep it in.

I smoothed her hair flat against her back. "Yeah," I said. "I know."

SCENE 4

Everything was canceled. The remaining performances of *Caesar*, and all of our regular classes before Thanksgiving. We had tea with Frederick twice at Hallsworth House, and Gwendolyn ate dinner with us once, but in the two remaining days before break, we saw no one else. On Tuesday we returned to the Castle to collect our things. Richard's death had been officially dismissed as an accident, but this revelation did surprisingly little to allay our unease. That evening, we were expected to attend his memorial service, where we would see—and be seen by—the other students for the first time since Saturday night.

The Castle was empty, but something in the surrounding woods had changed. There was a foreign smell in the air, of chemicals and equipment, rubber and plastic, the trace odors of a dozen unseen strangers. The stairs leading down to the dock were cordoned off by a bold yellow X of police tape. Up in the Tower, I dragged my suitcase out from underneath my bed and packed without paying attention, piling shirts and pants on top of mismatched shoes and socks and rolled-up scarves. For the first time, I was looking forward to a few days at home for Thanksgiving. Normally Filippa and Alexander and I stayed on campus over break, but Dean Holinshed had informed us that the school would be closed for the holiday, for the first time in twenty years.

I bullied my suitcase down the helical staircase to the second floor, swearing and grunting as I pinched my toes under the wheels and crushed my fingers against the banister. I emerged into the library, sweating and irritated, dragging the suitcase behind me. The others had already gone except Filippa, who stood alone in front of the fire with the long brass poker in her hand, pointed down at the floor like a sword. She looked up as I clattered in and threw myself into a chair—deliberately avoiding the closest one, which I still thought of as belonging, somehow, to Richard.

"Has the fire been going all this time?" I asked.

"No," she said, lifting the poker to stoke the two skinny logs there. "I lit it."

"Why?"

"I don't know. It just felt wrong."

"Everything feels wrong," I said.

She nodded absently.

"Are you coming with us to the airport?"

"Yes," she said.

Camilo had offered to drive the fourth-years to O'Hare. From there, Meredith would fly to New York, Alexander to

Philadelphia, James to San Francisco. Wren would ride with her aunt and uncle and fly with them to London. (They had arrived the previous day, and Holinshed had arranged for them to have a room in Broadwater's only nice hotel, Hallsworth House being occupied.) I was bound for Ohio. When pressed, Filippa told people she was from Chicago, but I had no idea whether she had family there.

"And after that?" I asked, trying and failing to make it sound offhand.

She didn't answer, just watched the fire, eyes hidden by the reflection of the flames on her glasses.

"Pip, I swear I'm not trying to pry—"

She stabbed at the embers again, a little savagely. "So don't."

I shifted in my chair. What I wanted to tell her seemed nonsensically important. "Look, you know you could come home with me if you wanted to, right?" I said, abruptly. "I'm not saying you do or you should, just—if you *needed* somewhere to go. I mean, they'd all freak out because I've never brought a girl home and they'd completely misinterpret it, but just—in case. That's all, I'm sorry. I'll shut up now."

She turned away from the fire, and I was relieved not to find her frowning. Instead, she looked at me with a sad, stricken expression. I was seized by the strange unfounded idea that she was debating whether or not to say *I love you*. But the difference between us was that she assumed people just knew those sorts of things, while I was always worried that they didn't.

"Oliver" was what she did say. She sighed my name out like it was a breath of something warm and sweet, then leaned back against the mantel, maybe too tired to stand up on her own. "I'm scared." She said it with a wry smile, as if it were somehow embarrassing.

"Of what?" I asked, not because there was nothing to be scared of, but because there were so many scary things to choose from.

She shrugged. "Of what happens now." Neither of us spoke again before the clock on the mantel chimed. Filippa glanced up. "It's five."

The memorial service was scheduled for five thirty.

"God," I said. "Yeah. We should go." I heaved myself out of my chair with great reluctance, but Filippa didn't move. "Coming?" I asked.

She blinked at me with a look of blank puzzlement, as if she'd just woken up from a dream she already couldn't remember. "You go ahead." She plucked at the front of her sweater, which was streaked with soot. "I ought to change."

"All right." I hovered, half in and half out of the doorway. "Pip?"

"Yeah?"

"Don't be scared." It was a selfish thing to say. If she lost her nerve, I couldn't imagine what would become of everyone else. She was the only one of us who never flinched.

She gave me a smile so fragile I might have imagined it. "Okay."

SCENE 5

I found James at the top of the trailhead, just standing there, staring down the path like he couldn't make himself take another step. If he heard me approach he didn't react, and I waited behind him in twilight silence, unsure of what to do. An owl hooted somewhere in the treetops—perhaps the same owl from Saturday night.

"Do you think it's a bit morbid?" he asked, without preamble, without even turning around. "Having the service on the beach."

"I guess the music hall felt a little too . . . festive," I said. "All that gold."

"You'd think they'd have it as far away from the lake as possible."

"Yeah." I glanced back toward the Hall. It might have been Halloween again—James and I lurking like shadows under the trees—but the air was too cold, pressing against my skin like a flat steel blade. "I don't trust it anymore."

"What do you mean?"

"First Halloween, now this," I said, with a shrug he didn't see. "It's like the lake's turned on us. Like there's some naiad down there that we've pissed off. Maybe Meredith was right and we should have gone skinny-dipping at the start of term." I didn't realize how stupid it sounded until it was out of my mouth.

"Like some kind of pagan ritual?" James asked, turning his head so I could just see the side of his face, the curve of his cheek. "Good Lord, Oliver. Sleep with her if you must, but don't let her get inside your head."

"I'm not sleeping with her." I could see that he was about to protest and added, "Not, you know, figuratively."

"Doesn't really matter, does it?" he asked, and turned to face me—the movement deliberately casual, not convincing.

"What?"

"Whether it's figurative."

"I don't understand."

He raised his voice so it cut through the soft forest silence like a razor blade. "No, you *must* not, because I really don't think you're that sort of idiot."

"James," I said, too mystified to really be angry, "what are you talking about?"

He looked away. "You," he said, staring off into the trees. "*You* and *her.*" He grimaced, as though saying the words together left a bad taste in his mouth. "Do you not understand how it looks, Oliver? It doesn't matter if you are or are not *actually* sleeping with her—it looks bad."

"What do you care how it looks?" I asked, forcing the show of indignation, more unnerved than anything else. His sarcasm was caustic, unfamiliar.

"I don't," he said. "I really don't. I care about *you*, and what might happen if you carry on like this."

"I don't—"

"I know you don't understand, you never do. Richard is *dead*."

I glanced back toward the Hall again, the quadrate silhouette at the top of the hill. "It's not like we killed him."

"Don't be naïve, Oliver, for once in your life. He's been dead two days and his girlfriend's already in bed with you every night?" He shook his head, thoughts tumbling out in a reckless, implacable rush. "People won't like it. They'll talk. They'll gossip, that's what people do." He cupped his hand around one ear and said, "*Open your ears; for which of you will stop / The vent of hearing when loud Rumor speaks?*"

My voice stuck in my throat, dry as chalk. "Why are you talking about this like we killed him?"

He grabbed the front of my jacket, like he wanted to throttle me. "*Because it fucking looks like we might have.* You think people won't wonder whether someone might have pushed him? You keep sleeping with Meredith and they'll think it was you."

I stared at him, too surprised to move. His hand was the only solid thing, the brunt of his anger thrust against my chest in the shape of a fist. "James, the police—they've said, it was an accident. He hit his head," I said. "He *fell*."

He must have seen the fear in my face, because the hard lines around his eyes and mouth vanished, like someone had cut the right wire to defuse him before he went off. "Yes, of course he did." He looked down, let go of my jacket, and brushed one hand across the front to smooth the wrinkles out. "I'm sorry, Oliver. Everything's gone sideways."

I offered an awkward shrug, still half trapped by my nervous paralysis. "It's all right."

"Forgive me?"

"Yeah," I said, a split second too late. "Always."

SCENE 6

The tiny fairy lights of a thousand candles flickered on the beach. Half the attendants held narrow white tapers in cardboard cups, and luminarias hovered at the end of each row like little spectral ushers. The fourth-year choral music students were gathered in a dense clump on the sand, singing softly, voices shimmering off the water, as if our capricious mermaids were in mourning. Beside them on the beach were an old wooden podium and a covered easel stand. White lilies bloomed at the base of each, their gossamer fragrance too delicate to disguise the earthy smell of the lake.

James and I filed down the center aisle through a thicket of whispers that parted reluctantly to let us through. Wren, Richard's parents, Frederick, and Gwendolyn were seated on the first bench on the right—Meredith and Alexander on the left. I sat beside them, James sat beside me, and, when Filippa arrived, Alexander and I shifted farther apart to make room for her. Why, I wondered, had they put us at the front, where everyone could stare? The rows of benches felt like a courtroom gallery, hundreds of eyes burning on the back of my neck. (The sensation would eventually grow familiar. It is a unique kind of torture for an actor, to have an audience's undivided attention and to turn your back on them for shame.)

I glanced across the aisle at the opposite bench. Wren sat beside her uncle, who so fiercely resembled Richard that I couldn't help staring. The same black hair, the same black eyes, the same cruel mouth. But the familiar face was older, lined, and streaks of silver had crept into the sideburns. This, I had no doubt, was what Richard would have become in twenty years or so. No more chance of that.

He must have felt my gaze, the way I felt everyone else's,

because he turned suddenly in my direction. I looked away, but not fast enough—there was a moment of contact, a jolt of electricity that rattled me from the inside out. I breathed in at a gasp, the lights of the candles dancing in my peripheral vision. *Why all these fires?* I thought. *Why all these gliding ghosts?*

"Oliver?" Filippa whispered. "You all right?"

"Yeah," I said. "Fine." I didn't believe me, and neither did she, but before she could say anything else the chorus fell silent and Dean Holinshed appeared on the beach. He was dressed in black except for a scarf (Dellecher blue with the Key and Quill embroidered on one end), which hung limply around his neck. Besides that ribbon of color he was a grim, imposing figure, his beaky nose casting an ugly shadow across his face.

"Good evening." There was a wilted, weary quality to his voice.

Filippa laced her fingers through mine. I squeezed her hand, grateful for something to hold on to.

"We are here," Holinshed said, "to honor the memory of a remarkable young man, whom all of you knew." He cleared his throat, folded his hands behind his back, and for a moment looked down at the ground. "How best to remember Richard?" he asked. "He is not the sort of person who will soon fade from your memories. He was, you might say, larger than life. It does not seem far-fetched to think that he is larger than death also. Of whom does this remind you?" He paused again, chewed on his lip. "It is impossible not to think of Shakespeare when one thinks of Richard. He has appeared on our stage many times, in many roles. But there is one role we never had the opportunity to see him play. Those of you who knew him well will likely agree he would have made a fine Henry Five. I, for one, feel cheated."

Gwendolyn's bangles jingled as she lifted her hand to her mouth. Tears rolled down her face, dragging long streaks of smeared mascara with them.

"Henry the Fifth is one of Shakespeare's best beloved and most troublesome heroes, much as Richard was one of ours.

They will, I think, be similarly lamented." Holinshed reached into the deep pocket of his overcoat, feeling for something. As he searched for it, he said, "Before I read this, I must ask Richard's fellow thespians to forgive me. I have never pretended to be an actor, but I wish to pay my respects, and I hope that, given the circumstances, both you and he will find it in your hearts to forgive me for my poor delivery." There was a breathy murmur of laughter. Holinshed unfolded a sheet of paper from his pocket. I heard a rustle of fabric and looked sideways. Alexander had taken Filippa's other hand. He stared straight forward, jaw jutting out.

> Holinshed: *"Hung be the heavens with black: yield, day, to night!*
> *Comets, importing change of times and states,*
> *Brandish your crystal tresses in the sky,*
> *And with them scourge the bad revolting stars*
> *That have consented unto Henry's death.*
> *England ne'er lost a king of so much worth."*

He frowned, crumpled the paper and returned it to his pocket. "Dellecher never lost such a student," he said. "Let us remember Richard well, as he would have wanted. It is my honor to unveil for you his portrait, which from today forward will hang in the lobby of the Archibald Dellecher Theatre."

He reached over to pull the limp black cloth off the easel. Richard's face emerged from behind it—it was his *Caesar* portrait, what it had looked like before it was recolored and resized—and my heart leapt up into my throat. I felt myself step off the dock again, plunge down into the frigid water of the lake. He glared across the beach at us—imperious, enraged, in some abhorrent way *alive*. I gripped Filippa's hand so hard her knuckles went white. Holinshed was wrong: Richard didn't want to be remembered well—he had never been so forgiving. He wanted to wreak havoc on the rest of us.

"I can only say so much on Richard's behalf," Holinshed went on, but I barely heard him. "I did not have the privilege of knowing him as well as many of you. So I will step aside, and let someone nearer and dearer speak for him now."

He finished without any grander gesture and retreated from the podium. I glanced down the bench in dismay, but Meredith hadn't moved. She sat, ashen-faced, with Alexander's left hand in her lap, clutched tightly between both of hers. Four of us were linked now, like dolls in a paper chain. I could feel Filippa's pulse between my fingers and loosened my grip.

A soft susurration made me look the other way. Wren was on her feet and moving toward the podium. When she got there she was barely visible, a pale face and fine blond hair hovering just above the microphone.

"Richard and I never had siblings, so we were closer than most cousins," she said. "Dean Holinshed was right to say that he was larger than life. But not everybody liked that about him. I know actually that a lot of you didn't like him at all." She looked up, but not at any of us. Her voice was small and unsteady, but her eyes were dry. "To be perfectly honest with you, sometimes I don't—didn't—like him either. Richard wasn't an easy person to like. But he was an easy person to love."

On the bench across from ours Mrs. Stirling cried silently, one hand clutching the collar of her coat. Her husband sat with his fists balled up between his knees.

"Oh, God," Alexander muttered. "I can't do this."

Meredith dug her fingernails into his wrist. I bit my tongue, clenched my teeth so tight I thought they would crack.

"The idea that I would have to . . . let go of him, before we were old and falling to bits, never even occurred to me," Wren went on, picking her words one by one, like a child stepping from stone to stone to cross a stream. "But it doesn't just feel like I've lost a cousin. It feels like I've lost part of myself." She let out a tragic sort of laugh.

James grabbed my hand so suddenly that I started, but he didn't seem to see me. He watched Wren with a kind of desperation in his expression, swallowing repeatedly, as if he might be sick at any second. Filippa trembled on my other side.

"Last night, I couldn't sleep, so I reread *Twelfth Night*," Wren said. "We all know how it ends—happily, of course—but there's sadness there, too. Olivia has lost a brother. So has Viola, but they handle it very differently. Viola changes her name, her whole identity, and almost immediately falls in love. Olivia shuts herself away from the world, and refuses to let love in at all. Viola is trying desperately to forget her brother. Olivia is maybe remembering him too much. So what do you do? Ignore your grief, or indulge it?" She looked up from the sand and found us, gaze drifting from face to face. Meredith, Alexander, Filippa, me, and finally James. "You all know that Richard refuses to be ignored," she said, speaking to us, and no one else. "But maybe every day we let grief in, we'll also let a little bit of it out, and eventually we'll be able to breathe again. At least, that's how Shakespeare would tell the story. Hamlet says, *Absent thee from felicity awhile.* But just awhile. The show's not over. *Now cracks a noble heart. Goodnight.* The rest of us must go on."

She stopped, stepped back from the podium. A few hesitant, heartbroken smiles had appeared in the audience, but not for any of us. We held one another's hands so hard we couldn't feel them anymore. Wren walked back to her bench on unsteady legs. She sank down between her aunt and uncle, stayed upright for a second or two, and then collapsed into her uncle's lap. He bent over her protectively, tried to shield her with his arms, and soon they were both shaking so badly I couldn't tell which one of them was sobbing.

SCENE 7

An impromptu wake happened at the Bore's Head. We were all in desperate need of a drink, and none of us wanted to return to isolation in Hallsworth House. Our table felt miserably empty. Richard's usual seat was unoccupied (nobody even wanted to look at the blank space where he should have been), Wren was already en route to the airport, and most other people only came over long enough to express their condolences and raise a glass to Richard before departing again. We didn't speak much. Alexander had paid for an entire bottle of Johnnie Walker Black, which sat uncapped in the middle of the table, the contents slowly diminishing until there was only an inch of liquid left.

Alexander: "What time is Camilo coming to pick us up?"

Filippa: "Soon. Does anyone have a flight earlier than nine?"

We all shook our heads together.

Alexander: "James, what time do you get in?"

James: "Four in the morning."

Filippa: "And your dad's coming to get you at that hour?"

James: "No. I'll take a cab."

Meredith: "Alexander, where are you even going?"

Alexander: "Staying with my foster brother in Philly. Fuck knows where my mom is. You?"

She tilted her glass, watched the watery dregs of Scotch trickle around the melting ice cubes. "My parents are in Montreal with David and his wife," she said. "So it'll just be me and Caleb in the apartment, if he ever comes home from work."

I wanted to comfort her somehow, but I didn't dare touch her, not in front of the others. There was a tightness in my chest, as if all the shock and horror of the last few days had strained my heart.

Me: "We have the most depressing holiday plans of all time."

James: "I think Wren's are probably worse."

Alexander: "God, fuck you for even saying that."

James: "Just providing some perspective."

Meredith: "Do you think she'll come back after break?"

Silence came crashing down on the table.

"What?" Alexander said, loudly.

Meredith leaned back, glanced at the next table. "I mean, think about it," she said, at a quarter of Alexander's volume. "She's going to go home, bury her cousin, have three days to mourn, and then come all the way back across the ocean for exams and auditions again? The stress could kill her." She shrugged. "Maybe she won't come back. Maybe she'll finish next year, or not at all. I don't know."

"Did she say something to you?" James demanded.

"No! She just—I wouldn't want to come back right away if I were her. Would you?"

"Christ." Alexander dragged his hands across his face. "I hadn't even thought of that."

Besides Meredith, nobody had. We stared down into our drinks, cheeks pink with shame.

"She has to come back," James said, looking from me to Meredith as if one of us could somehow reassure him. "She has to."

"That might not be best for her," Meredith said. "She may need some time away. From Dellecher, and—all of us."

James was still for a moment, then stood and left the table without another word. Alexander watched him go, gloomily. "And then there were four," he said.

SCENE 8

My family home in Ohio was not a place I enjoyed visiting. It was one of twelve mostly identical houses (all clapboard, painted barely different shades of beige) on a quiet suburban street. Each came complete with a black mailbox, gray driveway, and jewel-green lawn dotted with little round boxwoods, some of which had already been wrapped in white Christmas lights.

Thanksgiving dinner (traditionally a dull affair made cheery only by the abundance of wine and food) was unusually tense. My mother and father sat on opposite ends of the table, wearing what I always thought of as their "church clothes": black slacks and embarrassingly similar pea green sweaters. My sisters bumped elbows on one side, and I sat alone on the other, wondering when in the world Caroline had gotten so thin, and when, for that matter, Leah had done the opposite and developed curves. Both of these changes seemed to have become points of contention in my absence—my father told Caroline to "stop playing with her dinner and eat it" more than once, and my mother's eyes kept flicking toward Leah's neckline as though the depth of it made her profoundly uncomfortable.

Oblivious to her scrutiny, Leah had peppered me with questions about Dellecher since we opened the wine. She, for some reason, took a keen interest in my alternative schooling, while Caroline had never displayed any interest at all. (I knew better than to be offended. Caroline rarely displayed an interest in anything unrelated to frenetic exercise or her 1960s fashion fetish.)

"Do you know yet what play you're doing spring semester?" Leah asked. "We've just read *Hamlet* for world lit."

"I doubt it'll be that," I said. "They did that last year."

"I wish I could have seen you do *Macbeth*," she went on, in a rush. "Halloween here was incredibly lame."

"Too old to dress up now?"

"I went to this absolutely awful party as Amelia Earhart. I think I was the only girl there not wearing some kind of lingerie."

The word "lingerie" coming out of her mouth was a little alarming. I hadn't been home much in the past four years and still thought of her as much younger than sixteen. "Well," I said. "That's—well."

"Leah," my mother said. "Not during dinner."

"Mother, please."

(When had she taken to calling her "Mother"? I reached for my wineglass and emptied it hastily.)

"Do you have pictures of *Macbeth*?" Leah pressed. "I'd love to see them."

"Don't give her any ideas, please," my father said. "One actor in the family is enough."

Privately, I agreed with him. The idea of my sister wearing only a nightgown and being ogled by all the boys of Dellecher made me feel slightly nauseous.

"Don't worry," Caroline said, slouched down in her chair, pulling at a loose thread on the cuff of her sweatshirt. "Leah's much too *smart* for that."

Leah's cheeks flamed pink. "Why do you always call me that like it's something horrible?"

"Girls," my mother said. "Not now."

Caroline smirked and fell silent, smearing mashed potatoes around with her fork. Leah sipped at her wine (she was allowed half a glass, and half a glass only), still blushing. My father sighed, shook his head, and said, "Oliver, pass me the gravy."

An excruciating half hour later, my mother pushed her chair back from the table to clear the dishes. Leah and Caroline began carrying things out of the dining room, but when I made to stand up my father instructed me to stay where I was.

"Your mother and I need to talk to you."

I sat up straighter, waiting. But he didn't say anything else, just returned his attention to his plate, picking at the broken bits of piecrust that were left. I poured myself a fourth glass of wine with clumsy, nervous hands. Had they heard about Richard somehow? I'd spent two days loitering around the mailbox and snatched the Dellecher newsletter out as soon as it arrived, hoping to prevent exactly that.

It was another five minutes before my mother came back. She sat beside my father in the chair that had been Leah's during dinner and smiled, a nervous twitch of her upper lip. My father wiped his mouth, set the napkin in his lap, and looked pointedly at me. "Oliver," he said. "We need to talk to you about something difficult."

"All right, what?"

He turned to my mother (as he always did when "something difficult" needed to be said). "Linda?"

She reached across the table and seized my hand before I could withdraw it. I fought the urge to squirm out of her grip.

"There's no easy way to say this," she said, tears already in her eyes. "And it'll probably come as a surprise to you, because you've been away from home so much."

Guilt crept down my spine like a spider.

"Your sister . . ." She let out a small, strangled sigh. "Your sister isn't doing well."

"Caroline," my father said, as if it weren't obvious which one of them she meant.

"She's not going back to school this semester," my mother went on. "She's been trying so hard to finish, but the doctor seemed to think it would be best for her health for her to take a break."

I glanced from her to my father and said, "Okay. But what—"

"Don't interrupt, please," he said.

"Fine. Sorry."

"You see, sweetheart, Caroline's not going back to school, but she's not going to stay here," my mother explained. "The doctors think someone needs to keep a closer eye on her than we can, being away at work every day."

Caroline had the least common sense of the three of us, but the fact that my parents were talking about her like she couldn't be left alone was more than a little unsettling.

"What does that mean?" I asked.

"It means that she's going to be . . . going away for a while, to stay with some people who can help her."

"What, like rehab?"

"We're not calling it that," my father snapped, as if I'd said something obscene.

"Okay, then what are we calling it?"

My mother cleared her throat delicately. "It's called a recovery center."

I glanced from her to my father and back again before I said, "What the hell is she recovering from?"

My father made an impatient sort of sound and said, "Surely you noticed she's not eating right."

I pulled my hand away from my mother. My mind was blank, stuck, unable to process this information. I took another unsteady sip from my wineglass, then put my hands in my lap, out of reach.

Me: "Right. That's . . . awful."

My father: "Yes. But now we have to talk about what it means for you."

Me: "For me? I don't understand."

My mother: "Well, I'm coming to that."

My father: "Please just listen, won't you?"

I squeezed my molars together and watched my mother.

"This recovery center, it's expensive," she said. "But we want to make sure she's getting the best treatment possible. And the problem is—the problem is that we can't afford the recovery center and your school at the same time."

My whole body went numb so fast I felt light-headed. "What?" I said, like I hadn't heard her.

"Oh, Oliver, I'm so sorry." Tears had spilled out of her eyes and were making dark spots on the tablecloth, like dripping candle wax. "We've agonized over this, but the truth is, right now we need to help your sister. She's not well."

"What about her tuition? You just said she's dropped out—what about that?"

"It's not enough," my father said, shortly.

I looked from him to her, openmouthed, disbelief turning my blood to sludge. It pounded and oozed slowly from my heart to my brain. "I have one semester left," I said. "What am I supposed to do?"

"Well, you'll have to talk to the school," my father said. "Think about taking out a last-minute loan if you really want to graduate."

"If I want— Why wouldn't I want to graduate?"

He shrugged. "I can't imagine a diploma really makes a difference to an actor."

"I— *What?*"

"Ken," my mother said, despairingly. "Please, let's just—"

"Let me get this straight." Anger kindled deep in the pit of my stomach, quickly devoured the little twigs of incredulity. "You're telling me I have to drop out of Dellecher because Caroline needs some celebrity doctor to spoon-feed her?"

My father banged his open hand down on the table. "I'm telling you you need to start considering monetary alternatives because your sister's health is more important than us paying twenty thousand dollars for you to play pretend!"

I glared at him for a moment in stupefied outrage, then thrust my chair back and left the table.

I spent four hours the following day locked in my father's office, on the phone with Dellecher's administrative staff. They patched me through to Frederick, to Gwendolyn, and even, eventually, to Dean Holinshed. They all sounded exhausted, but they each assured me that we'd work something out. Loans were suggested, along with work-study and late scholarship applications. When I finally hung up, I retreated to my room, lay on my bed, and stared at the ceiling.

Inevitably my eyes wandered down to the desk (cluttered with old production photos and programs), to the bookshelf (stuffed with tattered paperbacks, purchased for single dollars and quarters from used bookstores and library sales), and from poster to poster tacked on the wall, a gallery revue of my high school theatre endeavors. Most of them were Shakespeare: *Twelfth Night, Measure for Measure,* even a leftover handbill from a wildly misguided production of *Cymbeline,* which was set in the antebellum South for no reason the director could ever satisfactorily explain. I exhaled with a strange fond sadness, wondering what on earth had occupied my thoughts before Shakespeare. My first fumbling encounter with him at the age of eleven had quickly blossomed into full-blown Bardolatry. I bought a copy of the complete works with my precious pocket money and carried it everywhere, all too happy to ignore the less poetic reality of the outside world. Never before in my life had I experienced something so undeniably stirring and *important.* Without him, without Dellecher, without my company of lyric-mad classmates, what would become of me?

I decided—soberly, without hesitation—that I'd rob a bank

or sell a kidney before I'd let such a thing happen. Reluctant to dwell on the possibility of such dire straits, I dug *Theatre of Envy* out of my bag and continued to read.

A little after seven, my mother knocked and told me dinner was ready. I ignored her and stayed where I was, but regretted the decision two hours later when my stomach began to growl. On her way to bed, Leah brought me a sandwich crammed with Thanksgiving leftovers. She perched on the edge of my mattress and said, "I guess they told you."

"Yeah," I said—through a mouthful of turkey, bread, and cranberry sauce.

"Sorry."

"I'll find the money somewhere. I can't not go back to Dellecher."

"Why?" She watched me with curious china blue eyes.

"I don't know. It's just—I don't want to be anywhere else. James and Filippa and Alexander and Wren and Meredith, they're like family." I'd omitted Richard without even meaning to. The bread was a sticky paste in my mouth. "Better than family, really," I added, when I managed to swallow. "We all just fit together. Not like here."

She tugged at the edge of my comforter and said, "We used to fit. You and Caroline used to like each other."

"No, we didn't. You were just too young to figure it out." She frowned at me, so I elaborated. "Don't worry. I love her, just like I'm supposed to. I just don't *like* her very much."

She chewed her bottom lip, lost in thought. She'd never reminded me so much of Wren; grief and affection welled up unexpectedly, both at once. I wanted to hug her, squeeze her hand, something—but as a family, we'd never been so physically demonstrative, and I was afraid she'd find it strange.

"Do you like me?" she asked.

"Of course I like you," I said, surprised by the question. "You're the only one in this house worth a damn."

"Good. Don't you forget it." She smiled grudgingly and slid off the bed. "Promise you'll come out of your room tomorrow."

"Only if Dad's not around."

She rolled her eyes. "I'll let you know when the coast is clear. Go to sleep, nerd."

I pointed at her, then at myself. "Pot. Kettle."

She stuck her tongue out before disappearing down the hall, leaving the door cracked behind her. Maybe she hadn't grown up too much yet.

I lay down again to finish Girard, but before long a few uncomfortably evocative words slipped in through the mental barrier I'd built up to keep Richard out: *This mimesis of conflict means more solidarity among those who can fight the same enemy* together *and who promise one another to do so. Nothing unites men like a common enemy.* On the next page Casca's name stopped me as suddenly as if it had been my own, and I snapped the book shut. Was Richard our enemy, then? It felt like a gross exaggeration, but what else could we call him? I strummed my thumb against the pages, marveling that we'd needed so little convincing to acquiesce to Alexander's *Nothing*. A few days removed from the moment, my horror was stale and cold, but I asked myself again what made me do it. Was it something so defensible as fear, or was it petty retribution, envy, opportunism? I fingered the edge of my bookmark. A number had been scribbled on the back in impetuous red ink. At the airport after the memorial service, I'd carried one of Meredith's bags to security, and when I handed it off to her (safely out of earshot of James and Alexander), she suggested I come and see her in New York before heading back to school. Richard was gone. What was there to stop me?

Guilt itched like a rash on my skin. It flared up whenever I brushed against Richard in my mind and faded to a dull discomfort when I could make myself forget him, for an hour or two. Worse than the guilt was the uncertainty. *I'm scared*, Filippa had told me, *of what happens now.* As I lay there in the past in my high school bedroom, the future had never seemed so murky. I thought about it in terms of dramatic structure, because I didn't know any other way to think. Richard's death felt less like a *dénouement* than a second-act peripeteia, the catalytic event that set everything else in motion. As Wren had said, the show wasn't over. It was the unknown ending that terrified me.

I pressed the heels of my palms against my eyeballs. The exhaustion that had crept into my bones at Hallsworth House clung to me, the lassitude left when a high fever breaks. Soon I was asleep on top of the blankets, wading through a dream in which I and the other fourth-years—just the six of us—stood hip-deep in a misty, tree-studded swamp, saying all at the same time, over and over, *"He is drown'd in the brook; look but in, and you shall see him."*

An hour or so later, I twitched awake. The bars of sky visible between the blinds on my window were pitch-black and starless. I propped myself up on my elbows, wondering what had woken me. A dull thud from somewhere downstairs made me sit up straighter, listening. Unsure if I'd really heard anything at all, I swung my legs over the side of the bed and pulled the door open. My eyes adjusted slowly to the semidarkness as I crept down the hall, but I had had plenty of practice sneaking around the house after nightfall and wasn't likely to stumble. When I got to the bottom of the stairs I paused, ears pricked, one hand on the banister. Something moved on the porch, too big to be a neighborhood cat or a raccoon. Another thud. Someone was knocking.

I crept across the foyer and peered cautiously out through the sidelight. Surprise pounced on me and I fumbled to unlock the door.

"James!"

He stood on the porch with a duffel bag by his feet, his breath a stream of white in the frigid night air. "I didn't know if you'd be up," he said, as if he were merely late for a meeting we'd arranged and not completely unexpected.

"What are you doing here?" I asked, looking at him a little blearily, unsure if I might still be dreaming.

"I'm sorry," he said. "I should've called."

"No, it's fine—come in, it's cold." I waved him over the threshold, and he came in quickly, grabbing his bag off the porch. I closed the door behind him and locked it again.

"Is everyone asleep?" he asked, voice dropping to a whisper.

"Yeah. Come up, we can talk in my room."

He trailed behind me up the stairs and down the hall, glancing at pictures on the walls, knickknacks piled on side tables. He'd never been in my house and I was self-conscious, embarrassed by it. I was painfully aware of the fact that we didn't have enough books.

My own room was less overtly deficient—over the years I'd insulated myself from the rest of the house (the rest of the neighborhood, the rest of Ohio) with layers of ink and paper and poetry, like a squirrel lining a nest. James followed me in and stood looking around with obvious curiosity as I shut the door. The room seemed, for the first time, small.

"Here, let me take that." I reached for his bag and set it in the narrow alley between the bed and the wall.

"I like your room," he said. "It looks lived-in."

James's bedroom in California looked like a set pulled from a home-decorating magazine for wealthy librarians.

"It's not much." I sat on the foot of the bed and watched him absorb his surroundings. He seemed out of place, but not in an entirely unpleasant way—like a student who had wandered into the wrong classroom and found the new subject intensely interesting. At the same time, I couldn't ignore how worn-out he looked. His shoulders drooped low, his arms hanging lifelessly at his sides. A messy map of creases showed on his sweater, as if he had slept in it. He hadn't shaved, and the faint shadow of stubble on his jaw was jarringly unfamiliar.

"It's perfect," he said.

"Well, you're welcome to it. But—and don't take this the wrong way, you have no idea how glad I am to see you—why on earth are you here?"

He leaned on the edge of my desk. "I needed to get away from home," he said. "Rattling around that house by myself during the day, tiptoeing around my parents at night—I just couldn't take it. I couldn't go back to Dellecher so I flew to Chicago, but the busyness was just as bad. I thought about getting a bus to Broadwater, but there wasn't one so I came here." He shook his head. "I'm sorry, I should've called."

"Don't be ridiculous."

"*Thy friendship makes us fresh.*"

"No offense, but you don't look it," I told him. "You look battered, actually."

"It's been a long night."

"Let's get you to bed, then. We can talk more in the morning."

He nodded, tired eyes warm with gratitude. I stared at him, momentarily brain-dead except for the nonsensical question of whether he'd ever looked at me quite like that before.

"Where do you want me?" he asked.

"What? Oh. Why don't you sleep here, and I'll crash on the couch downstairs."

"I'm not going to kick you out of your own bed."

"You need the sleep more than I do."

"No, why don't we just— We can share, can't we?"

My synapses fizzled out again. His expression was one part puzzled, one part expectant, and so utterly boyish that in that instant he looked more like himself than he had in weeks. He shifted, eyes flicking away toward the window, and I realized he was waiting for an answer.

"I don't see why not," I said.

His mouth inched shyly toward a grin. "We're not such strange bedfellows."

"No."

I watched as he bent down to unlace his shoes, then pulled my own socks off and climbed out of my sweatpants. I glanced at the clock on my nightstand. It was well after two in the morning. I frowned, calculating how long he'd been on the bus. Five hours? Six?

"Which side do you want?" he asked.

"What?"

"The bed." He pointed.

"Oh. Whichever."

"Okay." He folded his jeans over the back of my desk chair and then pulled his sweater off over his head. Ghosts of bruises still stained his wrists and forearms green.

I sat gingerly on the near edge of the bed and found myself thinking, unexpectedly, of the summer we'd spent in California— taking turns behind the wheel of the old BMW that had once belonged to James's father, driving all the way up the coast to some gray, fog-blurred beach where we got drunk on white wine, swam naked, and fell asleep in the sand.

"Do you remember that night in Del Norte," I said, "when we passed out on the beach—"

"And when we woke up in the morning all our clothes were gone?"

He said it so readily that he must have been thinking of it, too. I almost laughed and turned to find him pulling back the comforter, eyes brighter than they'd been before.

"I still wonder what happened," I said. "Do you think it could have been the tide?"

"More likely someone with a sense of humor and a very light step liked the idea of us having to hike back to the car in the nude."

"It's a miracle we didn't get arrested."

"In California? It would take more than that."

Suddenly the old story—the water and the gray morning and James's remark, *It would take more than that*—was too familiar, too close for comfort to more recent memories. He averted his eyes and I knew we were still thinking the same thing. We climbed into bed, pushed the pillows around, and pretended to get comfortable in disconcerted silence. I lay on my back, dismayed that the five or six inches of space between us suddenly felt like a hundred miles. My petty fears from the memorial service were confirmed—death wasn't going to stop Richard tormenting us.

"Can I turn out the light?" James asked.

"'Course," I said, glad that his thoughts and mine were no longer wandering in the same direction.

He reached for the lamp, and darkness fell down from the ceiling. With it came a soft, senseless panic—I couldn't see James anymore. I fought the impulse to grope across the bed until I found his arm. I spoke out loud, just to hear him reply.

"You know what I keep thinking of? You know, when I think about Richard."

He was slow to answer, like he didn't really want to find out. "What?"

"The sparrow, from *Hamlet*."

I felt him shift. "Yeah, you said. *Let be*."

"I've never understood that speech," I said. "I mean, I understand it, but it doesn't make sense. After trying for so long to settle the score and restore some kind of order, suddenly Hamlet's a fatalist."

The mattress moved under him again. He might have rolled over to face me, but it was too dark to see. "I think you understand it perfectly. Nothing makes sense to him either. His whole world is falling apart, and once he realizes he can't stop it or fix it or change it, there's only one thing left to do."

My eyes adjusted slowly, maddeningly. "What's that?"

His shadow shrugged in the gloom. "Absolve yourself. Blame it on fate."

SCENE 10

The following morning I returned gradually to consciousness, floating on the surface of sleep, eyes still closed. Something fluttered against my shoulder and I remembered: James. Unlike the few nights I'd spent lying next to Meredith at Hallsworth House, I was instantly, acutely aware of him.

I opened one eye, unsure if I should move but reluctant to risk waking him. He'd rolled toward me sometime in the night, and his head was tucked against my shoulder, breath racing down my arm every time he exhaled. The strange sudden thought that I didn't *want* to move struck me, with the surprising lucidity of a sunbeam slanting right in my eyes. His warm drowsy weight in the bed beside me felt natural, comfortable, *comme il faut*. I lay impossibly still, wondered what I was waiting for, and slowly fell asleep again.

I didn't sleep long or deeply enough to dream. What seemed like seconds later I was awake, dimly conscious of hushed voices nearby. The whispers took shape, crescendoed until a giggle escaped and was sharply stifled. I pushed myself halfway up; James stirred beside me but didn't wake completely. I blinked furiously and, when I could see in the stark morning light, glared at my sisters. They were both in their pajamas, crowded together in the doorway. Leah tucked her bottom lip behind her teeth and continued giggling silently. Caroline leaned on the doorjamb, leering at me, her skinny legs poking out of her huge Ohio State sweatshirt like a pair of chopsticks.

"Both of you get out," I said.

Leah dissolved into audible laughter. James opened his eyes, squinted up at me, and followed my glare to the door. "Good morning?" he said.

Caroline: "Who's your boyfriend, Oliver?"

Me: "Fuck off, Caroline."

James: "I'm James. Lovely to meet you both."

Leah found this hilarious.

Caroline: "Are you going to come out to Mom and Dad?"

Me: "Seriously, get out of my room."

Caroline (to James): "What *do* you see in him?"

James: "Don't tease. Oliver's hooking up with the hottest girl in our year."

Caroline: "The redhead?"

James: "The same."

A pause.

Caroline: "Bullshit."

Leah: "No *way*. I thought she was with Richard!"

Caroline: "Yeah, what happened to him?"

Me: "Nothing happened to him, okay? Both of you out."

I kicked the blanket back, slid off the bed, and shooed them into the hall. Leah goggled at me like she'd never seen me before. "Oliver," she said, in a bad stage whisper. "Oliver, are you and Meredith *really*—"

"Knock it off, I'm not going to talk about it."

I nudged her toward the stairs and she reluctantly started down, but Caroline lingered at the top to say, "Mom wants to know if you and your boyfriend will be joining us for breakfast."

"Why don't you eat it instead?"

Her smile soured, turned to a scowl. I immediately regretted the remark but didn't apologize. She muttered something that sounded like "asshole," and went quietly down the stairs. I trudged back into my room. James was out of bed and digging through his bag.

"So those are your sisters," he said. If he was at all embarrassed, he didn't let on.

"Sorry."

"It's okay," he said. "I never had siblings."

"Well, don't waste a lot of time wishing you did." I glanced toward the door, considering for the first time how hazardous it was to have him in the house. I didn't care much what my family thought of James, but I cared what he thought of them. Compared to my father, my sisters were harmless. "Do you want breakfast?"

"I wouldn't say no. I'd like to meet the rest of your family."

"I take no responsibility for anything they say to you."

"Are you not coming down?"

"Yeah," I said. "I will in just a minute. Think you can find your way?"

He put his head through the collar of a clean blue sweater. "I'll manage."

When he left the room, I quickly pulled on a new T-shirt and the same sweatpants from the previous night. I took my bookmark from *Theatre of Envy* and tucked it in my pocket. On the landing I listened for voices from downstairs. By the sound of it, Leah was bombarding James with questions about California. My mother could hardly get a word in edgewise, but when she did she somehow managed to sound polite, puzzled, and slightly suspicious all at the same time. Relieved that my father seemed to have left the house already, I snuck down the hall to his office, slipped inside, and shut the door. It was a small, ugly room, where a mammoth computer monitor sat humming on the desk like a prehistoric beast in hibernation. I picked up the phone, pinned it under my ear, and fished the bookmark out of my pocket again. After the Thanksgiving dinner debacle, I'd considered defecting to Manhattan for the weekend. It was a reckless plan, but the prospect of Meredith and an empty penthouse—regardless of what happened there—was vastly more appealing than spending another three days closeted in my high school bedroom, hiding from my parents and Caroline. But then James appeared on the porch, like some kind of divine interference.

The telephone rang loudly in my ear. I squeezed the handset a little too hard, half hoping she wouldn't pick up.

"Hello?"

Maybe it was the distance or the quality of the call, but she sounded woozy, disoriented, like she'd just woken up. That one low note of her voice made an ember flare in the pit of my stomach. I glanced toward the door to make sure it was closed.

"Meredith, hi. It's m—Oliver," I said. "Listen, James showed up on my porch last night. I had no idea he was coming, but I can't just leave him here. I don't think New York is going to happen."

There was a short, shallow silence before she said, "Of course."

SCENE 11

The first day of December was bright and crisp and freezing cold. Classes were scheduled to resume the following day, and we were told when we arrived on campus that we'd be allowed to move back into the Castle at four o'clock in the afternoon. Alexander and Filippa settled into our usual booth at the Bore's Head, warming their hands with mugs of spiked cider, while James had tea with Frederick. Meredith was waiting on a delayed flight out of LaGuardia. We had no word from Wren.

I hauled my bags up the stairs to the third floor of the Hall for a brief meeting with Dean Holinshed, where he presented the solution to my sudden lack of funding: a combination of loans, unused scholarship dollars, and work-study. I listened and nodded and thanked him profusely and, when he dismissed me, shouldered my bag again and started down the trail through the trees. One of my work-study occupations, Holinshed explained, would be to take over the cleaning and maintenance of the Castle. It didn't even occur to me to be humiliated. I was so desperately glad not to be leaving Dellecher that I would have scrubbed every toilet in the Hall if he had asked.

The place was as much of a mess as it had been when we left. I decided to begin in the kitchen, where refuse from the disastrous *Caesar* party was scattered on every surface. Cleaning supplies, I'd been told, were under the sink—a place I'd never before bothered to explore. But first, I lit a fire in the library. It was painfully cold in the Castle, as if winter had crept in between the stones and made a home there in our absence. I crumpled a few sheets of newspaper from the basket on the hearth and wedged them underneath two new logs without clearing away the old ashes. A few minutes' fumbling with the fireplace matches yielded a small but persistent flame, and I rubbed my hands over it until I could feel them again.

As I straightened up, I heard a door open downstairs. I froze, waiting. Had Alexander snuck back in three hours early? I cursed him silently and tiptoed down the stairs, hoping to head him off in the kitchen, racking my brains for a plausible excuse for why I was already there. (I didn't want to burden him or any of the others with my family drama. We had enough drama of our own.)

An unfamiliar voice stopped me two steps from the bottom.

"Remind me again why we're here?"

"Because I want to have a look around before all those kids move back in."

"Whatever you say, Joe."

I squatted on the last step and peered through the doorway. Two men were standing in the dining room, with their backs to me. I recognized the taller one—or, rather, I recognized his brown bomber jacket. Colborne. The shorter one was wearing a blue quilted coat and a knobby yellow scarf that was almost certainly handmade. A crop of unruly blazing-red hair gave the impression that his head was on fire. (His name, I would eventually learn, was Ned Walton.) He rolled back and forth on the balls of his feet and glanced around. "What're we looking for, Chief?"

"Don't call me Chief," Colborne said, with a sigh that suggested it wasn't the first time he'd given that instruction. "I'm not the chief. And don't touch anything."

As Walton wandered toward the window, he pulled his gloves off by the fingertips, with his teeth, and stuffed them in his pockets. I wondered if he could see the dock from where he was standing.

Walton: "Is this the first time they've lost a student?"

Colborne: "A dancer committed suicide about ten years ago. Found out she didn't make the cut for fourth year, went up to her room, and slit her wrists."

Walton: "Jesus."

Colborne: "I'd seen her around. Pretty girl. Looked like she was made of tissue paper. The media went wild over it, accused the school of 'driving students to desperation.'"

Walton: "Is that what happened to this kid?"

Colborne turned on the spot, hands on his hips—expression pinched, contemplative. "No. He was the star of the program, from what I understand. Did you see those big red posters around town? *I am Caesar*?"

"Yeah."

"That's him."

"Scary dude," Walton said.

Colborne nodded. "The kids have all shut right up about it, but I get the sense that not everyone liked him."

"Oh no?" Walton asked, one ginger eyebrow rising.

"No."

Walton frowned across the room at Colborne. "Is that why we're here?" he asked. "I thought we ruled it an accident."

"Yeah." A shadow flitted across Colborne's face. "We did."

"Okay," Walton said, and the word had an interrogative upward tilt. He leaned on the windowsill, arms folded. "Take me through it."

Colborne took one slow step forward, eyes fixed on the floor.

"About nine days ago," he said, "the fourth-years and bunch of other drama students are all in a show up at the Fine Arts Building." He pointed northeast, in the direction of the FAB. I sat back on my heels, put one hand on the wall to steady myself. My breath came light and fast through my nose, the cold air stinging in my lungs. Colborne kept walking, putting one foot carefully in front of the other, making a wide circle around the room. "The show ends around ten thirty," he went on, "and the kids come down through the woods to here, where the party's already in full swing. Music, dancing, drugs, booze. Richard holes himself up in the library with a bottle of Scotch."

"If he was the star, why was he lurking up there?"

"Well, that's what nobody seems to want to tell me. He was in a mood, everyone agrees on that, but why? One of the third-years suggested he was having girlfriend trouble."

"Who's the girlfriend?"

"Meredith Dardenne, another fourth-year."

"Why's that name sound familiar?"

"Her family makes the fancy watches. They could buy the whole town if they wanted to."

"You think that's why no one's pointing at her?"

Colborne shrugged. "Couldn't say. But apparently the two of them had a knock-down, drag-out fight in front of everyone, and by the end of the night she was making out with someone else."

Walton let out a low, dangerous whistle. I leaned forward, my hands on my knees. Blood had rushed up from my chest and limbs and was swimming in my ears.

Walton: "Who was that?"

Colborne: "Nobody really wanted to say, but someone suggested Oliver Marks. He's another fourth-year. He admitted to going upstairs with her, but according to him they were just 'talking.'"

Walton: "Seems unlikely."

Colborne: "You haven't seen this girl. You don't understand how unlikely."

Walton chuckled. "What did she have to say about it?"

"Well, her story matches his," Colborne said. "She claims they went up to her room, where they talked until Richard came up and tried to break the door down. They didn't let him in and eventually he stormed off. And this is where it gets fuzzy."

"Fuzzy how?"

Colborne stopped, standing face-to-face with Walton, scowling, like his own confusion annoyed him. "At about this time— and nobody seems to be able to say for sure what time it was—pretty much everyone but the fourth-years is gone. Richard storms away from his girlfriend's room, where maybe she's hooking up with one of their mutual friends or maybe they're just talking, grabs a bottle of Glenfiddich, and heads outside. He's already drunk—he was a belligerent drunk, too, everyone agrees on that—and he stumbles out into the yard, where his cousin is talking with James Farrow."

Walton: "Another fourth-year?"

Colborne: "Marks's roommate. They live in the attic room upstairs."

Walton: "All right, then what?"

"Wren—the cousin—tries to talk him down, but he 'shakes her off.' Farrow's words. When I asked him what that meant he clammed up. Makes me wonder if it might have been a little violent, because neither one of them went after him. Anyway, Farrow stays with the cousin, and Richard disappears into the trees." Colborne's face darkened, his thick eyebrows sinking low over his eyes. "Nobody sees him again until the following morning when Alexander Vass—he's the last of the fourth-years—goes down to the dock for a smoke and finds him in the water. So, we have about three hours where we don't know where Richard was or what he was up to."

They were both quiet for a moment, looking out the same

narrow window. The day outside was awash with stark white sunlight that did nothing to soften the bitter cold.

"What did the ME have to say?" Walton asked.

"Well, there was a hard blow to the head, but she couldn't say with what. Originally we assumed that was what killed him."

Walton's forehead wrinkled. "Wasn't it?"

"No." Colborne exhaled heavily, and his shoulders sank down an inch or two. "He was alive when he hit the water. Alive, but unconscious or too stunned to roll himself over. Whatever it was hit him right in the face, and the damage was bad, but it shouldn't have been fatal."

"How did he die, then?"

"He drowned," Colborne said. "In a manner of speaking. Choked on his own blood."

I turned away from the door, pressed my back flat against the wall. I felt light-headed, the thrum of my pulse faint and far away, and I wondered if that was what it felt like—the slow loss of air, life seeping out into the surrounding water, and your own blood, thick as an oil spill, creeping into every empty space until it reached your eyes and the whole world went red. Asphyxia. System failure. Fade to black.

Colborne's voice came in sharp and clear from the next room: "It doesn't add up. We're missing something."

"Did we find the Scotch bottle?"

"In the woods, about a quarter mile from the dock. We thought that's what he might've been hit with, but it was intact. Empty, intact, no blood on it, and nobody's fingerprints but his. So what the hell was he doing between three in the morning and six?"

"Was that the time of death?"

"As close as the ME could figure it."

They were both silent for a while. I didn't dare move in my hiding place.

"What are you thinking?" Walton asked, eventually.

Colborne made a soft, impatient sound. I eased forward slowly until I could see him again, shaking his head, tongue pinched between his teeth. "These kids," he said. "The fourth-years. I don't trust them."

"Why not?"

"They're a bunch of fucking *actors*," Colborne said. "They could all be lying through their teeth, and how would we know?"

"Christ." They were quiet again until Walton said, "What do we do?"

"We keep a close eye on them. Wait for one of them to snap." He glanced around the empty dining room. "The six of them holed up out here, alone? It won't take long."

The floorboards groaned as they moved toward the kitchen.

"My money's on the cousin," Walton said.

"Maybe," Colborne said. "We'll see."

"Where to?"

"I want to walk through the woods to where we found the bottle, see if I can sort out how Richard got down to the dock from there."

"Okay, then what?"

"Don't know. Depends if we find anything."

Walton replied, but his voice had faded low enough that I couldn't hear what he said. The door closed behind them with a scrape and a thud. I slid to the floor, my legs weak and boneless underneath me. Richard loomed enormous in my mind, and if I could have spoken, I would have said to him, *Had you such leisure in the time of death / To gaze upon the secrets of the deep?*

To which he in my fantasy replied, *Methought I had; and often did I strive / To yield the ghost: but still the envious flood / Kept in my soul, and would not let it forth / To seek the empty, vast and wandering air.*

Awaked you not with this sore agony? I asked.

At last he abandoned his Shakespeare and said only, *No.*

SCENE 12

Our first day back in class was surprisingly quiet. Wren hadn't appeared, and Meredith arrived so late Monday night that none of us saw her, and she was given permission to sleep through Tuesday. With only the boys and Filippa in attendance, our teachers seemed content to simply explain what the short winter term between Thanksgiving and Christmas would include: *Romeo and Juliet*, our introduction to weapons combat, and midterm speeches.

Evening found the four of us in the Castle library (vigorously tidied by me the previous day), writing out our new monologues and beginning to scan them. Pens, pencils, highlighters, notebooks, and wineglasses were strewn on every table. A towering fire lit the whole room but didn't keep the cold entirely at bay. Filippa and I sat toe-to-toe on the couch, one thick wool blanket stretched over both of us. My eyelids had begun to droop an hour before, and at last I let them close. I might have fallen asleep if not for the constant motion of Filippa's left foot, which wiggled persistently against my leg as she wrote.

The words of my newest piece tumbled around between my ears, disconnected and chaotic, not yet regimented and committed to memory. They'd given me something surprisingly robust—Philip the Bastard's rousing battle speech from *King John*:

> *Your royal presences be ruled by me:*
> *Be friends awhile and both conjointly bend*
> *Your sharpest deeds of malice on this town:*
> *And when that we have dash'd them to the ground,*
> *Why then defy each other and pell-mell*
> *Make work upon ourselves, for heaven or hell.*

I sat up when a small voice said, "Hello. Sorry I'm late."

"Wren!" James launched himself out of his chair.

She was standing in the doorway, eyes dreamy and tired, a carry-on bag slung over her shoulder.

"We thought you weren't coming back," Alexander said, shooting a dirty look down the hall toward Meredith's room.

"Had enough of me?" Wren asked, as James pulled her bag off her shoulder and set it on the floor.

"Of course not. How are you?" Filippa stood up with her arms already open.

Wren drifted into her embrace and hugged her tight around the waist. "Better now."

I followed Filippa off the couch and, in a moment of foolish affection, put my arms around them both. "Us, too."

Alexander snorted. "Really?" he said. "Group hug? Are we going to do this?"

"Shut up," Wren said, her cheek squashed against Filippa's shoulder. "Don't spoil it."

"Fine." A second later Alexander's long monkey arms crushed us all together, and then James latched on as well. We lost our balance, swayed, Wren trapped and laughing at the heart of our human knot. The sound shivered through us, moving fluidly from one body to the next like a breath of warm air.

"What's going on in here?"

I looked over everyone's heads toward the hall. "Meredith."

She stood in the doorway, barefoot, barefaced, in leggings and a long T-shirt I was fairly sure had once belonged to Richard. Her hair was tousled, her eyes dusky and slow. I hadn't seen her since the airport and I felt slightly winded.

Our little clutch broke apart, each of us retreating half a step until Wren emerged again from the middle. Meredith's stern expression softened. "Wren."

"Me." She smiled weakly. Meredith blinked, staggered into

the room, and crashed into her. The two of them were hugging and laughing and falling over all at the same time, and Filippa and I barely caught them before they hit the coffee table.

When we were all upright again, smarting from colliding elbows and trodden-on toes, Meredith let go of Wren and said, "It's about time. *Best of comfort / And ever welcome to us.*"

Filippa: "You must be exhausted. When did you leave London?"

Wren: "Yesterday morning. I'd love to hear about Thanksgiving, but I don't want to offend anyone by falling asleep."

Alexander: "Don't be stupid. *Get thee to bed and rest; for thou hast need.*"

James: "Where's your suitcase?"

Wren: "Downstairs. I couldn't face carrying it up just yet."

James: "I'll get it."

Wren: "You sure?"

"Let him go," Meredith said, brushing Wren's hair back off her forehead. "You look like you might need someone to carry you."

"Come on," Filippa said. "I'll help you get settled."

They disappeared down the hall together, while James vanished into the stairwell. Alexander gave me a soporific smile and said, "The gang's all here." His eyes moved lazily from me to Meredith and the grin slid off his face. All of her gentleness seemed to have left the room with Wren, and she stood staring at me with a hard, unassailable sort of look. "So," Alexander said. "I think I'll go have a smoke before bed." He wound his scarf tightly around his neck and left the room, whistling "Secret Lovers" under his breath. (I considered running after him and kicking him down the stairs.)

Meredith was in Flamingo Pose again, one foot perched on the inside of the opposite knee. She made even that look graceful. I didn't know what to do with my hands, so I slid them into my back pockets, which felt far too casual.

"How was New York?" I asked.

"You know, hustle and bustle," she said, dryly. "We had a parade."

"Right."

"How was Ohio?"

"It sucked," I said. "It always does."

The fact that I could have come to New York and didn't hung so heavily in the air between us that there was no need to mention it.

"How's your family?" I asked.

"No idea," she said. "I only saw Caleb once and everyone else is in Canada."

"Oh."

I could picture her rambling around in an empty apartment, nothing to distract her from Richard's death. Our holidays weren't so different, probably—hours of reading and staring at the ceiling, isolated from siblings and parents so unfamiliar that they might as well have been a different species. Of course, I'd had the windfall of James's company, and she hadn't been so lucky. An impossible apology glued my tongue to the roof of my mouth.

She folded her arms and said, "I'm going to bed unless you've got something to say."

I didn't. I desperately wanted to, but my mind was blank. For someone who loved words as much as I did, it was amazing how often they failed me.

She waited, watching me, and when I said nothing, her mask of apathy cracked for a moment and I saw the quiet disappointment underneath. "Well," she said. "Goodnight, then."

"I—Meredith, wait."

"What?" she asked, the question dull and tired.

I shifted my weight, uncertain, unsure, cursing my own ineloquence. "Do you, um, want to sleep alone?"

"I don't know," she said. "Do you want to sleep with me or would you rather sleep with James?"

I glanced away, hoping to hide the rising warmth in my cheeks. When I looked back again she was shaking her head, one corner of her mouth tugged upward, caught between pity and disdain. She didn't wait for an answer—just turned and walked down the hall again. I watched her go, mental gears whirring and churning out weak, inadequate replies until she was gone and it was too late to say anything at all.

I lingered by the fireplace, debating whether to go after her— barge into her room, then throw her against the wall and kiss her until she was too out of breath for such harsh words—or just retreat to the Tower and try to sleep. I was too much a coward for the former, too restless for the latter. Unable to commit to either course of action, I reached for my coat instead.

The night was so cold that stepping outside felt like a slap in the face. I set off through the trees, shoulders hunched up to keep my ears warm, watching the ground for roots and rocks that might trip me in the dark. I reached the dock almost without realizing where I was. My feet had brought me there automatically, as though there were no other logical place to go. By night the lake was black and as still as a mirror, five hundred stars perfectly reflected on the surface. There was no moon—just a small round gap in the field of stars where the moon should have been. Alexander sat on the dock by himself, legs dangling over the water.

I walked to the end and stopped behind him. He must have heard me approach, but he didn't react, just sat staring out at the lake with his hands folded between his knees.

"Can I join you?" I asked, and my words emerged in a cloud.

" 'Course."

I sat beside him, and for a moment neither of us spoke.

"Smoke?" he said, eventually.

"Yeah, I could use one."

He reached inside his coat without looking, then passed a spliff to me and fumbled in his pockets for a lighter. He flicked a flame to life and I inhaled as deeply as I could, the smoke scorching hot in my throat.

"Thanks," I said, after my second pull, and passed it back to him.

He nodded, eyes pointed forward. "How'd it go?"

I assumed he meant my conversation with Meredith.

"Not well."

We sat in silence for a while, the smoke and our breath swirling and mingling as they drifted out over the water. I tried to push Meredith out of my head, but there was no safe distraction. In every corner of my mind, doubts and fears crouched on all fours, prepared to spring and sink their teeth in me at the slightest provocation.

"Colborne was in the Castle," I said, without really planning to. I hadn't told any of them what I'd overheard, but it was dangerous knowledge to have, and I didn't trust myself with it.

"When?" he demanded.

"Yesterday."

"Did you talk to him?"

"No, but I heard him talking to another cop. Young ginger guy. Hadn't seen him before."

Alexander swallowed a mouthful of smoke, and it unfurled from his nostrils in a distinctly dragonish way. "What were they talking about?" he asked, with a diffidence that suggested he didn't really want to know.

"All . . . this." I made a loose, unspecific gesture that included the lake, the dock, and both of us.

"You think he suspects something?" Alexander asked. To someone who didn't know him so well, he might not have sounded scared.

"He knows we lied. He just doesn't know about what."

"Shit."

"Yeah."

He sucked on the spliff and the end flared orange, a single bright ember in the bleak Illinois wilderness. There wasn't much left but the roach. He passed it to me; I took one last drag and stubbed it out.

"So what do we do?"

"Nothing, I guess," he said, and that empty word, "nothing," made me clench my fists in my pockets. "Stick to our story. Try to keep our wits about us."

"We should tell the others. He's just waiting for one of us to slip up."

He shook his head. "They'll start acting funny if they know."

I chewed on my bottom lip, wondering how much danger we were really in. I thought of meeting James in the bathroom the night of the party. By some unspoken agreement, we hadn't mentioned it to the others. It was trivial, unimportant. But the possibility that we weren't the only ones keeping secrets made my heart drum a little faster. If we'd all lied to one another the way we'd lied to Colborne—I couldn't finish the thought.

"What do you think happened to him?" I asked. "After he left the Castle."

"Dunno." He knew who I meant. "I can't imagine he just stumbled around in the woods."

"Where were you, anyway?"

He gave me a shifty sort of look and said, "Why?"

"Just curious. I missed everything that happened after I, uh, went upstairs."

"If I tell you, you have to swear to keep your mouth shut."

"Why?"

"Because, unlike you," he said, loftily, "I don't kiss and make sure the whole school knows about it."

Half curious and half annoyed, I said, "Who were you with, jackass?"

He turned away from me, with a smug little smile on his mouth. "Colin."

"*Colin?* I didn't think he liked guys."

Alexander's smile broadened just enough to show his sharp canine teeth. "Neither did he."

I laughed, grudgingly, which would have seemed impossible two minutes before. "*Call up the right master constable—we have here recovered the most dangerous piece of lechery that ever was known in the commonwealth!*"

"Look who's talking."

"Fucksake," I said, "she started it."

"Obviously. No offense, Oliver, but starting things isn't exactly your MO."

I shook my head, my amusement dampened by the lingering bitterness of my conversation with Meredith. "I am so stupid."

Alexander: "If it makes you feel any better, I'd have done exactly the same thing."

Me: "What *are* you?"

Alexander: "Sexually amphibious."

Me: "That's the grossest thing I've ever heard."

Alexander: "You should try it."

Me: "I've had enough sexual misadventures for one year, thanks."

I sighed and looked down at my own reflection on the surface of the water. My face seemed somehow unfamiliar, and I squinted, trying to work out what was different. The realization hit me like a blow to the stomach: with my dark hair a little wilder than usual and my blue eyes hollowed out by the weak starlight, I almost resembled Richard. For one sickening moment he stared back at me from the bottom of the lake. I looked up sharply.

"You okay?" Alexander asked. "For a second there it looked like you were going to throw yourself in."

"Oh. No."

"Good. Don't." He climbed to his feet. "C'mon. It's fucking freezing and I'm not leaving you out here alone."

"All right." I stood, brushing little bits of ash out of my lap.

Alexander buried his hands deep in his pockets, searching the darkness that shrouded the opposite shore. "I was on my way back from Colin's room," he said, and it seemed random until he added, "when I found him. Wandered down here for a smoke and . . . there he was. I didn't even think to check if he was alive, he seemed so totally dead. Must not have heard me."

I didn't know why he was telling me. Perhaps he relived that terrible moment of discovery every morning, the same way I felt my stomach drop and found myself neck-deep in memory almost every time I closed my eyes.

"Know what's weird, though?" he said.

"What?"

"There was blood in the water, but not on the dock."

I glanced down at my feet. The wood was clean and dry, bleached like bone by years of wind and sun and water. Not a speck of red. Not a stainèd spot.

"So?"

"So his face was smashed in. If he hit his head and fell in the water . . . what the hell did he hit?"

The stub of our spliff smoldered on the very edge of the dock. Alexander nudged it off with the toe of his shoe. Ripples moved outward from the point of impact, warping the reflection of the sky so the stars wobbled and winked in and out of existence.

"I keep thinking of the bird." I didn't even want to say it. It was a tic, a compulsion, as though I might get the image out of my head if I got the words out of my mouth.

He looked sideways at me, completely nonplussed. "What bird?"

"From *Hamlet*. That's what he reminded me of."

"Oh," he said. "Not sure I can see him as a *sparrow*. Too . . . delicate."

"So what sort of bird would he be?"

"Dunno. The sort that smacked into a window trying to have a go at its own reflection."

It was my turn to look at him strangely, but as soon as our eyes met, I wanted to laugh. I was horrified until I realized he was fighting it, too.

"Oh my God," I said, shaking my head. Alexander let the breath he was holding burst out, chuckled softly. "When did we become such terrible people?"

"Maybe we've always been terrible." He shrugged and watched the white cloud of his laughter shimmer and fade. His good humor seemed to vanish with it, and when he spoke again his voice was brittle. "Or maybe we learned from Richard," he said.

That scared me more than Colborne did.

SCENE 13

A week later, we arrived in the refectory for breakfast and found it humming with holiday excitement. At every table people were tearing invitations open and chattering about the Christmas masque—which was to go forward as usual, in defiance of recent events. The commotion was surprisingly refreshing after weeks of bowed heads and stiff, unsmiling faces.

"Who wants to gather the mail?" Alexander asked, digging into a pile of hash browns with characteristic relish. (Filippa had bullied him out of bed for breakfast, insisting that if he skipped any more meals he'd simply vanish into thin air.)

"Why bother?" I asked. "We know what it says."

Filippa blew steam off her coffee and said, "You don't think it might be a little different this year?"

"I don't know. Sort of seems like they're trying to get back to normal."

"And thank God," Alexander said. "I'm sick of being stared at."

"It could be worse." Wren pushed eggs around on her plate, not eating. She looked thin and wan, as if she hadn't eaten anything for days. "People keep looking around me and through me like I don't exist."

We sat in tongue-tied silence—avoiding one another's eyes and Richard's empty chair—while the other students continued to jabber at one another about the masque, what they'd wear, and how spectacular the ballroom would be. The spell of isolation broke when Colin appeared at the edge of our table, one hand alighting (unnoticed by everyone but me) on the back of Alexander's chair.

"Morning," he said, and then frowned. "Everyone all right?"

"Yes." Alexander speared a sausage on the end of his fork, a little violently. "Just considering starting our own leper colony down at the Castle."

"They do stare, don't they?" Colin said, glancing around as if he'd just noticed the wide berth everyone was giving our table.

"Voyeuristic little shits," Alexander said, and bit the sausage in half, teeth snapping down like a guillotine. "What brings you into exile with the rest of us?"

Colin held up a familiar envelope, small and square, a black splash of Frederick's writing on the front. "We've been given *R and J* assignments," he said. "Thought you'd like to know."

"Oh?" Alexander twisted around his chair, glancing across the room to the wall where all our mailboxes were.

"Want me to grab them?"

"No, that's all right." Meredith pushed her chair back and threw her napkin down in her seat. "I need another coffee. I'll go."

She left the table, and as she crossed the room people drifted automatically out of her way, like they were afraid her misfortune might be contagious. I felt a little snag of anger or anxiety (I couldn't tell the two apart anymore; after Richard's death they were somehow indistinguishable), tore a piece of bacon in half, and proceeded to crumble it into oblivion. I didn't realize I was ignoring everyone else until Filippa said loudly, "Oliver?"

"What?"

"You're torturing your bacon."

"Sorry, I'm not hungry. I'll see you guys in class."

I stood and carried my plate to the kitchen. I dumped it in the bin without bothering to scrape it off and went back out again. Meredith was still picking through the mailboxes, collecting our letters. I glared at a table of language students who were watching her until they bent their heads over their breakfasts again, whispering fiercely in Greek.

"Meredith," I said, when I was close enough that only she would hear me.

She looked up, eyes flicking dispassionately across my face before she turned back to the mailboxes. "Yes?"

"Look," I said, without hesitating. My annoyance with the rest of the student body had somehow made me bolder than usual. "I'm sorry about the other night, and I'm sorry about Thanksgiving. I'll be the first one to admit I don't know what we're doing here. But I want to figure it out."

She stopped rifling through the mailboxes, her hand perched on the edge of the one labeled *Stirling, Wren*. Right next to it was Richard's mailbox, empty. They hadn't removed his name. I forced myself to ignore it and look at Meredith. Her expression was inscrutable, but at least she was listening to me.

"Why don't we go get a drink or something?" I asked, leaning a little closer. "Just us. I can't think straight with everyone watching like we're a reality show."

She folded her arms, said skeptically, "Like a date?"

I wasn't sure what the right answer was. "I guess. I don't know. We'll figure it out when we get there."

Her face softened, and I was startled all over again by how pretty she was.

"All right. We'll get a drink." She put a pair of envelopes in my hand and left me alone by the mailboxes, staring dumbly after her. It was a moment or two before I realized the language students were gawping at me in her absence. I sighed, pretended not to see them, and opened my first envelope. The script on the front was long and loopy, not at all like Frederick's compact, tilted scribble. A blue silk ribbon had been fixed to the back with a wax seal bearing the Dellecher coat of arms. I slid my finger underneath it and flicked it open. The note was short, and the same as it had been the last three years except for the date.

You are cordially invited to the annual

CHRISTMAS MASQUE

Please arrive in the Josephine Dellecher Ballroom
between 8 and 9 p.m. on the evening of
Saturday, 20th December.
Masks and formal attire are required.

The second envelope was smaller, less ornate. I tore it open, quickly scanned the writing inside.

Please be in the ballroom at 8:45 p.m. on December 20th.
Come prepared for Act I, Scenes 1, 2, 4, and 5;
Act II, Scene 4; and Act III, Scene 1.

You will be playing BENVOLIO.

Please report to the costume shop at 12:30 p.m.
on December 15th for a fitting.
Please report to the rehearsal hall at 3 p.m.
on December 16th for combat choreography.
Do not discuss this with your peers.

I left the refectory without going back to our table. Colin had taken my seat. All of their envelopes were open, and they took turns glancing at one another, wondering whose note from Frederick said what. For the first time, I decided I didn't really want to know.

SCENE 14

Our winter-term schedule was so chaotic that it was five days before Meredith and I found a free minute to sneak away from the Castle. James and Wren and Filippa were locked in their various rooms—likely learning lines; we hardly had enough time to do them justice—and Alexander had disappeared early in the evening (probably, I thought, with Colin, though I kept this hypothesis to myself). What with *R and J* and work to do on our midterm speeches, we were all unusually high-strung. The idea of a quiet drink was wonderfully appealing, but even as I held the door to the bar for Meredith to precede me, I wasn't sure either one of us really had the time.

I had expected the place to be mostly empty, considering the day (Sunday) and the amount of work we all had to do before the twentieth (staggering). But the Bore's Head was surprisingly crowded, our usual table commandeered by a gaggle of philosophy students who were arguing loudly about the significance of Euclid of Megara's cross-dressing habit.

"What are they all doing out?" I asked, as Meredith led me to a small table on the opposite side of the room. "Don't they have homework?"

"Yes, but they don't also have half a play to memorize," she said. "Our perspective's a little skewed."

"Must be," I said. "Let me get us a drink."

She sat and pretended to look at the cocktail card (as though we didn't know it by heart) while I slid between chairs and stools to get to the bar. The guy to my left—a third-year dance student, I thought—gave me a dirty look when I asked for a pint and a vodka soda with lemon. He shook his head as I paid and lifted his glass to his mouth without a word.

"Thanks," I muttered at the bartender, and carried both drinks across the room, careful not to spill anything on myself as I dodged outstretched ankles and chair legs and wet spots on the floor. Meredith accepted her vodka gratefully and sucked half of it down before we said another word to each other.

Our conversation was unexpectedly awkward. We made superficial, silly remarks about our speech assignments and the upcoming masque, all the while acutely aware that we weren't really alone. Ours was the third of five tables in a row, and the small groups seated on either side of us had grown suspiciously quiet when we sat down. (They were almost all girls, I noticed, and all Dellecher students. Had girls always whispered so much? I couldn't decide if it was a new development or something I simply hadn't noticed. Admittedly I had never before been worth whispering about.) Meredith finished her drink and I jumped on the opportunity to get her another one. While I was waiting for it, I considered buying myself a shot. I couldn't help wondering how differently the night might have been going if we actually had some privacy, and decided that if everything proceeded in the same dreadful way, I'd suggest we finish our drinks and head back to the Castle, where we could at least lock a door or escape to the garden and breathe a little more freely.

When I sat back down Meredith smiled at me with obvious relief.

"It's weird, not being at our normal table," I said. "I don't think I've ever even sat on this side of the room."

"We haven't been in much," she said. "I think we forfeited our claim."

I glanced over my shoulder at the philosophers, still debating Euclid's possibly homoerotic obsession with Socrates. (It sounded like wishful thinking to me.)

"We can probably win it back," I said. "If we got everyone down here we could storm the beach."

"We'll have to arrange that." She smiled again, but the smile was uncertain.

Her hand rested on the table, and in a moment of rare bravery, I reached out and set my own on top of it. Four of her fingers curled around two of mine.

"You all right?" I asked, in a stage whisper. "I mean, really all right."

She stirred her drink around. "I'm trying. In spite of what everyone thinks, I'm sick of the staring, too." I couldn't keep my eyes from darting toward the other tables. "It sounds callous but I don't care. I don't want to just be the dead guy's girlfriend anymore."

I wanted, immediately, to let go of her hand. "And you want to be what?" I said, without thinking. "My girlfriend?"

She glared at me, surprise wiping every other emotion off her face. "What—"

"I'm not Richard's understudy," I said. "I'm not going to step in and play his part now that he's left the stage. That's not what I want."

"I don't want that either. That's exactly what I *don't* want. Jesus, Oliver." Her eyes were hard—green bottle glass, sharp-edged and brittle. "Richard and I were done," she said. "He was a bastard and a bully to me and everyone else and I was done with him. I know nobody wants to remember that now that he's gone, but you should."

I lowered my voice. "I'm sorry," I said. "I just—maybe it's because you're you, and I mean, look at you—but I don't understand. Why me? I'm nobody."

She looked away, biting hard on her bottom lip, like she was trying not to cry, or maybe not to scream. Her hand was limp and cool under mine, as if it were no longer connected to the rest of her. The tables on either side of us had stopped talking altogether.

"You know, everyone calls you 'nice,'" she said slowly, expression drawn and thoughtful. "But that's not the word. You're *good*.

So good you have no idea how good you are." She laughed—
once—a sad, resigned sort of sound. "And you're real. You're the
only one of us who isn't acting all the time, who isn't just playing
whatever part Gwendolyn gave you three years ago." Her eyes
found mine again, the echo of that laugh lingering around her
mouth. "I'm as bad as the rest of them. Treat a girl like a whore
and she'll learn to act like one." Her shoulders inched up, barely
a shrug. "But that's not how you treat me. And that's all I wanted."

I squeezed my eyes shut, then looked up at the ceiling. It was
the only safe place to look, the only place I knew I wouldn't find
five other sets of eyes staring back at me. "I'm sorry," I said
again, wishing I had never spoken, wishing I'd had the sense to
sit there with her and marvel at the fact that she wanted to sit
there with me, and not ask why. It should have been so easy, but
nothing between us ever would be. If this was what we wanted,
we'd played foully for it. We could leave the bar and escape the
scrutiny of other students, but locked doors didn't matter when
it was Richard watching us.

Meredith seemed weary more than angry. "Yeah, well, I'm
sorry, too."

"So, where does that leave us?" I asked, afraid to put too much
hope into the question. *Courage, man*, Romeo told me again, the
lying bastard, *the hurt cannot be much.*

"I don't know. Nowhere." She pulled her hand away. "Let's
just go back to the Castle. Better there than here."

I stood and gathered our empty glasses in bashful silence. I
helped her into her coat, let one hand linger on her shoulder.
She didn't seem to feel it, but at the table next to ours, I heard
one girl mutter to the others, "Fucking shameless."

But shame burned hot on my face and neck as I followed
Meredith out into the deep December darkness. The first flur-
ries of snow danced against a black sky, and I found myself hoping they would tumble down in millions, stick fast, and bury
everything.

SCENE 15

The schedule for our midterm speeches was posted on the call-board in the crossover on Monday. I was slated to go first, during what ordinarily would have been rehearsal time on Wednesday afternoon, and Wren would follow me. James and Filippa were scheduled to read at the same times on Thursday, Alexander and Meredith at the same times on Friday.

Snow had fallen thick and fast from Sunday night through Tuesday morning, doing its best to fulfill the reckless wish I'd made on the way out of the bar. Our feet and fingers were perpetually numb, our cheeks and noses rosy pink, ChapStick suddenly a valuable commodity. On Wednesday Frederick and Gwendolyn ushered us into the drafty rehearsal hall, where we shed scarves, coats, and gloves and were subjected to a rigorous warm-up exercise of Gwendolyn's selection.

I rushed headlong into my speech while Wren waited in the hallway. "*I'd play incessantly upon these jades / Even till unfencèd desolation / Leave them as naked as the vulgar air*" forced me to slow down, and the strength of the imagery carried me more steadily through "*How like you this wild counsel, mighty states?*" when I felt obliged to gather speed again. At the end, I was winded but weirdly elated, relieved to be someone other than myself for a while—more willing to go to war than face my own ugly, meager demons.

Frederick and Gwendolyn were both smiling at me—Gwendolyn's mouth a bold slash of her dark winter lipstick, Frederick's a small, creased bow.

"Very good, Oliver," Gwendolyn said. "A little hurried at the top, but you fell into it very nicely."

"I found it entirely persuasive," Frederick told me. "Which argues great success on your part."

"Thank you," I said.

"You'll get the rest of our comments in your mailbox tomorrow," Gwendolyn said. "But I wouldn't worry. Have a seat."

I thanked them again and went to sit beside their table, gulping down water from the bottle under my chair while we waited for Wren. Gwendolyn summoned her from the crossover, and when she appeared, I was alarmed by how small and frail she looked.

"Good morning," she said, her voice only an echo in the cavernous room.

"Good morning," Frederick said. "How are you?"

"All right," she said, but I didn't believe it. Her face and hands were pale, dark circles showing beneath both her eyes. "A little under the weather."

"With this sort of weather, everyone's under it," Gwendolyn said, and gave her a wink.

Wren tried to laugh but lurched into a deep cough instead. I glanced uneasily at Frederick, but I couldn't see past the glare on his glasses.

"What do you have for us today?" he asked. "Lady Anne, isn't it?"

"That's right."

"Lovely," Gwendolyn said. "When you're ready."

Wren nodded, then squared her feet on the floor, ten paces back from the table. I frowned across the room at her, unsure if it was my imagination or if she was trembling.

Wren: *"I would to God that the inclusive verge*
  Of golden metal that must round my brow
  Were red-hot steel, to sear me to the brain!
  Anointed let me be with deadly venom,
  And die, ere men can say, 'God save the Queen!' "

Her words rang high and clear under the vaulted ceiling, but they wavered, too. She continued bravely, her small body contracting even smaller under the crushing weight of Anne's pain—I didn't doubt that she felt it as intensely as if it were her own.

Wren: *"This was my wish: 'Be thou,' quoth I, 'accursed,*
For making me, so young, so old a widow!
And, when thou wed'st, let sorrow haunt thy bed;
And be thy wife—if any be so mad—
As miserable by the life of thee
As thou hast made me by my dear lord's death!'"

Her voice cracked, the sound too harsh to be an actor's affection. She struck her chest hard with one fist, but whether it
was a wordless expression of her grief or a desperate attempt to
dislodge whatever was choking her, I couldn't tell. Gwendolyn
leaned forward on the table, brow creased with concern. But
before she could speak, Wren's voice came stammering out again,
broken and disjointed. She was bent almost in half, one hand still
on her chest, the other digging violently into her stomach. I froze
in my seat, gripping the sides of my chair so hard my fingertips
went numb.

Wren: *"Lo, ere I can repeat this curse again,*
Even in so short a space, my woman's heart
Grossly grew captive to his honey words
And proved the subject of my own soul's curse,
Which ever since hath kept my eyes from sleep,
For never yet one hour in his bed . . ."

She stopped, faded out, and swayed on the spot. She blinked
ponderously and murmured, "*. . . sleep.*" I knew she was going to
fall, but I was too slow leaping out of my chair to catch her before
she crumpled to the floor.

SCENE 16

I returned to the Castle an hour later, the cold gnawing at my
limbs even as I climbed the stairs. I was still shivering (or maybe
shaking, like Wren, a symptom unrelated to the temperature
outside) when I appeared in the library doorway. James and

Filippa were on the couch, noses buried in their scripts until they heard me come in. Stale shock must have lingered in my expression, because they both jumped to their feet.

Filippa: "Oliver!"

James: "What's wrong?"

I tried to speak, but at first no sound came out, lost in the clamor of immediate memories crowding my brain.

James grabbed both my shoulders. "Oliver, look at me," he said. "What is it?"

"It's Wren," I said. "She just—collapsed—in the middle of her speech."

"What?" He spoke so loudly that I flinched away from him. "What do you mean, collapsed? Is she all right? Where—"

"James, let him talk!" Filippa pulled him back a step and said, more gently but still white-faced, "What happened?"

I told them, in a monologue fraught with awkward stops and pauses, how Wren had keeled over in the rehearsal hall, how after an abortive attempt to revive her, I'd gathered her up off the floor and run full tilt to the infirmary with Gwendolyn and Frederick close on my heels, struggling to keep up.

"She's stable now, that's what they said. She was just opening her eyes when the nurses shoved me out. They wouldn't let me stay." The last piece I said, apologetically, to James.

He opened his mouth, moved it wordlessly, like a man speaking underwater, then said, suddenly, "I have to go."

"No, wait—" I reached for his arm but only brushed his sleeve. He was already out of reach, moving toward the door. He gave me one pained look, trying to communicate something I didn't have time to grasp, before he turned and dashed down the stairs. When he was gone the adrenaline drained out of my body all at once and my knees buckled. Filippa guided me into a chair, but not the nearest one—not Richard's.

"Just sit here awhile and be quiet," she said. "You've done enough."

I grabbed her wrist, squeezed it much too hard, in a strange fit of despair. Wren had lost her grip and slipped so quickly I couldn't catch her, and now James had vanished, too, out the door and into the night, like water trickling through my fingers. I was reluctant to be left alone, more reluctant still to let another friend out of my sight, as though one or the other of us might simply disappear. Filippa sank to the floor beside my chair and rested her head on my knee, saying nothing, simply waiting until I didn't need her there anymore.

After ten minutes or so I let her go, but it wasn't until Alexander and Meredith arrived that I felt like standing up again. I told the story to them, more coherently, and we spent an hour clustered close around the fire, not speaking much, waiting for news.

Me: "Do you think they'll go ahead with the masque?"

Filippa: "They can't cancel it now. People would panic."

Alexander: "Someone else will have to learn her part. No one will even know it was supposed to be her."

Meredith: "I don't know about the rest of you, but I'm sick of all this mystery."

We retreated into silence, watched the fire, and waited.

It was midnight before James came back. Alexander had slumped sideways on the couch and fallen asleep—his face ashen, his breathing shallow—but the girls and I were awake, bleary-eyed and restless. When we heard the front door open we all sat up straighter, listening for footsteps on the stairs.

"James?" I called.

He didn't reply, but a moment later he appeared in the doorway, snow clinging to his hair. Two vivid red spots glowed on his cheeks, as if he'd had his face rouged by a little girl who had no idea what was too much.

"How is she?" I asked, pushing myself off the couch to help him out of his coat.

"They wouldn't let me see her." His teeth chattered, making his words quiver and stall.

"What?" Meredith said. "Why not?"

"I don't know. Other people were in and out and back and forth like it was Grand Central Station, but they made me sit in the hall."

"Who was there?" Filippa asked.

"Holinshed, and all the nurses. They brought a doctor in from Broadwater. The cops were there, too—that guy Colborne and another one, Walton."

Alexander had woken at James's entrance, and I looked straight at him. His mouth made a grim, hard line. "What were they doing there?" he asked, eyes on me.

James fell heavily into a chair. "I don't know. They wouldn't tell me. Just asked if I knew what she'd been up to lately."

"Well, it's exhaustion, isn't it?" Meredith said. "Fatigue. She's had this terrible . . . *experience*, and she comes back here to have everyone skirting around her, and on top of that five hundred lines to learn. It's a miracle the rest of us are on our feet."

I was only half listening. Walton's words bounced around my brain like a stray pinball. *My money's on the cousin.* I sat quietly at the table, folded James's coat, and clutched it in my lap, hoping nobody would pay any attention to me. Keeping Colborne's ongoing investigation secret from the rest of them no longer felt fair, and I doubted I'd be able to maintain my silence if anyone asked me even an unrelated question. Alexander watched me like a hawk, and when I risked lifting my eyes to meet his, he shook his head, just barely.

"What do we do?" Filippa asked, looking from James to Meredith.

"Nothing," Alexander said, before either of them could speak, and I wanted to ask, *Is that your answer to everything?* I wondered how many ways he could use that word, and if my soul would squirm and shrink away every time he said it. "We carry on as usual, or they're going to want to ask all kinds of questions we don't want to answer."

"Who?" Meredith said. "The police?"

"No," he said, swiftly. "The school. They'll pull all of us in for fucking counseling if we get any more jumped up than we are."

"We have every reason to be jumped up," she said. "One of our classmates is *dead*, and another one's just had some kind of nervous breakdown."

"And how do you think that looks?" he asked. "I get that we can't pretend not to be affected by it, but if we all start acting like we killed somebody, they're going to start to wonder whether we did."

"We did not kill him," Meredith said, instantly, angrily. I recognized the reflex, guilt kicking out against an allegation too close to the truth.

"No, of course not," Alexander said, and made every word sting. "We just *let him die*."

At the time, it had seemed such an important distinction. But in the weeks that followed, as we recovered from the temporary madness of that morning, it grew more and more tenuous. Alexander's words snapped the last thread of pretense. We knew by then as well as Richard did that there was no difference at all.

Alexander stood, including everyone in a sweeping glare as he patted his pockets. "I need a smoke. Come find me if there's news." He left the room abruptly, a cigarette already sticking out of his mouth. James watched him go, then slumped and let his head sink into his hands. Filippa perched on the arm of his chair, one hand alighting on the back of his neck, bending low to say something I couldn't hear. As soon as Alexander was out of sight, Meredith shot me a look of mingled indignation and confusion.

"The fuck is wrong with him?" she said.

"I have no idea."

SCENE 17

Three days later I was alone in the Tower, getting ready for the masque and our truncated performance of *Romeo and Juliet*. The costumers had dressed us in a style they described as *"carnevale couture,"* which as far as I could tell adhered to no particular time period but called for a lot of velvet and gold embroidery. I checked my reflection in the mirror, turned from side to side. I looked like a musketeer, but a particularly flamboyant and well-funded one. The half cape they'd given me was slung over one shoulder and tied with a sparkling ribbon in the middle of my chest. I tugged at it self-consciously.

James and the girls had already gone (except Wren, who as far as we knew was still bedridden in the infirmary), and I had only a few minutes to spare. I tried to pull my boots on standing up, but quickly toppled sideways onto my bed and finished the job from there. My mask sat on the nightstand, watching me with hollow eyes. It was a beautiful, enchanted sort of thing—crisscrossed with lines of gold and painted with diamonds in shimmering blue and black and silver. (As they'd been measured and made for us by the art students and wouldn't fit anyone else properly, we'd been told that we could keep them.) I tied the silk ribbon behind my head with fumbling fingers, muttering my first lines under my breath, then took one last look at myself and hurried down the stairs.

Alexander was in the library, but at first I didn't even recognize him and he startled me so badly that I stumbled backward. He looked up from where he was crouched over a fine line of white powder on the coffee table. His keen eyes watched me through two deep holes in a green and black mask, wider and less delicate than mine, tapering to a sharp devilish point at the end of his nose.

"What are you doing?" I asked, more loudly than I meant to.

He twirled the tube of a ballpoint pen between his fingers and said, "Just getting a bit of a buzz before the ball. Would you like to join me?"

"What? No. Are you serious?"

"*I am more serious than my custom; you / Must be so too.*" He bent his head over the table and sniffed hard. I turned away, unwilling to watch, furious with him for some elusive, incoherent reason. I heard him exhale and looked around again. The line was gone, and he sat with his hands on his knees, his head tilted back, eyes half closed.

"So," I said. "How long has this been going on?"

"Are you going to scold me?"

"It would be well warranted," I said. "Do the others know?"

"No." He lifted his head again and watched me with unnerving intensity. "And I expect it to stay that way."

I glanced at the clock, mind whirring. "We're going to be late," I said, shortly.

"Then let's go."

I left the library without waiting to see if he would follow. We were on the trail, halfway to the Hall, when he finally caught up and fell in step beside me.

"Are you going to cold-shoulder me all night?" he asked, so casually that I was sure he wouldn't care if I did.

"I'm considering it, yeah."

He laughed again, but the sound had a false ring to it. I moved impatiently forward. I wanted to get away from him, lose myself in a press of people I didn't know and avoid thinking about it for another few hours. The cape hung heavily on my shoulders, but the cold crept underneath, gnawing at my skin through the thinner layers of my shirt and doublet.

"Oliver," Alexander said, and I ignored him. He could barely keep up with me, lungs working hard to convert the frigid air to something breathable. Snow crunched under our feet—brittle and icy on top; soft, dense powder underneath. "Oliver. Oliver!" The third time he said my name he grabbed me by the arm and wrenched me around to face him. "Are you really going to be a twat about this?"

"Yes."

"Fine. Look." He was still holding my arm, too hard, fingers crushing down through the muscle until they reached bone. I gritted my teeth, almost sure he didn't even realize he was doing it, unwilling to acknowledge the more troubling possibility that he did. "I just need an extra little kick to get me through exams. I'll be clean when you see me in January."

"You'd better be. Have you even thought about what'll happen if Colborne finds that shit in the Castle? He's just looking for a reason to tear this whole thing open again, and if you give him one, I swear I'll kill you."

He stared at me, mask to mask, with a wary, suspicious look I didn't quite recognize. "What's gotten into you?" he said. "You don't sound like yourself."

"Yeah, well, you're not acting like yourself." I tried to drag my arm out of his grip, but his fingers were locked around my bicep. "You're smarter than this. I'm not keeping any more secrets for you. Get off me. Let's go."

I tore my arm free and turned my back on him, plunging forward into deeper snow.

SCENE 18

Alexander shadowed me up three flights of stairs. The ballroom stretched skyward from the fourth floor to the fifth, with a long balcony and a sparkling glass atrium that stabbed up at the moon.

The Christmas masque was traditionally spectacular, and the

winter of 1997 was no exception. The marble floors had been polished to such a high shine that the partygoers might as well have been walking on mirrors. Weeping fig trees, which grew out of deep square planters in each corner, were bedecked with tiny white lights and strands of ribbon and wire that sent flashes of gold darting around the room. The chandeliers—strung on thick chains that stretched from wall to wall ten feet above the balcony—let a warm glow fall across the crowded floor. Tables cluttered with bowls of punch and platters of tiny hors d'oeuvres lined the west wall, and the students who had already arrived clustered around them like moths around a lantern. Everyone was dressed their absolute best, though their faces were hidden—the boys all in white *bauta* masks, the girls in small black *morettas*. (Our masks were overwhelmingly elaborate by comparison, made to stand out in a sea of blank, anonymous faces.) The orchestral students had gathered on one side of the room with their instruments, sheet music propped up on elegant silver music stands. A waltz—airy and beautiful—swelled under the ceiling.

As soon as we entered, heads turned toward us. Alexander went immediately forward into the crowd, a tall imposing figure in black and silver and serpentine green. I lingered at the door, waited for the staring to subside, and then began a slow, inconspicuous walk around the edge of the room. I searched for sparks of color, hoping to spot James, or Filippa, or Meredith. As on Halloween, we didn't know how it would begin. Expectation vibrated in the room like an electrical current. My hand rested on the hilt of the knife in my belt. I'd spent two hours on Tuesday afternoon with Camilo, learning the combat of the play's first duel. Who was Tybalt, and where had he hidden himself? I was ready.

The orchestra fell silent, and almost immediately a voice called out from the balcony, "*The quarrel is between our masters and us their men.*"

Two girls—both third-years, I thought—were leaning out of the balcony on the east wall, plain silver half masks hiding their eyes, their hair drawn tightly back from their faces. They were dressed as boys, in breeches, boots, and doublets.

"*'Tis all one*," the second one said. "*I will show myself a tyrant: when I have fought with the men, I will be civil with the maids, and cut off their heads.*"

"*The heads of the maids?*"

"*Ay, the heads of the maids, or their maidenheads; take it in what sense thou wilt.*"

They affected bawdy, masculine laughter, which was enthusiastically rejoined by the onlookers below. I watched and wondered how best to enter to stop their dispute. But as Abraham and Balthasar (also third-year girls) entered on the ballroom floor, Gregory and Sampson swung their legs over the balcony wall and began to climb down the nearest column, fingers gripping tightly in the greenery wound around it. As soon as they touched the floor, one of them whistled, and the two Montague servants turned. The biting of thumbs—accompanied by more indulgent laughter—turned quickly to an argument.

Gregory: "*Do you quarrel, sir?*"

Abraham: "*Quarrel, sir! No, sir.*"

Sampson: "*If you do, sir, I am for you: I serve as good a man as you.*"

Abraham: "*No better.*"

Sampson: "*Yes, better, sir.*"

Abraham: "*You lie!*"

They dissolved into a clumsy four-way duel. The audience (pushed back now to the edges of the room) watched in keen delight, laughing and cheering their favorites. I waited until I felt the fight was ripe to be interrupted, then ran forward, drew my own dagger, and drove the girls apart. "*Part, fools!*" I said. "*Put up your swords; you know not what you do.*"

They fell back, panting hard, but the next voice came ringing from the opposite end of the room. Tybalt.

"What, art thou drawn among these heartless hinds? / Turn thee, Benvolio, look upon thy death."

I wheeled around. The crowd had parted around Colin, who stood staring at me through the eyes of a black and red mask, the sides cut sharply back from his cheekbones, angular and reptilian, like dragons' wings.

Me: *"I do but keep the peace: put up thy sword,*
 Or manage it to part these men with me."

Colin: *"What, drawn, and talk of peace! I hate the word,*
 As I hate hell, all Montagues, and thee:
 Have at thee, coward!"

Colin charged at me, and we crashed together like a pair of gamecocks. We lunged and parried until the four girls threw themselves into the fray, jeered on by the hundreds of masked students watching. I took an elbow to the chin and fell heavily to the floor on my back. Colin was on top of me in an instant, reaching for my throat, but I knew Escalus would arrive in time to forestall my strangulation. He—or, rather, she—appeared at the top of the balcony stairs in staggering royal splendor.

"Rebellious subjects, enemies to peace, / Profaners of this neighbor-stainèd steel— / Will they not hear?"

On the contrary, we all ceased squabbling at once. Colin let go of me, and I rolled onto my knees, gazing up at Meredith in mute amazement. She looked no less a prince than one of us boys would have—rich red hair tied back in a long braid, shapely legs hidden in high leather boots, face shielded by a white mask that shimmered as if it had been dipped in stardust. A floor-length cape swept the stairs behind her as she descended.

Meredith: *"What ho! you men, you beasts,*
 That quench the fire of your pernicious rage
 With purple fountains issuing from your veins,
 On pain of torture, from those bloody hands
 Throw your mistemper'd weapons to the ground
 And hear the sentence of your movèd prince!"

We obediently threw our daggers down.

Meredith: *"Three civil brawls, bred of an airy word,*
   Have thrice disturb'd the quiet of our streets,
   And made Verona's ancient citizens
   Cast by their grave beseeming ornaments,
   To wield old partisans, in hands as old,
   Canker'd with peace, to part your canker'd hate."

She walked slowly between us, head held high. Colin stepped back and bowed. I and the other girls had each sunk to one knee. Meredith looked down at me and lifted my chin with one gloved hand. *"If ever you disturb our streets again, / Your lives shall pay the forfeit of the peace."* She turned on her heel, the hem of her cape snapping across my face. *"For this time, all the rest depart away."*

The girls and Colin bent to gather their discarded weapons and lost bits of costume. But the prince was impatient.

"Once more, on pain of death, all men depart!"

We scattered from the center of the room, which erupted in applause as Meredith ascended the stairs to the balcony again. I hovered at the edge of the crowd, watching her feet on the steps until she was gone, then turned to the nearest reveler—a boy, I didn't know who, only his brown eyes visible through the holes in his mask—and said, *"O, where is Romeo?"* To another spectator, *"Saw you him today? / Right glad I am he was not at this fray."*

At exactly that moment, Romeo emerged from a door on the east wall, clad all in blue and silver, his mask gently curving back toward his temples. He seemed almost a mythical figure, Ganymede, caught beautifully between man and boy. I knew it would be James, had guessed as much, but his appearance was no less affecting.

"See, where he comes," I said, to the girl nearest me, in a softer tone. That strange possessive pride washed over me again. Everyone in the room was watching James—how could they not?—but I was the only one who really knew him, every inch. *"So please you, step aside: / I'll know his grievance or be much denied. / Good morrow, cousin!"*

James looked up, looked right at me. He seemed surprised to

see me standing there, though I didn't know for the life of me why he should be. Was I not always his right-hand man, his lieutenant? Banquo or Benvolio or Oliver—little difference.

We argued lightly about his unrequited love, a game emerging wherein I blocked his way each time he tried to leave, attempted to evade my questions. He was content to play along until at last he said, more firmly, *"Farewell, my coz."*

"Soft!" I said. *"I will go along; / An if you leave me so, you do me wrong."*

"Tut, I have lost myself; I am not here; / This is not Romeo, he's some other where."

He turned to go, and I darted around to bar his path again. My desire to keep him there had, at some point, transcended the alignment of an actor's motivation and his character's. I desperately wanted him to stay, seized by the nonsensical idea that if he left, I would lose him, irretrievably. *"Tell me in sadness, who is that you love,"* I said, searching the parts of his face I could see for a flicker of reciprocal feeling.

James: *"A sick man in sadness makes his will:*
   A word ill urged to one that is so ill!
   In sadness, cousin, I do love a woman."

For a moment, I forgot which line of mine followed. We stared at each other, and the crowd faded around us into indistinct shadow and set dressing. With a jolt I remembered my words, but not quite the right ones.

"Be ruled by me," I said, a few lines too soon. *"Forget to think of her."*

James blinked rapidly behind his mask, but then he stepped back, detached, and carried on. I stood still and watched him pace around: his words, his footsteps, his gestures—everything restless.

A servant entered with news of the Capulets' upcoming feast. We gossiped, planned, and plotted, until a third masker finally entered: Alexander.

He spoke his first line from where he was sitting on the edge of the punch table, his arms draped around the two nearest audience members—one of whom was giggling uncontrollably behind her mask, while the other shrank away from him, obviously terrified.

"*Nay, gentle Romeo, we must have you dance.*"

He slid off the table so smoothly that he might have been made of liquid and approached with his loping feline gait. He nudged me out of his way, walked around James in a small circle, pausing to eye him from every intriguing angle. They volleyed words and quips between them, easy and inconsequential until James said, "*Is love a tender thing? It is too rough, / Too rude, too boisterous, and it pricks like thorn.*"

Alexander released a purring laugh and seized James by the front of his doublet.

Alexander: "*If love be rough with you, be rough with love!*
    Prick love for pricking, and you beat love down.
    Give me a case to put my visage in:
    A visor for a visor."

The foreheads of their masks knocked together, Alexander holding James so tightly I heard him grunt in pain. I started toward them, but as soon as I moved, Alexander shoved him backward, right into my arms.

Alexander: "*What care I*
    What curious eye doth quote deformities?
    Here are the beetle brows shall blush for me."

I pushed James upright again and said, "*Come, knock and enter; and no sooner in / But every man betake him to his legs.*"

Alexander: "*Come, we burn daylight, ho!*"

James: "*Nay, that's not so.*"

Alexander (impatiently):   "*I mean, sir, in delay,*
    We waste our lights in vain, like lamps by day.
    Take our good meaning, for our judgment sits
    Five times in that ere once in our five wits."

James: *"And we mean well in going to this masque;*
      But 'tis no wit to go."
Alexander: *"Why, may one ask?"*
James: *"I dream'd a dream tonight."*
Alexander: *"And so did I."*
James: *"Well, what was yours?"*
Alexander: *"That dreamers often lie."*
James: *"In bed asleep, while they do dream things true."*
Alexander: *"O, then I see Queen Mab hath been with you!"*

I retreated two steps to watch the peculiar monologue unfold. Alexander's Mercutio was razor-edged, unbalanced, barely sane. His sharp incisors flashed in the light when he smiled, his mask glittering mischievously as he danced around, first toying with one spectator, then another. His voice and movement both grew more sensual and more savage, until he completely lost control and lunged at me. I staggered backward but not fast enough—he grabbed me by the hair, bent my head back against his shoulder, snarling in my ear.

Alexander: *"This is the hag, when maids lie on their backs,*
      That presses them and learns them first to bear,
      Making them women of good carriage:
      This is she—!"

I strained against his hold but his strength was iron, over-wrought, at odds with the delicacy of one fingertip tracing the embroidery on my chest. James, who had been watching, frozen stiff, fought off his paralysis and pulled Alexander off me. *"Peace, peace, Mercutio, peace!"* He took Alexander's face in his hands. *"Thou talk'st of nothing."*

Alexander's distracted eyes latched onto James's, and he spoke more slowly.

Alexander: *"True, I talk of dreams,*
      Which are the children of an idle brain,
      Begot of nothing but vain fantasy,

Which is as thin of substance as the air
And more inconstant than the wind."

When it was my turn to speak again I spoke carefully, wondering if Alexander was truly, now, safe. Our conversation from earlier in the evening was too close, too recent to ignore, like a fresh smarting scratch on my skin.

Me: *"This wind you talk of blows us from ourselves;*
　　Supper is done, and we shall come too late."

James turned his face skyward, squinting up at the pyramid of glass that seemed so distant, searching in the wash of light from the chandeliers for the secret, far-off glimmer of a star. I thought of the night of the party, when he and I had stood together in the garden, peering up at the heavens through a jagged hole in the treetops. Our last isolated, innocent moment; the stillness that precedes the blows and billows of a storm.

James: *"I fear, too early: for my mind misgives*
　　Some consequence yet hanging in the stars
　　Shall bitterly begin his fearful date
　　With this night's revels and expire the term
　　Of a despisèd life closed in my breast
　　By some vile forfeit of untimely death."

He paused, gazing upward in soft surprise, sadness like drops of blue in both his eyes. Then he sighed and, smiling, shook his head.

James: *"But He that hath the steerage of my course*
　　Direct my sails! On, lusty gentlemen."

I had almost forgotten where we were—who we were, even—but then the orchestra struck up again and reality came rushing back. Another soaring waltz filled the atrium and breathed life into the audience that had gone silent during the previous scene. The Capulets' ball was suddenly in full swing.

Alexander grabbed the nearest girl and dragged her forcefully into a dance. The other players appeared from the makeshift wings and did the same, choosing partners at random, pushing other par-

tygoers together. Soon the room was a whirl of movement, surprisingly graceful considering the number of couples. I found a partner
at my elbow—indistinguishable from all the other girls except for
a black ribbon tied around her throat—and bowed to her before
we began to dance. As we turned and revolved and changed places,
my attention was constantly elsewhere. Filippa appeared in the
corner of my eye, her mask black, silver, purple—she, too, was
dressed as male, dancing with another girl, and I wondered if she
might be Paris. I turned and lost sight of her again. I looked for
James, looked for Meredith, but could not find them, either one.

The song persisted (in my opinion) overlong. When it ended,
I bowed again, hastily, and ducked out of the room, making a
beeline for the back stairs to the balcony. It was quiet there, and
deeply dark. A few couples had sought that secrecy and were
maskless now, joined at the lips, pressed close against the walls.
The music had begun again but slower. The lights dimmed,
burned blue, except for one bright white circle where James
stood alone. When the light struck him the surrounding dancers
drew back, fell silent.

James: *"What lady's that which doth enrich the hand*
    Of yonder knight?"

The audience turned to see what he was staring at. And there,
faint and ephemeral as a ghost, was Wren. A blue and white
mask framed her eyes, but she was unmistakably herself. My fingers curled around the edge of the balustrade; I leaned as far
forward as I could without falling.

James: *"Did my heart love till now? Forswear it, sight!*
    For I ne'er saw true beauty till this night."

The music rose again. Wren and her borrowed partner turned
slowly on the spot, and in pantomime bade farewell. James's feet
carried him closer, his eyes fixed on her as if he were afraid that she
would simply disappear if he lost sight of her. When he was close
enough, he caught her hand, and she turned to see who had
touched her.

James: *"If I profane with my unworthiest hand*
    This holy shrine, the gentle sin is this:
    My lips, two blushing pilgrims, ready stand
    To smooth that rough touch with a tender kiss."

He lowered his head and kissed her palm. Her breath ruffled his hair when she spoke.

Wren: *"Good pilgrim, you do wrong your hand too much,*
    Which mannerly devotion shows in this;
    For saints have hands that pilgrims' hands do touch,
    And palm to palm is holy palmers' kiss."

Partway through her speech, they eased into motion together, palm to palm, revolving slowly. They paused, changed hands, and stepped together in the opposite direction.

James: *"Have not saints lips, and holy palmers too?"*

Wren: *"Ay, pilgrim, lips that they must use in prayer."*

James: *"O, then, dear saint, let lips do what hands do;*
    They pray, grant thou, lest faith turn to despair."

Wren: *"Saints do not move, though grant for prayers' sake."*

James: *"Then move not, while my prayer's effect I take."*

They were motionless. James's finger brushed her cheek; he turned her face up toward his and kissed her, so softly that she might not have even felt it.

James: *"Thus from my lips, by thine, my sin is purged."*

Wren: *"Then have my lips the sin that they have took."*

James: *"Sin from thy lips? O trespass sweetly urged!*
    Give me my sin again."

He kissed her once more, this time long and lingering. My mask was hot and sticky on my face, my stomach twisted inside out and aching like an open wound. I leaned heavily on the balustrade, trembling under the weight of parallel truths that I had, until then, been able to ignore: James was in love with Wren, and I was blindly, savagely jealous.

ACT IV

PROLOGUE

"It's shorter than I remember," I tell Colborne, as we stand looking down the dock toward the water. "Back then it felt like it went on for miles." We've wandered through the woods to the south side of the lake, talking quietly. Colborne listens with unfailing patience, weighing and evaluating every word. I turn to him and ask, "Are the kids even allowed down here anymore?"

"We can't exactly stop them, but once they realize it's just a dock and there's nothing to see, they lose interest. We have more of a problem with people stealing stuff that used to be yours."

This has never occurred to me, and I stare at him. "Like what?"

He shrugs. "Old books, costume pieces, the photo of your class in the hall behind the theatre. We got that one back, but not before someone scratched your face out." He sees the confusion in my expression and adds, "It's not all bad. I still get letters trying to convince me that you're innocent."

"Yeah," I say. "I get those, too."

"Are you convinced yet?"

"No. I know better."

I walk down the dock and Colborne follows, one step behind. I know I owe him a new ending for our old story, but I find it unexpectedly difficult to continue. Up until Christmas, we could pretend that we were mostly all right—or that we would be, someday.

I stop at the end, looking down into the water. I've aged well, one might say. My hair is still dark, my eyes still clear bright blue, my body firmer and stronger than it was before prison. I need glasses now to read, but besides that and a few extra scars, I haven't changed much. I feel older than thirty-one.

How old is Colborne now? I don't ask, but I could. Our

relationship is not inhibited by expectations of politeness. We stand with our toes peeking over the edge of the dock, not speaking. The green smell of the water is so familiar that I feel a soft tug at the back of my throat.

"We didn't come down here as much when it was cold out," I say, without prompting. "Between Thanksgiving and Christmas, we mostly kept to the Castle and sat around the fire, scratching out speeches and scansion. It almost felt normal, except that empty chair. I don't think I ever saw anyone sit in it after he died. We were a bit superstitious, I guess—plays full of witches and ghosts will do that to you."

Colborne nods vaguely. Then his expression changes, shifts, brow furrowing. "Do you blame Shakespeare for any of it?"

The question is so unlikely, so nonsensical coming from such a sensible man, that I can't suppress a smile. "I blame him for all of it," I say.

He mimics my smile, though his is tentative, unsure of where the humor really is. "Why's that?"

"It's hard to put into words." I pause, waste a minute trying to collect my thoughts, then proceed without having collected anything at all. "We spent four years—and most of us years before that—*immersed* in Shakespeare. Submerged. Here we could indulge our collective obsession. We spoke it as a second language, conversed in poetry, and lost touch with reality, a little." I reconsider. "Well, that's misleading. Shakespeare is real, but his characters live in a world of real extremes. They swing from ecstasy to anguish, love to hate, wonder to terror. It's not melodrama, though, they're not exaggerating. Every moment is crucial." I glance sideways at him, unsure if I'm making any sense. He's still wearing that uncertain half smile, but he nods, so I continue. "A good Shakespearean actor—a good actor of any stripe, really—doesn't just *say* words, he *feels* them. We felt all the passions of the characters we played as if they were our own. But a character's emotions don't cancel out the actor's—instead you feel both at once. Imagine having all your own thoughts and feelings tangled up with all the thoughts and feelings of a whole other person. It can be hard, sometimes, to sort out which is which."

I slow down, come to a stop, frustrated by my own inability to express myself (a frustration exacerbated by the fact that, after ten years, I still think of myself as an actor). Colborne watches me with keen, curious eyes. I wet my lips with my tongue and proceed more carefully.

"Our sheer capacity for feeling got to be so unwieldy that we staggered under it, like Atlas with the weight of the world." I sigh, and the freshness of the air derails me. How long will it take, I wonder, for me to get used to it again? My chest aches, and maybe it's the unfamiliar purity of the air, but maybe not. "The thing about Shakespeare is, he's so eloquent . . . He speaks the unspeakable. He turns grief and triumph and rapture and rage into words, into something we can understand. He renders the whole mystery of humanity comprehensible." I stop. Shrug. "You can justify anything if you do it poetically enough."

Colborne lowers his eyes, looks down into the white glare of the sun on the water. "Do you think Richard would agree?"

"I think Richard was under Shakespeare's spell as much as the rest of us."

Colborne accepts this without protest. "You know, it's strange," he says. "Every now and then I have to remind myself that I never actually knew him."

"You would have loved or hated him."

"What makes you say that?"

"That's how he was."

"What about you? Did you love him or hate him?"

"Usually both at once."

"Is this what you mean about feeling everything twice?"

"Ah," I say. "You see, you do understand me."

The quiet that follows is comfortable, at least for me. I forget why we're there for a moment and watch as a leaf breaks loose from a tree and comes twirling down on the breeze to land on the water. Rings ripple out toward the edges of the lake but disappear before they ever get there. I can almost see the seven of us running along the bank through the trees, tearing our clothes off, racing to the water, ready to fall in all together. Third year, the year of the comedy. Light and delightful and distant. Days we can't have back.

"Well," Colborne says, when he's waited long enough for me to speak. "What's next?"

"Christmas." I turn away, toward the forest. The Castle is close now, the Tower soaring up out of the trees, its long shadow falling over the ramshackle boathouse. "That's when everything went wrong."

"How did it start?" he asks.

"It had already started."

"Then what changed?"

"We were separated," I say. "James went to California, Meredith to New York, Alexander to Philadelphia, Wren to London, Filippa . . . who knows where. I went back to Ohio. Being trapped together in the Castle with our guilt and Richard's ghost, it was terrible in a way. But being divided from each other, flung to every corner of the world to face it on our own—that was worse."

"So what happened?" he asks.

"We cracked up," I say, but the phrase feels wrong. It was not so simple, or so clean, as a piece of fractured glass. "But we didn't really shatter until we were all back together again."

SCENE 1

Christmas in Ohio was disastrous.

I survived the four preceding days by maintaining a state of mild intoxication and conversing only when required. Christmas Eve passed uneventfully, but Christmas dinner (the thrilling sequel to Thanksgiving dinner a month before) ended in an uproar when Caroline left the table for a suspiciously long time and my father caught her in the bathroom, flushing most of her food down the toilet. Three hours later she and my parents were shouting at one another in the dining room. I had fled the scene and was already packing my suitcase, which gaped open in the middle of my unmade bed. I balled up half a dozen scarves and about as many socks and flung them in.

"Oliver!" Leah blocked the doorway, sobbing at me, as she'd been doing for the last ten minutes. "You can't leave now!"

"I have to." I swept an armful of books off my desk and dumped them on top of the scarves. "I can't take this. I need to get out of here."

My father's voice thundered from the floor below, and Leah whimpered.

"You should get out, too." I nudged her out of the way and grabbed my coat off the hook on the back of the door. "Go to a friend's house or something."

"Oliver!" she wailed, and I turned away, unable to look at her when her face was screwed up like an infant's, slick and shining with tears.

I threw a pile of clothes—dirty or clean, I had no idea and it didn't matter—into the suitcase and slammed it closed. The zipper skated easily around the edge because I'd only packed half of what I'd come home with. Downstairs, my mother and Caroline were both screaming at the same time.

I pulled my coat on and yanked the suitcase off the bed, nearly crushing my sister's foot. "C'mon, Leah," I said. "You've gotta let me go."

"You're just going to leave me?"

I clenched my teeth against a surge of guilt coming up like bile from the pit of my stomach. "I'm sorry," I said, then pushed past her through the door.

"Oliver!" she yelled, hanging over the banister as I rushed down the stairs. "Where are you going?"

I didn't answer. I didn't know.

I dragged my suitcase down a driveway dusted with powdered-sugar snow and waited on the curb for the cab I'd called before packing my bag, wondering what on earth to do next. Dellecher's campus was closed for Christmas. I couldn't afford a hotel room in Broadwater or a plane ticket to California. Philadelphia wasn't far, but I was residually angry with Alexander and didn't want to see him. Filippa would have been my best option, but I had no idea where she was or how to get in touch. I had the cab drop me at the bus station, where I called Meredith from a pay phone, explained what had happened, and asked if her Thanksgiving offer still stood.

There was no bus Christmas night, so I had six hours to sit outside the station, shivering and second-guessing my decision. By morning I was so cold I didn't care how bad an idea it was and immediately bought a ticket to Port Authority. I slept almost the whole way, with my face crushed against the grimy window. When we arrived, I called again, and she gave me an address on the Upper East Side.

Her parents, eldest brother, and sister-in-law were once again in Canada. Even with me and her and Caleb (the middle sibling, unattached, going kicking and screaming into his thirties), the apartment felt empty and untouched, like a set from a television show. The furniture was expensive, stylish, and uncomfortable, the décor done in blinding white and dull slate gray. In the living room the *Architectural Digest* aesthetic was blighted by evidence of occupation: a dog-eared copy of *Bonfire of the Vanities*, half-drunk bottles of wine, an Armani overcoat tossed carelessly over one arm of the couch. The only indication that a holiday had come and gone was a menorah with four half-melted candles sitting crookedly in the window. ("We suck at being Jewish," Meredith explained.)

Her room was smaller than I expected, but a high sloped ceiling kept it from feeling cramped. Compared to her room in the Castle it was ferociously tidy, her clothes tucked away in closets and drawers, books neatly arranged by subject on their shelves. What first caught my eye was the vanity table. It was cluttered with black tufted brushes, sleek tubes of lipstick and mascara, but so many photos had been stuck in the frame that the mirror itself was hardly usable. Though one picture of her and her brothers (they were striking children, all auburn hair and green eyes, sitting three in a row like Russian nesting dolls on the bumper of a black Mercedes) was wedged in the topmost corner, the rest were of *us*. Wren and Richard, faces painted black and white for our second-year mime class. Alexander in the gallery, pretending to share a cigarette with Homer. Meredith and Filippa in cutoff shorts and bikini tops, sprawled in the shallow water on the north shore of the lake as if they'd fallen from the sky and landed there. James, smiling but not at the camera, one hand shyly raised to push the lens away, the other arm hooked around my neck. Me, unaware that we were being photographed, laughing into the distance, a bright autumn leaf caught in my hair.

I stood staring at the wistful collage she'd created until I felt a lump form in my throat. When I glanced over my shoulder at the pristine impersonality of the rest of the room—the smooth flat bedspread, the bare hardwood floor—it occurred to me at last how alone she was. Unable (as always) to find the words to express my own belated understanding, I said nothing.

For three days Meredith and I lounged around—reading, talking, not touching—as Caleb came and went, indifferent to my presence, rarely sober, always on the phone with someone. Like his sister he was almost unfairly good-looking, their shared features strangely (though not unpleasantly) delicate and feminine in him. He had a quick smile, but his eyes were distant, as though his mind was perpetually preoccupied with important

business, elsewhere. He did promise, though it made little difference to us, an extravagant New Year's party. Caleb, for all his
shortcomings, was a man of his word.

By nine thirty on December 31, the apartment was packed
with people in glamorous party attire. I knew none of them,
Meredith only a handful, Caleb a quarter of them at best. By
eleven everyone was drunk, including me and Meredith, but
when people started snorting lines of coke off the kitchen
counter, we slipped out, unnoticed, with two bottles of Laurent-
Perrier.

Times Square, like the apartment, was teeming with people,
and Meredith clung to my arm to keep from being swept away
down the sidewalk by the crowd. We laughed and stumbled and
drank pink champagne straight from the bottle until it was con-
fiscated by an exasperated police officer. Snow fell like confetti
on our heads and shoulders and stuck in Meredith's eyelashes.
She glimmered in the night like a precious stone—vivid and
flawless. I drunkenly told her as much, and at midnight we kissed
on a Manhattan street corner, one of a million couples all kissing
at the same time.

We wandered the city until the champagne wore off and the
cold set in, then clumsily made our way back to the apartment.
All was dark and quiet, the last partygoers sprawled on the living
room furniture, asleep or too high to move. We crept to Meredith's room, stripped off our wet layers, and huddled under the
blankets on her bed. The search for warmth turned slowly but
predictably to more kissing, then gradual undressing, cautious
touches, and eventually, inevitably, sex. Afterward I waited for
the guilt to come, the compulsion to beg Richard's phantom for
forgiveness. But for once, when I most expected to open my eyes
and find him standing over me, he declined to show himself.
Instead the silhouette I saw on the wall belonged, inexplicably,
to James—who had no business in that room, in my thoughts, at
that moment. Anger rushed through me, but before it went to

my head Meredith moved, nestled closer, interrupted the illusion. I exhaled, relieved to think she'd woken me from some disturbed half dream. I let my fingertips trail from the tip of her shoulder to the smooth inward curve of her waist, comforted by how soft and feminine she was. Her head rested on my chest, and I wondered if she felt the fleeting stillness of my fitful, troubled soul.

The next three days passed in much the same way. By night we drank just barely too much, tolerated Caleb as long as we could, then tumbled into bed together. By day we roamed New York, wasted time and the Dardennes' money in bookstores and theatres and cafés, talking about life after Dellecher, realizing at last that it was only a few months away. We'd had so much else on our minds.

"They'll have scouts down for the spring production," Meredith said one afternoon as we wandered away from the Strand, empty-handed only because we'd been there once already. "And then we'll have showcase in May. I haven't even thought about what I'll read." She nudged me with her elbow. "We ought to do a scene together. We could be . . . Oh, I don't know. Margaret and Suffolk." She tossed her head and said, airily, "Would you carry my heart like a jewel in a box?"

"I dunno. Would you carry my head around in a basket if I got decapitated by pirates?"

She looked at me like I was crazy, but then—to my relief and my delight—she laughed, the sound wild and lovely, like a tiger lily bursting open. When her mirth had subsided she glanced around at the other people on the sidewalk, moving in a steady stream toward Union Square. "How odd it'll be," she said, more soberly, "to have everyone here in the city."

"It'll be fun," I told her, wondering if we'd all stay with her the week of showcase, sleep on the floor like it was a middle school slumber party. "Like a test run. This time next year we'll all probably be living here."

"You think so?"

"Well, we've got to go somewhere there's Shakespeare. Will you stay in the apartment?"

"God, no. I need to get out of there."

"Then I guess you'll have to move into some hovel in Queens with the rest of us." I leaned toward her until our shoulders bumped together and she gave me a tentative smile.

"We're all going to live on top of each other, like it's the Castle all over again?"

"I don't see why not."

The smile slipped and she shook her head. "It won't be the same."

I looped one arm around her neck, pulled her close, and kissed her temple. I felt her sigh, and when she breathed her sadness out, I breathed it in. No, it wouldn't be the same. I couldn't argue with that.

On Sunday evening we flew back to O'Hare, first class—Caleb's treat. We were the first to arrive at the Castle, as classes didn't resume until Wednesday. (I was grateful for this. Whatever Meredith and I were doing—we hadn't actually talked about it since our unfortunate "date" at the Bore's Head—I wasn't ready to discuss it with anyone else.) I tore the LaGuardia tag off my suitcase and left it at the foot of my bed. For a moment I paused, staring into James's corner of the room. What with family histrionics and the enormous distraction of Meredith, I'd managed to push him, for a week or two, out of my mind. I'd told myself that the jealous dismay that seized me during the Christmas masque was merely a moment of insanity, a side effect of manipulative theatre magic. But as I stood there in the Tower with his shadow in the room, I felt it come creeping slowly back again.

I went unsteadily down the stairs and spent one more night with Meredith—the only cure I could think of.

SCENE 2

Second-semester auditions were posted on the call-board first thing Wednesday morning.

All fourth-years, second-years, and invited third-years,
please prepare a two-minute monologue for

KING LEAR

The audition and rehearsal schedules were posted below. Alexander would audition first, unobserved. Then he'd watch Wren's audition, she'd watch mine, I'd watch Filippa's, she'd watch James's, and he'd watch Meredith's.

We spent the next week scrambling to prepare new audition pieces, universally surprised by the choice of production. *Lear* had never in fifty years been attempted at Dellecher, likely because (as Alexander pointed out) having a tender twentysomething in the title role would be entirely absurd. How Frederick and Gwendolyn intended to address this problem, we couldn't guess.

At eight on the evening of the auditions, I sat alone in our usual booth at the Bore's Head, attracting dirty looks from larger parties waiting for a table. Meredith had just left me to prepare for her own reading, and Filippa, I guessed, would be arriving shortly. I'd watched her audition—an excellent take on Tamora—and was eager to discuss casting with somebody else who had already read. (Alexander and Wren were nowhere to be found.) I finished my beer, but I didn't leave the table, certain it would be stolen if I got up to go to the bar.

Fortunately, Filippa breezed in from outside after only five minutes or so. Her hair was windswept and tangled, cheeks glowing pink from the sting of the cold gusts blowing snow down the street. As she sat down I said, "Drink?"

"God, yes. Something warm."

I slid out of the booth as she piled her outer layers—scarf, hat, gloves, coat—in the corner. I returned from the bar with two mugs of hot cider, and Filippa raised hers in a silent toast before gulping down a mouthful.

"I think hell may have frozen over," I said, brushing bits of snow that had fallen from her hat and scarf off the bench beside me.

"I'll believe that when I see the cast list." She wiped a sticky drop of cider from her lips. "What do you think they'll do?"

"If I had to guess? No clue about Lear, but obviously Wren will be Cordelia. You and Meredith will be Regan and Goneril. I'll probably be Albany, James'll be Edgar, and Alexander'll be Edmund."

"I wouldn't be too sure about that last bit."

"Why not?"

She shifted in her seat and glanced at the next booth, where a trio of dancers sat sipping long-stemmed glasses of white wine. When she leaned low over the table I instinctively mimicked her. We were so close that a strand of her hair tickled my forehead.

"So, I just watched James's audition," she said.

"What did he read?" I asked. "He wouldn't tell me."

"Richard Plantagenet, *Two Henry Six*. *And force perforce I'll make him yield the crown / Whose bookish rule hath pulled fair England down.*"

"Really? That speech is so . . . I don't know, aggressive. Doesn't really seem his style."

"Yeah. As soon as he got to *A day will come when York shall claim his own*, it was like he was a different person all of a sudden." She shook her head slowly. "You should have seen it, Oliver. He scared me, honestly."

I was mute for a moment, then shrugged. "Good for him."

She gave me a look so deeply skeptical that I almost laughed.

"Pip, I mean it," I said. "Good for him. He said at the beginning of the year he was tired of playing a type, and he's always had that kind of range, he's just never had a chance to show it because those sorts of roles were always going to go to Richard. Why bother? He's got a chance now to do something new."

She sighed. "You're probably right. God knows I'd like a chance to do something new."

"Maybe they'll change it up this time around. It's a different dynamic." I nodded vaguely toward the end of the table, where, six weeks before, Richard might have been sitting. He had become a perpetual blind spot in my—and, I suspected, the others'—peripheral vision.

"Well, you're not wrong," Filippa said, looking away, toward the door, at nothing in particular. "At any rate, I'll be surprised if they don't cast James as Edmund."

I didn't set much stock by her prediction (the more fool I). Our conversation changed course, and two hours passed without incident before Meredith came in from outside, bringing a little whirl of snow in with her. "The list is up and you'll never believe it," she said, slapping the paper down on the table. I didn't have time to ask where everyone else was.

Filippa and I nearly cracked heads trying to see the list at the same time; she choked and spluttered cider across the booth. "*Frederick* is going to play Lear?"

"*Camilo* is Albany?" I said. "What the hell?"

"That's not all," Meredith said, struggling to unwind her scarf. "Read the whole thing, it's utterly insane."

We bent our heads again, more cautiously. Frederick and Camilo were listed first, followed by the fourth-years, below that the third-years, and finally the second-years.

The cast for *King Lear* is as follows:

KING LEAR	—	Frederick Teasdale
ALBANY	—	Camilo Varela
CORDELIA	—	Wren Stirling
REGAN	—	Filippa Kosta
GONERIL	—	Meredith Dardenne
EDMUND	—	James Farrow
EDGAR	—	Oliver Marks
FOOL	—	Alexander Vass
CORNWALL	—	Colin Hyland

I stopped reading after Colin's name and gaped up at Meredith. "What on earth have they done?"

"Fuck knows," she said, still fiddling with the scarf, which was tangled in her hair. I instinctively lifted my hand to reach over and help, but my wrist smacked against the underside of the table and I thought better of it. "It's like they mixed all the boys around and then decided that moving the girls was too much effort."

Filippa: "Alexander's going to be thrilled."

Me: "For what it's worth, *I'm* thrilled."

Meredith: "Honestly, Oliver, you act like they've done you a favor. It's not as if you haven't earned it."

Her face disappeared as she gave up on untangling the scarf and pulled it off over her head. Filippa looked at me and raised her eyebrows. I could have blamed the cider for the warm, melting sensation in my stomach, but my mug had long been empty.

Meredith resurfaced and tossed the offending scarf on top of Filippa's things. "Is it just you two?" she said.

"It was just me for a while," I said. "Where is everyone?"

"Wren went back to the Castle after her audition and went straight to bed," Meredith said. "Don't think she wants to risk another 'episode.'" This was what we had taken to calling Wren's fainting spell during her Lady Anne speech. What exactly was wrong with her, nobody seemed to be able to say. "Emotional exhaustion" was how the Broadwater doctor described it, but Alexander's diagnosis of "guilt complex" seemed more likely.

"What about James?" Filippa asked.

"He sat through my audition, but he was in an absolute state the whole time," Meredith said. "Moody. You know." (This directed at me, though I did not, in fact, know anything of the sort.) "I asked if he was coming to the bar and he said no, he wanted to go for a walk."

Filippa's eyebrows climbed higher—so high they nearly disappeared into her hair. "In this weather?"

"That's what I said. And he said he wanted to clear his head and that he didn't much care what the cast list said; it would say the same thing in the morning."

I glanced from Meredith to Filippa and said, slowly, "Okay. Where does that leave Alexander?"

Filippa: "Probably he's with Colin."

Me: "But—how did you know?"

Meredith: "It's not like it's a secret."

Me: "He said it was!"

Filippa: "Please. The only person who thinks it's a secret is Colin."

I shook my head, glanced around the crowded barroom.

Me: "Why do we even pretend anything is private around here?"

Meredith: "Welcome to art school. It's like Gwendolyn always says: 'When you enter the theatre, there are three things you must leave at the door: dignity, modesty, and personal space.'"

Filippa: "I thought it was dignity, modesty, and personal pride."

Me: "She told me dignity, modesty, and self-doubt."

All three of us were silent for a moment before Filippa said, "Well, this explains a lot."

"Do you suppose she has three different things for every student she talks to?" I asked.

"Probably," Meredith said. "I'm just surprised she thought personal space was my biggest issue."

"Maybe she wanted to prepare you to get ogled and groped and borderline sexually assaulted in every play we put on," Filippa said.

"Ha ha, I'm an object, very funny." Meredith rolled her eyes. "I swear, I should have just been a stripper."

Filippa smirked into her mug and said, "Everyone needs a backup plan."

"Yeah," Meredith said. "You could always get a sex change, become a boy on a permanent basis and start calling yourself 'Philip.'"

They scowled at each other, and in an effort to lighten the mood I said, "I guess my other option is an existential crisis."

"Not so bad," Filippa said. "You can just play Hamlet."

We drank six more ciders between the three of us, waiting in vain for one of the others to make an appearance. Never before had there been so little interest in a new cast list. Even as we drank and talked and laughed halfheartedly, it was impossible to ignore the fact that everyone's priorities had changed. Wren was too fragile to make the usual walk from the FAB to the bar. James too distracted. Alexander, otherwise occupied. The whims governing the Dellecher staff were similarly unfathomable. Why had they suddenly lifted their half-century boycott of _Lear_ and wedged Frederick and Camilo in with the rest of us? I told myself as I gathered my coat and gloves at the end of the night that they were simply trying to fill the hole Richard had left behind. But another nagging voice at the back of my mind kept asking whether there might be an ulterior motive. Was it possible that they, like Colborne, didn't trust us? Perhaps Frederick and Camilo were more than cast mates and teachers. Perhaps they'd at last begun to realize what danger we were in.

SCENE 3

As we made our first foray into the tragic morass of *King Lear*, little was clarified. What became painfully clear to me, however, was that we had greatly underestimated the enormousness of Richard's absence. He was more than a vacant bedroom, an unoccupied seat in the library, a chair at our refectory table where he sat like Banquo's ghost, invisible to everyone but us. Often I thought I saw him out of the corner of my eye, a passing shadow, slipping out of sight around the corner. By night he was a recurring character in my dreams—as my midterm scene partner, or my silent companion at the bar—twisting the most mundane scenarios into something dark and sinister. I was not the only victim of these nocturnal torments; James had taken to muttering and fidgeting in his sleep, and on the nights I shared a bed with Meredith, sometimes I woke to find her trembling beside me. Twice we were all woken by sounds of screaming and sobbing from Wren's room. He was as much a bully in death as he was in life, a giant who left behind not an empty space so much as a black hole, a huge crushing void that swallowed up all of our comforts, sooner or later.

But as we were moving cautiously into the shortest calendrical month, our comfort was mostly my responsibility.

Cleaning the Castle had become my primary occupation outside of classes, rehearsals, and homework. My custodial schedule was irregular, determined largely by when I had a free hour and nobody else was in the building. These coincidental opportunities were few and far between, and I was forced to seize them whenever they arrived, regardless of how tired I was. The second day of February found me on my hands and knees in the library, finally doing what I had put off for weeks and thoroughly cleaning out the fireplace.

The remains of a few logs rested in the grate like a pile of blackened bones. I lifted them delicately for fear they would crumble and leave streaks of soot on the carpet, and deposited them one by one in the paper sack I had appropriated for the purpose. Despite the persistent winter chill I was sweating, fat salty beads falling from my forehead onto the hearth. When the logs were all safely stowed in their bag, I reached for a dustpan and brush and started on the pile of ash, which had built up like a mountain against the back of the chimney. As I swept, I muttered Edgar's lines under my breath:

> *"Who alone suffers suffers most i' the mind,*
> *Leaving free things and happy shows behind:*
> *But then the mind much sufferance doth o'er skip,*
> *When grief hath mates, and bearing fellowship."*

Unable to remember the following line, I stopped and sat back on my heels. What next? I had no idea, and so crawled farther into the fireplace, beginning the speech again as I resumed my sweeping. The densest mound of ash collapsed under my brush, but as I pulled it forward, something dragged beneath the bristles. A long twisted line, like a snakeskin, had appeared on the floor of the fireplace. Fabric.

It was nothing more than a scrap, five inches long and two inches wide, curling in at the edges. One end was heavier, double-stitched—a shirt collar, maybe, or the seam of a sleeve. I bent my head low over it and blew gently, so a few little puffs of ash whirled up. It had been white once, but it was badly singed and badly stained with something dark deep red, like wine. I stared at it for a moment in consternation, then froze where I was kneeling on the hearth—so horror-struck I didn't hear the door downstairs. But the footsteps in the stairwell grew louder as they ascended, and I came back to life with a jolt, seized the insidious thing off the floor and stuffed it into my pocket. I grabbed the dustpan and brush and jumped to my feet with one held at each side, like sword and shield.

I was still standing in this rigid, ridiculous way when Colborne appeared in the doorway. His eyes barely widened, quickly adjusted from surprise at my presence to recognition. "Oliver."

"Detective Colborne," I said, clumsy and cotton-mouthed.

He pointed into the room. "May I come in?"

"If you want to."

He slid his hands into the pockets of his jeans. His badge glinted on one hip, and the butt of a handgun bulged under the hem of his coat on the other. I deposited the brush and pan in the closest chair, waiting for him to speak.

"Aren't you usually in rehearsal this time of day?" he asked, tugging the curtains apart in order to peer out the window, toward the lake.

"I'm not called for combat until five." I rummaged through my mental archives for one of Gwendolyn's breath control routines, hoping to clear my head.

He nodded and gave me a quizzical smile. "And what exactly are you doing? If you don't mind my asking."

"Cleaning." I counted four beats to breathe in.

His mouth twitched, as if there were a genuine smile hiding under the superficial one. "I never thought Dellecher students the sort who did their own cleaning."

"We don't, usually. I'm on scholarship." Five beats to breathe out.

He chuckled, like he couldn't quite believe it. "So they've got you cleaning this place?"

"Among other things." My pulse began to slow. "I don't mind."

"You're from Ohio, is that right?"

"You've got a good memory. Or have you got a file on me somewhere?"

"Both, maybe."

"Should I be nervous?" I asked, but I felt markedly less so. Colborne was a more discerning audience than I was used to, but an audience nonetheless.

"Well, you'd know that better than I would."

We stared at each other. He still had that two-layer smile on, and it occurred to me that under any other circumstances I would have liked him.

"Hard not to be nervous when the police are in and out of your house so often," I said, without thinking. He didn't know I'd overheard his conversation with Walton a month before. If he noticed my blunder, he didn't let on.

"Fair enough." He glanced out the window once more, then crossed the room and sat down on the couch in front of me. "You all read a lot, or are these just for decoration?" He pointed at the nearest bookshelf.

"We read."

"You read anything besides Shakespeare?"

"Sure. Shakespeare doesn't exist in a vacuum."

"How so?"

I couldn't tell if he was truly interested or if it was some kind of ploy.

"Well, take *Caesar*," I said, unsure what sort of incriminating information he might hope to get from the question. "Ostensibly it's all about the fall of the Roman Republic, but it's also all about the politics of early modern England. In the first scene, the tribunes and the revelers talk about trades and holidays like it's London in 1599, even though it's supposed to be 44 BC. There are a few anachronisms—like the clock in Act II—but for the most part it works both ways."

"Clever man," Colborne said, after a moment's consideration. "You know, I remember reading *Caesar* in school. They never told us any of that, just dragged us through it. I must have been about fifteen and I thought I was being punished for something."

"Anything can feel like punishment if it's taught poorly."

"True. I guess I'm just wondering what makes a kid about that age decide to devote his whole life to Shakespeare."

"Are you asking me?"

"Yeah. I'm intrigued."

"I don't know," I said. It was easier to keep talking than to stop. "I got hooked early. The high school needed a kid for *Henry V* when I was about eleven, so my English teacher took me to the audition—she thought it might make me less shy, I guess—and somehow I wound up onstage with all these boys with swords and armor, who were all twice my size. And there I was, shouting, *'As young as I am, I have observed these three swashers,'* just hoping people would hear me. I was terrified until opening night, but after that it was all I wanted to do. It's a kind of addiction."

He was silent for a moment, then asked, "Does it make you happy?"

"Sorry?"

"Does it make you happy?"

I opened my mouth to respond—*yes* seemed the only possible answer—but then I closed it again, uncertain. I cleared my throat and spoke more cautiously. "I won't pretend it's not difficult. We're always working and we don't sleep much and it's hard to have normal friendships outside of our sphere, but it's worth it just for the rush we get, being onstage and speaking Shakespeare's words. It's like we're not really alive until then, and then everything just lights up and the bad stuff disappears and we don't want to be anywhere else."

He sat inhumanly still, keen gray eyes fixed on mine. "You paint a very good picture of addiction."

I tried to backtrack. "It sounds overdramatic, but that's just how we're wired. It's how we feel everything."

"Fascinating." Colborne watched me, his fingers laced between his knees, the pose casual but every muscle in his body taut with expectation. The ticking of the mantel clock was enormously loud, beating directly against my eardrums. The scrap from the fireplace felt like a ball of lead in my pocket.

"So," I continued, anxious to change the subject, divert it away from what I had just said. "What brings you back down here?"

He leaned back, more relaxed. "Sometimes I get curious."

"About what?"

"About Richard," he said, and it was jarring to hear him say it so easily, the name we all avoided like a curse word, something even more profane than the oaths and obscenities we used so liberally. "Don't you?"

"Mostly I try not to think about it."

Colborne's eyes flicked from my feet to my face and back. An evaluative look. Measuring the depth of my honesty. "I can't help but wonder what happened that night," he said, one hand drumming idly on the arm of the sofa. "Everyone seems to remember it differently." There was a subtle, cloying challenge in his voice. Answer if you dare.

"Everyone experienced it differently, I think." My own voice was cool and flat, my nerves settled again by the fact that he'd given me a part to play, and as a casting director he was no more imaginative than Gwendolyn. I was peripheral, a bystander, an unwilling witness who just might be won over. "It's like watching the news. When there's a disaster, does anyone really remember it the same way? We all saw it from different angles, different vantage points."

He nodded slowly, considering my rebuttal. "I suppose I can't argue with that." He pushed himself to his feet. When he was upright again he rocked back on his heels, looked up at the ceiling. "Here's what I struggle with, Oliver," he said, speaking more to the light fixture than to me. "*Mathematically*, it doesn't make sense."

I waited for him to elaborate. He didn't, so I said, "Math was never my strong subject."

He frowned, but there was a flicker of amusement in his expression. "Surprising. After all, Shakespeare is *poetry*—most of it, anyway—and there's a certain mathematical pattern to poetry, isn't there?"

"You could say that."

"In any mathematical equation, a series of known and unknown variables add up to the given solution."

"That's about what I remember of algebra. Solve for x."

"Precisely," he said. "Well, here we have an equation with a known outcome—Richard's death. We'll call that x. And on the other side of the equals sign we have your—that is, the fourth-years'—accounts of the event. A, b, c, d, e, and f, if you will. And then there's everyone else. We'll call them y. Nine weeks later we have all the variables accounted for, but I still can't solve for x. Can't get the two sides of the equation to balance." He shook his head, the motion measured and deliberate. "So what does that mean?"

I stared at him. Didn't answer.

"It means," he went on, "that at least one of our variables is wrong. Make sense to you?"

"To a certain extent. But I think the premise is flawed."

"How so?" he said, the question wry, almost teasing.

I shrugged. "You can't quantify humanity. You can't measure it—not the way you mean to. People are passionate and flawed and fallible. They make mistakes. Their memories fade. Their eyes deceive them." I paused, just long enough that he might believe I hadn't planned what to say next. "Or sometimes they drink too much and fall in the lake."

Colborne blinked and a kind of profound confusion surfaced in his expression—as though he wasn't sure whether he might have miscalculated me. "Is that really how you think it happened?"

"Yes," I said. "Of course it was." We'd been saying it for weeks. Yes. He fell. Of course he did.

Colborne sighed, his breath heavy in the lukewarm library air. "You know, Oliver, I like you. Mostly in spite of myself."

I frowned, unsure if I'd heard him right. "Strange thing to say."

"Well, truth can be stranger than fiction. My point is, I'd like to trust you. But that's a lot to ask, so instead I'm just going to ask a favor."

I realized he was expecting a reply, so I said, "All right."

"I'm guessing you'll get a good look at this place as you clean it," he said. "If you find anything unusual . . . Well, let's just say I wouldn't mind being kept in the loop."

A pause followed, like a scripted beat between lines in a play. "I'll keep that in mind."

Colborne's eyes lingered on me a moment longer, and then he walked slowly back across the room to the stairs, where he stopped. "Be careful, Oliver," he said. "As I said, I like you. And—let me put this in such a way that you'll be sure to understand—*Something is rotten in the state of Denmark.*"

With that he left, a small smile on his mouth, at once sad and mocking. I stood motionless as his footsteps creaked on the stairs, and only when I heard the front door close behind him did I unclench my fist in my pocket. The blood-spotted scrap there was crumpled and damp with sweat.

SCENE 4

I gave Colborne a five-minute head start because I didn't want him to catch me leaving the Castle. I stashed my cleaning supplies under the kitchen sink, pulled my coat and gloves on, and left through the back door. I ran the whole distance to the FAB without stopping, frost crunching under my feet. By the time I arrived my limbs were numb, my eyes watering from the sting of the sharp February air.

I let myself in through a side door and listened carefully. The third-years were in the auditorium, stumbling through the second act of *Two Gentlemen of Verona*. Hoping not to run into anyone loitering backstage, I hurried into the stairwell, one hand skating along the railing as I took the steep steps to the basement two at a time.

A sprawling undercroft lurked beneath the Archibald Dellecher Theatre and all of its tributary hallways and anterooms. Usually only the technical crew ventured into that low-ceilinged, dimly lit warren, to unearth old props and furniture long ago deemed irrelevant and doomed to eternal storage. I hadn't planned to go there, hadn't even thought of it until I was halfway to the FAB, desperate at first just to get the hell away from the Castle. But as I crept down two or three shadowy corridors crowded with theatrical refuse, I realized my own accidental brilliance. Nobody could ever find anything in the undercroft, even if they knew exactly what they were looking for. Before long I stumbled into a cobwebbed corner where a bank of lockers (probably ripped out of the crossover sometime in the eighties) leaned tiredly against the wall. Rust leaked from their gills like old dried blood and crept across their gaping, sharp-edged doors. It was as good a place as any.

I shoved a battered trestle table out of my way, then waded through the rubbish piled up in my path. The first locker had a padlock hanging on the door, the catch spotted with rust like a bad tooth. I removed it, pulled hard on the handle, and swore as loudly as I dared when the door sprang open and cracked against my shin. The locker was empty except for a chipped mug bearing a faded Dellecher coat of arms, a black ring of coffee clinging to the bottom. I reached into my pocket to find the scrap of fabric I'd plucked from the fireplace. I squinted at it in the dim light, and that ominous red stain glared back. I wasn't even sure it was blood, but my own paranoia dragged me back to the day of Richard's memorial service, when I'd found Filippa alone by the fireplace. I thrust the thought away with alarm. There were no locks on the library doors, so it might have been any one of us. The air in the undercroft felt frigid. Any one of us might have done what? Suddenly nauseous and impatient to get the thing out of sight, I bent down and stuffed it into the mug. If anyone else found it there, they'd just think it a rag—stained with paint or dye or some other innocuous thing. For all I knew, it was. I chastised myself for being excitable. Alexander was right about that much: if we didn't keep our wits about us, everything would come undone. I slammed the door, then hesitated. I didn't know the lock's combination. I didn't want to return to it, ever, but just in case, I left it dangling, open.

I shoved the trestle table back in front of the lockers, hoping that maybe nobody else would bother moving it, that nobody would even know I'd been there. I stepped back and stood staring at the small wheel of the lock, the tiny gap between the shackle and case. How tremendous the agony of unmade decisions.

SCENE 5

I got lost on my way out of the basement and was late for combat call. James, Camilo, and three second-years were already there.

"Sorry," I said. "Sorry, I lost track of the time."

"Where've you been?" James asked, with a strange deadpan expression. I was burning to ask him the same question, but not in front of other people.

Camilo interjected. "Let's talk later. We've got a lot to get through and not a whole lot of time to do it. Did you two work this over the weekend?"

I glanced at James, who said, "Yes," before I could answer. We'd only run through the blocking twice, because he'd been out of the Castle most of the day Saturday and all day Sunday.

"Then let's get started," Camilo said. "Shall we go from Edgar's challenge?"

The set for *Lear* had been outlined on the floor in blue spike tape. It was a curious design, the proscenium stage stretching into a catwalk that ran down the center aisle of the audience. We called it the Bridge; the elevation was marked at four feet.

I took my place upstage, my rapier hanging on my left hip. James and the rest of them were already in place—he at the top of the Bridge, the soldiers on stage left, Camilo and the herald on stage right. Meredith should have been there, too, but there was no sense summoning her when all she did was watch.

Me: "*What's he that speaks for Edmund Earl of Gloucester?*"

James: "*Himself. What say'st thou to him?*"

I glared at him, fists clenched against the churning of my stomach. There was no need to impress anyone with emotions for a fight call, but I was already on edge.

Me: "*Draw thy sword,*
   That, if my speech offend a noble heart,
   Thy arm may do thee justice. Here is mine."

I drew my sword, and James raised his eyebrows, faintly amused. I crossed downstage to the top of the Bridge.

Me: "*Despite thy victor sword and fire-new fortune,*
   Thy valor and thy heart, thou art a traitor,
   False to thy gods, thy brother, and thy father,
   Conspirant 'gainst this high illustrious prince,
   And from th' extremest upward of thy head
   To the descent and dust below thy foot,
   A most toad-spotted traitor."

Somewhere in the middle of my speech, James's wry amusement faded from his face and was replaced with a cold, ugly look. When it was his turn to speak I watched him closely, uncertain whether he was acting only, or if he and I both were gnashing secrets between our teeth.

James: *"What safe and nicely I might well delay*
  By rule of knighthood, I disdain and spurn.
  Back do I toss those treasons to thy head!"
He may as well have spat at me.
James: *"With the hell-hated lie o'erwhelm thy heart,*
  Which, for they yet glance by and scarcely bruise,
  This sword of mine shall give them instant way
  Where they shall rest for ever. Trumpets, speak!"

We raised our weapons, bowed to each other without breaking eye contact. He attacked first; my block was sloppy and his blade slid along mine to the hilt with an angry hiss. I threw him off and clumsily recovered my balance. Another blow, another block. I parried, struck at his left shoulder. The foils clattered together, their blunt edges colliding with the rattle and snap of a snare drum.

"Easy," Camilo said. "Easy, now."

We danced a rapid grapevine down a narrow aisle between two long lines of tape. That was the choreography: I beat him to the end of the Bridge, where he would fall, one hand on his stomach, blood blossoming beneath his fingers. (How this would happen, we had yet to be informed by the costume crew.) We fought with our bodies parallel, swords flashing between us. He staggered, lost his footing, but when I raised my arm to deliver the killing stroke, his fingers curled more tightly around the hilt of his sword. The pommel and guard cracked across my face, white-hot stars burst through my field of vision, and pain hit me like a battering ram. Camilo and one of the soldiers shouted at the same time. The rapier slipped loose from my fingers and crashed down beside me as I fell backward onto my elbows, blood gushing from my nose like someone had turned on a faucet.

James dropped his foil and gaped down at me with wide, bulging eyes.

"What the hell do you think you're doing?" Camilo yelled.

James stepped back like a sleepwalker, slowly, entranced. His fingers flexed at his side, his knuckles gleaming red. I tried to speak, but my mouth was full of iron, blood dribbling down my chin, soaking the front of my shirt. The two soldiers propped me up, and my head drooped heavily forward, like all the tendons in my neck had snapped.

Camilo was still shouting. "Unacceptable! What the hell's gotten into you?"

James looked up at him instead of me. "I—" he began.

"Get out," Camilo said. "I'll deal with you later."

James's mouth moved wordlessly. Water suddenly welled in his eyes, and he turned and ran out of the room, leaving his coat and gloves and everything else behind.

"Oliver, are you all right?" Camilo crouched beside me, lifting my chin. "You got all your teeth?" I closed my lips, swallowed blood, and gulped hard against the reflex to vomit. He pointed first at the taller of the two soldiers, then at the other one. "You, help me get him to the infirmary. You, run and find Frederick, tell him I need to see him and Gwendolyn immediately. Move."

The world reeled as they hoisted me up, and I hoped dully that I'd lose consciousness and never wake up again.

SCENE 6

I didn't get out of the infirmary until after eleven. My nose was broken, but not badly. A splint had been taped over the bridge to keep it straight, and beneath that, red and purple bruises were spreading under both my eyes. Gwendolyn and Frederick had been to see me, asked what happened, apologized profusely, and then requested that I keep it as much to myself as possible and call it an accident if other students asked. We didn't, they said, need any more gossip or any more trouble. By the time I got back to the Castle, I hadn't decided whether I would comply or not.

I went immediately upstairs, but not to the Tower. It seemed unlikely that James would be there, but I didn't want to risk it. Instead I knocked softly on Alexander's door. I heard a drawer scrape shut, and a moment later he appeared, one hand on the doorknob.

"Fuck, Oliver," he said. "Pip told me what happened, but I didn't think it'd be this bad." His eyes were bloodshot, his lips dry and cracked. He didn't look much better than I did.

"I don't really want to talk about it."

"Fair enough." He sniffed, wiped his nose on his sleeve. "Can I help?"

"My head hurts like a bitch and right now I'd rather not feel anything above the neck."

He opened the door wider. "The doctor is in."

I didn't go in Alexander's room often, and I was always surprised by how dark it was. Sometime in the last few weeks, he'd tacked a tapestry over the window. His bed was buried under a pile of books, which he gathered up and dropped on the already cluttered desk. Crumpled rolling papers, broken matches, and dirty clothes littered the floor. He gestured at the bed, and I sank gratefully down on the mattress, my pulse pounding hard between my temples.

"Can I ask what happened?" he said, as he rummaged in the top drawer of his desk. "I won't make you talk about it. I just want to know whether I should shove James in the lake next time I see him."

Unsure if the remark was simply Alexander's morbid sense of humor or something more deliberate, I shifted on the bed, chalked it up to lingering paranoia, and decided to ignore it.

"Have you seen much of him lately?" I asked. "I feel like he's never here."

"He comes in and out. You'd know better than I would."

"He usually comes in after I've gone to bed, and by the time I get up, he's gone."

Alexander shook a few little florets of weed out of a film canister and crumbled them into a cigarette paper. "If you ask me, he's getting a little too deep into his role. Method, you know? Doesn't know where he stops and Edmund starts anymore."

"Well, that can't be good."

He looked up at me and my busted nose. "Clearly." He made a face like he'd just bitten his tongue. "Did they give you some kind of painkillers for that?"

I produced a bottle of little white pills from my pocket.

"Grand," he said. "Gimme two of those."

I handed them over. He crushed both under the film canister and sprinkled the resulting powder on top of the weed in the paper. Then he reached into the drawer again, came up with another mysterious pill bottle. He popped the top off, tapped it on the heel of his palm. Another white powder, finer. He added this to the joint without telling me what it was. I didn't ask.

"So what happened?" he said, as he started rolling. "You guys were doing the Five-Three combat and he just clocked you?"

"Basically."

"What the fuck. Why?"

"Believe me, I'd love to know."

He ran his tongue along the sticky edge of the paper, then pasted it down with one fingertip. He twisted the end into a tiny curl and handed the joint to me. "There," he said. "Smoke that in one go and you won't feel anything for a week."

"Terrific." I stood and grabbed onto the back of his chair. My head was throbbing.

"You all right?"

"I will be in a few minutes."

He didn't sound convinced. "You sure?"

"Yeah," I said. "I'll be fine." I felt my way to the door like a blind man, hands moving from one piece of furniture to the next until I reached the wall.

"Oliver," he said, as I opened the door to let myself out.

"Yeah?"

He tossed me a lighter when I turned, then pointed at his nose and smiled sadly. I reached up to my face. There was a fresh spot of blood on my upper lip.

As a rule, we didn't smoke in the Castle. I exited through the side door and stood in the driveway with the joint, spliff, whatever it was pinched tightly between my lips. I inhaled how Alexander had taught me two years before, deep into the lungs. It was cold, even for February, and my breath and the smoke came out of my mouth together in one long spiral. My sinuses felt heavy and thick, like they'd been plugged up with clay. I wondered when the bruises would fade, if my nose would look the same in three weeks' time.

I leaned against the wall and tried not to think anymore, certain I'd drive myself crazy if I did. The forest was quiet and at the same time brimming with small sounds—the distant hoot of an owl, the dry rustle of leaves, a breeze slithering through the treetops. Somehow, slowly, my brain disconnected from the rest of me. I still felt pain, still twisted in the grip of indecision, but there was something between me and thought and feeling and everything else—a fine mist, a backlit scrim, shadow-puppet silhouettes moving softly on the other side. Whether it was the cold or Alexander's joint I couldn't say, but inch by inch I began to go numb.

The door opened, closed. I looked toward it without expectation or curiosity. Meredith. She hesitated on the porch for a moment, then came down. I didn't move. She took the joint out of my mouth, threw it on the ground, and kissed me before I could speak. A dull throb of pain went up the bridge of my nose to my brain. Her palm was warm on the side of my face, her mouth magnetic. She took my hand like she had so many weeks ago and led me back inside.

SCENE 7

I slept through most of the following day, regaining consciousness for only a moment or two when Meredith slid out of bed, brushed my hair back off my forehead, and left for class. I murmured something at her, but the words never really took shape. Sleep crawled back on top of me like an affectionate, purring pet, and I didn't wake again for eight hours. When I did, Filippa was sitting cross-legged on the bed beside me.

I gazed up at her blearily, groping through my muddled memory of the previous night, unsure whether I had any clothes on under the blanket. She pushed me back down when I tried to sit up. "How do you feel?" she asked.

"How do I look?"

"Honestly? Awful."

"Coincidence? No. What time is it?"

The windows were already dark.

"Quarter to nine," she said, and her forehead creased. "Have you slept all day?"

I groaned, shifted, reluctant to lift my head. "Mostly. How was class?"

"Very quiet."

"Why?"

"Well, without you there were only four of us."

"Who else was missing?"

"Who do you think?"

I turned my head away from her on the pillow, stared hard at the wall. The movement produced a painful thud in my sinus cavity that distracted me, but only for a moment.

"I suppose you're waiting for me to ask where he is," I said.

She plucked at the edge of the comforter where it was folded across my chest. "Nobody's seen him since yesterday. After fight call he just disappeared."

I grunted at her and said, "There's a 'but,' I can hear it coming."

She sighed, her shoulders rising slightly up and sinking down much farther. "But he's back now. He's up in the Tower."

"In which case I will be staying right here until Meredith kicks me out."

Her mouth made a flat pink line. Behind her glasses—I didn't know why she was wearing them, she wasn't reading anything—her eyes were drowsy ocean blue, patient but tired. "Come on, Oliver," she said quietly. "It can't hurt to go up and talk to him."

I gestured at my face. "Um, apparently it can."

"Look, we're all mad at him, too. I think Meredith left a scorch mark on the floor where she was standing when he came in. Even Wren wouldn't talk to him."

"Good," I said.

"Oliver."

"What?"

She leaned her cheek on one hand and inexplicably, grudgingly, smiled.

"What?" I said again, more warily.

"You," she said. "You know I wouldn't even be in here if you were anyone else."

"What does that mean?"

"It means that you have better reasons than the rest of us to hold a grudge, but you're also the first one who's going to forgive him."

The unsettling feeling that Filippa could see right through

my skin made me squirm deeper into the mattress. "Is that so?" I said, but it sounded weak and unpersuasive, even to me.

"Yeah." Her smile faded. "We can't afford to be at one another's throats right now. Things are bad enough." She seemed frail, all of a sudden. Thin and transparent, like a cancer patient. Unflappable Filippa. I felt a weird overwhelming urge to just *hold* her, ashamed that I had, however briefly, suspected her of anything. I wanted to pull her under the blanket and wrap my arms around her. I almost did it before I remembered that I (probably) wasn't dressed.

"Fine," I said. "I'll go talk to him."

She nodded, and I thought I saw the flash of a tear behind her glasses. "Thanks." She waited a moment, realized I wasn't moving, and said, "Okay, when?"

"Um, in a minute."

She blinked, and all traces of the tear—if it had ever been there—were gone. "Are you naked?" she said.

"I might be."

She left the room. I took my time getting dressed.

As I climbed the stairs to the Tower, I found myself walking in slow motion. It didn't feel like I was going up to see James for the first time in only a day or two. I felt like I hadn't really seen him, spoken to him, communicated with him in any significant way since before Christmas. The door at the top of the stairs was cracked. I nervously licked my lip and pushed it open.

He was perched on the side of the bed, eyes fixed on the floor. But it wasn't his bed—it was mine.

"Comfortable?" I said.

He stood swiftly and took two steps forward. "Oliver—"

I raised one hand, palm out, like a crossing guard. "No—just stay over there, for a minute."

He stopped in the middle of the room. "Okay. Whatever you want."

My feet were unsteady on the floorboards. I swallowed,

choked down a surge of strange, despondent affection. "I want to forgive you," I blurted. "But James, I could kill you right now, honestly." I reached toward him, clenched my fist on empty air. "I want to—God, I can't even explain it. You're like a bird, you know that?" He opened his mouth—a question, some expression of confusion caught on the tip of his tongue. I made a harsh, inelegant gesture, a chop of the hand, to keep him from speaking. My thoughts tumbled out manic and disorganized. "Alexander was right, Richard's not the sparrow, it's you. You're—I don't know, this fragile, elusive thing, and I feel like if I could just catch you, I could crush you."

He had this terrible, wounded look on his face, and he had no right to it, not in that moment. Half a dozen conflicting feelings roared up in me at once, and I took a huge, ungainly step toward him.

"I want so badly to be so mad at you that I could do that, but I *can't*, so I'm mad at myself instead. Do you even understand how unfair that is?" My voice was high and stringent, like a little boy's. I hated it, so I swore, loudly. "Fuck! Fuck this, fuck me, fuck *you*— God damn it, James!" I wanted to throw him to the floor, fight him down—and do what? The violence of the thought alarmed me, and with a strangled noise of outrage, I seized a book off the trunk at the end of his bed and flung it at him, threw it at his knees. It was a paperback copy of *Lear*, limp and harmless, but he winced as it hit him. It fluttered to the floor at his feet, one page hanging crookedly out from the binding. When he looked up at me I averted my eyes immediately.

"Oliver, I—"

"Don't!" I jabbed a finger at him for silence. "Don't. Just let me—just—for a minute." I dragged my fingers through my hair. A hard ball of pain had lodged behind the bridge of my nose, and my eyes were beginning to water. "What *is* it about you?" I asked, my words thick from the effort of keeping my voice steady. I glared at him, waiting for an answer I knew I wouldn't get. "I should hate you right now. And I want to—*God*, I want to—but that's not enough."

I shook my head, utterly at a loss. What on earth was happening to us? I searched his face for a hint of it, some clue to seize on, but for a long time all he did was breathe, with his face twisted up like breathing hurt.

"*My name, dear saint, is hateful to myself,*" he said. "*Because it is an enemy to thee.*"

The balcony scene. Too mistrustful to guess at the meaning, I said, "Don't do that, James, please—right now can we just be ourselves?"

He crouched down, lifted the mangled script from the floor. "I'm sorry," he said. "It's easier now to be Romeo, or Macbeth, or Brutus, or Edmund. Someone else."

"James," I said again, more gently. "Are you all right?"

He shook his head, eyes downcast. His voice crept out of his mouth with fearful, cautious steps. "No. I'm not."

"Okay." I shifted my weight, foot to foot. The floor still didn't feel firm enough. "Can you tell me what's wrong?"

"Oh," he said, with a strange, watery smile. "No. Everything."

"I'm sorry," I said, and it sounded like a question.

He moved forward, one step, closed the small space between us, and lifted his hand, touched the bruise that had spread beneath my left eye. A sliver of pain. I twitched.

"I should be the sorry one," he said. My eyes flicked from one of his to the other. Gray like steel, gold like honey. "I don't know what made me do it. I've never wanted to hurt you before."

His fingertips felt like ice. "But now?" I said. "Why?"

His arm fell lifelessly to his side. He looked away and said, "Oliver, I don't know what's wrong with me. I want to hurt the whole world."

"James." I took his arm, turned him back toward me. Before I could decide what to do next, I felt his hand on my chest and glanced down. His palm was pressed against my shirt, his fingers splayed across my collarbone. I waited for him to pull me closer or push me away. But he only stared at his hand, like it was something strange he'd never seen before.

SCENE 8

February didn't linger long. The middle of the month had come and gone before I'd even stopped writing *January* on all my papers by mistake. Our midterm performance exams were approaching fast—and though Frederick and Gwendolyn had been unusually kind in their scene assignments, we were fighting to stay afloat in a sea of lines to learn, reading to do, text to scan, and papers to hand in. Early one Sunday evening, James and I and the girls huddled in the library, running lines for the scenes we were scheduled to perform in class the following week. James and Filippa had Hamlet and Gertrude; Meredith and Wren were reading Emilia and Desdemona; I was waiting for Alexander to show up and read Arcite to my Palamon.

"Honestly," Filippa said, as she tripped over the same line for the fourth time, "would it have killed them to make me Ophelia? I am not by any stretch of the imagination old enough to be your mother."

"*Would it were not so!*" James said.

She sighed enormously. "*What have I done that thou dar'st wag thy tongue / In noise so rude against me?*"

"*Such an act / That blurs the grace and blush of modesty.*"

They continued to argue quietly. I leaned back on the couch, watched Meredith brush Wren's hair for a moment. They made a pretty picture, the firelight playing softly on their faces, gleaming on the curves of lips and eyelashes.

Wren: *"Wouldst thou do such a deed for all the world?"*
Meredith: *"The world's a huge thing: it is a great price,*
　　For a small vice."
Wren:　　　　　　*"In troth, I think thou wouldst not."*

I lifted my own notebook again. My text was slashed through
and underlined in four different colors, so chaotically annotated that it was difficult to find the original words. I muttered
to myself for a while, the others' voices drifting gently on the
whisper and crack of the fire. Fifteen minutes ticked by, then
twenty. I was beginning to grow restless when the door opened
downstairs.

I sat up straighter. "Finally." Footsteps came quickly up the
stairs and I said, "It's about time, I've been waiting on you all
night," before I realized that it wasn't Alexander.

"Colin," Wren said, breaking out of her scene.

He nodded, hands moving uneasily in his coat pockets.
"Sorry to barge in."

"What's up?" I asked.

"I'm looking for Alexander." His cheeks were pink, but I
doubted it had much to do with the cold.

Filippa exchanged a fast glance with Meredith, who said,
"We thought he was with you."

Colin nodded, eyes darting around the room, strategically
avoiding all of our faces. "Yeah, he said he'd meet me for a drink
at five, but I haven't seen him or heard anything." He shrugged.
"Starting to worry, you know?"

"Yeah." Filippa was already climbing out of her chair. "Does
someone want to check his room? I'll look in the kitchen, see if
he left a note."

"I'll go." Colin nearly ran out of the library, clearly desperate
to get to the hall, where we wouldn't all be staring at him.

Meredith: "What do you suppose that's about?"
Me: "Don't know. Did he say anything to any of you?"
Wren: "No, but he's been a bit odd lately."

James: "Haven't we all."

Wren frowned at me. I had nothing to add, so I shrugged. She opened her mouth—but to say what, I never found out, because Colin came thundering in again, all the rosy color gone from his face. "He's in his room—something's wrong, something's really wrong!" His voice cracked on the last word, and we were all on our feet at once. Filippa's voice chased us down the hall from the kitchen, high and nervous, calling, "Guys? What's going on?"

The door cracked hard against the wall as Colin flung it open. Books and clothes and crumpled papers were strewn around the room like the refuse of a bomb blast. Alexander lay stretched on the floor, his limbs bent at awkward angles, head thrown back as if his neck had been broken.

"Oh my God," I said. "What do we do?"

James shoved past me. "Get of the way. Colin, prop him up, can you?"

Wren pointed across the room. "What is all that?"

Under the bed, the floor was littered with pill bottles and film canisters, pushed almost out of sight behind a low-hanging corner of his comforter. Prescription labels had been torn off some, leaving streaks of fuzzy white paper behind.

James knelt beside Alexander, squeezing his wrist in search of a pulse. Colin lifted his head off the floor—and some small sound escaped between his lips.

"He's alive," I said, "he must be, he just—"

James's voice was thin and strained. "Shut up a minute, I can't—"

Filippa arrived behind us in the doorway. "What's happening?"

Alexander murmured something, and Colin bent his head low over his face.

"I don't know," I said. "He must've taken too much of something."

"Oh, God. What? What was he on, does anyone know?"

"His pulse is really erratic," James said, talking fast and low. "He's got to go to the hospital. Someone get downstairs and call for an ambulance. And someone gather up all of that shit." He pointed at the pill bottles under the bed.

Colin blanched, cradling Alexander's sweaty head in his lap. "You can't send that stuff to the hospital—do you want him to get expelled?"

"Would you rather he died?" James said, fiercely.

Before Colin could answer, Alexander's whole body seized up, teeth clenched, muscles twitching.

"Do what he says," Meredith ordered. "Somebody get to the phone, now." She crouched down beside James and started sweeping bottles out from under the bed. Alexander moaned, one hand groping across the floor. Colin grabbed it and squeezed hard, rocking slightly forward. Wren had backed into a corner and crouched there, hugging herself, looking sick. My stomach tried to crawl out of my mouth.

Filippa grabbed my arm. "Oliver, can you—"

"Yeah, I'll go, you look after Wren."

I left the room and flew down the stairs, my feet numb and clumsy underneath me. I grabbed the phone out of its cradle and dialed 911.

A voice answered. Female. Indifferent. Efficient. "Nine-one-one, what's your emergency?"

"I'm at the Castle on the Dellecher school grounds and we need an ambulance, immediately."

"What is the nature of your emergency?" She was so cool, so calm. I fought an urge to shout at her, *Emergency! Does it mean nothing to you?*

"Some kind of drug overdose, I don't know. Get help here, now."

I dropped the phone, letting it fall out of my hand, pull the cord taut with a jerk, and swing like a dead man on the end of a rope. As I listened to the tinny voice droning from the phone, the distant sounds of dismay and agitation from upstairs, all I could think was, why? Why the drugs, why the overdose, *what has he done what has he done what has he done?* I couldn't go back up, but I couldn't stay where I was, terrified of what I might say when the police or paramedics wanted answers. I left the phone dangling and threw the door open, without taking my coat, scarf, gloves, anything.

I gained momentum as I walked down the driveway, the gravel like little chunks of ice under my socks. By the time I hit the dirt—buried under a muddled blanket of old snow and pine needles—I was running full tilt. My heart pumped hard against the cold, and blood slammed through my veins, thundered and roared in my ears until the dam in my sinus cavity burst and it came streaming out of my nose again. I ran straight into the trees, where branches and thorns tore at my face and arms and legs, but I barely felt them, tiny pricks of pain lost in the tumult and snarl of panic. I turned off the path and plunged deeper into the woods, so deep I didn't know if I'd be able to find my way back, deep enough that no one would hear me. When I thought my heart or my lungs would burst, I fell on my hands and knees in the icy leaves and howled into the trees until something in my throat broke.

SCENE 9

There were only four of us in class on Tuesday morning: James, Filippa, Meredith, and me. Alexander hadn't yet come back from Broadwater's emergency clinic—though he was stable by then, or so we'd been told. The rest of us were pulled from class one by one on Monday to undergo psychiatric evaluation. The school shrink and a doctor from Broadwater took turns asking us invasive questions about ourselves, one another, and our collectively bad track record with substance abuse. (We each left with a pamphlet on the dangers of drug use and a stern reminder that attendance of the upcoming alcohol awareness seminar was mandatory.) Beyond the obvious problems of stress and exhaustion, both James and Wren, from what I'd overheard outside Holinshed's office on my way to the bathroom, were exhibiting symptoms of post-traumatic stress disorder. She'd taken an additional day off class to rest, but when I suggested that James do the same, he said, "If I'm shut up in the Castle by myself all day, I'll lose my mind." I didn't argue with that, but as it turned out, he wasn't much better off in Studio Five.

"Well," Gwendolyn said as soon as we sat down, "I don't think anyone's up for new material today, and besides there aren't enough of you. I'd be teaching the same lesson tomorrow." Her solution was to work problem scenes from *Lear* that couldn't be more thoroughly dissected during rehearsal for the sake of time.

James and I watched for an hour while Gwendolyn dug her nails into Meredith and Filippa, searching for sparks of real-life sibling rivalry to fan into a flame for the stage. She had her work cut out for her; Meredith barely knew her own brothers, and Filippa claimed not to have any siblings. (I still don't know whether this is true.) Gwendolyn startled me out of a stupor by asking about *my* sisters, a subject I was not then—nor ever had been—fond of. She stopped just short of outing me as the Castle's new custodian and mercifully moved on. When she'd hassled the girls to distraction, she gave us a five-minute water break and instructed James and Meredith to come back prepared for Act IV, Scene 2.

When we returned, Gwendolyn opened the scene work with a lecture on the last week's lackluster performance. "I mean, really," she said. "This is one of the most passionate moments of the play, between two of the most powerful people in it. The stakes are as high as they can be, so I don't want to feel like I'm watching a bad pickup at the bar." Meredith and James listened without comment and, when she finished, took their places without so much as acknowledging each other. (After James had broken my nose, Meredith's attitude toward him went from lukewarm to icy, which undoubtedly contributed to their complete lack of chemistry onstage.)

Filippa fed them a cue line—it wasn't hers, but Gwendolyn couldn't be bothered—and they went through the motions with a woodenness that made me cringe. Their words fell flat; their touches were forced and awkward. Beside me, Filippa watched the scene collapse with a grim, pained expression, like she was being tortured.

"Stop, stop, stop," Gwendolyn said, waving one hand at James and Meredith. "Stop." They moved gratefully apart, like magnets with the same polarity. Meredith folded her arms; James scowled at the floor. Gwendolyn glanced from one of them to the other and said, "What on earth is the matter with you two?" Meredith stiffened. James sensed it and tensed to match but didn't look at her. Gwendolyn put her hands on her hips and studied them shrewdly. "I'll get to the bottom of it, whatever it is," she said, "but let's talk about the scene first. What's happening here? Meredith?"

"Goneril needs Edmund's help, so she bribes him the only way she knows how." She sounded utterly bored by it.

"Sure," Gwendolyn said. "That's a fine answer, if you're dead from the neck down. James? Let's hear from you. What's happening with Edmund?"

"He sees another way to get what he wants and he plays the hand she gives him," he said, in a toneless, automatic sort of way.

"That's interesting. It's also bullshit," Gwendolyn said, and I looked up from my knees in surprise. "Something *huge* is missing from this scene, and it's staring you in the face," she went on. "Goneril's not going to kill her husband just so she can have a new captain in the field, and Edmund's not going to risk losing Regan's title unless there's a more compelling offer on the table. So why do they do this?"

Nobody spoke. Gwendolyn whirled around and said, "Oh, for God's sake—Oliver!" so loudly that I jumped. "I know you know—*Murder's as near to* what *as flame to smoke?*"

The old familiar line from *Pericles* shot through my head. "Lust?" I said, wary of the word, as afraid of being right as I was of being wrong.

"Lust!" she barked, and shook her fist at James and Meredith. "Passion! If you just play the logic and not the feelings, the scene doesn't work!" She waved at the two of them again. "Clearly you two *don't* feel it, so we're going to have to fix that. How? First, we stand facing each other." She took James by the shoulders and turned him sharply, so he and Meredith were almost nose to nose. "Now, we dispense with all the he/she nonsense and start talking like real people. Stop saying 'Edmund' like he's some guy you met at a party. It's not about *him*, it's about *you*."

They were both watching her blankly.

"No," she said. "No. Don't look at *me*." They turned and glowered at each other until she added, "It's not a staring contest."

"This isn't *working*," Meredith snapped.

"And why not?" Gwendolyn said. "You two don't like each other right now? That's too damn bad." She stopped, sighed. "Here's the thing, kids—and I know this because I've lived a long and scandalous life—here's the thing about lust: you don't have to like each other. Ever heard of hate sex?"

Filippa made a small gagging noise, and I swallowed a nervous laugh.

"Keep looking at each other, but stop me if I'm wrong," Gwendolyn continued. "James, you don't like Meredith. Why not? She's beautiful. She's intelligent. She's fiery. I think she intimidates you, and you don't like to be intimidated. But there's more than that, isn't there?" She began to walk a slow circle around the pair of them, like a prowling jungle cat. "You look at her like she disgusts you, but I don't think that's it. I think she distracts you, like she distracts every other man with a pulse. When you look at her, you can't help having filthy, sexy thoughts, and then you're disgusted with yourself."

James's hands curled into fists at his sides. I could see how carefully he was breathing—his chest rising and falling in perfect clockwork time.

"And then there's Miss Meredith," Gwendolyn purred. "You're not afraid to get filthy and sexy, so what is it? You're used to everyone you walk past looking at you like you're a goddess, and I think you're offended by the fact that James resists you. He's the only boy here you can't have. How badly does that make you want him?"

Unlike James, Meredith seemed not to be breathing at all. She stood perfectly still, lips barely parted, a vivid dart of pink on each cheek. I knew that look—it was the same reckless, burning look she'd given me in the stairwell during the *Caesar* party. Something squirmed under my lungs.

"Now," Gwendolyn instructed, "for once I want you to forget about eye contact and look at every other inch of each other. Do it. Don't rush."

They obeyed. They looked at each other, stared, indulged, and I followed their eyes, saw what they saw—the line of James's jaw, the triangle of smooth skin visible in the V of his collar. The backs of his hands, the delicate bones, precise as lines carved by Michelangelo. And Meredith—the soft clamshell pink of her mouth, the curve of her throat, the slope of her shoulders. The tiny mark I'd left with my teeth on the heel of her palm. Anxiety flickered through every nerve in my body.

"Now look each other in the eyes," Gwendolyn said. "And do this like you mean it. Filippa?"

Filippa glanced down at the script in her hand and said Oswald's last line. "*What most he should dislike seems pleasant to him; / What like, offensive.*"

Meredith inhaled in a rush, like someone waking up. Her

hand landed on James's chest before he could move, held him at arm's length.

Meredith: *"Then shall you go no further.*
It is the cowish terror of his spirit,
That dares not undertake. He'll not feel wrongs
Which tie him to an answer. Our wishes on the way
May prove effects."

She toyed with the collar of his shirt, perhaps distracted by the warmth underneath the fabric. He reached up to find her wrist, traced the blue lace veins there with his fingertips.

Meredith: *"Back, Edmund, to my brother.*
Hasten his musters and conduct his pow'rs.
I must change arms at home and give the distaff
Into my husband's hands."

He watched her mouth as she spoke, and she let her arm bend at the elbow, inviting him closer, as if she'd forgotten why he ought to be kept at a distance.

Meredith: *"This trusty servant*
Shall pass between us. Ere long you are like to hear
(If you dare venture in your own behalf)
A mistress's command."

Her hand moved toward the neck of her sweater and his moved with it, hovering a hairsbreadth from her skin as she found her handkerchief and drew it out.

"Wear this," she said. *"Spare speech. / Decline your head—"*

In one sudden motion he snatched the handkerchief and kissed her so hard he nearly knocked her over. She seized his shirt in both fists like she wanted to choke him, and I heard the hitch in his breath, the little answering gasp. It was violent, aggressive, the handkerchief and its delicate seduction crushed and forgotten. If they'd had claws they would have mauled each other. I felt hot, sick, light-headed. I wanted to look away but couldn't—it was like watching a car crash. I clenched my teeth so hard my vision started to swim.

Meredith broke loose, thrust James back a step. They stood four feet apart, staring at each other, disheveled and breathless.

Meredith: *"This kiss, if it durst speak,*
Would stretch thy spirits up into the air.
Conceive, and fare thee well."

James: *"Yours, in the ranks of death."*

He turned, exited the wrong way, walked right out of the room. As soon as he was gone Meredith turned away from the place where he'd stood, and her words were sharp and furious as she said, "*O, the difference of man and man! / To thee a woman's ser-vices are due; / My fool usurps my body.*"

The bell rang, not a moment too soon. I bolted for the hall, skin crawling with the hideous feeling of all their eyes on me.

SCENE 10

I shoved my way up the stairs, nearly hurling a philosophy student over the banister in my rush to get away from Studio Five. I dropped a book but didn't go back for it—someone would pick it up; my name was in the cover. When I got to the gallery I threw the door open without knocking, closed it behind me, and pressed my back flat against it. A sneeze began to form under the splint on my nose, and for a moment I didn't dare breathe, afraid of how much it would hurt.

"Oliver?" Frederick peered out from behind the blackboard, a chalk rag in one hand.

"Yes," I said, exhaling all at once. "I'm sorry, I just—wanted some quiet."

"Understandable. Why don't you sit, and I'll pour tea?"

I nodded, eyes watering from the effort of holding back the sneeze, and crossed the room to look out the window. Everything was bleak and gray, the lake dull and lusterless under a thin layer of ice. From so far and so high, it looked like a fogged mirror, and I imagined God reaching down to smear the glass clean with his sleeve.

"Honey?" Frederick asked. "Lemon?"

"Yes, please," I said, my mind distant from my mouth. James and Meredith were tangled and wrestling in my brain. Sweat prickled on my scalp and between my shoulder blades. I wanted to fling the window open, let a cold blast of winter wind deaden my creeping fever, freeze through me until I couldn't feel a thing.

Frederick carried my cup and saucer over, and I gulped down a mouthful of tea. It scalded my tongue and the roof of my mouth and I tasted nothing, not even the sour sting of lemon. Frederick watched me bemusedly. I tried to smile at him, but it must have been more like a grimace because he tapped the side of his nose and said, "How is it?"

"Itchy," I said. A knee-jerk reply, but honest enough.

His face was blank at first and then he chuckled. "You, Oliver," he said, "are truly indomitable."

My smile cracked like plaster.

He shuffled back to the sideboard to continue pouring tea. I rolled my fingers into the tightest fists I could make, fighting an impulse to scream or maybe let that crazy laugh out, finally, even though my throat was still raw and sore from the night Alexander overdosed.

The late bell rang and I glanced up at Frederick, who was checking the little gold watch on his wrist. "Is everyone else tardy?" he said.

"I don't know." My voice was stiff, brittle. "Alexander's in the clinic, and Wren's coming back tomorrow, but . . ."

"The rest of them?"

"I don't know," I said again, unable to suppress a flash of panic. "They were all in Gwendolyn's class." The small rational part of my brain spat out a list of reasons they might be late. They were rattled after our last lesson, most likely. Tired. Not feeling well. PTSD.

Frederick peered out through the hall door, looking first one way, then the other, like a child preparing to cross the street. I reached for my tea, hoping it would settle my nerves, but the cup slipped from my unsteady hand. Blistering hot liquid splashed across my skin—I yelped in pain, and the china shattered on the floor.

Frederick moved faster than I had ever seen him do, starting and whirling around at the door. "Oliver," he said, in a tone of surprise that was almost reproachful.

"I'm sorry!" I said. "I'm sorry, it slipped and I—"

"Oliver," he said again, closing the door behind him. "I am not concerned about the cup." He reached for a napkin on the sideboard and brought it to me. I dried my hands as best I could while they were shaking so badly and breathed in short, strange hiccups, gulping the chalky air down like it might run out. Frederick lowered himself into the chair that James usually occupied. "Look at me, please, Oliver," he said, sternly but softly. I raised my eyes. "Now. Tell me what's wrong."

"Everyone's—" I shook my head as I shredded the napkin with seared and smarting fingertips. "We're all falling apart."

I knew by then the way the story went. Our little drama was rapidly hurtling toward its climactic crisis. What next, when we reached the precipice?

First, the reckoning. Then, the fall.

ACT V

PROLOGUE

The climb from the first floor to the Tower takes a decade. I ascend slowly, like a man on the steps to the gallows, and Colborne comes haltingly behind me. The smell of the place—old wood and old books under a soft sprinkling of dust—is overwhelmingly familiar, though I never noticed it ten years ago when I lived here. The door is barely cracked, as if one of us, twenty-something, left it open in our rush to get to the theatre, Studio Five, the Bore's Head, wherever. For one instant I wonder if James is waiting on the other side.

The door opens silently when I push—it hasn't rusted the way I have. The empty room gapes at me as I step over the threshold, braced for the pain of recollection to hit me like a thunderbolt. Instead there's only a faint whisper, a sigh like the slightest breeze on the other side of the window glass. I venture farther in.

Students still live here, or so it seems. The layer of dust on the empty bookshelves is only a few weeks deep, not years. The beds are stripped of everything, and they look naked and skeletal. Mine. James's. I reach for one of his bedposts, the spiraled wood smooth as glass. I exhale the breath I didn't know I was holding. The room is just a room.

The window between my wardrobe and James's bed—narrow, like an arrow slit—squints down at the lake. If I crane my neck I can see the end of the dock, jutting into the summer's emerald water. I wonder (for the first time, oddly) if I would have watched it happen from here, had I not spent the night of the *Caesar* party one floor down in Meredith's room. Too dark, I tell myself. I wouldn't have seen a thing.

"This was your room?" Behind me, Colborne is looking up

at the ceiling, the faraway central point where all the beams con-
verge, like spokes on a wheel. "You and Farrow."

"Yes, James and I."

Colborne's eyes slowly descend and find my face. He shakes
his head. "The two of you. I never understood it."

"Neither did we. It was easier not to."

He struggles, for a moment, to find words. "What *were* you?"
he asks, finally. It sounds rude, but it's just exasperation at his
own inability to better craft the question.

"We were a lot of things. Friends, brothers, partners in crime."
His expression darkens, but I ignore it and continue. "James was
everything I desperately wanted to be and never could: talented,
intelligent, worldly. The only child of a family that prized art
over logic and passion over peace and quiet. I stuck to him like a
burr from the day we met, hoping some of his brilliance might
rub off on me."

"And him?" Colborne asks. "What was his interest in you?"

"Is it so hard to believe that someone might just like me, Joe?"

"Not at all. I've told you more than once that I like you, completely in spite of myself."

"Yes," I say, dryly, "and it never fails to give me a warm fuzzy
feeling."

He smirks. "You don't have to answer the question, but I
won't withdraw it."

"Very well. This is guesswork, of course, but I think James
liked me for the opposite reasons that I liked him. Everyone
called me 'nice,' but what they really meant was 'naïve.' I was
naïve and impressionable and shockingly *ordinary*. But I was just
clever enough to keep up with him, so he let me."

Colborne gives me a queer, evaluative look. "That's all there
was to it?"

"Of course not," I tell him. "We were inseparable for four
years. It's not something you can explain in a few minutes."

He frowns, pushes his hands into his pockets. My eyes automatically flick to his hip, searching for the gold glint of a police badge, before I remember he's changed jobs. I glance up at his face again. He hasn't aged so much as discolored, the way old dogs do.

"You know what I think it was?" he asks.

I raise my eyebrows, intrigued. People often wanted my explanation of my relationship with James—which seemed inherently unfair, expecting one half of an equation to account for the whole—but no one has ever offered their own diagnosis.

"I think he was enamored with you because you were so enamored with him."

("Enamored." I note that this is the word he chooses to use. It doesn't feel quite right to me, but it's not entirely wrong either.)

"It's possible," I say. "I never asked. He was my friend—much more than that, truthfully—and that was enough. I didn't need to know why."

We stand facing each other in a silence that is awkward only for him. There's another question he's itching to ask, but he won't. He gets as close as he can, starts slowly, perhaps hoping I'll leap in and finish the thought for him. "When you say 'more than friends' . . ."

I wait. "Yes?"

He abandons the attempt. "I suppose it doesn't matter, but I can't help wondering."

I give him a smile nondescript enough that he will probably go on wondering—about this much, at least—for a good long while. If he'd had enough nerve to ask, I would have told him. My infatuation with James (there's the word, never mind "enamored") transcended any notion of gender. Colborne—regular Joe, happily married, father of two, not unlike my own father in some respects—does not strike me as the sort of man who would understand this. No man is, perhaps, until he experiences it himself and deniability is no longer plausible.

What *were* we, then? In ten years I have not found an adequate word to describe us.

SCENE 1

As soon as the third-years finished *Two Gentlemen of Verona*, the set was ripped down with unceremonious haste. Three days later, the set for *Lear* had overtaken the stage, and we walked through the transformed space for the first time. During what normally would have been combat class, we shuffled in through the wings, one by one, numb to the usually exciting prospect of a new set. (Alexander was back from the clinic by then. He brought up the rear—hollow-eyed, stiff and lifeless, a walking cadaver. He looked so utterly broken that I hadn't yet had the heart—or perhaps the nerve—to confront him, about anything.)

"Here it is," Camilo said, as he flicked the work lights on. "They've really outdone themselves this time."

For one precious moment, I forgot my tiredness, the weight of constant worry that had settled on my shoulders. It was like wandering into a dreamland.

Taped out on the floor, the set was deceptively simple: a bare stage and the narrow Bridge stretching down the center aisle like a runway. But the artistic design seized the imagination like a drug. An enormous mirror covered every inch of the floor, reflecting the deep shadows beyond the border curtains. Another mirror rose at the upstage wall where the backdrop should have been, tilted just enough that it, too, only reflected black and emptiness—not the audience. Meredith was the first to venture out onto the stage, and I fought a ridiculous urge to grab her arm and pull her back. Her identical twin appeared upside down, reflected in the floor. "God," she said. "How did they do it?"

"It's mirrored plexiglass," Camilo explained, "so it won't crack and it's perfectly safe to walk on. The costume crew is fitting special grips to the bottoms of our shoes so we don't slip."

She nodded, gazing down a sheer vertical drop to—what? Cautiously, Filippa stepped out to join her. Then Alexander, then Wren, then James. I waited in the wings, uncertain.

"Wow," Wren said, in a small, awed voice. "What does it look like with the stage lights on?"

"Why don't I show you?" Camilo said, turning to the monitor in the prompt corner. "*Voilà.*"

Wren gasped as the lights came up. It wasn't the hot, sweltering yellow we were used to, but bright dazzling white. We blinked, blinded, until our eyes adjusted. Then Meredith pointed upward and said, "Look!"

Overhead, between the backdrop mirror and the grand drape (where normally there were only a few bare battens and long vines of rope), a million tiny fiber-optic cables hung, burning bright blue like stars. The mirror beneath everyone's feet had been transformed to an endless night sky.

"Go on," Camilo said to me. "I promise it's safe."

I obediently inched out of the wings and set my foot down, worried it would simply go through the floor and I would plummet. But the mirror was there, deceptively solid. I walked gingerly to center stage where my classmates stood in a tight little group, alternately looking up and down, faces slack with amazement.

"They've done actual constellations," Filippa said. "That's Draco." She pointed, and James followed her gaze. I glanced down toward the Bridge, where another line of fiber-optic wires hung from the ceiling in the house.

"Trippy," Alexander said, softly.

Below us, our reflections stretched down into a starry abyss. My stomach rolled unpleasantly.

"Take your time," Camilo said. "Walk around. Get used to moving on a three-dimensional floor."

The others dispersed, drifting quietly away from me, like ripples on the surface of the lake. I realized, with a funny little jolt behind my solar plexus, that this was what it reminded me of: the lake in middle winter, before freezing, the vast black sky reflected like a portal to another universe. I closed my eyes, feeling seasick.

The last few weeks had passed in a whirl and rush, time sometimes moving so slowly it was unbearable, sometimes so fast that it was impossible to catch our breath. We had become a small colony of insomniacs. Outside of classes and rehearsals, Wren rarely left her room, but more often than not the light stayed on all night. Alexander, once released from the hospital, spent two hours every week with a nurse and the school shrink, and lived under threat of expulsion should he put another toe out of line. In the Castle he was constantly observed by Colin and Filippa as he suffered through withdrawal. They suffered with him—watching, worrying, not sleeping. I slept fitfully, at strange hours, and never for very long. When I spent the night downstairs with Meredith she lay cool and quiet beside me, but always kept one hand on my arm or my back or my chest while she read (sometimes for hours without ever turning a page), perhaps just to be certain I was there. If I couldn't sleep in one room, I crept to the other. James was a fickle companion. Sometimes we lay on our opposite beds in companionable quiet. Sometimes he tossed and muttered in his sleep. Other nights, when he thought I was already dreaming, he slid out of bed, took his coat and shoes, and disappeared into the dark outside. I never asked where he went, worried he wouldn't ask me to follow.

I still saw Richard, almost nightly, more often than not in the undercroft. Blood leaked out from underneath the locker door, and when I opened it I found him crushed inside, red dripping from his nose and eyes and mouth. But he was no longer the only player in my oneiric repertory; Meredith and James had both joined the company, cast sometimes as my lovers, sometimes my enemies, sometimes in scenes so chaotic that I couldn't tell which.

Worst of all, sometimes they clashed with each other and seemed not to see me at all. In my subconscious dramas they, like violence and intimacy, became somehow interchangeable. More than once I woke with a guilty start, unable to remember which bedroom I was in, who else's breath stirred softly in the silence.

I opened my eyes, and my own vertiginous reflection stared up at me. My cheeks were gaunt, my skin blotchy with fading bruises. I lifted my head, looked from one friend to another. Alexander had made his way to the end of the Bridge and sat staring out at the empty house. Meredith stood at the very edge of the stage, looking down into the orchestra pit, like a jumper contemplating suicide. Wren, a few paces behind her, put one foot carefully in front of the other, arms outstretched, tightrope walking. Filippa had retreated to the left wing; her face was turned up toward Camilo, who had leaned close to whisper something without interrupting the lull.

I found James standing against the backdrop, one arm outstretched, palm to palm with his own reflection, his eyes slate blue in the cold cosmic light.

I shifted and my shoes squeaked on the mirror. James turned and caught my eye. But I stayed where I was, afraid to move toward him, afraid I might lose my footing on solid ground, detach from what had anchored me before and drift out into the void of space—a vagabond, wandering moon.

SCENE 2

Our first performance of *Lear* went smoothly enough. Posters done in white and midnight blue had appeared on every blank wall on campus and in town. One version showed a white-robed Frederick, Wren limp and unmoving at his feet. Beneath that:

COME NOT BETWEEN THE DRAGON AND HIS WRATH

On the other, James stood alone on the Bridge, sword at his side, a bright spot in the darkness. A few of the Fool's wise words were scattered among the stars reflected under him:

TRUST NOT IN THE TAMENESS OF THE WOLF

The house was full on opening night. When we all appeared onstage for curtain call, the audience rose to their feet in one oceanic surge, but the clapping didn't drown out the small sounds of grief that had persisted from the final tragic scene. Gwendolyn sat in the front row beside Dean Holinshed, tears shining on her cheeks, a tissue pinched beneath her nose. We returned to the dressing rooms in suffocating silence.

We'd planned to have the cast party as usual on Friday night, though none of us, I was certain, really felt like having a party at all. At the same time, we were desperate to pretend that everything was all right—or something like it—and to prove as much to everyone else. Colin, who died at the end of Act III, had taken it upon himself to hurry back to the Castle before curtain call and have everything ready for us when we arrived. In a halfhearted show of respect for the school's recent crackdown on reckless drinking, we'd only bought half the booze we normally did, and Filippa and Colin made it clear to prospective guests that if any illegal substance came within a mile of the Castle—or Alexander—there would be hell to pay.

We took our time undressing after the show, partly because our costumes were complicated (we'd been dressed in a neoclassical Empire style, in shades of blue and gray and lilac), and partly because we, poor sleepers all, were too tired to move any faster. James changed more quickly than I or Alexander, hung his costume on the rack, and left the room without a word. When we emerged into the crossover, there was no sign of him.

"He must have already left for the Castle."

"You think?"

"Where else would he go?"

"Who knows. I've stopped wondering."

The night was cold, a gusty, merciless wind blowing down out of the sky. We pulled our coats close around us and walked briskly, heads down. The wind was so loud that we were nearly at the front door before we heard the music. Unlike our last party, there were no lights outside—only a dim yellowish glow seeping out from the kitchen. Upstairs, a candle guttered in one of the library windows.

We let ourselves in and found the kitchen sparsely populated. Only two handles had been cracked, and most of the food was untouched.

"What time is it?" I asked.

"Late enough," Alexander said. "There should be more people here."

We accepted a few soft congratulations from the small crowd gathered at the counter before Wren and Filippa came in from the dining room. They'd changed into their party clothes, but they looked strangely colorless—Filippa in sleek silvery gray, Wren in pale ice pink.

"Hey," Filippa said, voice raised just enough to be heard over the bounce and thud of music from the next room, which felt incongruously upbeat. "Feel like a drink?"

Alexander: "Might as well. What have we got?"

Wren: "Not much. There's some Stoli stashed upstairs."

Me: "Fine by me. Have either of you seen James?"

They shook their heads in unison.

Filippa: "We thought he'd come back with you."

Me: "Yeah. We did, too."

"He might just be taking one of his walks," Wren suggested. "I think he needs a few minutes to come down from being Edmund, you know?"

"Yeah," I said again. "I guess."

Alexander surveyed the room, neck craned to see over everyone's heads, and asked, "Where's Colin?"

"In the dining room," Wren said. "He's hosting more than
we are."

Filippa touched Alexander's elbow. "C'mon," she said,
"he's been waiting for you," and they disappeared into the dining
room together.

Wren offered me a weak smile. I mimicked it without conviction and said, "I don't suppose you've seen Meredith."

"In the garden, I think."

"Will you be all right if I leave you?"

She nodded. "I'll be fine."

I left her, a little reluctantly, and slipped outside.

Meredith was sitting on the table again. It would have been
a familiar sight, reminiscent of that now infamous November
night, if not for the empty, barren feeling of the yard. The wind
whirled around me, darted under my shirt and jacket, and sent
goose bumps skating across my skin. Meredith huddled on the
table, elbows folded close to her body, knees pressed tightly together. She was wearing black again, but she looked more like
she was ready for a wake than a party. Her hair blew in a wild
auburn gust around her face.

As I walked across the yard, the tree branches rustled and
swept together, a soft hiss and clatter in the shadows. Music
limped and lilted from the Castle, drowned out by the wind one
moment, carried through the trees like the smoky-sweet scent
of incense the next. I sat beside Meredith on the table, and her
hair tangled around her fingers as she pushed it out of her face.
At first it was hard to see in the gloom, but the tender skin under
her eyes glistened, and little black smudges had rubbed off beneath her lashes. Raggedy Ann. She breathed in short little bursts
through her nose, but was otherwise silent. She hadn't looked at
me since I set foot outside, and I didn't know if a touch would be
comforting or unwelcome, so I did nothing.

"Are you okay?" I asked, when the wind settled for a moment. The same question I'd asked James in the Tower a month before—the same because I already knew the answer.

"Not even a little bit."

"Can I help?" I glanced down at my hands, lying limp and useless in my lap. "I still—I want to help."

The breeze kicked up again, tossed a few locks of her hair into my face. It brushed my lips, tickled my nose. Her perfume was familiar by then, amber and jasmine. Something ached deep in my chest. The squall passed, and her hair fell down around her shoulders again. She picked at the rim of her cup with short, bitten-down fingernails she'd tried to hide with wine-red polish.

"Oliver," she said, her voice strained and plaintive, "I have to tell you something."

The ache in my chest sharpened, the scab on my soul threatening to split wide open. "Okay," I said. A single loose tear dragged a line of watercolor black down her cheek. I wanted to brush it away, kiss both her eyelids, take her hands and rub some warmth into them. Instead, I waited.

She lifted her head suddenly, wiped underneath her eyes, and looked sideways at me. "You know, let's talk about it tomorrow."

"Really?" I said. "I don't—"

I felt her hand on the inside of my knee. "Tomorrow."

"All right. If you're sure."

"I'm sure," she said. "Let's try to have some fun tonight."

The ache faded to a sick, sad feeling and sank down into my stomach. "Sure." I pointed at the corner of my own eye. "Do you want to—?"

"Yeah. Let me put myself back together and then I'll come find you." She handed me her mostly empty cup. "You want to get me a drink?"

"Will it help?"

"It won't hurt."

She slid off the table, her hand trailing down off my knee. I watched her silhouette as she crossed the yard, the wind rising again and lifting her hair, dragging it behind her. When she disappeared inside, the wheels and cogs of my brain began to turn, slowly at first. What did she want to tell me that was so tremendous it had drawn tears from her, a woman made of marble?

I had tortured myself asking whether my own selfish desire to pursue her with impunity was a stronger factor than fear of Richard when I agreed to let him die. But I had never considered the possibility that Meredith might be guilty of something just as bad—or something worse. The past six months splintered into sharp little fragments of memory: the firelight flashing on Meredith's teeth as she laughed, sand and water and a wet sheet clinging to her body on the beach. Her, falling on the stage, blood creeping down out of her sleeve. Arms rigid at her sides as she shouted at Richard in the kitchen. His fingers clenched in her hair. A scrap of bloody fabric in the fireplace. Could she have done it? Left me sleeping in her room, crept out of the Castle and down to the dock and killed him, then stripped her clothes off and crawled back into bed with me? I felt light-headed just thinking about it. But it was absurd, almost impossible. I would have woken, surely.

Another image, another flash, half dream and half recollection, came unbidden into my brain. Studio Five. Her. James. I squeezed my eyes shut tightly and shook my head to dissolve the picture, disarrange it, like a drawing in dry sand. In an effort to distract myself, I tipped her cup to my lips to taste the drops on the bottom. Vodka. I climbed down off the table and stepped through the back door just as the wind began howling again.

Voices and music swelled in the Castle, trapped there by the gales sweeping past outside. In the kitchen, Wren and Colin talked with the second-years from *Lear*. Filippa and Alexander were nowhere to be seen, and Meredith, too, had disappeared by then. I slid between a few first-years discussing their summer plans with little enthusiasm and made my way toward the stairs. Wren had said the Stoli was stashed upstairs, but never specified where. Not Alexander's room, which had been declared a substance-free zone. The library seemed most likely. I ducked in from the stairwell and stopped, surprised not to find it empty.

"James."

He was standing on the table with his back to me, hands in his pockets. He'd opened the window and the wind rolled into the room, ruffling the tails of his shirt, which he hadn't bothered to button. An open fifth of vodka stood on the table beside him, but I didn't see a glass.

"What are you doing?" I asked. All of the candles—which normally we never lit, considering the number of books in the room—burned and flickered at the caprice of the breeze and sent shadows chasing one another across the shelves and floor and ceiling. It looked like he was having some kind of séance.

"You know you can see the boathouse if you stand up here."

"Great," I said. "Will you get down? You're making me nervous."

He turned around and stepped off the edge of the table, hands still in his pockets. He landed with surprising ease for someone who'd drunk a pint of vodka in less than an hour, then wandered across the room until he was standing right in front of me. He hadn't washed his face since the show—his pale powder makeup and the pencil smudged along his lower lash line gave the impression that his eyes were retreating deep into his skull.

"*Brother, a word,*" he said, with an odd lopsided leer.

"Okay, but can we close the window first?"

"*Shut up your doors, my lord: 'tis a wild night.*"

I stepped around him, went to the window, and pulled it shut. "You're in a weird mood."

"*This cold night will turn us all to fools and madmen.*"

"Stop that. I can't understand you."

He sighed and said, "*They'll have me whipp'd for speaking true; thou'lt have me whipp'd for lying; and sometimes I am whipp'd for holding my peace.*"

"What is the matter with you?"

"*Sick, O, sick!*"

"Drunk, more like."

"*By an enforc'd obedience of planetary influence!*" he said, insistently. "*And pat! He comes, like the catastrophe of the old comedy.*" He climbed up on the table again and sat with his legs dangling off the side. He was drunker than I'd ever seen him, and unsure of what else to do, I decided to play along.

"*How now, brother Edmund?*" I asked. "*What serious contemplation are you in?*"

"*I am thinking, brother, of a prediction I read this other day,*" he said. "*Death, dearth, dissolutions of ancient amities, menaces and maledictions, banishment of friends, nuptial breaches, and I know not what.*"

"*Do you busy yourself with that?*"

He jumped several lines ahead. "*If you do stir abroad, go arm'd.*"

"*Arm'd, brother?*"

"*I advise you to the best. Go arm'd. I am no honest man.*"

I waited for the "if" that should have followed, but it never came. He skipped ahead again, nonsensically.

"*I have told you what I have seen and heard; but faintly, nothing like the image and horror of it.*" He leapt off the table and ran to the window, thrust it open again. "*He's coming hither; now, i' th' night, i' th' haste!*" He gripped the windowsill with white-knuckled fingers, leaning as far out as he could, eyes flicking back and forth through the bone-bare branches of the trees. "*Here stood he in the dark, his sharp sword out.*"

I laid a hand on his shoulder, afraid he might fall if he leaned too much farther, and said, "*But where is he?*" Who did he mean? Richard? He wasn't just playing—I could tell that much by the way he was breathing, staring, not blinking.

He dragged one hand across his face and gasped, "*Look, sir, I bleed!*" He brandished his naked palm, pushed it into my face. I swatted it down, patience rapidly running out.

"*Where is the villain, Edmund?*" I asked.

He smiled crazily at me and echoed, "*Where is the villain, Edmund? A pause, for punctuation, yes?* But not the playwright's—commas belong to the compositors. *Where is the villain Edmund? Here, sir, but trouble him not—his wits are gone.*"

"You're scaring me," I said. "Snap out of it."

He shook his head, his grin shrinking until it disappeared. "*Pray ye, go,*" he said.

"James, just talk to me!"

He pushed me back a step. "*Pray you, away! I do serve you in this business.*"

He shouldered past me, moved rapidly toward the door. I ran after him, caught his arm, and yanked him around. "James! Stop!"

"*Stop, stop! No help? The enemy's in view!*" He was shouting by then, and he beat one hand hard against his bare chest, where it left an angry red mark. I struggled to keep hold of his other wrist. "*The wheel is come full circle; I am here!*"

"James!" I jerked on his arm. "What are you talking about? What's wrong?"

"*No less than all—and more, much more. The time will bring it out!*" He wrenched his arm away and smoothed the front of his shirt, as if he were trying to wipe his hands clean. "*Some blood drawn on me would beget opinion / Of my more fierce endeavor.*"

"You're drunk. You're not making sense," I decided, unwilling to believe the opposite. "Just calm down and we'll—"

He shook his head grimly. "*I have seen drunkards / Do more than this in sport.*" He took a step back toward the stairs.

"James!" I reached for his arm again, but he moved more quickly, one hand darting out to knock a pair of candles off the nearest shelf. I swore and leapt out of the way.

"*Torches, torches!*" he cried. "*So farewell!*"

He dashed into the stairwell and disappeared. I swore again and stamped the candles out. The corner of a folio facsimile on the bottom shelf had caught fire. I ripped it out from underneath the others and smothered the flames with the corner of the carpet. When it was out I sat back on my heels and wiped one sleeve across my forehead, which by then was spotted with sweat, despite the cold March air blowing in from the window.

"What the fuck. What the *fuck*," I muttered, and climbed shakily to my feet again. I crossed the room and shut the window, locked it, then turned and eyed the vodka bottle on the table. It was two-thirds empty. Meredith and Wren and Filippa had had some, certainly, but they were mostly sober. James had never been a drinker. He'd made himself sick at the *Caesar* party, but—but what? He hadn't had half so much then.

His disjointed words echoed in the empty room. An actor's rambling, I told myself. Method touched with madness. No meaning in it. I put the bottle to my lips. The vodka burned my tongue, but I swallowed it in one ugly gulp. Watery saliva gathered at the back of my throat like I myself might be sick.

I hastily blew the candles out, then started down the stairs, clutching the bottle, determined to find James. I'd march him out into the bracing air and keep him there until he sobered up enough to make some kind of sense.

I nearly crashed into Filippa at the bottom of the stairs.

"I was just coming up for the vodka," she said. "Jesus, did you drink all that yourself?"

I shook my head. "James. Where is he?"

"God, I don't know. He came through the kitchen a minute ago."

"Right," I said.

She caught my sleeve as I tried to brush past her. "Oliver, what's wrong?"

"I don't know. James is just about unhinged. I'm going to see if I can find him and figure out what the hell's going on. You keep an eye on the others."

"Yeah," she said. "Yeah, of course."

I pushed the Stoli into her hand. "Hide that," I said. "It's definitely too late for James and it might be too late for Meredith, but keep Wren and Alexander sober if you can. I've got a weird feeling about this night."

"All right," she said. "Hey. Be careful."

"Of what?"

"Of James." She shrugged. "You said, he's not himself. Just . . . remember what happened last time."

I stared at her until I realized she was talking about my broken nose. "Yeah," I said. "Thanks, Pip."

I slid past her, out through the hall and into the kitchen. The only people there were third-years, mostly from the theatre class. They stopped talking, looked my way when I came in. Colin wasn't among them, so I addressed the group at large, raising my voice just enough to be heard over the music from the next room. "Any of you seen James?"

Nine of the ten of them shook their heads, but the last one pointed toward the front door and said, "That way. Bathroom, by the look it."

"Thanks." I nodded at her and went the way she'd indicated. The foyer was dark and empty. Wind rushed against the front door, rattled the panes in the transom window. The bathroom door was closed, but a light peeked out underneath and I opened it without knocking.

The scene there was even stranger, more unsettling than the one in the library. James leaned over the sink, his weight on his fists, the knuckles of his right hand split and bleeding. A huge fractal crack in the mirror stretched in jagged lines from corner to corner, and a long black streak on the counter led to the tip of an uncapped mascara wand. The tube had rolled onto the floor and gleamed against the baseboard, a flash of metallic purple. Meredith's.

"James, what the hell," I said, pins and needles prickling down my spine. His head jerked up as if he hadn't heard the door, didn't know I'd come in. "Did you break the mirror?"

He glanced at it, then back at me. "Bad luck."

"I don't know what's going on, but you've got to talk to me," I said, distracted by the drumming of my pulse in my ears and the mismatched thud of music through the wall—persisting, unimpeded. "I just want to help. Let me help, okay?"

His lip was trembling and he tucked it behind his teeth, but his arms were quivering, too, like they couldn't support his weight. A crack split his face into four different pieces in the mirror. He shook his head. "No."

"C'mon. You can tell me. Even if it's bad, even if it's really bad. We'll find a way to fix it." I realized I was begging and swallowed hard. "James, *please*."

"No." He tried to push past me, but I blocked him in. "Let me go!"

"James! Wait—"

He threw his weight against me, drunkenly, heavily. I braced myself against the door with one arm, caught him around the shoulders with the other. He shoved harder when he felt my hand on him and I crushed him against me, fighting to keep him from knocking me aside or toppling both of us to the floor.

"Let me go!" he said, voice muffled where his face was caught in the crook of my arm. He strained against me for a moment longer, but I had him in a strangely solid grip, his arms trapped between us, hands pushing futilely against my chest. He seemed so *small* all of a sudden. How easy it should have been for me to overpower him.

"Not until you talk to me." My throat tightened, and I was

afraid I would cry until I realized James was crying already, sobbing even, huge clumsy breaths making his shoulders shudder and jerk in my grip. We wavered in what had somehow become an embrace until he lifted his head, found his face too close to mine. He writhed away from me, then stumbled out into the foyer and said, with a child's petulant anger, "*Don't* follow me, Oliver."

But I pursued him blindly, idiotically, like a man in a dream compelled by some great mysterious force to move forward. I lost him in the press of people dancing in the dining room, the lights hazy and indistinct, blue and purple, electric shadows moving dizzily from wall to wall. I pawed my way between dancers, searching for James's face in the blur of people. I caught a glimpse as he slipped into the kitchen and followed close on his heels, almost falling in my haste to catch up with him.

Wren, Colin, Alexander, and Filippa had joined the third-years. James looked over his shoulder, saw me, then grabbed Wren's arm and pulled her away from the others.

"James!" she squeaked, tripping after him. "What are you—"

He was already dragging her out of the kitchen, toward the stairwell tower.

"Don't—!" I said, but he talked over me.

"Wren, come up to bed with me, please."

She stopped dead, and we all froze around her, watching. But all she could see was James. Her lips moved soundlessly and then she stammered, "Yes."

He looked over her head at me, something strange and bitter and vindictive in his expression, but for only a split second. Then he was gone, pulling her out of the room behind him. In disbelief I tried to follow them, but Alexander caught me by the shoulder. "Oliver, no," he said. "Not this time."

He and Filippa and I all stood staring at one another, while the silent third-years stared at us. Music surged on obliviously behind us, and the wind roared outside. I stood paralyzed in the middle of the room, too dismayed to speak or move. To notice, at first, that Meredith was missing.

SCENE 3

I woke up alone in Filippa's room. After James disappeared into the Tower with Wren, I'd spent the night wandering the Castle in a daze, wondering where Meredith had gone and more worried than I would confess to anyone. By the time the place emptied and everyone else was in bed, I came to the unnerving conclusion that she wasn't coming back. At half past three I knocked on Filippa's door. She opened it wearing an oversized flannel shirt and wool socks pulled halfway up her calves.

"I can't go up to the Tower," I told her. "Meredith's gone. I don't want to sleep alone." Finally I understood the feeling.

She opened the door, tucked me into bed, and curled up in a ball beside me, all without saying a word. When I shivered she shifted closer, draped one arm over my side, and fell asleep with her chin perched on my shoulder. I listened to her breath and felt her heart beat against my back and tricked myself into thinking that maybe, when we woke up, everything would be back to normal. But what kind of normal did we have to go back to?

In the morning, everyone was gone. I didn't know where, but they'd be expecting to come home to a Castle cleaned and scoured, all evidence of the party washed away. I needed distraction like a drug, something to occupy and exhaust my mind, to keep it from wandering back into the memory labyrinth of the previous night. So I spent hours on my hands and knees, dizzy from the smell of bleach, my hands raw from scrubbing. It seemed to me that the Castle hadn't been cleaned properly in years, and I attacked the grime that had settled into the grooves between the floorboards, possessed by the idea that I could purge the place, baptize it, absolve it of its sins and make it new again.

From the kitchen I moved through the downstairs bathroom, the dining room, the foyer. There was nothing I could do about the broken mirror—I'd have to contact the custodial staff at the Hall—but I wiped away the red smear of James's blood, the black slash of Meredith's mascara. The tube was still on the floor. I picked it up, pocketed it, wondering when I'd have the chance to return it to her.

I crawled up the stairs, rag and polish in hand, and by the time I reached the second floor, my knees were aching. I couldn't fix the burn mark on the library carpet, so I left it as it was. I cleaned the bathroom, mopped the floor in the hall, wiped down bedroom windows, and tidied where I could without disturbing anyone's things. I made the bed in Filippa's room. The sight of Wren's bed, smooth and unslept in, made my stomach wind up in a tight little knot. I closed her door, didn't venture in. Alexander's room was such a mess that I couldn't do much. I glanced under his bed and through his drawers, checking for drug paraphernalia, but didn't find anything. (He'd learned his lesson, I hoped.) Meredith's room looked exactly as we'd last left it, cluttered but not chaotic: books piled on the desk, empty wineglasses on the nightstand, clothes thrown across the foot of the bed. I didn't see her dress from the night before.

When I emerged again, Richard's door seemed to be watching me from the end of the hall. Someone had closed it after he died, and as far as I knew none of us had opened it since. I blinked, unable to even really remember what his room looked like. Without realizing I had made the decision to move, I found myself walking down the hall, turning the handle. The door opened without protest, without so much as a squeak. Early evening light, touched with the pink of sunset, streamed in through the window and lay decadently across the bed. The rest of the room stood in quiet gray-blue shade, patiently waiting for night to fall. So many of his things were still there; hardback books, naked without their dust jackets, were stacked on the shelf above the bed, and his watch (I knew without wanting to know that Meredith had given it to him for his birthday, third year) lay discarded on the desk. A pair of brown leather boxing gloves hung over one corner of the closet door, and inside I could see a row of hangers, the white undershirts he'd liked so much hung up beside button-downs that might actually wrinkle. An old, forgotten affection stirred and I looked away, searching for something to remind me why I'd be a fool to regret for one minute that he was gone. A collection of wooden chess pieces stood like a row of soldiers awaiting orders on the windowsill. They were all upright except the white horsemen, one of which had fallen sideways. The other was missing from the place where it should have stood. Wondering if it might have toppled off the ledge, I crouched down to peer underneath the bed, and felt the tiny muffled voice of my conscience cry out. A pair of shoes lay crookedly where he'd last kicked them off, laces plucked at and tangled. I knew him well enough to know he never would have left them that way if he'd thought he wasn't coming back.

Grief seized me so suddenly I thought I might black out. He was there, in that room where we'd tried to lock him up, shut him out of sight, with all our deadly sins to keep him company. I staggered to my feet, blundered into the hall, and slammed the door.

I climbed the stairs to the Tower, unsure of what I would find but desperate to put as much distance between myself and Richard's room as possible. At first glance, it looked like it always did, and for a moment I stood swaying in the doorway, hoping to find comfort in its tame familiarity. Our little attic room, with its two beds, two bookshelves, two wardrobes. When my legs felt steady enough, I wandered in. My own messy bed I made with meticulous care, delaying the inevitable cross to James's side of the room. When I could find nothing else to straighten, nothing to fold, nothing to hide in a drawer or tuck out of sight in the wardrobe, I moved from my corner into his.

I straightened the books, shook the dust from the curtains, picked up a pencil that had rolled off a shelf and onto the floor. James was unfailingly neat, always had been, and there wasn't much to keep me occupied. Finally, I reached for the bedspread, pulled it and the sheet beneath it flat against the mattress, trying not to think of him and Wren and how each wrinkle and crease had been pressed into place.

A corner of the sheet was hanging out from under the mattress. I crouched down to fix it, but paused when I felt something unexpectedly soft between my fingers. As I lifted my hand a tuft of white floated away from my palm and settled on the floor again. I tugged the corner of James's bedspread loose and found another little cluster of cotton tufts gathered around one leg of the bedframe, as if they'd been gradually swept there by careless passing feet. I folded the blanket farther back. If there were bedbugs, or a spring was poking through, I'd need to add a new mattress to my list of requests for the real custodial staff.

I pulled the fitted sheet up off the foot of the bed. There was a jagged rip in the end of the mattress, like a grinning mouth six inches long. I checked the footboard for a nail, a protuberant splinter, but didn't find anything that could have torn through the fabric. The split gaped, laughed at me, and I didn't realize I was leaning closer until I saw the narrow red smudge on the edge of the tear, like a dash of lipstick. I sat staring at the mattress for a moment like I'd been fused to the spot. Then I reached in through the hole.

I groped through a tangle of springs and cotton and foam until I felt something severely, indisputably solid. It didn't come easily—something at the end kept catching—but with one good yank I wrenched it free and let it clatter to the floor. It looked alarmingly wrong lying there—anachronistic, almost Gothic, stolen out of time from a darker age. In the back of my brain I knew what it was, really: an old boat hook, curved at one end like a claw, snatched from the long-forgotten rack of tools at the back of the boathouse. The talon and pole had been hastily wiped clean, but blood still clung to the crevices, cracked and flaking away like rust.

My lungs struggled for air. I grabbed the boat hook off the floor and fled the room, one hand clapped over my mouth, afraid I might vomit my heart out onto the floor.

SCENE 4

I sprinted through the forest to the FAB like I had only a few weeks before, then with a scrap of fabric clutched in my fist. I ran with the boat hook at my side like a spear, feet churning the earth to a pulp. When the building was in sight I realized my mistake—I'd forgotten the time. People were already lining up outside to see the show, playgoers in their evening clothes, talking and laughing and clutching glossy programs. I dropped into a crouch and crept along the bottom of the hill, head bent low.

The side door to the stairwell opened with a crunch. I caught it when it tried to slam behind me, let it shut more softly, then took the stairs down to the basement so fast I almost fell. Sweat prickled on my face as I shoved my way through the mass of furniture piled up in the undercroft. After three harrowing minutes I found the room with the lockers again, the open padlock glaring at me like a single Cyclopean eye. I dragged the trestle table aside, removed the lock, and threw the door open. The mug was sitting there, untouched, that guilty bit of fabric stuffed in the bottom like a crumpled napkin. I thrust the boat hook in beside it, slammed the door and kicked it until it latched, heedless of the sound. The lock scraped as it slid back through the loop, and I pushed the shackle toe into place without hesitating. I staggered back, stared for a moment, then scrambled out to the stairwell again, panic rising from the soles of my feet to the crown of my head in a hot, delirious rush.

I ran down two backstage hallways, the clatter and murmur of the audience seeping through the walls. In the crossover, two second-years hurried past me to get to the wings, pointing and whispering as I charged by. I flung the dressing room door open, and everyone looked up at once.

"Where in the *fuck* have you been?" Alexander demanded.

"I'm sorry!" I said. "I just—I'll explain later. Where's my costume?"

"Well, Timothy's fucking wearing it because we didn't know where you were!"

I turned on the spot to find Timothy (a second-year who usually played Cornwall's mutinous servant) already on his feet, looking green, a script clutched in his hand.

"Shit, I'm sorry," I said. "Tim, give me that."

"Thank God," he said. "Oh, thank fucking Christ, I was trying to learn your lines—"

"I'm sorry, something happened—"

I threw my clothes on as he pulled them off, struggling with my boots, sword belt, coat. The audience chatter from the overhead speaker crackled and died out. A small gasp rippled in from the house and I knew the lights had come up on Lear's empyreal palace.

Kent: "*I thought the King had more affected the Duke of Albany than Cornwall.*"

Gloucester: "*It did always seem so to us; but now, in the division of the kingdom, it appears not which of the Dukes he values most, for equalities are so weigh'd that curiosity in neither can make choice of either's moiety.*"

Kent: "*Is not this your son, my lord?*"

I glanced down at Alexander, who was on his knees lacing

my boots as I fumbled with the buttons on my waistcoat. "Is James already onstage?" I asked.

"Obviously." He jerked on my laces so hard I nearly lost my balance. "Hold still, damn you."

"And Meredith?" I reached for my cravat.

"In the wings, I assume."

"So she's here," I said.

He stood and started feeding my belt through the loops. "Why wouldn't she be?"

"I don't know." My fingers were clumsy, unsteady, unable to form the familiar knot. "She stayed out last night."

"Worry about it later. Now's not the time." He buckled my belt too tight and grabbed my gloves off the counter. I glanced in the mirror. My hair was wildly disheveled, sweat glistening on my cheeks. "You look awful," he said. "Are you sick?"

"*I am sick with working of my thoughts,*" I said, before I could stop myself.

"Oliver, what—"

"Never mind," I said. "I have to go." I slipped out into the crossover before he could speak again. The door closed heavily behind me, and I waited with my hand on the knob, forced to stand still by the enormous concentration it took—in that moment—just to breathe. I closed my eyes, mind blank but for inhale, exhale, until the last line of Scene 1 brought me back to life. Meredith's voice, low and resolute: "*We must do something.*"

I made my way to the wings.

I stumbled along the line sets in the merciless dark backstage until my eyes adjusted to the cool glow of the work lamp in the prompt corner. The ASM spotted me and hissed into his headset, "Booth? We have a live Edgar. No, the original. Looks a little worse for wear, but he's dressed and ready to go." He cupped his hand over the microphone, muttered, "Gwendolyn's going to have your balls, friend," and turned his attention back to the stage. I wondered briefly what he would say if I told him that Gwendolyn was the least of my worries.

Onstage, James stood with his head bent in deference to his father.

Gloucester: *"We have seen the best of our time. Machinations, hollowness, treachery, and all ruinous disorders follow us disquietly to our graves. Find out this villain, Edmund—"*

James's mouth twitched, and I remembered his unsettling repetitions of the previous night. Gloucester finished his speech and strode across the star-strewn floor toward the opposite wing.

"This," James said, when he had disappeared. *"This is the excellent foppery of the world, that, when we are sick in fortune—often the surfeit of our own behavior—we make guilty of our disasters the sun, the moon, and the stars . . . as if we were villains on necessity; fools by heavenly compulsion; knaves, thieves, and treachers by spherical predominance; drunkards, liars, and adulterers by an enforc'd obedience of planetary influence; and all that we are evil in, by a divine thrusting-on!"* He looked heavenward, made a fist, and shook it at the stars. A laugh blossomed from his lips and rang in my ears, bold and unabashed. *"An admirable evasion of whore-master man, to lay his goatish disposition to the charge of a star!"* He raised one finger, pointed out a single constellation among a hundred, and spoke more thoughtfully. *"My father compounded with my mother under the Dragon's Tail, and my nativity was under Ursa Major, so that it follows I am rough and lecherous."* He laughed again, but now the laugh was bitter. I shifted my feet on the spot, every hair on the back of my neck standing on end. *"I should have been that I am, had the maidenliest star in the firmament twinkled on my bastardizing. Edgar—"*

He hesitated, whether due to doubt that I would appear or some greater unease, I didn't know. I emerged into our star-world with one cautious step.

"How now, brother Edmund?" I asked, for the second time in eighteen hours. *"What serious contemplation are you in?"*

We moved smoothly through the same conversation we had had the previous night brokenly, bit by bit. James's face might as well have been a mask. He delivered his lines as coolly as he always had, oblivious to the disbelief and fright and fury threatening to rip me in half every time I looked at him. My words were harsh and stringent as I said, "*Some villain hath done me wrong!*"

"*That's my fear,*" he said, slowly, but as he continued he slid back into his same silky drawl. I forgot my blocking, stood motionless, my responses flat and mechanical.

When he finished again I said, sharply, "*Shall I hear from you anon?*"

"*I do serve you in this business,*" he said. It was my time to leave, but I didn't. I waited too long, long enough that he was forced to look through Edgar and see me instead. Recognition flickered in his eyes and, with it, a spark of fear. I turned to go, and as I walked toward the wings I heard him speak again, a little faintly.

James: "*. . . A brother noble,*
>*Whose nature is so far from doing harms*
>*That he suspects none; on whose foolish honesty*
>*My practices ride easy!*"

His bravado sounded suddenly false. He knew what I knew. For the moment, that was enough. The play would falter on.

SCENE 5

I wasted ten scenes or so waiting in the dressing room for James to appear. He never did, but I knew better than to go looking for him in the wings. The kind of confrontation we were doomed to have couldn't be confined to the alleys and walkways backstage. Intermission would be my best chance to catch him before he could slip away. As the last scene of Act III approached its violent climax, I climbed out of my chair, pulling a jacket on over my bare chest. My madman's rags made me feel naked and vulnerable.

The crossover was empty, the lights glowing dull autumnal yellow. I was reaching for the backstage door when Meredith emerged at the other end of the hall. I hadn't really laid eyes on her all night, and for a moment I was frozen in place. She looked like a Grecian princess, draped in pale blue chiffon and voile, a band of gold across her forehead, curls falling loosely down her back. I turned and walked right at her, unsure of when I'd find her alone again, or what the rest of the night might bring. The sound of my footsteps made her look up, and surprise flashed on her face before I caught her and kissed her, as deeply as I dared.

"What was that for?" she asked, when I leaned back.

She knew she was beautiful. I didn't need to tell her that.

"You know, you scare the hell out of me," I said, clutching the fabric of her dress to keep her close.

"What?"

"I don't know, it's like I look at you and suddenly the sonnets make sense. The good ones, anyway."

Whatever either one of us had expected me to say, it wasn't that. She blushed, and a little thrill of joy went through me—improbable, inexplicable, given all the other circumstances of the evening. But then it was extinguished like a candle flame, blown by doubt out of existence.

"Where were you last night?" I asked.

She looked away. "I just—I had to go somewhere."

"I don't understand."

"I'll tell you," she said, absently tracing the notch of my collarbone with one fingertip. "Tonight. Later."

"All right." I couldn't help wondering if there would be time later. What "later" even meant. "Later," I agreed, anyway.

"I have to go." She brushed my hair back off my forehead—a sweet affectionate gesture of hers, by then familiar and per-petually hoped for. But worry and misgivings made my knees weak.

"Meredith," I said, as she moved toward the girls' dressing

room. She paused at the door. "The other day, in class——" I didn't want to say it, but I couldn't stop myself. "Don't kiss James like that again."

She stared in blank incomprehension for a moment; then her expression hardened and she asked, "Who is it that you're jealous of? Him or me?" She made a soft sound of disgust and disappeared through the door before I could reply. My throat seized up. What had I even meant to do? Protect her, warn her, what? I slammed my open hand against the wall, and the impact stung.

It would have to wait. Act III was coming to a close; I could hear Colin gasping through the speakers.

Colin: *"I have receiv'd a hurt. Follow me, lady.*
  Turn out that eyeless villain! Throw this slave
  Upon the dunghill. Regan, I bleed apace.
  Untimely comes this hurt. Give me your arm."

I waited by the stage-left door, my back against the wall. The lights went out and the audience applauded, weakly at first and then with greater fervor, shell-shocked by the gruesome tearing out of Gloucester's eyes. Second-years spilled out of the wings and hurried past without seeing me. Then Colin, then Filippa. Then James.

I grabbed him by the elbow and steered him away from the dressing rooms.

"Oliver! What are you doing?"

"We need to talk."

"Now?" he said. "Let go, you're hurting me."

"Am I?" I had a brutally hard grip on his arm—I was bigger than he was, and for the first time I wanted both of us to be keenly aware of it.

I shoved the hall door open, pulling him through after me. The loading dock had been my first thought, but Alexander and some of the second- and third-years would have gone out to smoke. I considered the basement, but I didn't want to be trapped down there. James asked two or three more questions—all variations on the same theme; where were we going?—but I ignored them and he fell silent, his pulse quickening under my fingers.

The lawn behind the Hall was wide and flat, the last open place before the ground sloped downward toward the trees. The real sky was enormous overhead, making our mirrors and twinkling stage lights seem ridiculous—Man's futile attempt to imitate God. When we were far enough from the FAB that I knew we wouldn't be seen in the dark, much less overheard, I let go of James's arm and shoved him away from me. He stumbled, found his footing, then glanced nervously over his shoulder at the steep drop of the hill behind him.

"Oliver, we're in the middle of a show," he said. "What's this about?"

"I found the boat hook." I wished, suddenly, for the wild howling wind of the previous night. The stillness of the world beneath the dark dome of the sky was suffocating, massive, unbearable. "I found the boat hook, shoved inside your mattress."

His face was pale as bone in the raw moonlight. "I can explain."

"Can you?" I asked. "Because I've got to open Act IV, so you have fifteen minutes to convince me that this isn't what I think it is."

"Oliver—" he said, and turned his face away.

"Tell me you didn't do it." I risked a step closer, afraid to raise my voice above a whisper. "*Tell me* you didn't kill Richard."

He closed his eyes, swallowed, and said, "I didn't mean to."

A steel fist clenched in my chest, crushing the air out of me. My blood felt cold, crawling through my veins like morphine. "Oh, God, James, *no*." My voice cracked. Snapped in half. No sound left.

"I swear, I didn't mean to—you have to understand," he said, coming desperately toward me. I staggered three steps back, where he couldn't reach. "It was an accident, just like we said— it was an accident, Oliver, *please*!"

"No! Don't come too close," I said, forcing words out when there was no air for them. "Keep your distance. Tell me what happened."

The world seemed to stop on its axis, like a top precariously balanced on its point. The stars gleamed cruelly overhead, shards of glass scattered in the sky. Every nerve in my body was a live wire, shrinking away from the touch of the cold March air. James was colder, carved from ice, not my friend, not even human.

"After you went upstairs with Meredith, something happened to Richard," he said. "It was like Halloween, but worse. He came crashing out of the Castle in this . . . *uncontainable* rage. You should have seen it. It was like watching a star explode." He shook his head slowly, terror and awe indistinguishable in his expression. "Wren and I, we were sitting at the table. We had no idea what was happening, but then he just appeared, with this look on his face like he would crush anything that got in his way. He was headed for the woods—to do what, I have no idea—and Wren tried to stop him." He faltered, squeezed his eyes shut, like the memory was too close, too painful, excruciating. "God, Oliver. He grabbed her, and I swear I thought he might just break her in half, but he threw her down in the grass, halfway across the yard. And he stormed off into the trees and left her there, just *sobbing*. It was horrible. I put her back together as best I could, and Pip and I put her to bed. But she wouldn't stop crying and she kept saying, 'Go after him, he'll hurt himself.' So I went."

I opened my mouth in disbelief, but he didn't give me time to say a word.

"You don't need to tell me how stupid it was," he said. "I know. I knew then. But I went."

"And you found him." I could already see it unfolding. A quarrel. A threat. A shove. Too much.

"Not at first," he said. "I stumbled around in the dark like an idiot, calling for him. Then I had the idea that he might have gone down to the dock." He shrugged, and the motion was so powerless and pathetic that I felt the knot in my chest loosen, just barely. "I climbed down the hill, but I didn't see him. I went as far as the boathouse, just to make sure he hadn't done something stupid, like jump in the water, and when I turned around to go back up, there he was. He'd been following me around in the woods the whole time, like it was some sick sort of game." He was talking faster by then, all the words he'd kept stopped up for months flooding out at once. "And I said, 'There you are. Let's go back up, your cousin's a wreck.' And he said, you can guess what he said, it was 'Don't you worry about my cousin.' So I said, 'Fine. Everyone's upset. Come back and we'll sort it out.' And he gave me that *look* again—God, Oliver, I've been dreaming about it for weeks—it was like all the hate in the world at once. Has anyone ever looked at you like that?" For a moment the same stupefied fear seemed to seize him, but then he shook his head and continued. "And that's when it started. The pushing. The—taunting." His voice climbed to a high, nervous pitch, and he rubbed at his arms, stamped one foot on the ground like he couldn't keep his body warm enough. "And he wouldn't *stop*. It was Halloween again— C'mon, let's play a game. I didn't take the bait and it just got worse. Why don't you fight back? Why won't you get your hands dirty? Let's play a game, little prince, let's play a *game*. That's all it was to him, but I was so scared, and I *tried*, I said, one more time, why don't you just come back to the Castle and we'll talk to Wren? We'll talk to Meredith, we'll fix it. And then he just—he said—" He stopped, his face flushed an ugly red, as if the words were so vile he couldn't repeat them.

"James, what did he say?"

He looked up at me sharply, his head tilted back, his mouth a cruel, flat line, eyes dark and fathomless. He looked like Richard;

he even sounded like him when he spoke. "'Why can't you and Oliver just admit you're queer for each other and leave my girls alone?'"

I stared at him, throat tight, the cold sweat sensation of dread spreading slowly through my limbs.

"So I said," James went on, in his own voice again, "'I don't know who told you otherwise, but you don't own Meredith and you certainly don't own Wren. Drink yourself to death if you like. I'm going.' And he wouldn't let me."

"What do you mean?"

"He wanted a fight. He wouldn't let me leave without one. I tried to walk past him, but he grabbed me, and he threw me against the doors of the boathouse. They're not solid, it's so old, and I kind of crashed inside, fell against all the stuff piled up in there. And he came at me again and I just reached for the nearest thing, and it was the boat hook."

He stopped, pressed his hand over his eyes, like he wanted to wipe the recollection away. His lip trembled. His whole body was trembling.

"And then what?" I didn't want to ask, didn't want to know, didn't want to hear another word.

"And then he *laughed*," James said weakly, from behind his hand. I could almost hear the sound, Richard's deep, dangerous laugh, ringing in the dark. "He laughed and said, do it, pretty boy, little prince, I dare you. And he pushed me again. Pushed me down to the end of the dock, saying, 'I dare you, I dare you, you won't do it.' And I looked behind me and the water was right there and all I could think of was Halloween, and who would keep him from drowning me this time? And he wouldn't shut up, he just kept saying it, you won't do it, I dare you I dare you I dare you, and I—" His hand slid down to cover his mouth, eyes wide with horror, as if he had just in that moment realized what he'd done. "I didn't mean to," he said, a soft little moan from behind his hand. "I didn't *mean* to. But I was so scared, and so angry."

I could see it just as it must have happened. A wild, unplanned blow. The painful jolt of impact. Surprise at the hot spray of blood on his face. Richard falling in slow motion toward the water. A sickening splash and even more sickening silence.

"Oliver, I thought he was dead," he said, so faintly I almost didn't hear him. "I swear, I thought he was already dead. And I didn't know what to do, so I just . . . ran. I think I lost my mind, for a minute. I ran back into the trees and I might have kept running all night if I hadn't run right into Filippa."

I felt numb, frozen, stunned into stillness. "You what?"

He nodded, distractedly, like he couldn't quite remember how the rest of it had happened. "I guess she was worried that I hadn't come back and came out to look for me and I ran right into her. It's a miracle I didn't hurt her, I still had the fucking hook in my hand—I don't know what made me take it."

"She knew," I said, that one fact skipping and repeating in my brain. "She knew?"

"She was so calm, it was like she expected it. She didn't even ask questions, really, just got me inside and up the stairs, somehow. I was shaking so badly she had to help me out of my clothes, but as soon as she left me in the bathroom, went to burn everything with blood on it, I just started throwing up and I couldn't stop until—" He fell abruptly silent, made a strange gesture toward me, like I was supposed to finish the sentence.

"Oh God," I said. "Me." Half asleep, half dressed. Him. Heart hammering, crouched on the floor. "You didn't tell me." I didn't realize until it was out of my mouth that that alone was worse than any of the rest of it. "Why didn't you tell me?"

"I didn't want you to know," he said. He took another step toward me, and this time I didn't move back. "Filippa—maybe she's crazy, I don't know, nothing fazes her—but you? Oliver, you—" His voice failed him, and in its absence he gestured at me again, but it was a thought I couldn't finish for him.

"I what, James? I don't understand."

He let his hand fall back to his side, and he gave me that same helpless, hopeless shrug. "I never wanted you to look at me the way you're looking at me right now."

And maybe there was a kind of terror in my expression, but not for the reason he thought. I looked at him in the cold moonlight, frail and small and scared, and the thousand questions that had come thronging around me every time I looked at him since Christmas melded and fused and shrank until there was really only one.

"Oliver?"

"Yes," I said, that single word accepting everything at once. I couldn't remember when he'd started crying, but tears glistened on his cheeks. He stared at me, mistrustful and confused.

"It's okay," I said, to myself as much as him. I glanced back toward the FAB, calmed somehow as I heard Hamlet in my head again: *The readiness is all.* "It'll be okay," I said, though I'd never been less certain of anything. "We'll sort it out, but now we have to go back." I had no idea what "it" meant or what he thought it was supposed to mean. "We have to go back and act like nothing's wrong. We've got to get through tonight, and then we'll worry about it. All right?"

Relief—hope—something—finally warmed his face. "Are you—"

"Yeah, I am," I said, the only possible answer to whatever he wanted to know. "Let's go." I turned toward the FAB. He caught my arm.

"Oliver," he said, a question clinging to the end of my name.

"It's okay," I said again. "Later. We'll figure it out." He nodded, eyes darting down, but I felt his fingers tighten on my arm. "Come on."

He followed behind me as we ran back to the theatre. We

slipped in through the side door and separated as I went to the wings and he went the other way, toward the bathroom, to wipe all evidence of distress from his face. In that one brief moment, I actually wondered if "okay" or something like it might still be possible. But that is how a tragedy like ours or *King Lear* breaks your heart—by making you believe that the ending might still be happy, until the very last minute.

SCENE 6

The second half of the show moved swiftly, recklessly forward. I was as mad and distracted as Tom o' Bedlam should have been, but Frederick and Gloucester must have noticed a change, for they were both eyeing me suspiciously by the end of the fourth act. Act V opened with James directing the movements of his army. He spoke with undeniable urgency—perhaps as desperate as I was to close the show, sequester ourselves in the Tower, and figure out what to do next. He spoke shortly to Wren, seemed not to see her, and treated Frederick with the same cold apathy. Camilo approached, flanked by Filippa and Meredith—who looked guilty enough that I believed she might have poisoned someone. I lurked in the shadows upstage, waiting for my entrance and the end.

Filippa grew quickly ill and reached for Camilo's arm to steady herself.

Filippa: *"Sick, O, sick!"*

Meredith (aside): *"If not, I'll ne'er trust medicine."*

James (to Camilo, throwing down his glove):
"There's my exchange. What in the world he is
That names me traitor, villain-like he lies."

His voice rose to call me from my hiding place. The heralds were summoned, the trumpets sounded; Filippa collapsed and was carried offstage by a bevy of second-years.

Herald (reading): "*If any man of quality or degree within the lists of the army will maintain upon Edmund, supposed Earl of Glouces-ter, that he is a manifold traitor, let him appear. He is bold in his defense.*'"

I breathed in through the scarf tied over my mouth and nose to disguise me, then entered upstage, one hand on my sword.

Me: "*Know my name is lost;*
       By treason's tooth bare-gnawn and canker-bit.
       Yet am I noble as the adversary
       I come to cope."

Camilo: "*Which is that adversary?*"

Me: "*What's he that speaks for Edmund Earl of Gloucester?*"

James: "*Himself. What say'st thou to him?*"

I spoke a litany of his sins to him, and he listened with keen and intimate attention. When he replied, it was without his usual malice, his usual arrogance. His words were thoughtful, humbly aware of their own falsehood.

James: "*Back do I toss those treasons to thy head;*
       With the hell-hated lie o'erwhelm thy heart,
       Which—for they yet glance by and scarcely bruise—
       This sword of mine shall give them instant way
       Where they shall rest for ever."

We drew our swords, bowed to each other, and our final duel began. We moved almost in unison, blades flashing and gleam-ing under the artificial stars. I began to gain the upper hand, delivering more blows than I received, maneuvering James toward the narrow mouth of the Bridge. Sweat glistened on his forehead and in the hollow of his throat, his footwork growing clumsier. I forced him deep into the unfriendly darkness of the house until he could go no farther. The last ring of steel on steel echoing in my ears, I thrust my rapier under his arm. He grabbed my shoulder, gasped, his own blade clattering down on the mir-rored floor of the Bridge. I let my sword fall, too, slid one arm around his back to take his weight and looked down to find him

staring past me, into the gloom of the stage left wing. Gwendolyn was standing there at the edge of the light, her expression
blank with shock. Holinshed stood beside her, and Detective
Colborne stood beside him, the badge on his hip glinting in the
fiber-optic starlight.

James's fingertips dug into my arms. I clenched my teeth and
lowered him slowly to the floor. Behind us, Meredith was being
ushered from the apron to the wings. Camilo watched her go,
his face dark with questions.

Meredith: *"Ask me not what I know."*

Camilo: *"Go after her. She's desperate; govern her."*

The last second-years left the stage. I crouched over James.
The violet sash we used for blood had emerged from the open
neck of his shirt, and I drew it out slowly as he spoke.

"What you have charg'd me with, that have I done," he said. *"And
more, much more. The time will bring it out."* He shivered under me,
and I laid one hand on his chest to keep him still. *"'Tis past, and so
am I."* A tired smile formed on his mouth. *"But what art thou / That
hast this fortune on me? If thou'rt noble, / I do forgive thee."*

"Let's exchange charity." I pulled the scarf away from my face.
There was nothing else to do to comfort him. *"My name is Edgar
and thy father's son."*

I glanced toward the wings. Meredith stood beside Colborne,
talking close in his ear. When she realized I was watching her, she
closed her lips and slowly shook her head. I turned back to James.
"The gods are just," I said, *"and of our pleasant vices / Make instruments
to scourge us."*

James laughed brokenly, and I felt something deep between
my lungs crack clean in two. *"Th' hast spoken right; 'tis true,"* he
said. *"The wheel is come full circle; I am here."*

Camilo spoke behind us, but I barely heard him. My next
line was meant for him, but I said it to James instead. *"Worthy
prince, I know't."*

He stared up at me for a moment, then lifted his head and

pulled me down to meet him. It was almost a brotherly kiss, but not quite. Too fragile, too painful. Soft whispers of surprise and confusion swept through the audience. My heart throbbed, and it hurt so badly that I bit his lip. I felt his breath catch and let him go, lowered him to the floor again. Silence lingered overlong. Whatever Camilo's line was, he had forgotten it, and so I spoke out of turn. "*List a brief tale; / And when 'tis told, O that my heart would burst!*"

I couldn't remember the rest. Didn't care to. Camilo cut my speech, perhaps to make up for his previous lapse, his voice stumbling and uncertain. James lay limp on the floor, as if Edmund's life had left him and whatever remained of his own was not enough to move.

Camilo: "*If there be more, more woeful, hold it in;*
    For I am almost ready to dissolve."

I didn't speak again. My voice was forfeit. A second-year, realizing that neither James nor I would say another word, came dashing in and shattered the spell of stillness that had descended over the stage. "*Help! O, help!*"

I let Camilo converse with her. Deaths were tallied and accounted. James's time came to be carried off, but neither of us moved, sorely aware of what waited on the other side of the curtain. Servants and heralds said our lines in shy, unsteady voices. Frederick entered, with Wren dead in his arms. He, too, sank to the floor and, despite what anyone could do, died, crushed under the weight of his grief. Camilo—the last bastion of our collapsing world—finished the play as best he could, with a speech that should have been mine.

Camilo: "*The weight of this sad time we must obey,*
    Speak what we feel, not what we ought to say.
    The oldest have borne most; we that are young
    Shall never see so much, nor live so long."

The stars all went out at once. Darkness came plunging down. The audience slid slowly, uncertainly into applause. I clung to

James until the lights came up again, then helped him to his feet. Wren and Frederick reanimated like the living dead. Filippa and Meredith and Alexander emerged from the wings, without raising their eyes from their feet. We bowed stiffly from the waist and waited for the lights to go out again. When they did, we walked single file toward the wings. The curtain closed behind us, a heavy sweep of velvet, shutting out the soft human noise of the audience—climbing to its feet, recovering.

The work lights burned back to life overhead. The first- and second-years shrank away from Colborne's unfamiliar face. He came slowly forward from his place beside the line sets, watching James as if there were nobody else in the world. "Well," he said. "We couldn't play make-believe forever. Are you ready to tell me the truth?"

James wavered beside me, opened his mouth to speak. Before he could make a sound I moved forward, the decision already made, made in the same instant it flashed into existence.

"Yes," I said. Colborne turned toward me in disbelief. "Yes," I said again. "I am."

SCENE 7

Lights and sirens. Outside in the insubstantial air, audience members in their best clothes, technicians in black, and actors in costume watched as Walton guided me into the back of a car with *Broadwater Police Department* branded on the side. Everyone was whispering, staring, pointing, but I could only see my classmates, huddled together just like that day on the dock all over again. Alexander's face was so full of sadness that there was no room left for surprise. In Filippa's expression there was only a desperate kind of confusion. In Wren's, emptiness. In Meredith's, something violent I couldn't find a word to describe. And on James's face, despair. Richard stood beside them, so solid it seemed a miracle that no one else could see him, eyes burning black, somehow still unsatisfied. I looked down to the handcuffs already glinting on my wrists and sank onto the cracked leather seat of the car. Colborne shut the door, and in the small, quiet darkness I struggled to breathe.

I spent the next forty-eight hours in windowless interrogation rooms, fingering tiny cups of lukewarm water and answering questions from Colborne, Walton, and two other officers whose names I forgot as soon as I heard them. I told the story as James had told it to me, with only necessary variations. Richard, enraged by my and Meredith's betrayal. Me, swinging the boat hook at his head in a fit of jealous fear. They didn't ask about the morning after.

Further performances of *Lear* were canceled. Following a map I had drawn on the back of Walton's legal pad, Colborne led five cops with flashlights down into the undercroft, where they broke into my locker with a crowbar and bolt cutter. Damning evidence, covered in my fingerprints. "Now," Colborne told me coldly, "might be the time to call your lawyer."

I didn't have one, of course, so she was provided for me. There was no question whether it was homicide, only of what degree. Our best chance, she explained, was to argue imperfect self-defense instead of murder two. I nodded and said nothing. I declined my phone call to my family. They weren't whom I wanted to speak to. On Monday morning I was informed of my new status as a pretrial detainee, but I wasn't sent to county right away. I stayed in Broadwater, because (according to Colborne) moving me to a bigger, more crowded facility might mean I never made it to my trial at all. It seemed more likely that he was stalling. Even after I had handed in my written confession, I could tell he didn't quite believe it. After all, he had come to the FAB expecting to arrest James, acting on information provided by an "anonymous source." Meredith, I assumed.

Perhaps that lingering doubt was why he let me have so many

visitors. Filippa and Alexander were the first. They sat side by side on a bench on the other side of the bars.

"My God, Oliver," Alexander said when he saw me. "What the hell are you doing in here?"

"Just . . . waiting."

"Not what I meant."

"We've talked to your lawyer," Filippa said. "She asked me to be a character witness."

"Not me, though," Alexander added, with a sad little twitch of a smile. "Drug problem."

"Oh." I looked at Filippa. "Will you do it?"

She folded her arms tightly. "I don't know. I haven't forgiven you for this yet."

I ran a finger along one of the bars between us. "I'm sorry."

"You have no idea, do you? What you've done." She shook her head, eyes hard and angry. When she spoke again her voice was the same. "My dad's been in prison since I was thirteen. They're going to eat you alive."

I couldn't look at her.

"*Why?*" Alexander asked. "Why did you do it?"

I knew he wasn't asking why I killed Richard. I squirmed where I was sitting on my cot, grappled with the question.

"It's like *Romeo and Juliet*," I said, eventually.

Filippa made an impatient sort of noise and said, "What are you talking about?"

"*Romeo and Juliet*," I said again, and risked glancing up at the two of them. Alexander had slumped against the wall. Filippa was glaring. "Would you change the ending, if you could? What if Benvolio came forward and said, 'I killed Tybalt. It was me.'"

Filippa hung her head, pushed her hands through her hair. "You fool, Oliver," she said. I couldn't argue with that.

They came back, from time to time. Just to talk. To tell me what was happening at Dellecher. To tell me when my family found out. Filippa was the only one brave enough to speak to my mother on the phone. I wasn't brave enough to speak to her myself. I never heard from my father, or Caroline, but I didn't expect to. Colborne found Leah outside the station one morning, sobbing and throwing rocks at the side of the building. (She'd fled Ohio in the dead of the night, as I had once done.) He brought her in to see me, but she wouldn't speak. She only sat on the bench, staring at me and biting her bottom lip raw. I spent all day apologizing, uselessly, and that night Colborne put her on a bus back home. Walton, he assured me, had called my parents to tell them where she was.

I didn't see Meredith before my trial, and heard of her only through Alexander and Filippa and my lawyer. I should have been desperate for a chance to explain myself, but what would I say? She had her answer by then, to the last question she'd asked me. But I thought of her often. More often than I thought of Frederick, or Gwendolyn, or Colin, or Dean Holinshed. I couldn't bear to think of Wren at all. Of course, the only person I really wanted to see was James.

He came halfway through the first week of my detention. I would have expected him sooner, but according to Alexander it was the first time in days he'd even managed to pick himself up off the floor.

I was asleep when he arrived, lying on my back on my narrow cot, stuck in the permanent daze that had persisted since intermission of *Lear*. I sensed someone outside the cell and sat up slowly. James was sitting on the floor in front of the bars, pale and somehow insubstantial, as if he'd been stitched together from scraps of light and memory and illusion, like a patchwork doll.

I slid down off the cot—feeling suddenly, unexpectedly weak—and sat facing him.

"I can't let you do this," he said. "I didn't come sooner because I didn't know what to do."

"No," I said, quickly. I'd played my part, hadn't I? I'd followed Meredith upstairs, without thinking what might happen when Richard found out. I'd convinced James to leave Richard in the water when no one else could. I'd made my fair share of tragic mistakes, and I didn't want exoneration. "Please, James," I said. "Don't undo what I've done."

His voice emerged scratchy and raw from his throat. "Oliver, I don't understand," he said. "Why?"

"You know why." I was done pretending otherwise.

(I don't think he ever forgave me. After my incarceration he visited often, at first. Every time he came he asked me to let him make things right. Every time, I refused. I knew by then that I would survive my time in prison, quietly counting down the days until all my sins had been atoned for. But his was a softer soul, sunk in sin to the hilt, and I wasn't sure he would. Every time he took my refusal a little bit harder. The very last time he came was six years after my conviction, six months since I'd seen him. He looked older, ill, exhausted. "Oliver, I'm begging you," he said. "I can't do this anymore." When I refused again, he pulled my hand across the table, kissed it, and turned to leave. I asked where he was going and he said, "Hell. Del Norte. Nowhere. I don't know.")

My trial was mercifully short. Filippa and James and Alexander were all dragged in to testify, but Meredith refused to say a word in my defense or otherwise, and gave every question the same useless answer: "I don't remember." My resolve cracked a little every time I looked at her. Other familiar faces I avoided. Wren's and Richard's parents'. Leah's and my mother's, blotchy and tearstained and distant. When it came time for me to speak for myself, I recited my written confession without emotion or embellishment, as if it were just another monologue I'd memorized. At the end, everyone seemed to be expecting an apology, but I didn't have one to give them. What could I say? *This thing of darkness I acknowledge mine.*

We settled on second-degree murder (plus time for obstruction of justice) before the jury ever reached a verdict. A bus took me a few miles downstate. I turned in my clothes and my personal belongings, and began my ten-year penance on the same day that the Dellecher school year ended.

Colborne's face was the last familiar one I saw. "You know, it's not too late," he said. "If there's another version of the truth you want to tell me."

I wanted, in some strange way, to thank him for refusing to believe me.

"*I am myself indifferent honest,*" I admitted. "*But yet I could accuse me of such things that it were better my mother had not borne me. What should such fellows as I do crawling between earth and heaven? We are arrant knaves, all. Believe none of us.*"

EPILOGUE

I feel, at the end of my story, sapped of life, as if I have been bleeding freely for the past few hours instead of simply speaking. "*Demand me nothing,*" I say to Colborne. "*What you know, you know: / From this time forth I will never speak a word.*"

I turn away from the Tower window and avoid his eyes as I walk past him, toward the stairs. He follows me down to the library in respectful silence. Filippa is there, sitting on the couch, a copy of *Winter's Tale* open in her lap. She looks up, and the fading evening light darts across her glasses. My heart is a little lighter at the sight of her.

"*It is almost morning,*" she says to Colborne, "*and yet I am sure you are not satisfied / Of these events in full.*"

"Well, I can't ask much more of Oliver," he says. "He's confirmed a few long-standing suspicions."

"Will you rest easier with one less mystery on your mind?"

"Honestly, I don't know. I thought some closure would make it more bearable, but now I'm not so sure."

I drift to the edge of the room and stare down at the long black burn on the carpet. Now that I've told Colborne everything I feel unmoored. I have nothing of my own now, not even secrets.

The sound of my name makes me turn back toward the others.

"Oliver, will you tolerate one last question?" Colborne asks.

"You can ask," I say. "I won't promise to answer."

"Fair enough." He glances at Filippa, then looks back at me again. "What's next for you? I'm just wondering. What happens now?"

The answer is so obvious I'm surprised it hasn't occurred to him. I hesitate at first, protective of it. But then I meet Filippa's eyes and I realize she's wondering, too.

"I'm supposed to go stay with my sister—you remember Leah. She's doing her doctorate at Chicago," I say. "I wouldn't blame the rest of my family if they didn't want to see me. But more than that—you *must* know—more than anything, I just need to see James."

Something strange happens now. I don't see in their faces the exasperation I'm expecting. Instead Colborne turns toward Filippa, eyes wide with alarm. She sits up straighter on the couch and lifts one hand to stop him speaking.

"Pip?" I say. "What's wrong?"

She stands slowly, smoothing invisible wrinkles from the front of her jeans. "There's something I haven't told you." I swallow, fighting an urge to run out of the room and never find out what she means to say next. But I stay where I am, glued to the spot by the fear that not knowing is worse. "I was afraid that if I told you while you were inside, you'd never want to come out," she says. "So I waited."

"Tell me what?" I say. "Tell me *what*?"

"Oh, Oliver," she says, her voice a distant echo of itself. "I'm so sorry. James is gone."

The world drops out from underneath me. My hand gropes blindly for the bookshelf beside me, for something to hold on to. I stare down at the burn on the carpet, listening for my own heartbeat and hearing nothing. "When?" is all I manage to say.

"Four years ago," she says, quietly. "Four years ago now."

Colborne bows his head. Why? Is he ashamed that he dragged the story out of me and all the while he knew, and I didn't?

"How did it happen?" I ask.

"Slowly. It was the guilt, Oliver," she says. "The guilt was killing him. Why did you think he stopped visiting?" There's a note of desperation in her voice, but I have no pity for her. There's no room for that. No room for anger either. Only a catastrophic sense of loss. Filippa is still talking, but I hardly hear the words. "You know how he was. If we felt everything twice, he felt it all four times."

"What did he do?" I demand.

Her words are tiny. Barely audible. "He drowned," she says. "He drowned himself. God, Oliver, I'm so sorry. I wanted to tell you when it happened, but I was so afraid of what you might do." I can tell she's no less afraid now. "I'm sorry."

I am wretched. Destitute.

Suddenly it seems there is a fourth person in the room. For the first time in ten years, I look at the chair that had always been Richard's and find it isn't empty. There he sits, in lounging, leonine arrogance. He watches me with a razor-thin smile and I realize that this is it—the *dénouement*, the counterstroke, the end-all he was waiting for. He lingers only long enough for me to see the gleam of triumph in his half-lidded eyes; then he, too, is gone.

"So," I say when I have just enough strength to speak. "Now I know."

I don't speak again until we bid goodbye to Colborne at the

Hall. The day is over now, night falling as we walked back through the woods to seal us in a world of darkness. There are no stars tonight.

"Oliver," Colborne says when we find ourselves standing in the shadow of the Hall again. "I'm sorry today ended this way."

"I'm sorry for a lot of things."

"If I can ever do anything for you . . . Well, you know how to find me." He looks at me differently than he ever has, and I realize he's forgiven me, finally, now that he knows the truth. He holds out one hand, and I accept it. We shake. Then we go our separate ways.

Filippa is waiting for me by the car. "I'll take you anywhere you want," she says, "if you promise I won't have to worry."

"No," I say. "Don't do that. We've worried enough for a lifetime, don't you think?"

"Enough for ten."

I lean on the car beside her, and we stand there for a long time, staring up at the Hall. The Dellecher coat of arms stares back down at us, in all its delusional grandeur.

"*Oh, is all forgot?*" I ask. "*All school-days' friendship, childhood innocence?*"

I wonder if Filippa will recognize the line. It was hers, once, in the easy days of our third year, when we all thought ourselves invincible.

"We'll never forget it," she says. "That's the worst part."

I scuff my toes in the dirt. "There's one thing I still don't understand, though."

"What?"

"If you knew all along, why didn't you tell anyone?"

"God, Oliver, isn't it obvious?" She shrugs when I don't answer. "You all were the only family I had. I'd have killed Richard myself if I thought it would keep the rest of you safe."

"I do understand that," I say, privately thinking that if it had been her, we probably would have gotten away with it. And really, it could have been any one of us. "But me, Pip? Why couldn't you tell *me*?"

"I knew you better than you knew yourself," she says, and I can hear ten years of sadness in her voice. "I was terrified you'd do exactly what you did."

My martyrdom is not the selfless kind. I can't look at Filippa, shamed by all the injuries I've inflicted—like a man with a bomb strapped to his chest, ready to blow himself up without a thought for the collateral damage.

"How are Frederick and Gwendolyn?" I say, grasping at something easier to talk about. "I forgot to ask."

"Gwendolyn's just the same," she tells me, with a shadow of a smirk, which fades as soon as it appears. "Except I think she keeps the students at a bit of a distance now."

I nod, don't comment. "And Frederick?"

"He still teaches, but he's slowing down," she says. "It took a lot out of him. Took a lot out of all of us. But they wouldn't need me directing if it hadn't, so I guess it's not all bad."

"I guess not," I say, a hollow echo. "And Camilo?" I don't know how it started, but I have my suspicions about Thanksgiving of our fourth year. How distracted we were, not to notice.

She gives me a small, guilty smile. "He hasn't changed at all. Asks about you every two weeks when I come home."

In the short pause that follows, I almost forgive her. Every two weeks.

"Will you marry him?" I ask. "It's been long enough."

"He says the same thing. You'd come back for that, wouldn't you? I'd need someone to give me away."

"Only if Holinshed officiates."

It's not as firm a promise as she wants. But she won't get that. James is gone, and I'm sure of nothing now.

We stand side by side for a little longer without speaking. Then she says, "It's getting late. Where can I take you? You know you're welcome to stay with us."

"No," I say. "Thanks. The bus station would be fine."

We climb into the car, and drive in silence.

I have not been to Chicago in ten years, and it takes much longer than it should for me to find the address Filippa reluctantly wrote down. It is an unassuming but elegant town house, which murmurs of money and success and a desire not to be disturbed. For a long time before I knock on the door I stand on the side-walk, staring up at the bedroom window, where a soft white light glows. It's been seven years since the last time I saw her, the only time she visited, to tell me I wasn't fooling anyone. At least, not her. "That shirt in the locker," she said. "It wasn't yours, not from that night. I ought to know."

I breathe in as deeply as I can (my lungs still feel too small) and knock. As I wait on the porch in the warm summer shad-ows, I wonder if Filippa warned her.

When she opens the door, her eyes are already wet. She slaps me hard across the face, and I accept the blow without protest. I deserve much worse. She makes a small sound of wounded satis-faction, then opens the door wide enough to let me in.

Meredith is as perfect as I remember her. Her hair is shorter now, though not by much. She wears her clothes a little looser, too, but again, not much. We pour wine but don't drink it. She sits on a chair in the living room and I sit on the couch beside it and we talk. We talk for hours. There's a decade of things we haven't said.

"I'm sorry," I say, when there's a pause long enough for me to screw my courage to the sticking-place. "I know I have no right to ask, but . . . what happened with you and James in Gwendo-lyn's class, did it ever happen offstage?"

She nods, not looking at me. "Once, right afterward. We thought we were going our separate ways, but then I walked into the music room, and there he was. I wanted to go right back out again, but he grabbed me and we just—"

I know what must have happened, without her telling me.

"I don't know what made us do it. I needed to understand, you and him and how he'd wrapped you quite so tight around his finger. I couldn't think of any other way," she says. "But it was over as soon as it started. We heard someone coming—Filippa, of course, she must have known something was wrong—and sort of came to our senses. Then we just stood there. And he said, 'What are you thinking about?' I said, 'The same thing you're thinking about.' We didn't even need to say your name." She frowns down into the red pool of her wine. "It was just a kiss, but God, it hurt like hell."

"I know," I say, without resentment. Which of us could say we were more sinned against than sinning? We were so easily manipulated—confusion made a masterpiece of us.

"I thought it was over then," she says, her voice strained and uncertain. "But the night of the *Lear* party—I was in the bathroom, fixing my makeup, and I felt a hand on my waist. At first I thought it was you, but it was him, and he was drunk, and talking like a crazy person. I shoved him off and said, 'James, what is the matter with you?' And he said, 'You wouldn't believe me if I told you.' He grabbed me again, but it was violent. Painful. He said, 'Or maybe you're the only one who would, but why object? What's done is done, and even-handed justice for us both.' And that was enough—I knew. I got away, barely. Got out of the Castle and went straight to Colborne. I told him everything I could. Not about the dock, not that morning, but everything else. And I wanted to tell you, right there in the crossover, but I was afraid you would do something stupid, like help him run off in the middle of intermission. I *never* thought . . ."

Her voice fades out.

"Meredith, I'm sorry," I say. "I didn't think. I didn't care what happened to me, but I should've thought about what would happen to you."

She won't look at me, but she says, "There's one thing I need to know, now."

"Of course." I owe her that much.

"Us. All that time. Was any of it real, or did you know all along, and we were just a get-out-of-jail-free card for James?" She glares at me with those dark green eyes, and I feel sick.

"God, Meredith, no. I had no idea," I tell her. "You were real to me. Sometimes I thought you were the only real thing."

She nods like she wants to believe me but there's something else in the way. She says, "Were you in love with him?"

"Yes," I say, simply. James and I put each other through the kind of reckless passions Gwendolyn once talked about, joy and anger and desire and despair. After all that, was it really so strange? I am no longer baffled or amazed or embarrassed by it. "Yes, I was." It's not the whole truth. The whole truth is, I'm in love with him still.

"I know." She sounds exhausted. "I knew then, I just pretended not to."

"So did I. So did he. I'm sorry."

She shakes her head, stares out the dark window for a moment. "I'm sorry, too, you know. About him."

It hurts too much to talk about. My teeth ache in my head. I open my mouth to speak, but what comes out instead is a gasp, a sob, and the grief that shock has kept at bay crashes through me like a flood. I pitch forward, that strange twisted laugh that's been stuck in my throat for ten years finally bursting out. Meredith lurches out of her chair and knocks her wineglass to the floor but ignores the sound of it shattering. She says my name and a dozen other things I barely hear.

Nothing is so exhausting as anguish. After a quarter of an hour I am utterly spent, my throat ragged and aching, my face hot and sticky with tears. I lie on the floor with no memory of how I got there, and Meredith sits cradling my head as if it's a fragile, precious thing that might, at any moment, break. When I've been silent for another half hour, she helps me to my feet and leads me to bed.

We lie side by side in solemn darkness. All I can think of is Macbeth—he has James's face in my imagination—shouting, *Sleep no more! Macbeth does murder sleep, so sleep no more!* Oh, balm of hurt minds. I want sleep desperately, but do not hope to have it.

But I wake up in the morning and blink with swollen eyelids as the sun rises and spills in through the window. Sometime in the night, Meredith has rolled over, and is sleeping now with her hair fanned out behind her, her cheek against my shoulder.

Though we never talk about it, it is somehow decided that I will stay with Meredith indefinitely. While her professional life is crowded with people, her personal life is a mostly solitary one, the long hours filled with books and words and wine. For a week we reenact Christmas in New York, but more cautiously. I sit on the couch with a mug of tea at my elbow and a book on my knee, sometimes reading, sometimes staring past the pages. At first she sits across from me. Then beside me. Then she lies with her head in my lap and I run my fingers through her hair.

When I explain all this to Leah, I can't tell if she's disappointed or relieved.

Alexander calls and we agree to meet for drinks next time he's in the city. I don't hope to hear from Wren—Meredith tells me she's in London, working as a dramaturg and living like a recluse, afraid of the outside world. We don't talk about James again. I know that whatever else happens, we never will.

Filippa calls and asks for me. She says there's something in the mail. Two days later it arrives, a plain brown envelope with a smaller white envelope inside. The sight of James's handwriting on the second one stops my heart for a moment. I hide it under a couch cushion, and resolve to open it when Meredith is gone.

The next week she's filming in Los Angeles. She puts a new key on the nightstand, kisses me, and leaves me sleeping in what

I've come to think of—prematurely, perhaps—as "our" bed. When I wake up again, I retrieve James's letter.

I know more by now about what happened. He drove north from the small apartment he'd occupied outside Berkeley and drowned in the icy winter waters of the San Juan Islands. In his car, abandoned on the ferry landing, he'd left his keys, an empty bottle of Xanax, and a pair of almost identical envelopes. The first was unmarked, unsealed, and contained a short handwritten farewell, but no explanation or confession. (He respected, at least, the last request I'd made of him.) On the second, he'd written only one word:

OLIVER

I open it with clumsy fingers. Ten lines of verse are scratched in the middle of the page. It's James's writing still, but more jagged, as if it had been written hastily, with a pen that had little ink left to give. I recognize the text—a disjointed, mosaic monologue, cobbled together from an early scene of *Pericles*:

> *Alas, the sea hath cast me on the rock,*
> *Wash'd me from shore to shore, and left me breath*
> *Nothing to think on but ensuing death.*
> *What I have been I have forgot to know;*
> *But what I am, want teaches me to think on:*
> *A man throng'd up with cold: my veins are chill,*
> *And have no more of life than may suffice*
> *To give my tongue that heat to ask your help;*
> *Which if you shall refuse, when I am dead,*
> *For that I am a man, pray see me buried.*

I read it three times, wondering why he would choose such a strange, obscure passage to leave me—until I remember I haven't heard these words since he chanted them to me, lying drunk in the sand on some beach in Del Norte, as if he'd been washed up beside me by the tide. I am all too aware of my own desperate need to find a message in the madness, and as it takes shape I am suspicious, afraid to hope. But the implications of the text and its small part in our story are impossible to ignore, too critical for a scholar as meticulous as James to overlook.

When I can't stand another moment's inaction, I race up the stairs to the office, my head full of what would have been Pericles's last words—if he had not asked for *help*.

The computer on the desk crackles to life when I touch the mouse, and after one interminable minute I am on the Internet, searching for every record I can find of James Farrow's death in the bleak midwinter of 2004. I devour five, six, ten old articles, all of which say the same thing. He drowned himself on the last day of December, and though the local authorities dragged the freezing water for days and miles, his body was never found.

Exeunt omnes.

Author's Note

In the writing of this book I have consulted so many different editions of the complete works and the individual plays that it would be impossible to list all of them without the bibliography becoming longer than the story itself. However, a few volumes do stand out as worthy of mention (and of my eternal gratitude). *The Riverside Shakespeare* (2nd ed.) has been a nearly constant companion not only in the writing of this book but in every Shakespearean endeavor I have embarked on since it first came into my possession in 2010. More recently and especially in the intricate process of revision, I came to rely on *The Norton Shakespeare* (3rd ed.), with its groundbreaking commitment to preserving both "wonder and resonance," as Stephen Greenblatt described it at the launch party in October 2015. Like the *Riverside* it has become indispensable, especially in navigating the textual maze that is *King Lear*. Two other books that it would be remiss not to mention are Patsy Rodenberg's *Speaking Shakespeare,* which had a significant influence on Gwendolyn's theatrical philosophies, and René Girard's *Theatre of Envy,* which might have prevented much of what goes wrong for the fourth-years had Oliver read it a little sooner.

Here I must also acknowledge that I have ransacked Shakespeare's entire oeuvre with giddy abandon. The fourth-year thespians speak a kind of Pidgin English so saturated with Shakespearean words and quotes and turns of phrase that it could almost be classified as a new (and, there is no denying, exceptionally pretentious) dialect. Because it is a natural and unregulated phenomenon, in some instances quotes borrowed from the

Bard—which for the sake of clarity have been italicized, regardless of whether they are verse or prose—are not borrowed word for word. This is the creative liberty of language. For the purposes of this particular story, the texts of Shakespeare and his collaborators (whomsoever they may have been) are always filtered either through the characters' mouths and/or Oliver's brain, and so are subject to small transformations. The vagaries of early modern orthography have been regularized for the contemporary reader, and I have punctuated the text in whatever manner best serves the speaker or the scene. As James remarks in Act V, "Commas belong to the compositors." But whatever small discrepancies there may be, every line of *If We Were Villains* is written with the intention of paying homage to William Shakespeare—who has had more than enough defamers, detractors, and deniers. (*Lord, what fools these mortals be.*)

Acknowledgments

I am indebted to Arielle Datz, who took a very big chance on a very young writer, talked her off various ledges, and walked her through the process of publication with unfailing patience and unflagging enthusiasm. To Christine Kopprasch, who laughed at my most terrible jokes and worked magic on my mess of a manuscript with remarkable instinct and insight about the art of storytelling. To everyone at Flatiron Books, whose dedication, creativity, and love of good books are nothing less than inspiring. To Chris Parris-Lamb, without whose guidance this book never would have made it past the query stage. To my fellow MA students at King's College, who vindicated my conviction that, yes, some people really are obsessed enough to have entire conversations in Shakespearean quotations. To Margaret, for giving ear to my every complaint. To my early readers (Madison, Crissy, and Sophie), all of whom were bribed with wine and offered invaluable input in return. To my friends in Chapel Hill (Bailey, Cary, and the Simpson family), whose goodwill never wavered, even in the face of my crippling artistic anxiety. To the teachers, directors, and professors (Natalie Dekle, Brooke Linefsky, Greg Kable, Ray Dooley, Jeff Cornell, and Farah Karim-Cooper), who have encouraged and enabled my infatuation with Shakespeare. To my grandmother, who fostered my love of literature from an early age and let me drink up all her tea and most of her liquor while I worked on my manuscript in the corner of her library. And to my parents, who drove me to and from countless rehearsals, sat through a number of truly atrocious plays, read a stack of similarly hideous first drafts, and never once decried my impractical passions. *Let me give humble thanks for all at once.*

If We Were Villains
by M. L. Rio

PLEASE NOTE: In order to provide reading groups with the most informed and thought-provoking questions possible, it is necessary to reveal important aspects of the plot of this novel— as well as the ending. If you have not finished reading *If We Were Villains*, we respectfully suggest that you may want to wait before reviewing this guide.

1. In the very first scene, Oliver says, "We did wicked things, but they were necessary, too—or so it seemed. Looking back, years later, I'm not so sure they were, and now I wonder: Could I explain it all to Colborne?" (page 5). Having finished the story, which of the "wicked" things do you think were necessary or inevitable? Which were not? What, in the last ten years, might have caused Oliver to change his mind?

2. Throughout the story the fourth-years perform four of Shakespeare's plays and quote the other plays and poems in their everyday conversation. Shakespeare's works—and especially the tragedies—are saturated with love, loss, jealousy, betrayal, and violence. How do these themes manifest themselves offstage? To what degree is life imitating art? Do you, like Oliver, "blame Shakespeare" for what happens in the story, or is he simply using Shakespeare as a scapegoat?

3. How does Dellecher's educational model affect the fourth-years' behavior? Oliver and Colborne both hypothesize that the highly competitive nature of the school contributes to the students' proclivity for passionate action and sometimes violence. Is this true? To what extent? Oliver remarks that "actors are

by nature volatile—alchemic creatures composed of incendiary elements, emotion and ego and envy. Heat them up, stir them together, and sometimes you get gold. Sometimes disaster" (page 53). Is this innate or learned behavior?

4. How does the usual "typecasting" of the seven fourth-years affect the course of the story? How do the changes in that typecasting affect their interpersonal relationships? To what extent does Gwendolyn's "psychological puppeteering" (page 49) influence the students' actions? Does she merely exacerbate existing tensions or does she create conflict where none existed before? Why do you think she does this?

5. Oliver repeatedly identifies himself as a bystander, secondary character, or interloper. How does his role as observer affect his role as storyteller? On page 102 he says, "I was quiet. Motionless. In my own estimation, pointless. A fuse with no fire and nothing to ignite." Is he really just a pawn between James and Richard, or is he more integral to the conflict from the outset?

6. A line from *Pericles*—"Murder's as near to lust as flame to smoke"—is quoted twice in the story, and in Act IV Oliver observes that in his subconscious mind, violence and intimacy have become "somehow interchangeable" (page 305). How are love, sex, and violence connected in the story? Does one necessitate or provoke the other? Why might that be true of this particular group of people?

7. Are the fourth-years justified in their decision not to save Richard's life? Are some more justified than others? What might have happened if they had? In their position, what would you do?

8. Oliver tells Colborne, "People always forget about Filippa... And later they always wish they hadn't"

(page 88). Why do you think this is? Why is she so easily overlooked, and what makes her so indispensable?

9. Oliver claims to love both James and Meredith, at different points throughout the story. Do you think he loves them in the same or different ways? Does he love one more than the other? Is it possible for him to love them equally, or simultaneously?

10. When Oliver ventures into Richard's room the morning after the *King Lear* cast party, he struggles with feelings of guilt and old affection but also insists that he "would be a fool to regret for one minute that he was gone" (page 320). Is this true, and if it is, why is he feeling so remorseful now and not earlier in the story?

11. After hearing James's confession, do you think he was justified in killing Richard? Would you categorize it as self-defense? Do you think he tells Oliver the whole truth or is there more to the story?

12. The ending of the story is deliberately ambiguous. What do you think might happen next?